CAPTURED

It felt unreal. He was flying through the rain, over the bridge, above the ocean. The white caps reached for him and splashed in the great sea in dismay when they could not touch him.

The beast's tentacles held him securely. He did not fight, did not even struggle. The final moments before death were met with an inner calm and wonder.

The sky opened. Rain pelted the ocean, fought the waves and built more froth. Enickor squinted into the grey blur, saw nothing and wondered how long the beast would hold him at the threshold of death's door before hurling him through it.

He did not have long to wait . . .

Other Avon Books by
Susan Coon

CASSILEE
RAHNE
THE VIRGIN

SUSAN COON

CHIY-UNE

AVON
PUBLISHERS OF BARD, CAMELOT, DISCUS AND FLARE BOOKS

CHIY-UNE is an original publication of Avon Books. This work
has never before appeared in book form.

AVON BOOKS
A division of
The Hearst Corporation
959 Eighth Avenue
New York, New York 10019

Copyright © 1982 by Susan Coon
Published by arrangement with the author
Library of Congress Catalog Card Number: 81-65073
ISBN: 0-380-79301-6

First Avon Printing, January, 1982

AVON TRADEMARK REG. U. S. PAT. OFF. AND IN
OTHER COUNTRIES, MARCA REGISTRADA, HECHO EN
U. S. A.

Printed in the U. S. A.

WFH 10 9 8 7 6 5 4 3 2 1

For my sisters,
Kathryne, Krysteen, Kaaren & Theresa

Introduction

CHIY-UNE WAS OLD, THE LAST OF HER KIND IN that quadrant of the Galaxy. Her first children had departed to follow the destiny of their evolution. One at a time they returned to the Mother. As the children had grown older, so had Chiy-une. The fruit spawn during her middle age had evolved into man, loving and caring, kind and giving. From them Chiy-une needed to select one who would save them all from the men who had jumped across the stars to kill her and the life she harbored.

Chapter 1

ENICKOR VAL DENSU WAS CLOSELY WATCHED. HE stormed down the main hall of Shirwall past a full complement of guards at the cross section and into the foyer. He showed not the slightest bit of fear when two guards, both easily as large as he, halted him at the massive doors. He eyed the decorative long swords strapped to their synthetic uniforms, silently comparing their ability to use the weapons with that of the natives to produce synthetics. Neither was a fact.

He stood poised, his chest solid against the crossed arms of the guards.

Two *kalases* were leveled upon him. If he went for his own weapon, he knew death would claim him before his body bounced on the shiny floor a second time.

From the rear hall came the bass voice of Hy-Commander Hoyiv Jeffires. "Allow him to pass. He will not be returning." It was the pronouncement of a sentence, the proclamation of a rift never to be mended.

Enickor val Densu belonged nowhere. The Porintel Loag, his mother's people, had refused him honor or a place in their villages. His father's people, the Star Followers, plundered the land and fouled the air. They considered him inferior, unfit to operate their complicated machines.

The guards stepped away with a precise click of their heels on the floor.

Enickor glared past them to the intricately-carved wooden doors.

The even manner in which the doors swung open just enough to permit him passage was another reminder of the technological superiority of the Star Followers over the natives. They could not fight back. They were separate. They had to endure. In time, the Star Followers would depart.

Life would continue.

But it would not be the same. Chiy-une's heavy metals would be gone, her riches gracing a hundred worlds no one from her lands would touch. It was a future belonging only to the Star Followers. Already, lung death was touching heavily upon the Harcel Loag in the south.

Chiy-une had become the stepping-stone to the riches beyond. None of those planets possessed the hospitable atmosphere or clime. They regaled in the ferocity of their fight against the mining ships marked by the Houses of Jeffires and Hadilka.

For the first time in the history of the Overeechy, two warring Houses voluntarily called for a truce. Both held legitimate claim to the territories. Both mined them avidly. Neither returned to the Overeechy and left the other behind. Trust was not part of the bargain. Overseers did not live long.

Enickor strode past the sentries and through the doors. He spun around, met Hy-Commander Hoyiv Jeffires's pale gray eyes for a moment, then turned down the steps. The word "brother" formed on his lips. This morning he had had one. This evening, he had neither brother nor father.

Now he did not know what he had expected upon his return to Shirwall. In truth, he had not anticipated his father's total rejection.

The Hy-Commander's pale gray eyes, the same shade as the ones he saw in the mirror each day, the same shade as their father's, seemed to look into his soul, sadly mocking the youth for his naiveté.

Head high, he strode down the winding stone walk until it became a mud-stained rock ledge turned sideways to form a bridge between Shirwall and the mainland. For a moment he paused, sniffing the air, feeling the portent of storm in the

2

ocean breeze, seeing the restlessness of whitecaps close to the bridge.

It was three kilometers to the safety of the mainland.

He glanced over his shoulder. There was no going back. If he did not make it ... Perhaps it was better that way, he mused, allowing his depression to surface. He felt that he had much to offer life, yet life refused him the slightest chance. He was an outcast neither camp would claim. There was nowhere left to go. He was a man of seventy seasons. Alone.

He started onto the land bridge, feeling the nip of winter in the air. Great volumes of dust in the atmosphere gave longer life to the harsher season and stretched spring almost into fall. The ninety days of summer were cool, the growing time stifled.

The pace he set along the rocky path was quick. The treacherous sea appeared to sense Enickor's fear, and responded by building frothy waves that washed at his boots.

The moss-slicked rock required all his attention. It narrowed to a dozen centimeters in places, falling straight down into the murky depth on either side. The narrows were what he feared most. Horrendous monsters lived in the sea. They frequented the deep pools around the land bridge, just waiting for an errant traveler to drop in. No man had lived to tell of the horror waiting below the moody waves.

The wind gusted, blowing stronger by the moment.

Enickor straightened, arms out for balance, and looked around. Someone was calling his name. He glanced at the shore.

Two young men from Ocandar Loag were hauling in nets.

He shook his head. They were occupied and would not waste time calling into the wind, even if they cared.

Carefully, he turned to look behind him.

Shirwall rose out of the sea. The failing light coaxed a false brilliance from the alien walls and piqued his fascination anew. There was no one on the steps.

Thunderclouds rolled out of the sea and clashed in the near north.

A metal rod, corroded by the weather, with a tattered flag wrapped around the top, marked the halfway point. He paused to catch his breath. Perspiration rolled down his ribs.

The storm built as he continued over the rough bridge. The waves grew stronger, summoning the tide from the ocean's opposite shore.

Again, the sound of his name rode the sea wind.

He stopped short, fell to his left, and scrambled to get his feet back under him.

The desperation in the voice calling his name created an urgency inside him. There was a pain in the tone, one which he sensed as an unrequited need.

It called again.

A tremor ran up his back, though his body was hot in the cold wind.

"Enickor val Densu..."

The sound touched his soul.

The water behind him bubbled and frothed for a distance of fifty meters.

It sounded like a woman. What woman would call to him?

A tentacle that spread into five-meter-long finger tendrils slithered across the rock. Behind that, the head of the monster rose from the water. It was pointed at the snout, easily three meters across and splotched with a mossy growth. Two nostrils as large as Enickor's chest fluttered in the spume, offended by the pungent atmosphere.

The woman pleaded with his name again.

"Where are you?" he cried into the wind.

"Everywhere," came her urgent response.

The monster slipped two tendrils around Enickor's right leg.

Before he realized what had happened, Enickor was in the water and struggling for air. The beast pulled him down into the lurid depths, where life was more alien than inside the Star Followers' settlements.

Even through his fear he heard the woman sobbing his name.

His lungs felt as though they were being crushed. He fumbled at the knife case strapped to his right hip.

Within seconds all he could hear was the thudding of his heart against his temples. He slashed at the two tendrils holding his leg. The knife sliced through them as though they were well cooked meat.

Immediately, he began to rise. He clawed at the water, trying to climb it like a ladder.

When his head broke the surface, he inhaled spume, gagged and sank. Desperate, he clambered on the rock wall, tearing his skin and clothing, shredding his elbows and knees. The water splashed pink onto the bridge.

He dug his boot tips into the wall and pushed, heaving himself onto the rocks. He clutched his knife. A tingling crawled up his spine, reminding him of his exposed side. He

4

expected to be sucked back into the sea, and could not be free of it quickly enough.

The beast rose to just below the breaking waves. White foam camouflaged his monstrous bulk.

Enickor threw his right leg onto the bridge and rolled, springing to his feet with the grace of a mountain torna-pok. The wind clutched at his wet clothes hanging in shreds about his arms. It slapped his hair across the angles and planes of his face and into his eyes.

The beast lifted his head from the water and roared.

Mouth open, Enickor's heart skipped two beats.

He renewed his grip on the knife. *There it is*, he thought, staring at the round, green eyes bulging above the beast's nostrils. *It's a mirror of all the atrocities beset upon Chiy-une. The injustice I am sentenced to live....*

The beast moved almost imperceptibly.

Enickor, the mountain hunter watching his prey, noticed it and shifted slightly to the left.

A lightning-quick set of tendrils scraped over the top of the rocks.

He jumped and landed hard on his left foot. Pain jabbed through his heel and up into his thigh. It almost gave way when he put his weight upon it.

The first sheet of rain reached the ledge. The drops, propelled by the wind, struck his exposed skin like small icicles.

He sidestepped along the ridge, groping his way with his weakened left foot, slanting his balance so that, if he fell, he would fall backwards, away from the monstrosity playing games in the water at his boot tips.

His name rode the wind once again.

He did not look around. Rather, he watched the beast, not even daring to wipe away water running into his eyes.

The beast marked him, and kept Enickor's grueling, slow pace effortlessly.

The frigid wind numbed his fingers. The sea turned into a thrashing ice melt and bit his toes. His ankle no longer hurt. The cold had sapped all feeling from it.

He stole a glance at the shore.

Less than a half a kilometer to go. With a sigh, he felt as though he were going to make it. The shallows began a few meters off to his left. Heart beating wildly, he allowed himself to hope and acknowledged how much he wanted to live.

Only a little more...

5

With a speed his eyes barely registered, the beast sent out a tentacle, wrapped him in the tendrils, and lifted him from the ridge.

The two youths from the Ocandar Loag watched from well back on the shore. The smaller one shrieked a cry of terror into the frigid wind.

It felt unreal. He was flying through the rain, over the bridge, above the ocean. The whitecaps reached for him, and splashed into the great sea in dismay when they could not touch.

The tendrils held him securely. He did not fight, did not even struggle. The final moments before death were met with an inner calm and wonder. He watched the horizon, expecting to be pulled into the ocean.

The ocean rangtur held him aloft. He slithered through the mounting waves pounding the shallows and headed for open sea.

The sky opened. Rain pelted the ocean, fought the waves and built more froth.

Enickor squinted into the gray blur, saw nothing and wondered how long the beast would hold him at the threshold of death's door before hurling him through.

He did not have long to wait. The beast dove, plunging Enickor into the sea like a heavy stone attached to a fallen mountain.

Pam-ella Jeffires fumed in the antechamber of her father's office. She was a slightly built woman approximately the same age as Enickor val Densu, her half-brother.

The door opened. Her brother, Hy-Commander Hoyiv Jeffires, marched out, scowling, not giving her so much as a glance.

She rushed in, hurried across the room and leaned over the desk. "How could you? How could you deny him his birthright?"

Anger and hurt overrode the healthy fear Pam-ella usually had of her father. Her wounds cut deeply into her emotions.

Lord Jeffires, her father, was an elderly man who had aged considerably in the past two days. His round face was lined deeply by the struggles to develop his territories and the years as a warlord in the Kriell's service. He had earned his mining grant to these territories. The small paunch growing around his middle was deplorable to him, yet he had neither the time nor the perseverance to be rid of it. Chiy-une and the rich worlds beyond demanded much to hold them secure in the black presence of Lord Hadilka and his henchmen. But he was part of the bargain.

"You loved him, child?" he asked, sadly. He did not look at her. A block holo of his son and daughter with Enickor at forty seasons, when first he came to live with them, filled his vision.

"Love him? He's my brother! He's your son." The tears came hard now. Voicing the loss magnified it. "Please, please, reconsider. I beg of you. There is no place for him to go out there. He'll die." Pam-ella sank back to the edge of a visitor's chair, covered her face and wept.

After a time, Lord Jeffires spoke. His long fingers, the ring of office dominating two knuckles of his index finger on his right hand, were pressed together under his chin.

"There can only be one line to my seat, child. Your brother Hoyiv is my heir. There is no room for contest."

Disbelieving what she was hearing, she stopped crying and lowered her hands. "You can't believe Enickor would want your title? You can't know him so little, Father. He loved you. He loved all of us. He has done as you asked. He returned to his mother's people and sought their help on your behalf. What more . . ."

Abruptly, her demeanor changed. She met her father's gaze. The gray of his eyes was the color of the cold ocean and rain beyond the heights of Shirwall. Her own were green like the forests of Chiy-une's mountain valleys.

"Bring him back. Claim him as a liege bastard and I will agree to marry Lord Hadilka in the spring." She swallowed hard, knowing how miserable the life she was agreeing to would be. Enickor's safety was worth that. She loved him. She felt guilty for that love, wanting him to be more than a brother, knowing his honor would not permit such a thing.

"Do not bargain with me, child. You will marry Lord Hadilka in the spring anyway."

Her answer was quiet. "No, father, I will not. He has no morals, no principles. He drinks too much, and compromises his women. The only way I would subject myself to that is to have your guarantee that Enickor will be given a place in the House of Jeffires. Lord Hadilka's word means nothing. We both know that, Father. But your word to me is binding. If I'm to be turned over to slavery, I should get some satisfaction of my own out of it." She stood, straightening the whole height of her scant meter and a half. Anger replaced the tears of sorrow.

"Does my own daughter think so little of her father? Enickor is not my son, Pam-ella." He smiled faintly.

Her stance betrayed her disbelief.

"Yes, I bedded his mother. Even my Lord the Kriell succumbed to her invitation. God! Half my survey party bedded his mother."

Pam-ella steeled her expression to one of noncommittal.

Lord Jeffires picked up a sheath of papers and flung them at his daughter. They gathered followers and skittered to the floor. "That, my child, is a report from Kal Pridain's very own lab. Enickor val Densu is not, nor could he possibly be, my son."

She was exhilarated by this sudden piece of hopeful information. "He was still a product of an act from someone representing the House of Jeffires. Claim him as a liege bastard, father. Please."

"No. I have given him more than he has a right to expect under the circumstances. And I have spared him the knowledge of his mother, just as his own people have done. He can ask no more, Pam-ella. Nor can you. You are my daughter, and will do as I command." He rose, a signal that her session was over. "As for Lord Hadilka, we will see when the time comes."

Gooseflesh ran across her body at the thought of the loathsome Lord's touch. She turned to leave.

"Do not think of sending emissaries to search for him, child. It would be a mistake for you both; one I would regret seeing you make." He sighed heavily as she continued to the door. "Headstrong daughter . . . would that she had been a boy." He lifted his head and called to her.

"If you had been a son, Pam-ella, I would beat you soundly for the insolence you have shown your Lord-Father today!"

"I just bet you would," she said under her breath, then slammed the door.

Chapter 2

STORIES TOLD AROUND THE COMMON FIRE OF PO-
rintel Loag included a legend purporting that one's life passed
in review during drowning. There had never been any reason
given why this phenomenon was limited to those unfortunate
enough to meet an early death by such heinous means. Since
no one had come back to refute the tale, there was no reason
to disbelieve it, either.

Lungs aching, his eyes stinging and bulging from the strain,
Enickor decided he had a credibility problem—either the tale
was a lie or he was not drowning.

The pressure of the depths forced the last of the air reserve
from his lungs. On the edge of oblivion, trying in vain not to
inhale the murky ocean, Enickor decided that the tale was a
lie.

The beast cradled him in a flexible network of tendrils.
Sensing his charge's resignation to die, the beast swung Enickor
out in front of him and stopped dead in the water. He arched
until his great maw was only a meter above the ocean floor.
Water eddies, flung across the sea bottom by the rangtur's
tremendous tail, churned up the sand and sent the pink kelp

streamers into a frenzy. He forced water from his enormous maw and belched air up from his gullet, which he then trapped.

When at last Enickor could no longer hold any control over his body, his mouth opened. His chest expanded. His lungs pulled. His tongue fluttered against the roof of his mouth.

Instead of water, putrid air filled his lungs. He gagged, coughed, and gasped, thinking stench never smelled so good.

Not until his head cleared of the ludicrous thought trend did he realize how dark it was in the place which gave him new life. He was lying on his side. The tendrils were still wrapped firmly around him.

When there was a slit of light, he wanted to scream, but would not waste the air. He was inside the beast's mouth.

Panicked, he inhaled deep, rapid breaths, trying to regain enough strength to put up a fight. But the tendrils remained secure. The sharp rows of brown teeth did not close on him. Instead, he was pulled back into the water. The rangtur continued his journey.

How long, and how many times Enickor was revived by the beast, he could not tell. He lost count. The hypnotic daze, a perpetual state of almost drowning, kept him shrouded in unreality.

At last, the journey ended. They had been at sea for days. It had to be that long, he knew, or longer. It had been an eternity, an infinity of watery hell.

Enickor's ears throbbed against the constant pulsing of his heart in his temples. An ache that began deep in his chest permeated his body. He no longer cared where he was or why he came to be there. Breathing regularly, he curled up against a rock and slept.

Welcome home, Enickor val Densu. You shall be my Warrior. I will train you well.

Enickor stirred, then sat up and looked around.

No longer did he hear the soulful call of his name.

But something had awakened him. He was in great need of a long rest. Content that he had been dreaming, he lay down again, asleep before three heartbeats passed.

You wish for a home, a place to stand, a woman to love. . . . You have all these. You have me. You will know this as I do. And when you are through with the ocean—the land shall know it, too.

When he woke, he thought there was someone with him. He looked around, called aloud, but found no one. He was alone. Even the rangtur was gone. Depressed, yet curious and hungry, he began to explore the cavern and headed toward the light around the bend. He had a feeling he would be here for a long time. It seemed that there was something he needed to do.

For several reasons, any one of which presented sufficient cause, Pam-ella readied to leave the safety of Shirwall. The decision had not been a hasty one wrought by the House of Jeffires's disclaimer of Enickor val Densu, nor the love she bore for him, which bordered upon the incestuous while she thought him her brother. Lord Hadilka weighed as heavily upon her mind in the matter as he was likely to weigh upon her body.

The storm raged outside. Enormous waves hammered the outer stone-plas walls, unable to shake them.

Pam-ella watched the hall outside her room. Sooner or later the guard her father placed there would tire or seek a momentary leave. That would be her chance.

She waited half the night. A bundle, half as large as she was, draped across her lap. The old jerkin and breeches she wore were of Porintel Loag vintage. They had been Enickor's when he first came to live at Shirwall.

She tucked in a fraying seam along the sleeve, realizing for the first time how large a child he had been. Even then he had towered over Hoyiv, and continued to do so until the last few seasons.

It had crossed her mind to seek out Hoyiv and beseech him to help her find Enickor. Surely he could not turn off his emotions as their father had done. But she did not ask his help, nor forewarn him of her plans. Something in the way he had stormed out of Lord Jeffires's office prevented her.

There was a look on his face that she had not seen before. It frightened her. Evil came to mind, unbidden. Was he glad Enickor was gone? she wondered. Hoyiv loved competition, but he loved to win, too. On a physical level, he had never come close to beating Enickor at anything. She knew Enickor's youth further annoyed Hoyiv.

There had been anger. She recalled how angry both Hoyiv and her father had been when they found out that she taught Enickor how to program the mining rigs through the computer. Then she had not understood. It was so simple—for her, for them—but not for Enickor, who spent the first decade of years

11

without electricity. Now she grasped the significance of their concern and smiled.

Knowledge, swiftly gained, showed him to be Hoyiv's superior again.

Voices disturbed her reverie. She turned off her listener, ran for the bed and shoved her bundle into the closet on the way.

When the door opened, she had her covers pulled over her shoulders and around her chin.

The layers of clothing and bedding compounded the heat generated by her fear of discovery. She began to think of the consequences if she did not successfully escape Shirwall. Her father would have her married off to Lord Hadilka, and secure not only the complete mining rights on Chiy-une, but two space station mining settlements over the planet Vaine as part of the agreement. It was a great deal. Not great enough for her, though. The transaction made her feel like a piece of merchandise being sold over the counter.

She had to outwait whoever was at the door.

It closed.

Unsure, her back burning as though two *kalases* were slowly boring through her rough garb, she waited, unmoving, afraid. Her heart pounded in her throat. Her breath wanted to come in hard, quick gasps. Perspiring, she controlled what showed on the surface and tried to concentrate on a deep, even rhythm of exchanging the air in the room with that in her lungs.

After what seemed like an eternity, the door opened and closed again. This time she knew she was alone.

The night was slipping away, as was the cover of the storm. A flick at the monitor turned on the listener. Retrieving her bundle from the closet, she glanced over at the screen.

The hall was empty.

As an afterthought, she grabbed an oversized rain poncho from the closet floor and smiled that she had thought to keep it after her last trip to the mainland.

Shirwall was quiet in the small hours before morning. Storms seemed to lull the inhabitants into sound sleep. Pamella crept down the hall, stepped into a lift, and descended to the kitchens. The high, ornately decorated walls looked down on her, chiding the folly of her departure, warning her of the harsh world beyond their splendid protection.

In the darkness she moved slowly, not wanting to disturb anything or make a noise. The lingering aroma of the evening's meal sparked hunger. Her stomach churned with fear and growled. She gathered several days' food supply, a few utensils, packed them in a separate bundle, and hung it on her shoulder. On the way across the spotless kitchen, she paused long enough to find a sweet fruit pastry, folded it, and stuffed her mouth.

She left the kitchens, closing the doors securely behind her.

Two levels lower, and beyond what seemed like a kilometer of barren hallways that echoed every noise, lay her destination.

In the dim light of the delivery bays, where supplies were brought to Shirwall almost daily, sat the water skimmers and the personal aircraft of the House of Jeffires.

Pam-ella smiled. It was an exciting memory. The races between Enickor and Hoyiv had clutched at the edge of death with a total abandon. The machines responded to skill, and both had more skill than any dozen men combined on the entire planet.

Her smile faded. It had been playing with death. Hoyiv could swim. Enickor could not.

She triggered the outside doors and let the storm in. She had to move fast now. The alarms were sounding in the security area. Armed guards would be all over the bays in minutes.

She hurled her bundles into her father's skimmer and climbed in after them. Her slight build and small weight were another advantage.

Moments later she was in the thick of the storm. The small pleasure craft, designed for smooth waters, was tossed about like a broken stick. If it remained intact, the guidance system would get her to shore. It did not concern her too greatly.

Pam-ella held on, praying that Enickor was camped on the beach opposite Shirwall.

As the storm worsened and she lost all sense of direction in the night, she wondered what she would do if Enickor was not camped on the beach.

A ray of light beamed down from a crack so high up on the steep, angular slope that Enickor could not see an end to the ascent he had begun. Behind lay a black cavern with a fluctuating water level. Enickor climbed, slid part way down the steep shaft several times, and continued climbing. It seemed the only rational thing to do, since he had not been permitted to die like any normal man who fell into the sea.

Once he laughed, wondering if all the people who were

swallowed by the sea were on separate little pockets on the continent's edge, waiting for "civilization"—as the Star Followers called it. It was a macabre thought.

The sun was directly overhead by the time he worked his way out of the top of the shaft.

A couple of hundred meters below the narrow perch he rested on, the ocean beat the very cliff he had climbed from the inside. Above rose a mountain the likes of which he had never dreamed. It went almost straight into the clouds and out of sight.

With a sigh, he looked for a way down the cliff face; yet even as he did, he felt compelled to revere the heights. The smooth black rock held few flaws and no visible joints. Sunlight glared from it. Heat danced and shimmered, playing along its surface. This rock did not crumble or mar when struck with his knife handle. It was harder than any rock he could remember encountering over his long journeys between loags.

The sun was a great orange ball teasing the western horizon by the time Enickor's prolonged labors were rewarded by a glimpse of a white sand beach in the distance. He hurried, his feet bleeding in his boots, his arms, legs, and torso scraped and scabbed over from the many falls in the shaft and desperate clutches against the rock face. Heat blisters formed around his eyes, puffing his lids almost shut.

Night came. The air grew cool. Perspiration continued to roll down Enickor's body. His lips were swollen, his tongue thick. Still he moved over the cliff, hearing the threat of the angry sea a hundred meters below.

The agonizing slowness of his progress made the night last even longer.

His name still rode the wind. There was a growing concern in the call.

He wanted to yell back, to vent his pain and rage. He did not. The slender ledge he worked to descend the face demanded all of his energies. It narrowed to less than a couple of centimeters in places, flared occasionally and allowed him a reprieve, then became almost nonexistent. He felt his way, trying each move before actually making it.

After a time he no longer searched for the white, elusive promise of safety on his left. His vision clouded. There was no part of his body that did not ache. And the ache was better than those times when his extremities went numb and he had

14

to wait for them to regain feeling. And those times were better than the awful cramps in his toes and calves.

Morning brought clouds gathering for another storm.

His eyes burned and watered. He cursed them. So little body water, and it spilled uselessly down his cheeks.

He kept moving, braced himself around a jut, then paused.

The beach edge began just ten meters ahead and twenty below.

It was the most beautiful thing he had ever seen. It was safety, within his grasp. Dividing his attention between the black rock and the white beach, Enickor's breathing quickened as he hurried. Five meters from safety, a blister on his left hand popped and coated his handhold with watery blood. He reached frantically for another jut. His fingers slipped away, bright red and dripping, as another blister split.

He tried to hug the mountain, lost his balance, and slid, hit a lower shelf and bounced off, awkwardly hitting the sand. He passed out from the pain, and woke when the sun was overhead and looking down on him like a great eye from a hole in the clouds.

He rolled against something.

It was his bundle. He pushed up on one elbow and looked out at the sea.

Beyond the shallows was a beast like the one who had brought him. Perhaps it was the same one. He did not know, nor did he care. He lay back down on the sand, his head on the bundle, and tried to will himself to sleep.

But the sound of his name thwarted his efforts, and lured him to his feet.

He dragged the bundle behind him and carried his boots. Wherever he walked, the white sand took on a pink tinge.

Entranced, he followed the sound of his name.

Lightning flashed out of the black clouds boiling over the sea from the west. The wind picked up again, blowing fine grit into his exposed sores.

He kept walking.

Rain began to fall, large drops that left the sand wounded where they hit.

Head back, he opened his mouth, grateful for the fresh water, even though it stung his cracked lips and beat his bruised face.

At last he turned and looked inland. Two mountain peaks rose into the cloud maelstrom.

Now he knew the voice's source. It frightened him. Even in Porintel Loag legends mountains did not reach across the sea and call a man's name. Surely they would never call an outcast bastard's name. He was tainted, unfit for the loags, unwanted by the Star Followers. There would be no family for Enickor val Densu.

Fear gripped him. He fell to the sand, lowered his head and covered his face. Enickor did not want to believe that he knew who was calling him. He did not want to know why. What he wanted was to hide. But there was nowhere to go.

Chapter 3

PAM-ELLA SAT STRAIGHT IN A BRIGHTLY DECO-
rated saddle fashioned and made by the Harcel Loag. The
exquisite craftsmanship was more functional than decorative.
It fit her small frame well, acting as an adaptor for the broad
back of her beige-spotted roh. She patted the roh's side.

He lifted his left head, shook the dark brown mane that
continued around his chest and down his front legs, and loosed
a series of guttural whines. She answered by crooning a promise
to him of an early camp. The muscular roh alternated nodding
his two massive heads. The left one, a darker brown than the
right, dropped to nibble at the brackish grass tufts poking from
sand. The right one, almost white over the top of his sloping
forehead, changing to tan around his slanted, expressive eyes,
kept watch.

Beyond the blowing sand and the ocean's relentless waves
stood Shirwall. It seemed a lifetime ago since she had taken
leave of those majestic walls. "Over three years . . . thirteen
seasons . . ."

Conversion from the standard years used throughout the
Overeechy to Chiy-uneite seasons still had to be thought over.

How far the Overeechy was from Chiy-une. How removed the Kriell and his court were.

Chiy-une had experienced rough seasons, the winters harsh, the summers short, intense; seasons that had both aged and developed Pam-ella mentally and emotionally. The land accepted her after a time, as did the roh, when the stench of Star Follower diffused. It was not easy to live on the land, especially for an outworlder woman with so few skills. Necessity taught her what her mechanized education had not. She survived with scars as diplomas.

When she left Shirwall her skin had been soft, fed by luxury. She retained the young suppleness of her years, but there was a toughness around her eyes, which never rested in one place for more than a few seconds, and the set of her jaw that extended down to the corners of her mouth.

She seldom smiled. The external toll that worry and hardship demanded showed in the sinewy network of muscles over her arms and legs. She could walk the land without a roh, and had done so for more than five seasons before the smell of Shirwall wore off sufficiently for her to hunt well. Hunger was no longer a stranger. Cold dampness that seeped into bone marrow was a constant companion, the worst of which was abated by bedding down with a roh.

A hint of spring rode the west wind, promising better times.

Pam-ella felt defeated. Her long quest to find Enickor had produced nothing but loneliness. Never had she regretted her departure from Shirwall. Often, she thought about her father and Hoyiv. They, too, were a part of her life—a life she left behind.

It befuddled her to think that Enickor could so effectively disappear. Listening to the arrhythmic beat of the waves on the rock bridge, she wondered if he had ever made it across to the mainland. Had her quest been for nothing?

The suspicion that he might not want her to find him nagged her repeatedly.

A grimace darkened her tan cheeks.

There was much to learn on the land. The devastation caused by the Star Followers shamed her. The rejection of the House of Jeffires sickened her. It was genocide. Worse. What was the term for planet killing? Ecocide? It didn't really matter. It was mass murder by any name.

Come back to Shirwall.

She fondled the crisp edges of a letter written by Lord

Jeffires. The green in her eyes took on a deadliness. The price for retrieving the letter had been great at the southern gem extraction site. She remembered the look on the Overlord's face upon learning who she was, and the fate of the two who sought to treat her as a traveling whore.

She had not gone there to receive another imploring or threatening letter.

She had wanted news of Enickor. She had wanted to find him working at the site, or hear something about a half-breed Chiy-uneite.

Rather than reject her family in the eyes of the subjects of the House of Jeffires, she had accepted the letter. It was easy, after all the time away from them, to rationalize that dedication to her quest did not mean she had to abandon her family forever. They were all she had.

Come back to Shirwall . . .

She could not bring herself to cross the stone ridge. Life was easy there, no hardships, no drudgery, clean air. Compromise.

The land called her, claiming her as one of her own. The freedom her unique position afforded was unparalleled anywhere. The loags treated her courteously, provided she did not linger longer than a mark. Most times, ten days were more than sufficient to rest herself and the roh in the midst of their hospitality.

Behind her back, in hushed whispers and guarded company, they called her "fraen-spu." The first time she heard the term she asked what it meant.

Denial was out of the question. If they thought she could speak to the land, change the rivers, ride the wind—well, she decided at that time, maybe they won't sell me to the next rider from the House of Jeffires.

The Porintel Loag equated her strangeness and small build to Enickor's mother directly to her face. Pam-ella knew well the blame the dead woman bore for each and every misfortune which had befallen the Porintel.

All the loags revered her from afar, tolerated her in their midst, and catered when necessary. Most loagers feared the fraen-spu would turn on them if they did not. Life had become too precious, too difficult, in the last hundred seasons to incur another menace.

As a rule, Pam-ella preferred the company of her two roh and the cold ground to the scrutiny of the loags or the soft bed

19

waiting at Shirwall that was being paid for by the methodical demise of Chiy-une and her children.

The spotted brown-and-black roh carrying her supplies sneezed on the left side.

Alerted to the danger, she listened to the wind. Her head did not turn, but her eyes moved across their range, searching. The move to arm herself was slight, virtually unnoticeable.

She waited.

Her mount double-sneezed.

The scent of Star Followers was strong.

Shifting, her feet pushed firmly into the stirrups. The reins filled her left hand. A tug checked the pack roh's rope. It was loose. She slipped the noose from the side hook and freed him.

The beasts, both of whom had come from the mountains during the off-season of migration and chose to serve her eight seasons earlier, knew her readiness to flee and shared the desire.

She turned abruptly, yelled like a mountain gries, and dug her heels into the big roh's fleshy sides. Bent low, her *kalase* tight in her right hand, she charged her beasts into the oris weeds.

Cape and wraps flying over the roh, it was difficult to tell which of the two beasts carried a rider or a supply load.

No native would risk the tall weeds. They were a place for the roh. Roh and fraen-spus.

Star Followers, unfamiliar with the natural defenses Chiy-une provided her children, would follow and become lost.

The roh galloped, their slender legs and wide, flat hooves eating up the meters, felling the tall, thin oris spears. The razor-edged flower tufts at the end fell away from Pam-ella.

Well camouflaged by the towering sheaths, the roh loped along an unseen path, heading inland. Pam-ella let them have their way. This was their territory. After a time they would stop. Then she would lay an ambush if she was still being pursued.

Far south of Shirwall, and an additional hundred and eighty kilometers out to sea was a lone island. Just outside its single lagoon the water began to boil, as though yielding her dead to the sun god worshiped by the Ocandar Loag. The rangtur Enickor had long ago named Meiska frolicked in the shallows off their island home.

The period of isolation had hardened and strengthened Enickor. The last traces of youth were gone, replaced by a wisdom

20

and conviction which denied that he had ever been a child. Gone, too, was the hesitancy, the uncertainty that had previously cloaked his future.

His destiny was clear.

When the time came, he would pursue it relentlessly and without question. Questioning was reserved for those who suspected themselves mad. He could not be mad, insane. Therefore, he must accept the fact that hearing voices and having an inner guidance that spoke in a soft female voice was normal.

He ran down to the beach, muscular legs drilling his feet into the sand, sending it flying behind him. The water slowed him. He waded out to his waist, pushed off, and swam toward Meiska.

Recurring dreams, one-sided conversations he could not consciously remember, impressions of the danger in the air, and an ability to direct the massive sea creatures were all a part of the realm he embraced. At first, he was afraid to believe his new world real. Now, he was master to it.

It had been an arduous task to conquer the loneliness and the mountain simultaneously. He longed to hold a conversation with another human being. The ethereal voice that called him, directed his every activity without letting up, had nearly driven him mad the first two seasons. Now, in winter, she was weak, her voice usually silent.

He visualized her in dreams, his body craving substance. And he wept when he realized her peril at the hands of the Star Followers. He wanted her to rebel, to cast them out, reject the atrocities which wounded her so sorely. But she would not, for to do so would be the death of the loags. She loved her human children. Not until twelve of the thirteen seasons he spent on the island had passed did she charge him with finding a way to achieve harmony.

In the warm sun it was difficult to believe that the harsh ice age descending rapidly upon them would kill every living creature, including Chiy-une. And if the sun did warm her some many million seasons from now, no seed would sprout, no fish would surface.

Powerful arms reached into the waves. He kicked hard, propelling himself at Meiska. The water was warm, like the air hugging the island. Thin, meter-long fish with weighty jowls under their gills split their school as he approached. Sea floor life was abundant in these shallows, more plentiful than the bounty that the Ocandar Loag prayed for to the black sea god.

Sun-streaked hair floated around his shoulders when he treaded water, pausing to summon Meiska with a wave.

There was a bitterness in him. The hurt he suffered from Lord Jeffires still weighed heavily on his heart. To be so totally cast out after compromising his principles, keeping his distance from Pam-ella, and soliciting loag help in the destruction of the land they loved was something he could never forgive his Lord-Father for doing.

But Lord Jeffires was not his Lord-Father anymore. He had said so. Enickor wondered if it was true, if he could have approached Pam-ella in a different manner . . . .

The rangtur stopped rolling in the backwash, and straightened. The sea calmed as Meiska coiled his fifty-meter length like a great spring. The mottled green moss growth on his white, shiny, reptilian flesh coalesced into a solid green on the top.

He shot out of the water, forming a perfect arch over the reef barrier, glistening in the sunlight, dropping a shower of salty rain back into the sea. He seemed to sail through the air and dive into the shallows as though they were waters of enormous depth. His pointed snout came out of the foam and into the air, dipped back, then out again, finally resting half a dozen meters short of Enickor.

Meiska was sleek when stretched to his full length. Tentacles, ending with the standard set of five tendrils, spiraled his body from both sides of his jaw to just short of his flat, doubly split tail. Twelve meters wide and tapering to a couple of centimeters at the flat edge, Meiska's tail was his real fighting weapon, and effective during battle with other predatory sea dwellers. Now it stuck out of the water just over the barrier reef.

Meiska reached for Chiy-une's Sea Lord. Two of his five tendrils were shorter than the others, having not quite grown back from when Enickor sliced them off thirteen seasons ago.

Relaxed, Enickor was lifted onto the rangtur's slick green back a couple of meters behind the head. Tendrils held him while he worked his feet and legs into the harness shield which would protect him during the long ride ahead.

Once secured, he hauled in a rope tied to his waist, hand over hand. The bundle at the end disappeared, then popped out of the water, buffeted by the waves rolling over each other to feed the white sand beach. A neat coil grew over a hooked appendage wrapped into the harness rigging.

His bundle was tied in front of him. It served as another means to deflect the spray.

For several minutes he held Meiska in readiness.

The island loomed out of the sea. The ring of sandy beach was an illusion that gave way to high rock cliffs lifting vertically from the water just beyond the bend. This was home. It was his. And it was his blood that had turned the black cliff face red, staining the trail from the top forever. He did not understand it, but the smeared red streaks gave him a sense of pride. It was a climb he would not want to undertake even now, skilled as he was with the mountains.

The island was the crux of his new strength.

Never again would he fear the sea or her beasts. There was a harmony among them no land creature knew, save him. And he would not share that secret. It was part of the key to Chiyune's heart.

The mountain, twin peaks thrust into the sky to snag the low clouds and wring the water from them, was dark, bathed in shadow and mystique. For seven seasons he had lived upon the western peak, scavenging for food, snaring animals, robbing nests—studying Star Followers' secrets laid bare by an errant ship which had struck the peak. A small craft originally designed for pleasure, it carried an abundant amount of knowledge concerning mineral and ore deposits and their subsequent extraction.

Most of his new knowledge saddened him. Much of it angered him. Always he felt grateful, and somewhat guilty, when the harsh winters forced him to give up the mountain and live near the sea and Meiska. He craved the freedom. He needed the time to assimilate his learnings without pressure.

"Meiska, Meiska," he murmured. "Do you think we will ever come back home?"

The rangtur snorted into the water, sending spray halfway to the beach. He was impatient.

"All right, my friend, we shall begin this distasteful venture and pray we survive it."

A gentle nudge against Meiska's lymph glands under Enickor's right foot turned them toward the roaring sea. Clouds dotted the blue/purple sky. From high above came a roar which had no visible source.

Enickor turned his head toward the sea and looked eastward. It had been many seasons since he last heard a ship. Little doubt but that it was one of Lord Jeffires's ships.

He prodded Meiska.

He had no father. No brother. Pam-ella...

She would be wed to Hadilka. He shuddered. Hadilka was worse than a gorbich and held no principles, save the ones which benefited him monetarily. The thought saddened him. No bastard could have ever had a sweeter sister.

It was good that he had not seen her to say good-bye when he left Shirwall.

"Probably just as well," he said aloud.

Now he served another mistress, one who denied any division in his loyalties.

Chapter 4

THE SEA BEYOND THE RIPTIDES LOOKED DECEP-
tively calm. Waves gently licked against the wall of white cliffs
rising from the water and capped with stringy green-red cetit
vines. The stillness of the wind allowed the pungent land stench
to roll far out onto the sea.

Meiska traveled low in the water to avoid the distasteful air.
Enickor, too, could not help noticing the noxious thickness.
It burned his nostrils and irritated his sinuses. The changes in
Chiy-une were drastic in the short interval of twelve hundred
days which had elapsed since Meiska pulled him from the sea
bridge.

The trip had been smooth, but the four days were long. He
had slept at night. Meiska's pace never changed.

When Enickor considered the enormous task and the responsibility with which Chiy-une entrusted him, time raced.
Mediums, where a balance could be struck, were no longer
feasible for him.

Meiska selected a cove where numerable juts grew out of
the secluded area. These served as baffles, further arresting the
waves in the recess for which he headed. Sensitive to the moods
of the sea, Meiska sidled up to the face of the cliff he had

chosen. He paused, sharing the reluctance of his rider to bid farewell for a length of time neither could guess.

Enickor gazed at the open sea, inexplicably lonesome. The white limestone cliffs gathered in the dull orange of the sunlight refracting over the edge of Chiy-une.

He gauged the difficulty involved in the climb facing him. Night added a negative dimension. Yet daylight guaranteed his detection by one of the cliff watchers from the Harcel Loag. Dusk was the optimum time, if such a condition did truly exist.

And there was little time to spare. Without a spoken farewell, he tied the free end of the rope resting on the hook he had fashioned into the harness around his waist, then tested the end attached to his bundle. It was secure.

Meiska coiled, braced against the white/orange cliff, then sprang, pulling his head high out of the water. His frontmost tentacle, Enickor grasped securely in the three longer tendrils, reached even higher onto the cliff face.

Enickor struggled to find a safe hold. For a split second, the old panic of pre-island days reached out and put an icy finger on his heart. But there was no secure hold for the past either.

He scrambled, reaching to the left and worked his fingers into a crevice which had not been weathered smooth. A few precarious moments lapsed before Meiska was confident in Enickor's placement on the cliff face, and released him.

The rangtur's collapse into the water formed tidal waves in the cove, destroying its sedateness with the oscillation of the water.

Driven to climb the island mountains time after time by the voice of his mistress in the wind, Enickor had learned easier ways to attack the seemingly impossible barriers the land posed. The white seacliffs were not so difficult, not while there existed a smattering of light. He hurried, pausing only to wipe his hands on his pants legs when they became moist and slipped on the smooth limestone.

Below, the sea thrashed for a while, then settled into the peaceful rise and fall of the incoming and outgoing water at the cliff base.

The final ten meters were the most difficult. The sun had sunk so far beyond the horizon that not even an orange/umber ribbon stained the west. The stars were bright overhead. A chill crept over the land and spilled down the cliff to press the sea. Enickor groped, rather than saw, his way toward the top. The

26

red/green vines with oblong, fleshy leaves the size of his fore-arm made the last couple of meters feel longer than they were.

He could not rely upon cetit vines to hold his weight, nor could he bull his way through them. Wherever he broke the pliable skin on the leaves a sticky juice oozed out. The insides were a series of cellular octagons, and spongy in consistency. He gathered the heartiest vines, stripped the leaves away one-handed, then regrouped. Testing the cluster of vines was as risky as using them.

He managed to get over the lip of the cliff by hurling his body upward. The slick cliff face was impossible to hold on to, with the cetit juice spreading from the flat where a large patch of leaves had been slashed.

In the darkness, the saccharine odor of the cetit grew stronger, overpowering the aroma from the sea. He stood, looked around briefly, then froze.

A hundred meters inland, on a small rise, a figure stood, outlined by starlight. He hoped it was a sea watcher from the Harcel. If it was a soldier . . .

A stream of angry curses silently moved over his lips. Either way, it was bad. If it was a watcher from the Harcel, the whole loag would speak of the Man Who Walked out of the Sea and feel the end of the world coming. It had been foretold in the legends.

The Harcel legends had seldom been wrong.

The mood faded. He could not think of the Harcel without remembering Keladine Ornasive. Thoughts of the great Leader were synonymous with his only daughter, Elisif. He always smiled when remembering her. It would be good to see her again. She had been open with him, bright and vivacious.

He debated cutting the rope attached to his belongings and chasing the watcher. He gazed down at the blackness of the cove, unable to see much more than a hint of light against the very tops of the opposite cliffs. When he looked back to the rise the figure was gone.

It solved the problem of which course he should choose, but gave him a new worry.

Dismayed, he hauled up the bundle. He could not risk calling to Meiska now.

On the other hand, the rangtur would not expect any emotional parting ceremony, even if it were limited to a word.

Meiska would linger around the cliff bases and the line of sandy beaches to the north until needed, or until he felt the life

27

force the Mistress had blessed Enickor with on the island dissipate.

The rangtur's view of his universe extended well beyond what he considered his temporary stay on Chiy-une. He would do his utmost to preserve his corporeal water world, lest the chain in the evolutionary path he followed be broken. Beginning anew was the dread of any rangtur ascending toward the goal of pure intelligence and energy.

He tolerated man, though he considered him so low on the evolutionary scale that he was a food source, much the way man viewed the torna-pok.

Enickor's knowledge of the rangtur was greater than man as a whole had been privy to over the eons that the rangtur had spent evolving throughout the galaxy. They had a hundred shapes and more than twice as many names, no two quite the same, each an increment above the level below.

With a tug the bundle came over the lip, dragging cetit vines in its wake. Enickor slung it across his chest to the left and the rope coil to the right.

He turned inland, ready to outrun the night and reach the heart of the Harcel Loag territory before dawn.

The cetit squished under his weight, coating his feet and ankles halfway up to his knees with juice. Several hundred meters inland the vines thinned. The ground was gritty. Sharp blades of grass grew in clusters and reached into the night, attempting to trip him. The cold crawling over the land aided him as he ran.

Beyond the Harcel he had no real destination. He felt compelled to see the land, assess the damage, and seek help as the opportunity arose. If there was no help to be had . . . Chiy-une would surely direct him.

He hoped.

When he slowed to rest he could smell death in the air. The foulness in the wind stank of Star Follower exploitation. It saddened him to know that they had penetrated so deeply into the Harcel Loag land.

Clouds rolled down from the north to blot out the faint starlight.

Enickor moved cautiously, alerted by the absoluteness of the dark. There were no gries, no night calls, no noise upon the land from foragers. It was deathly silent.

For the second time since leaving the island, the icy touch of fear lingered upon his heart.

28

The advent of night imposed a slower pace on the roh. Pamella, too, felt the strain of their forced journey through the oris. Her promise of an early camp had fallen by the wayside.

Whoever penetrated the oris had to have an excellent mount, one capable of navigating the deceiving grasses. He was also a Star Follower, or lived among them. The stench made the roh sneeze when they doubled back and the wind shifted.

The proximity of her pursuer was such that she could not stop and prepare an ambush, yet she was unable to outrun or outmaneuver him. The stealth he employed assured her that it was only one man or woman. And one on one she was not too afraid of losing. However, it seemed more prudent to try to outlast the pursuer. Surely it was safer.

The roh were tired. She had pushed them hard to reach the ocean, only to retreat into the oris. A bit ashamed, she prodded the roh a final time and urged the pack roh to move on its own to the north. She laid low over her saddle and veered south.

The oris weed parted for the last time. Ahead lay a small clearing strewn with boulders. Beyond that were trees and grass signaling the first swell of the Gorbich Hills and the Lyndirlyan Mountains.

Pam-ella made her decision instantly. She pulled up the pack roh and unfastened the lead rope. Next she dug her heels into her mount, and hung on. The awkward leaps of the beast, surmounting the hurdles before him, tossed her about on his back. Twice she was nearly thrown from the saddle.

The pack roh followed and slowed under his burden. He nickered and turned north.

The roh's gait smoothed on the soft grass terrain below the trees. Pam-ella regained control of both her position and the roh, and chose a more southerly course. She kept to the rocky trails and watched the sky, dreading the midnight moon.

The night was unusually silent. Only the cry of an errant gries startled Pam-ella. The steady plod of the roh was next to silent until they hit an occasional patch of drum rock. She dismounted and walked, leading the beast and watchful for the glint of silver flickering in the starlight.

She hurried, head moving from side to side, listening, smelling the air.

Rolling hills hid them while they remained in the valleys. But the valleys were often sodden with spring rains and the plentiful snow-melt rivers running through an underground network to find the sea.

When the moon did rise, large, round, and luminous, it lit the land with a false daylight. Streamers of clouds heralding a new storm raced to veil it, but like the night friend it was, light poked through to the land and cast shadows.

Pam-ella could not allay the growing concern, almost a fear, which obsessed her. She had not heard the pursuer since parting with her pack roh.

She crested a hill, using the trees for camouflage, halted the roh, and mounted.

"Soon, Philiar," she whispered, patting his right neck, "we will find a place and camp." The weariness in her voice seemed to instill a second wind in the mount. He traversed down the steeper back side of the hill, mindful of the excellent cover the trees and scrub provided.

The breeze came from behind her. That was not a good tactic, she knew. These hills belonged to the gorbich and were seldom frequented even by the loags. It was too dangerous.

In a fashion, she wished for the return of her pack roh. He would come. In time. Hopefully not so soon that he dragged along the follower, but soon enough to be of help should the gorbich gather and attack.

Thwak!

It sounded on her downhill side. Instantly she guided the roh to her left, angling uphill. Then almost as quickly, she jerked the reins in the direction of the sound.

The air turned heavy with the scent of Star Followers. The roh would have sneezed if he had not been breathing hard with the sudden burst of exertion. He galloped straight into the brush, leaping the lower ones.

The sound came again.

This time Pam-ella felt something strike her right shoulder. Her grip tightened on the *kalase* strapped to her wrist and ready for firing.

She could hear them now. There were three of them. Possibly four.

A faint light flash from the right was answered by her *kalase*. There was a scream.

Her roh slacked his pace so abruptly that she almost toppled forward. Once recovered, she turned in the saddle, picked out one of the two charging shapes, and fired again.

The shot passed narrowly to the left of the shape.

The thing piercing her shoulder felt like a lead weight. Her arm numbed.

Using her left hand, and nearly out of the saddle, she aimed and fired again. It was a bright, quick burst.

One more adversary was eliminated.

Another dim light flash surprised her from the left. It struck her. She could feel herself falling forever and ever. There was no pain when she hit the ground, bounced twice, and rolled into a rumpled heap between two boulders.

She was conscious, aware of everything going on around her, even the angry spider whose web she had ruined. No pain rushed her senses and, strangely, no fear. Resignation was all she had.

Philiar sneezed, then wandered over to investigate. An opening in the trees created a search beacon from the moon. Pam-ella saw the ugly mark on the beast's near neck. She wanted to cry out when he staggered, then crumpled, striking his black jaw on the boulder. The sound of his bones breaking sickened her.

She wanted to turn away, to get up and run.

Yet only her mind knew what was best. Her body could not respond.

She listened to the remaining two approach her. They were cautious, as though they were either well-trained or unsure of themselves.

Their feet were clumsy upon the land. The scrub was loud, snapping and rustling a warning of their approach.

When at last she could see them, a cry of surprise died in her throat. They wore the House of Jeffires battle garb.

The lead man examined her roh quickly, drew back his foot and loosed several hard kicks into his side.

The beast exhaled loudly with each kick, snorting at the final one, which broke two of his ribs.

The way Pam-ella's head was twisted prevented her from missing the cruelty meters away from her. She studied their faces in the splashes of moonlight. She would remember them as long as she lived.

Angry, afraid, she watched the soldier change the setting on his weapon. It was not the standard *kalase* that she used, but something new, foreign.

He aimed at the roh's near head and fired, changed direction for the one with the shattered jaw and fired again.

It was quick. Final.

Philiar died without a whimper.

Pam-ella's eyes opened wider as the weapon was brought to bear on her. Often she had considered the possibility of meeting her death while roaming across the land, but in all those times she had never considered that possibility arriving in the form of soldiers from the House of Jeffires.

The second man shone a light on her. By the way the light moved she knew she was badly twisted among the rocks. Still, she felt nothing.

"Look what we have here," said the first one.

"Is that the old Lord's daughter? The wild one who ran away?" The light flicked off.

"I believe so." He picked his way through the rocks and squatted beside her.

She tried to look away when he touched the back of his hand to her face.

He chuckled. "Yes. It is the hauteur of royalty isn't it, Mistress Pam-ella? You fail to remember me?"

In truth, she did not remember him from the past, but she would not forget him easily in the future. His pinched features added to an already gaunt appearance. He looked dehydrated.

"There is a nice reward for your return to m'Lord Hoyiv."

The comment forced her eyes to seek him.

He laughed loudly.

The sound alarmed his partner. "Quiet! These woods have ears, fool!"

As though the land heard, a stronger breeze sprang up and riffled the trees.

"Yes, your brother, Mistress. Would you like to know about your father?" As he taunted, he fumbled with her cape tie, pausing occasionally to run his hand over her breasts.

She continued to look directly at him, blinking only when necessary, relieved she could not feel his intimate touches. She hoped that he would continue his banter and tell her some news of her father. Something had to be amiss for the soldier to mention him. In fact, something had to be terribly wrong for there to be soldiers on the land at all.

"Podel, my friend, royalty?" He was delighted by his suggestion, which was lost on the vigilant Podel.

Podel kept a nervous watch and turned his back, making it obvious he had no taste for what his friend planned.

"She is small, but I think she will last." Once busy with the layers of clothing she wore, he lost his verbosity.

Pam-ella became detached from what she knew would follow, and turned inward. She thought he would either kill her or leave her to die when he finished. He could not afford to take her to Hoyiv. No. Chiy-une would claim her life with the cold that crept out of the north and moved across the land, killing the unprotected along with the more fragile vegetation.

Hooting gorbich sounded from the north. A flash of light came from the other side of the hill and reached against the stars.

"Do what you will. I am leaving this place," Podel said quietly, stood and began walking. "Those damn gem finders crossed into Hadilka territory, and now there's no place safe for us. Especially here."

"Come now, can't you spare me a few minutes?"

"Do what you want. I'm leaving. I don't like the feel of this place. That nekka leader, Illeuro, got away. I'm not sticking around to find out how one of them acts when he's separated. No, thanks." Podel walked faster, his steps harsh on the land. "It will be difficult enough explaining why and how we lost a whole nekka, a supply line, and all our officers."

Disgusted, he threw her cape over her. Loudly he addressed Podel, "Once again, you are right. She has already cost us Vagod and Tad. Wait up, Podel. Maybe we ought to go hunt down Illeuro. The last thing we need is one of them Quniero to give a different story than we do. There are actually men who can understand them."

He straightened, watching Podel. "When I was on a sender detail at Lord Hadilka's main house I also heard that those gem finders never lie, and they always know what their mates are thinking." He shuddered and squinted at the dark.

"What about her?" Podel glanced nervously at Pam-ella.

"Leave her. What damn good is she? We don't have time to use her. We can't take her back to Lord Hoyiv without worsening our chances of getting off this rock alive and in one piece." He looked at the mountain. "No. We better get moving."

She wanted to cry out for them not to just leave her for the gorbich and the cold sweeps.

Podel's reluctance to abandon her needed little convincing before he recognized the wisdom in his friend's logic. They began to walk away from the boulders and the roh and the half-naked woman on the ground.

She strained to hear the last sound of their untrained feet

beat on the ground, hoping they would have a change of heart and return, knowing they would not. A tear rolled out of the corner of her left eye. The clouds gathered around the moon, and an icy spring drizzle began to fall.

Light flashed from the other side of the hill once again. She wished the two soldiers dead.

Chapter 5

ENICKOR TRAVELED THROUGH THE NIGHT. HIS mood had swung toward the positive for a moment when the full moon rose in the east. The glow aided his journey by allowing him to travel more swiftly.

The first cold ribbon that snaked across the ground forced him to delve into his bundle for his boots and warmer clothing. Moonlight highlighted the bleak desolation facing Enickor from all directions.

For the entire night there was not one sound from any living creature save Enickor.

With the morning came a new depression. The vastness of the ruins extended as far as Enickor could see. He knew he was not wrong about the direction he had chosen. Harcel Loag boundaries were too familiar.

Mounds of churned and charred soil dotted the scape in all directions. These were similar in both size and shape to the ones he had been walking around all night. There numbers were uncountable, and there seemed no end to them.

How could this have happened in only twelve hundred days?

Too well he knew that nothing would grow in this barren,

poisoned soil. Not for at least four hundred seasons. And that was too late for Chiy-une's children.

Ice would be upon the land. It could not be stopped now.

It was too late. The plight of the land could not be reversed. He wanted a future for Chiy-une. He wanted a rebirth after the ice was gone.

He walked the entire day, realizing the possibility that the Harcel Loag may have ceased to exist. The idea struck fear in him. It had to exist. It must survive! It was somewhere other than where it had been since the beginning of the loags.

By noon, white bones began to appear between the mounds on his left. He assumed a north-easterly course and followed the bleached trail. It physically hurt him to count the horrendous number of animals that had been slaughtered in the Star Followers' wake. He hoped to climb over a rise and see lush country where a few early sprouts of spagus might be dug and eaten. In truth, he had not expected the condition of the land to be so desecrated, and had anticipated finding food much earlier in his journey.

During late afternoon he saw an ominous dark brown stain spread across the eastern sky. Within minutes the air turned cold and difficult to breathe, as though the molecules were being sucked away and only a few were strong enough to resist the pull.

Angry, Enickor ran to the largest, most stable-looking mound he could find, and began to scoop out a niche on the east side.

He worked frantically, feeling the effects of the oxygen-stripped air, pulled and pushed by the wind being generated by the Star Followers' mining.

The recess was barely large enough for him, but greater protection than he expected. Sitting, elbows on knees, he held his head in his hands and worked on stabilizing his breathing.

He called upon the discipline learned as a child in the Porintel Loag. How many hours had he stood among the roh, barely breathing, concentrating, waiting, wishing with all his heart one of them would accept him? Might look his way?

It did not matter now. No roh grazed in this country. The Porintel was far away. Ardinay, the Metaliary, no longer demanded perfection from him. Now he demanded it from himself.

Thoughts of his childhood and his burning desire to be accepted by the Porintel as one of them soured. Those were days long ago, when the most important thing in the world was to belong to a family. Today, he had no family save Chiy-une.

He watched the sky move at tremendous speeds over the mounds.

It still boggled his mind when he thought about the harnessing of a planet's atmosphere; churning it with the ground and converting the energy the mixture created into a vehicle that killed the planet. The greater the atmospheric disturbance, the more energy released, the more power available to harness. With that power, Chiy-une's metals were extracted from the ground and hurled through the atmosphere at more than eight kilometers a second, a speed at which the mined material achieved orbit around the planet.

He had seen the calculation on what was lost at the critical point when the mass was brought up to orbital speed. He had also seen the exorbitant price they were paid for the percentage of Chiy-une's precious material that achieved the pick-up orbit.

They would strip all of Chiy-une.

The wind grew stronger. The sky turned dark, darker than quarter moon.

Dust and grit flowed over the ground, eroding the mounds, redistributing their masses to form new barchan dunes. Enickor pressed his body against the back of his shelter. The brown wind howling along the ground could flay the skin from his bones as cleanly as it had the animals whose remains ran the northern lines.

Half the night had passed before Enickor was able to breathe the air without filtering it through several layers of his old shirt. Hungry, he set out again, feeling his way through the debris and light dust rain. It would continue to fall from the sky for days, perhaps even a quarter-season, depending upon how big a strike they found and how deep it was.

Lightning and thunder warred in the east. Seldom was the powerful flash visible. He had seen the aftereffects up close, from the helix ship itself. That was many seasons ago, but he would never forget it. Power of so great a magnitude could not be forgotten—especially by a Chiy-uneite.

Caught in the reverie of the happier events that filled his life at that time, Enickor continued through the ruins. He wondered about Pam-ella and Hadilka, figuring that they would be living in opulence and journeying for visits into the Kriell's tight circles.

It saddened him.

"She was brought up for that," he whispered into the night. "Maybe she found a lover for him." He shuddered, fervently hoping she had, remembering how she cringed each time Hoyiv teased her about marrying the powerful lord.

He kicked a dried mudball. It shattered in a dozen directions.

It did not make sense that Pam-ella's unhappiness with Hadilka should buy so much power for Hoyiv.

That was an anomaly he had never been able to sort out and hit a wall of silence each time he asked, regardless of whom he asked.

He tried to push Pam-ella from his thoughts. She lingered, reminding him that he still loved her and probably always would.

From out of the dark came a shout, followed by the uneven pounding of running feet on the caked and cracking ground.

Enickor looked around, seeking a shelter.

Unable to see them, he could hear them coming, loud and thunderous enough to drown the power maelstrom in the east.

He ran quietly, wanting to create confusion, hoping they could not see any better than he, knowing better than they how uneven a match it was.

He hugged the dust wall and rounded a barchan, angled hard north and charged head-on into a runner. Though he expected the collision and locked his extended forearms, the impact staggered him. He recovered quickly and pressed on.

Wrongness scathed his mind. It was more than the presence of the Star Followers, as surely these men were. No loagers would attack *en masse* in the cloak of night unless at war. Loagers did not wage war. They could only commit suicide at the hands of the Star Followers.

There was no time to think about it.

He ran into two men, both smaller than he, but strong. He swung and caught one in the throat, bolted, and used both fists to pummel the second man in the abdomen.

Again he was free.

Their numbers were great.

These last two had been waiting for him.

He veered westward and climbed a mound. He pressed his body into the dust. Perspiration ran freely under his clothing, soaked it, and lapped up the dust.

For a short time confusion dominated the ground. Enickor lay perfectly still, controlling his breathing and using layers of cloth to keep from sneezing.

"Damn! Where did he go?"

"We didn't get him?" asked a second voice, surprised.

"No." There was a pause before he continued. "Search this whole area, centimeter by centimeter. I want a survivor!"

Gaediv? Gaediv? I am lost. Call to me. Bring me home. The Quniero moved through the brush, his sturdy paddle tail flicking twigs and leaves. The call had gone out. He thought of his katelings and sent yet another call.

Aloneness was unnatural for the Quniero, not being alone, but being emotionally separate from the leah, from Gaediv and the katelings. Illeuro asa Khatioup fought the dismal isolation crushing his spirit. To yield was to die, mad, insane, dispossessed of mind, his memory unabsorbed by Gaediv.

Illeuro asa Khatioup was a nekka leader. Strength had made him so.

The disaster compelled him to seek advice from Gaediv. The caretakers had fought among themselves, then deserted them.

His nekka had located and mined a half a metric ton of the substance called diamond, moved over the hills, and located a pure vein of titanium. The caretakers should have been pleased.

They were not.

Illeuro did not understand, nor did he question.

Gaediv had told him to work for the caretakers and obey. He had led his nekka in accordance with her wishes. Molecular mutation had been forbidden by the Gaediv. As a consequence, they had known hunger for the first time in the collective memory of the leah.

He tried to ignore the soulful cries of this land. He thought only of the nekka, of Gaediv, of home and the katelings. Unbidden, the knowledge that the Quniero aided in the destruction of a living world came to fetter his mind.

The high caves of Alidanko called to him from across the light years. Memories of the katelings, their foreclaws barely formed, hind legs beginning to sprout, and baby fuzz sprouting between their soft lapped scales, cajoled him through the heart of the Gorbich Hills.

Where had the caretakers gone? Why had the supply lines died? Where had the strange caretakers taken his nekka?

He did not understand the differences between caretakers. Some wore bright crimson-colored skins over their skins. Others, the ones who took his nekka, wore gold and yellow. Surely the find they had mined was sufficient for all the caretakers?

Perhaps not. He reminded himself that the differences between caretaker and Quniero were infinitely greater than appearance and ability. Caretakers shared neither possessions as a whole nor thoughts.

He ached to commune with the leah, to know the warmth of a thought and partake in the emotional anesthesia of oneness.

The drone of insects in a rocky clearing on his left caught his attention. His slender body waved from side to side around the ipcar trees and the scrub. Perched on a boulder he surveyed carnage which sparked terror in his heart.

What might have been a two-headed beast indigenous to this land had been killed. Illeuro's sensitive glands detected a violence of tremendous power. Caretaker weapons.

A small caretaker lay turned on the rocks. The scent of death was so great, he did not know if it lived. Its small size suggested that it had been a kateling not long ago.

The territorial beasts hooted. They were near. Illeuro had felt the fear born in the caretakers when hordes of the beasts massed outside the mining camp. Then he had been fascinated, savoring all he could gather on the emotional wind for Gaediv's analysis. Now the isolation made him vulnerable to the same disease of the mind that the caretakers had experienced.

A malevolence rode the breeze. The offensive scent found him.

He did not know whether to run or stay to protect the small caretaker. Without Gaediv to direct him, without the nekka to provide incentive, he was lost.

Undecided, he turned away. His shovel paws curved over the boulder, his iron claws clacking against the surface. Skittish, the fine tendrils which usually remained coiled above his two heavily-lidded eyes whipped in the air. All three meters danced. His long body, built close to the ground for swift traveling and easy tunneling, rose at the base of the boulder. His elongated snout was crowned by two raised nostrils that grew beards as filters for the fine sense of smell which made the Quniero the best gem finders in the galaxy. Nothing could smell out a hard mineral—except a Quniero.

They were coming, the beasts whom the caretakers feared.

Illeuro sought Gaediv and his nekka one final time, received emptiness, then scurried through the brush. He would go west, follow the sun, just as Gaediv had told him to do when he was a kateling. If a Quniero follows the sun long enough, he will find a leah. A leah loves.

He knew the beasts would follow him for a while. When they got too close, he would tunnel. They could not follow. He was Quniero, a nekka leader, and strong. This he told himself over and over, holding to the promise of communion with the leah.

Pam-ella had slept. The sun was well into the sky, though where she could not tell exactly. She felt watched and sniffed. Gorbich had an unmistakable stench.

The tingling in her fingers and toes birthed hopes that her paralysis was temporary, and recovery imminent.

In time, she thought. *Everything comes in its own time*.

Diligently she tried to move, increasing the range of feeling and fighting the stark alternatives which cropped into her mind.

The dead roh drew insects. These settled on Pam-ella, too, and, receiving no resistance, went about their work.

The insects were inconvenient at best, but could not do her irreparable harm if she regained feeling in her body before the next cold wave ran over the ground. That could kill her. Or the gorbich would be attracted by the roh carcass and find her more appetizing. They preferred live meat.

She grieved for her dead comrade. The hardships and service they had shared with one another deepened the loss. Were it possible, she would have sobbed openly, letting her hurt wail through the forest as a Metaliary of the Harcel would do for so great a love. But her vocal chords remained mute.

The forest turned silent with midafternoon lethargy.

Tears rolled from the outside corner of her right eye, and ran down her temple into the dirty mat of her hair.

Her grieving deepened in the aura of depression which had plagued her for more days than she cared to count. It did not seem possible for things to become worse, though she was certain they would. The gorbich lived here.

The searching and the amount of time since Enickor's disappearance had almost convinced her that he never made it across the bridge. The storm probably swept him out to sea, or one of the monsters that terrorized the Ocandar Loag claimed him.

In retrospect, the futility was even more dismal, but she would have done it all again, if given the option.

The odds had always been against her. She thought about

dying, and wished she could make some kind of peace with her father for casting her into the role of Lord Hadilka's wife. Surely, there had to be another way? Were the money, the mining rights, the long-term political gain great enough to justify a forced marriage? Was he so afraid of Hadilka's prestige and power with the Overeechy?

She could appeal to the Kriell.

What price peace between the two most powerful, influential Great Houses?

She doubted that the Overeechy would even hear her case. Would they give up the harmony between the two Houses in court just to force her right to choose who she married? Not likely.

Hadilka had managed to gain dependency from many of the minor Houses. They had no choice but to ally with him. The financial backing of those puppet houses and their holdings during critical times had kept the Overeechy solvent, their coffers full. A powerful man, Lord Hadilka manipulated people and their holdings with the same whims found in a spring storm.

Lord Jeffires was not without his influence, too. Yet both men had a lust for new territories and expansion of their empires within the Overeechy. And both knew they had to hold on tightly while the other was near. They were rival predators, political brothers of the gorbich.

Pam-ella could not see herself as the bond between the two Great Houses. Perhaps it was selfishness, but she feared nothing would cement the rift which had existed for more than two hundred standard years.

Hadilka had been cordial last time she had seen him. He had gone out of his way to be kind to her. Yet it felt like a game in which she was the pawn, tossed and bargained for by two seasoned opponents.

By the time the sun began to hide below the horizon and the shadows were a blanket descending over the Gorbich Hills, feeling had returned to Pam-ella's legs up to her knees, her arms to above the elbows, and parts of her buttocks and rib cage. Her head pounded. A dull ache in her back served as a portent of the pain in store for her when feeling returned in full. Still, she could not move.

The first gorbich hooted just before the shadow line stole up the opposing hillside. Pam-ella listened.

He had a dinner find.

A flurry of gries sounded in the sky, going home for a change of hunters. At night the male rested while the female hunted; their tastes in food differed. They too had spotted an easy dinner, but would pass.

The gorbich must be close, she thought, trying to move. And there must be several of them.

It seemed odd that she could be so objective about the death that certainly faced her when they converged upon the carcass of her friend. It was an unreality. The detachment, which grew in proportion to the nearness of the gorbich, imparted the sensation that she was watching herself from some point in the trees and could see all the peril ready to shred the flesh from her bones.

She could smell them before their passage through the brush reached her ears. The musk-and-damp-fur odor seeped into the stone. How they managed to sniff out their prey was a mystery.

The odor permeated her sinuses, stung, then passed into her lungs, carrying with it a dread which killed any foolish hopes of escape she may have nurtured. It seeped into the very nuclei of her being and manufactured a fear greater than anything she thought possible.

They began circling.

Occasionally one showed his yellow-eyed, gigantic head. Saliva dripped from double rows of fangs, which fit together like a complex three-dimensional puzzle. The long streamers of perpetually-wet hair that hung from the round, floppy jowls matched the shaggy coat hanging on the two-meter-long body. Talons, instead of hooves on the front two legs, clicked on a rock slab approximately fifty meters into the forest in the direction of her feet. The clatter of their hooves was a hollow sound. They were not fast runners, but had the stamina to pursue their prey until the victim dropped in its tracks.

The faster they circled, the more fear they managed to generate in Pam-ella. Had her vocal chords been in better shape, she would have been screaming instead of whimpering.

Their movements were ritualistic, weaving a spell, intensifying the fear they generated by combining psyches.

The fear acted as a catalyst against the paralytic state. Without her realizing it, partial mobility had returned to her left side. The pain in her spine blended into her emotional trauma until it was merely a contributory aspect to the over-all condition of borderline hysteria.

The gorbich became braver in direct porportion to the thickness of the shadows and the blackness of the eastern horizon. Several of the mightiest stars had already staked claims on the ecliptic plane for their constellations.

Abruptly, the fear ceased to be sent.

Pam-ella still whimpered; desperate to be free and away from the Gorbich Hills, disappointed with her failure to find Enickor, disgusted by her role in the hardships Star Followers had thrust upon the peaceful loags.

The night had completely pressed the sun from the sky before Pam-ella realized the absence of the fear created by the gorbich. She could still hear them. Their circle was growing tighter, drawing them closer to her. She could not get used to the stench, and noted an added pungency as they drew near.

The wind stilled. The fetid air rested heavily upon the ground.

She used the time. Many seasons upon the land had taught her to maintain a presence of mind, which, coupled with a much-needed optimism, was often her best chance of survival.

She used the mobility in her left side and hand to push herself off the sharp rock jabbing into her backbone.

A shrill scream escaped though she had promised herself it would not. There were spots of feeling in her leg. These compounded the difficulty she had coordinating her flight, centimeter by centimeter, away from the roh carcass and toward a large tree. A visual search for her *kalase* showed it to be strapped to her right hand.

Death so close, she thought bitterly. Had she known . . . Had there been a way to make the arm move . . . She would have killed both the soldiers wandering the hills. *I hope the gorbich got them!*

She was not concerned about covering her body, only that she be able to drag along her clothing to the tree. The rocks cut into her flesh, rolled over one another, and sometimes fell, landing on a tender area just regaining feeling.

Pam-ella fixed her gaze on the tree, ignoring the yellow eyes stopping to watch her. They glowed like lighted signs advertising death.

The pain, like the fear, was set aside.

When the gorbich resumed sending terror her way she did her utmost to close her mind, look only at the tree, and make it a singularity.

They began to hoot. The tones ranged the octaves and shook the leaves in the trees with resonance.

Pam-ella felt the blood oozing from her shoulder wound and faltered.

The tree was a few centimeters from her fingertips when the first gorbich broke into the clearing and made a pass at the roh, taking the entire front leg and shoulder. The leg was stiff in the gorbich's mouth. He ran toward Pam-ella, dipped the hoof, and struck her right hip before leaping over her to clear the way for the next gorbich.

Chapter 6

RAIN CAME WITH THE MORNING LIGHT. IT WAS A black rain filled with ice crystals whose cores were bits of Chiy-une. The force driving it seemed angry at the gravity trying to reclaim the Star Follower waste.

Cold seeped through the dust and rock cover hiding Enickor. Gradually the thin layer turned to mud, undermined the larger particles, and began to slip away.

He listened hard, trying to ascertain the soldiers' proximity. He hoped they had enough sense to seek shelter, just as he would have to. The grit and ice in the wind could separate the skin from healthy muscle, then that too, right down to the bone, once the storm approached its fury.

The roar of the maelstrom grew until he was left no choice but to seek protection. He fell, then slid down the side of the mound, losing patches of clothing and skin on the way. The ground was soft and cold. The dust had been beaten into a frothy mud by the rain. It was difficult to stand. Running was next to impossible.

Using the sides of the mounds, Enickor called on all his instincts to put him in the direction from which the soldiers had come. The rope crossing his chest became heavy with water. For a brief moment he toyed with getting rid of it.

He fell often. Several times he brought some of the outer layers of the mounds protecting him along. Twice, slag covered him completely and he had to burrow his way back to the storm or smother.

There came a place where the mounds ceased to exist. Nothing aided him in avoiding the storm. Nothing broke the wind or sheltered him from the driving ice. His skin began to burn with pain. Despair grew out of his realization of how desperate his predicament was becoming.

Enickor . . .

The first time he heard the Mistress he thought he was hallucinating.

To the left, Enickor. Go to your left.

It hardly seemed possible to hear anything over the incessant roar of the wind and clatter of the ice on the rocks, but he followed. It made as much sense as going straight.

She guided him out of the dead area and into a place where the land and the rock were still alive.

When the voice stopped, Enickor stopped. It took him several minutes to realize that the ice was no longer battering him. He touched his face. It was bleeding. The pain began to catch up with him.

He turned, seeking to divert himself through the worst of it.

The lightning flashes lit the sky briefly from time to time. Their presence indicated a new intensity to the storm.

Enickor gazed into the darkness, waiting for a time when a new flash would come, so he could see more of the world around him. He was in a cave only four or five meters deep and a couple of meters wide. The ceiling arched high enough for him to stand straight, but he could not stretch.

A tremendous lightning fork lit the sky brighter than day, then left it darker than before. Enickor stared at a spot on the ground several meters from the mouth of the cave. It seemed to have shifted.

A lesser flash came, confirming that there was something just beyond the cave mouth. Enickor dashed into the storm, squatted beside the form and ran his hands over it. It was a man, his uniform torn by the ice knives.

Enickor rolled him face up, grabbed his arms and jerked

him through the sucking grasp of the mud to the cave. His arms ached and his skin bled.

Once inside, Enickor pulled the man to the very back of the cave, where his own bundle was, and tried to lay him on his back. The unnatural bend in the way the man lay had Enickor check his back. Under his jacket he wore a pack.

A sword had been strapped to the soldier's waist with an improvised belt. Enickor paused, laid the man gently on the rock and stared at the sword for several moments before he cut it free.

His surprise turned to anger.

The scabbard was lustrous, ornately decorated by each of the Metaliary craftsmen who had sat in service of a loag Leader. It was the scepter of the Harcel, the Holy upon which vows were made and promises sealed by blood against the sword's edge. It had belonged to Keladine Ornasive. Enickor remembered the Harcel Leader as a large man, perhaps as big and powerful as he was now. He longed to speak with him again and listen to his bragging complaints centered around Elisif, his only daughter.

The sword slipped from the scabbard with the ring of metal against metal. It sang in the tiny shelter. To Enickor, it was a dirge for the death of a loag, a lament for Ornasive. Softly, he hummed the death song of the Harcel, having forgotten, or never learned, the words during his time with them. The sword warmed, the serrated grip as perfect to the form of his hand as if it had been designed. It was a strangely exhilarating sensation.

After a time, Enickor proceeded to carefully remove the soldier's jacket and pack. The shallow breathing and constant shiver bespoke the nearness of death.

He rifled the pack. The inside was dry. There were a couple of things Enickor recognized and one that he did not. What he wanted most for the man was at the bottom. He removed a small pouch, opened it and began pulling out a heat sheet.

He covered the man immediately. Next he examined the hardware. He ignited the blower, sat back, and enjoyed the light and warmth filling the back of the cave.

The heat had a way of easing the pain in his skin. A mild headache replaced the thrumming which had kept time on his scalp with his heart. Exhaustion settled over him. He gazed at the man lying on the only flat spot in the cave, and wondered if he was the last guard they posted before the storm broke.

He hoped so.

When he woke, it was day. The rain continued. It was more gentle. The ice storm had played itself out in this area and moved on to pelt the forests further inland.

He was hungry. It had been two days since his last meal. It seemed longer.

He rummaged in the man's pack again, found some protein bars, and ate.

The nourishment improved his outlook.

The man on the floor moaned.

Enickor turned off the blower and moved to his side. A touch of the man's face told of the fever burning his life away. Enickor pulled the heat sheet back and scraped enough mud from the fasteners to remove both his shirt and uniform tunic.

Upon closer examination, Enickor recognized the uniform. It was the crimson battle garb of the House of Hadilka.

"Help me." The man's voice was weak.

"What are you doing here?"

"The mines . . . we have to save the mines." His eyes opened to the ceiling. His head did not turn. "Help me."

"I'll help you," Enickor said after a silence. "But I want some answers."

"Help me."

"What is threatening the mines?"

"M'Lord, the Kriell . . . Jeffires . . ."

In wonderment, Enickor mused, "Lady Hadilka is fighting with her own House?"

"No Lady Hadilka. Just fighting . . . Quniero miners run . . ." The man closed his eyes and slept.

Enickor turned the blower on, wrapped the man tightly in the heat sheet and watched the rain.

Occasionally he glanced at the Hadilkan soldier, hoping he lived long enough to answer a few of the thousand questions rumbling around in his mind. Something must have gone terribly wrong for the political climate to have changed so significantly in such a short time.

No Lady Hadilka? he thought over and over, afraid of what might have happened to Pam-ella, determined to find out. "Pam-ella . . ." The words left his lips with an echo of the want inside him when he thought of her.

Nothing had really changed. He still cared for her. She was family, even if the House of Jeffires was not. Family.

* * *

The gorbich took turns at the carcass, each one leaping over Pam-ella on his way back to the forest, where the circle never ended.

She was beyond tears. Pinned as she was by the unending line, she could not reach the tree, nor could she establish any position from which to counter. The *kalase* warmed in her hand. She considered turning it on herself when the gorbich were through with the roh and started on her. There were too many of them for her to summon the slightest bravado. And they were tough. The most she could hope for was to kill even one before they began skinning her with their talons.

No, she thought, remembering a grisly sight from the borders of the Gorbich Hills two seasons earlier, *I've lost, lost it all . . .*

A treble shriek cut the darkness. Its ferocity stunned the gorbich.

For a dozen heartbeats no sound pierced the night save the restlessness of the wind among the new leaves anxious to reach maturity.

The gorbich looked, became nervous, and barked at shadows. Several howled, then retreated.

Pam-ella listened, straining to determine if Theller was alone in his attack. The thought of him being shredded by the gorbich talons made her nauseous.

There was movement beside her. The fetid, moist breath of a gorbich hit her hand in a quick rhythm. The beast made a slow journey up her arm, to her shoulder, undaunted when the roh challenged a second time and his comrades answered.

Pam-ella watched the glint of starlight in the gorbich's yellow eyes. The putrid blood breath he exhaled into her face quelled her nausea with the reality of her fate should a sign of weakness show. In that instant, the gorbich would be on her and have her partially skinned before she could raise her *kalase* to fire.

Unmoving, she maintained the staring duel with the gorbich. All around her the forest erupted with the beasts. Some made last-minute runs at the roh carcass disappearing into the night with a final chunk. Others gathered for an assault on the challenger.

A second call split the chaos and brought silence once again.

This one took Pam-ella and the gorbich by surprise. Both blinked. Neither had heard such a melodious call. Its musical range was greater than any human voice and vastly superior to that of the gorbich. The cry not only hinted of death; it promised it with an ethereal beauty that was macabre. The message reached inside the body and touched the core of the listener's existence. It made him believe he was alone and helpless.

Pam-ella was resigned to being alone and helpless.

All of the gorbich, with the exception of the one hovering over her, staged a careful, deliberate retreat. Whines and whimpers replaced the brave retorts of moments earlier.

Teeth bared, saliva dripping from the rows of side fangs, the gorbich lifted his right front leg and rested his talons on Pam-ella's arm. He flexed. The tips penetrated her skin.

She did not cry out, nor did her eyes waver.

Two gorbich emerged from the thicket on the other side of the boulder to her left. They had returned to take a stand over the carcass. Snarling, clawing at the night, they accepted the challenger in the darkness.

The roh came out of the brush, both heads high in the air, teeth bared, eyes glazed over with the emotion of his loss.

Pam-ella looked when he shrieked. He was raised on his hind legs, taunting the gorbich.

The one nearest the carcass charged.

The roh seemed to be perched on an invisible platform, his balance perfect, unflinching. He hung in the air until the exposed fangs of the gorbich were half a meter from his tender belly. His weight crashed down, his entire body hurled onto his front hooves. The wide surfaces struck; one on the gorbich's head, the other on his back.

Two quick bone snaps preceded the exhaling moan of the gorbich. The roh immediately put his balance on his front hooves and kicked with his back feet.

A second gorbich died.

The balance and cunning of the roh proved awesome under attack.

The gorbich beside the carcass used the moment to stage his own assault. He lunged, talons primed, and caught the roh on the near neck.

Agony screeched from the unencumbered head before it turned and sunk its teeth into the gorbich's throat, for he had picked the wrong head. The predatory teeth of the roh's right head sank several times before pulling free.

The melodious call sounded again. Closer.

The talons in Pam-ella's arm withdrew.

She looked at the beast.

His eyes were wild with fear. He turned slightly and lifted his leg. Any hope she once may have held died with the onslaught of urine soaking her clothing. His territory had been claimed. He would die protecting it.

Her arm began to burn. The pain in her shoulder connected with that in her upper arm. It reached so great an intensity that she did not realize the talons had sunk in a second time.

The roh stepped over thrashing gorbich in the throes of death. He nudged what remained of the carcass with his right head while looking over at Pam-ella with his bloody left.

Things began to blur.

Delusions seemed to take a special joy and beset her with a vision of a delicate beast which held a massive rider aloft in the night. The twosome came and left her peripheral vision.

The gorbich sank his talons into her thigh.

She screamed.

From the direction of the shimmering rider a *kalase* opened fire. The instant brilliance left streaks running through her distorted vision. The gorbich collapsed. The pungency of seared hair and flesh clung to the corpse. His talons remained imbedded in her thigh, twisting as his mass fell. His head dropped to rest on her right upper arm.

Pam-ella felt herself shrieking internally. She screamed and screamed, terrified, aware of the thin fiber of sanity being stretched to the limit—perhaps beyond.

On the outside, nothing showed. She regarded the stranger dismounting his alien beast with skepticism.

"Migod!" His voice had a slight tremor. The agility of his movements as he leaped the carcasses without a glance and made his way to her was something she would have to take into account in the future.

He lifted the gorbich's head from her arm. She watched his preference for his right hand with a cold detachment.

He was gentle.

Extracting the individual claws was both time-consuming and difficult. The gorbich had not retracted them in death; instead he had extended them to the limit.

"Feel free to scream." He sounded as though he was the one in pain and hated touching the talons. "This has got to hurt."

The screams rattling every fiber of her being were unheard by Chiy-une.

He pulled an object from his belt and turned on a light. It was adjusted to shine on the wounds. After working for several minutes, he was breathing hard. He checked to see if she was still conscious.

Pam-ella had retreated from the pain. The mixed emotions she suffered over being alive waged their own war.

"You are tougher than most men," he said, flinging the gorbich's leg aside. He pulled a scarf from inside his great coat and wrapped it around her leg.

"Let's get out of here." He straightened, then squatted, prepared to pick her up.

With the little strength that remained charged by her iron will, she brought the *kalase* upward to bear on him. "Touch me again and I'll kill you."

Stunned, the man froze.

His features were indiscernible in the night. She was glad and hoped that she sounded stronger than she knew she looked or felt. "Get the saddle from the dead roh." She inhaled, listening before she continued. "Slip the packs back on the other one and saddle him. Then leave." If he did that, she would let him live. He had to be a hunter, but he had helped her. It was to his advantage. Lord Hadilka would not marry a corpse.

He did not move right away. When he did, it was not toward the roh, but toward his own mount. "I thought you needed help. Apparently I was wrong. You had this situation completely in order. Sorry I interfered.

"I had hoped to have a few of my questions answered when I saw you on the beach near Shirwall. But you don't seem in a very congenial frame of mind right now." He walked to his mount, keeping his back to her.

"Perhaps some other time. When you feel like company."

"I said, saddle the roh." Her tone was steel, though faint. It was hard to retain control. If she could just get on Theller...

"Saddle it yourself."

Her hand shook. She held her breath and tried to steady herself, then fired.

A branch directly above and behind the stranger split from the tree and fell.

For a fraction of a moment the Gorbich Hills were deathly quiet. Unwarned, they erupted with a barrage of curses in four languages, all from the stranger. He whirled and threw himself on Pam-ella with an anger she had not anticipated. The ensuing pain hurled her across the threshold of consciousness before the *kalase* had been wrestled from her hand.

Chapter 7

THE HADILKAN SOLDIER DIED WITHOUT REGAINING consciousness. The bits of information that rambled out of his delirium were absorbed with interest and alarm.

Enickor gazed down at the spent soldier. The last traces of color faded beneath the scabbed and scraped patches on his hands and face. The lips were bluer. The corpse's features appeared animated, carved out of a life-like substance and ready to spring alive. The eyes reminded Enickor of the primitive glass the Ocandar Loag made: dull, cloudy.

Outside, the rain fell steadily. The streams and rivers eroded the tender land fringing the ruins under cut trees and old shrubs. Lake-sized puddles lapped the higher ground, pulling it down a mud layer at a time.

His conflict lasted only minutes before he decided to strip the Hadilkan of his all-weather gear. It was a distasteful chore. The soldier was no more cooperative in death than he had been with his information in life. Already he was stiffening.

He picked up the Holy. The scabbard clanked against the rock floor. Holding it in both hands he faced the entrance and pointed the sword at the world. "I am the Harcel," he said, raising the sword slightly. The exquisite silver figure forming the handle looked back at him. "Until such time as I find a survivor of the Harcel to claim you rightfully. And until that time we shall seek a just vengeance for the loag who have had the Holy taken from them."

It was easier to finish stripping the soldier of his gear with the sword in plain view. Great horrors had been perpetrated on the Harcel. Placing a minuscule of blame on the corpse did not harm the conviction growing into a rage inside of Enickor. And the Harcel Holy seemed to emanate approval as well as provide company.

He was methodical when stuffing the pack. By the time it was sealed, it held all the soldier's important gear plus his own belongings and was waterproof, provided it was layered correctly.

Moments later he entered the downpour and resumed the journey north. He looked back toward the shelter.

Either it was not there, or he had lost track of the direction he was going. He faltered, then went on. The eerie feeling of something being wrong vanished with the mental impression of Chiy-une's smile.

He skirted the ruins, avoiding the quagmires formed by the low spots. The skeleton trees were black and gray against the solid metallic-colored sky. No vegetation survived the upheaval that formed the ruins and left so great a depression in the land.

By evening he had travel far northward and found occasional pieces of hearty green thriving in the desolation. The terrain took on the gentle roll of ancient hills worn by the kindness of time.

He paused at a stack of rounded boulders to use them as a shelter while he opened the pack and withdrew another ration. Star Follower food was not tasty, not like the lavish feasts at Shirwall, but it was filling and kept him from being hungry for long periods of time.

An intense heat struck the rock beside his cheek.

He glanced around, then ducked into the center, drawing the more familiar weapon he had confiscated from the Hadilkan.

The granite served as a protection, but hindered his ability to view the attacker. He listened. Nothing but the rain made noise. He nestled between two granite towers enjoined for mutual support and waited.

It is all so strange, he mused. *Fighting? On Chiy-une? Between Star Follower Houses? For Quniero?*

It made no sense and added to the frustration that bewilderment set upon him. He contemplated the changes he had seen since his return until dusk.

The first noise came from his left. He pressed further into the shadow-blackened recess the granite provided and flexed his fingers around the *kalase*.

From his right came the clumsy movements of a man unfamiliar with the terrain and heavy on his feet.

Enickor smiled at the night. He reached down by his right foot and selected a fist sized rock, shifted the *kalase* to his left hand, and watched the darkness in front of him.

The man on the left appeared first, only seconds before the clumsy one on the right.

Enickor threw the rock into the air, arcing it sharply to make it fall between the two.

No sooner did it strike the ground than the two men fired, first in the direction of the noise. A later flash was aimed at the man on the left.

Silently, Enickor cursed.

The man on the left had been too good a soldier to fall for such a trick. He was dead now, but the novice still moved around the granite pillars.

The darkness grew as the rain poured out of the sky with new zeal. Enickor slipped from between the rocks, kept his back to the granite and inched his way toward the open country. He had no desire to fight or kill the clumsy man, nor did he want to be around when he discovered his comrade.

He had not quite made good his escape when the man confirmed his target and found his friend. Yells and shouts roused the bushes. On his far left, two lights went on, off, then remained lit.

Chagrined, he got down on his hands and knees, then onto his belly. He elbowed and kneed his way through the mud and sharp rocks to the first line of bushes. Lights passed above him and intersected. No longer concerned with secrecy, men shouted orders and questions at one another. All the while the rain beat down and tried to muffle the cacophony they created.

What do they want? Who are they looking for? he wondered. *And why?* He could not stop wondering why all of this was happening in the midst of mining country.

I must go to the Ocandar. Perhaps they know. Someone must know. Someone has to know what has happened and why . . .

His thoughts were cut short by the feel of cold steel against the side of his neck.

"I'd suggest you stand up. Very slowly. Very slowly, or you might not make it."

A female egg emerged from the Gaediv. The time was right. The old Gaediv wearied. The journey away from the main leah on Alidanko had forced her confinement to a cargo hold. The prohibition of kateling births disturbed the old Gaediv's cycles. She had remained small, like the nekka leaders. The single egg she carried insured the establishment of another leah. Once hatched, it also insured her death.

The dark security of the tunnels consoled the drones. The new world held many incongruities, but rock was rock. Though its composition changed from place to place, its function, durability, and the rapport the Quniero had with it did not.

Young Gaediv sniffed the quartz content of the intrusive granite and knew Chiy-une's age. She tasted the peridotite, knew the danger the planet faced, and wept.

Within hours the young Gaediv was as large as a nekka drone. The leah under the western edge of the Lyndirlyan Mountains quieted. No man knew of the Quniero presence. Nor would they. The ceremony was underway.

The shriveled reproductive glands of the old Gaediv flapped along her sides. She eagerly awaited the end. The deprivation of her function as kateling birther had killed her insides, dried up the glands, crystallized the juices, and left her with a sadness greater than the collective memory of the leah knew.

Yet a high function had been completed. There was joy in that knowledge. The leah would build. There would be katelings. There would be harmony. There would be a future for the Alidanko Quinero on this new, troubled world.

Using their tongues as feelers, tasting their way to the corbancoob, the drones moved through the hundreds of tunnels honeycombing the lower crust of the Lyndirlyan. The hiss of breathing through their dilated nostrils contrasted sharply with the clack of their steel claws against the polished floors.

The old Gaediv waited patiently in the center of the corbancoob. Blue phosphorescence coated the top of the domed nursery. Eighteen papkoes lined up side by side on the other side of her.

She did not fight when the young Gaediv closed in on her, nor did she expose her throat too soon. Death meant little to her mind, but for her dried up body it was an end to suffering and unfulfillment.

The young Gaediv sank her teeth into the old one's throat. She tasted the blood and absorbed the thoughts of millennia. The history of the Quniero became her memories, without bias, without error. What each Gaediv had known and experienced through the ages was a part of her.

This would be different, the young Gaediv realized from her great base of wisdom. There was more than one Gaediv now. Alidanko lay behind.

A new chapter in the evolution of the Quniero had begun with her. She felt properly honored.

The papkoes commended the old Gaediv to the rock by encasing her cadaver in plain granite. Drones would go to work mutating the rock into a pure ore caretakers would not find. They knew the rock. The rock of this planet knew the Quniero.

Once the old Gaediv's ritual had been completed, the papkoes realigned themselves before the Gaediv.

She chose one. He became head, forever honored.

The Gaediv held still in the center of the soon to be nursery. The head papkoe mounted her, his tail lifted high, his back legs straddling the blunted end of her body where no tail would ever grow. He thrust twice, lowered his tail and removed himself to the line.

The silence in the corbancoob erupted with a whoosh of air and clacking of claws on the stone.

Kateling eggs would be laid in a matter of days, birthed a short time later.

The leah was happy. There would be a future here. A leah forever.

A fire brightened the night and kept the chill of the cold sweeps from the pile of softness on which Pam-ella lay. Fire also burned in her arm and leg where the gorbich had made his marks. She woke, alarmed, afraid, unsure of where she was, and in more pain than she thought she could endure.

"Yes, indeed, Lady Jeffires," the stranger said with a heavy sigh, "I am not sure if you're stupid or tough."

He spoke as if there had been no lapse in the conversation since she had fired the *kalase* at him. He took one of her pots from the fire and poured a liquid into a cup, turned, and brought it to her.

She did not see the steaming brew, just his face. Dazed,

she wondered if she looked older too. "Enickor . . ." She began to cry, joyful that the long search had finally ended. A spinning in the center of her brain blurred his image.

Heat from the fire and her body fostered an illusion of a sunny day on the beach across the water from Shirwall.

She was running, yet she could see herself run and feel the hot, wet sand as her feet slapped on it. Enickor ran behind her, allowing her the edge, able to catch her any time.

She began to laugh uncontrollably. God, how she loved being free in the wind and sun, how she loved being with him.

She slowed, exhausted, threw herself to the sand and tripped him when he tried to jump over her. Still laughing, she crawled to him. He pushed her head away and caught her before she landed on the sand.

They lay in the remnants of the waves until each stopped laughing and met the other one's gaze. The sensation lasted only a moment, but that was long enough. There was guilt in the painful expression which caught Enickor by surprise before he averted his face.

The gaiety of the day had died. There was no innocence in the feelings they shared. They rose, brushed the wet sand from their clothes and walked silently to the ocean skimmer waiting beside the land bridge.

Childhood was over.

"Enickor," she said again.

"No," the voice behind the blurred face said, "I'm not Enickor, but I'll help you find him."

Vaguely she felt herself lifted and something slip down her throat.

"Who? Who are you?" It took a tremendous effort to speak. Staying awake was so hard, so necessary. . . . He's a head hunter. *Probably is,* she mused through spotty reality. *Hoyiv would pay well. And Hadilka . . .*

The thought of Lord Hadilka still had the ability to make her feel worse.

"My name is Friedo."

They were moving. She opened her eyes. Stars played games with the black leaves high in the trees. Her dizziness increased.

"Who is?" What was he talking about?

Lord Hadilka followed two soldiers clad in ostentatious crimson battle garb from the shuttle bearing his crest. He was more repugnant than she had remembered. An aura of deceit clung to him.

She held the branch she was lying on and giggled softly.

Half a dozen soldiers followed the lord from the shuttle. They formed a loose phalanx around him.

Pam-ella could not hear their conversations. The kalase in her right hand was aimed at Hadilka's head, framed by two metallic battle helmets. She maintained her threat as the lord's entourage moved into the clearing with the regimentation of an enormous organism being sucked toward nutrition.

The sound was faint at first. As it grew, Pam-ella looked to the north. The Arch of the Lyndirlyan seemed to glow a radiant silver. The roughness of the tarnished ore was gone. A green passage leading down from the Upper Lyndirlyan spread into the serene meadow, then spilled down another narrow trail which led to the base of the Gorbich Hills.

She turned, put the kalase away, and began to retreat. Down two branches and with the tree trunk between her and the clearing, she glanced at Hadilka's party.

They were heading for the tree line.

Torna-pok thundered down the mountain at top speed. Each one polished the Arch a little more. The lands shook from the combined weight of the beasts on their way to the mating ground.

Pam-ella stopped. Through the maze of delirium she reexperienced the horror she felt when she realized that Hadilka and his men were there for the same reason she was, that he had picked the best spot on the route ...

They were magnificent beasts. As they entered the clearing their speed seemed to die, and they wound down to slow motion. The leader was blacker than a starless night. His saber fangs formed a jade network above and below his wide snout. Two meters high at the foreshoulder, he was easily four meters long before his forked tail began. His six legs, almost hidden by the long curly fur bouncing with momentum, carried him gracefully over the terrain.

The leader sensed a wrongness and turned the herd in the middle of the clearing. They veered away from the mating grounds at the bottom of the mountain and toward the trees.

Pam-ella began screaming. Only her roh heeded the warning.

A light storm erupted. The origination point was Hadilka's party.

The torna-pok leader took four hits before his three green eyes opened wide enough to show the surrounding white. He fell, leaving the herd in chaos. She knew that for the rest of her life she would see those three eyes, feel the terror of the beast, and know the bitterness of death when it touched her heart. The torna-pok had branded her soul. Though she did not want to be a part of such an act, she could not be rid of the certainty of its occurrence.

The ensuing slaughter did not take long. The beasts tried to climb the growing mountain of corpses to get to the tree line. As they reached the pinnacle, or ventured around it, Hadilka and his men picked them off.

The stench of burning air and flesh filled the breeze and brought the gries.

Pam-ella sat in the tree for the rest of the afternoon, watching Hadilka's men round up the last of the grayish torna-poks for their lord to target-practice on. When they left, the clearing was filled with mounds of death.

She had wanted to kill Hadilka with every fiber of her being. For several hours she followed him, with her kalase set to kill and aimed at his head. Even when the tears stopped flowing and the sickness let up she could not fire. Her weakness fed the revulsion curdling her insides.

The next day she selected the most perfect coat and skinned the beast for the fur. She barely finished when Hadilka's shuttle returned to torch the clearing, destroying even the food value the gries were deriving from the slaughter.

The sun was warm. Everything was warm. It was hot. Getting hotter.

"I must get you to Shirwall," said the voice from the blurred Enickor-face. "They're your best chance of keeping the leg."

"No." She reached down and touched her right thigh. It was swollen, the source of the fire which heated the cold day.

"You fail to understand. Your leg is badly infected. The few drugs I have won't save it."

She looked at the man. Gradually he became clear. He wasn't Enickor. Who was he? It didn't matter. He was a Star Follower and had the same Star Follower solution to everything—go to Shirwall.

"No. I won't go to Shirwall." She tried to sit up and failed. The dizziness returned immediately and lingered after the first wave dissipated.

"You will lose the leg if we don't get help for you."

His touch on her face was cool. His hands were calloused, but not hard like a worker's hands. "Then I'll lose the leg. Just put me on the roh. Please."

"No. I can't do that. Where will you go? Those beasts will attack you before you go half a kilometer." He pulled a heat blanket around her shoulders and tucked the edges around her.

"You're the one who doesn't understand." Drowsy, she felt the fire return to consume her. "He can save me. You can't."

She slept.

Several times she woke for a few moments. Reality and delirium played cruel tricks. Before she drifted back to oblivion each time, she buried her fingers in the mane of her roh, and prayed that Theller was real.

She was vaguely aware of the stranger. Somehow, he did not matter.

They climbed, leaving the Gorbich Hills behind as they entered the Lyndirlyan Mountains where the torna-pok roamed and guarded their tauiries.

She was awake when they approached the first tauiri. The leader pawed the ground and blocked the way. His nostrils flared. When he snorted, volumes of steam jetted more than a meter before they dissipated into curls.

"Get out of the way!" The stranger moved beside her, roughly trying to turn the roh from the torna-pok. Theller held his ground.

Her eyes burned. She doubted that she would survive the night even with the aid of the torna-pok. With the last bit of energy she could muster, she turned on the stranger. "Kill. That's the only answer you people have. If you kill him, you kill me, and they will kill you and that thing you're riding."

Pam-ella beckoned to the tauiri leader, uttering a low guttural moan. The roh chimed a dual intonation.

The tauiri leader approached.

She lunged for the thick fur of the torna-pok and found that she was strapped to the roh. She looked, pleading, at the stranger.

Beligerently, Friedo leaned to the left. A silver blade cut the straps which held her to the saddle.

The tauiri leader made it easy for her. She rolled onto his broad back, crying out when her weight shifted to her right leg.

The roh followed the torna-pok into the brush.

Two torna-pok immediately flanked the stranger to prevent his following.

"Enickor?" she murmured, then closed her eyes and accepted the pain which pushed her into unconsciousness.

Chapter 8

"COMMANDER! COMMANDER! I GOT ONE. I GOT a survivor!" The excitement in the soldier's voice contrasted sharply to Enickor's heart-sinking depression. Being pinned to the ground by a sword the holder did not know how to use was humiliating. The youth evident in his voice added to Enickor's degradation. He had crawled right to the man's feet, given himself up without a fight.

Stupid, he thought. *I should have stayed in the rocks where the cover was good.*

The mud and rocks quivered under the onslaught of running feet that converged around Enickor. At first no one spoke. The brilliance around and on him lit the area until there were no shadows left, save those hiding directly under the rocks.

The ranks parted. Whispers faded into the rain. A separate pair of boots came to a halt in front of Enickor's head. The blade retreated.

There was the sound of a second sword being drawn, whipping through the air, then the cold, wet night slapped against the back of Enickor's neck where the all-weather hood had been connected to the suit.

Out of the disgrace came an anger foreign to his nature. He

rolled hard to his left, hurling his body against the bystanders. They toppled over him, groping at one another in a futile effort to stay upright. They succeeded only in pulling more soldiers down into the quagmire.

Enickor bulled through their feet, keeping the momentum, picked a spot near the edge, and bolted. The Holy of the Harcel Loag was unsheathed before he considered the consequences.

"The lad has spirit," said the commander, sword raised in half-salute over the tangle of men pushing to their feet. "Are you indeed as agile with the blade as with your brawn?"

Enickor did not answer. He sidestepped. His gaze roamed the enemy scowling before and beside him. Small moves kept the inertia broken. The lights created roving shadows and eye-squinting stabs at the clouds from the chaos struggling in the mud.

"Who are you?" the commander asked, waving men away.

He watched the man approach, and continued backing toward the rocks.

"Pretty clever trick you used in there. I've tried it myself a time or two." The commander continued to advance.

Enickor chose his ground, confident that there was not more than a man or two between him and the rocks. Beyond them lay his only hope for escape.

"Your gear is Hadilkan." The commander's grin, from under the transparent weather shield over his face, was bright, even in the half-shadows.

For the first time Enickor scrutinized the soldiers. It jolted him. He was reproachful for not noticing they were from the Kriell's army. Inwardly, he groaned.

The inexperience of the soldiers with the commander meant only one thing—the commander was among the best in the Overeechy at combat.

"Speak." The commander began a slow circle to his left, marking off boundaries for the impending battle.

Enickor studied the way he moved. The man was older than he, much older, but graceful, light on his feet. The fluidity of his movements evoked a healthy respect from Enickor. *A little fear is good for the courage,* he mused, squinting through the rain.

"No matter. Soon I will know how well the House of Hadilka trains its soldiers." He continued circling, gauging his opponent.

Enickor valued the excellent balance of the Harcel Holy as

66

it molded to his hand. The blade was easily ten centimeters longer than the commander's. His reach was also greater. He would have to guard against letting the man get on the inside where his effectiveness would be at a maximum.

As though some prearranged signal had been given, Enickor and the commander moved against one another. The night took on a new tenseness. Only the sounds of the combatants penetrated the steady fall of rain.

Thrusts were met with parries as Enickor and the Overeechy Commander tested one another.

The next series of moves, the ground, the rocks, the lights, and the man facing him filled Enickor's mind. His opponent was masterful with the sword, the like of which he had not seen since childhood when he had been taught to use the sword and strove for perfection. He had sought recognition, if not a blessing, from the Porintel Loag.

Enickor grinned.

The commander returned the grin from behind the rain shield.

The fight began in earnest, each knowing he held the admiration of the other regardless of the outcome.

Metal chimed against metal. The clang reached into the darkness. The duo moved in regular, then irregular, patterns, wearing deep paths into the ground and churning the lighter mud into a mild froth.

Both were feeling the strain of the battle. Neither could score. For each lunge there was a counter, the mud too thick to permit a return swift enough to inflict the first wound.

The commander's defogger spat into the rain as it labored to keep the inside of his face shield clear.

Enickor scrutinized the man, memorizing each detail, searching for a pattern while trying to keep his moves random. Gradually he detected a flaw in the commander's tactics.

He thrust low to the commander's right hip, expecting and receiving the counter. The blade slid down. He let his opponent direct it halfway, then raised it sharply and sliced it across the all-weather control joints.

A mild gasp rose from the soldiers. An uneasy shuffle followed.

The commander's shield fogged immediately. It was difficult to tell whether he was grinning or grimacing when he yanked it back. There was more admiration than confidence in his expression. "Well done. You're the best opponent I have had in many years. So it is obvious to me that you are not an Hadilkan. You are too good."

Enickor lifted the tip of his sword several centimeters and bowed his head, keeping his line of sight to the commander clear. The compliment acknowledged, he returned to the business of combat.

The commander glanced at his troops, then at Enickor. His whole demeanor changed. The seriousness of the battle took a new tactic.

The charges at Enickor were more fierce, the intensity greater. He retreated, moving in a backward semicircle, not wanting to be pinned against the boulders where the smaller man could get to his inside. The savageness grew, as did the tinge of fear nestled close to Enickor's heart.

The situation began to come clear to him. The commander had something to prove to his men. He saw little chance of escape, and even less for survival, if he won the duel.

Angered by the futility, he began pressing a fresh attack of his own.

"Star Followers," he hissed, reversing the tide.

"Desecrators! You kill a whole world and care nothing for it, for the people." He began slashing, using brute strength to drive the commander backwards. "You slaughter everything in your path to steal and waste..." His sword moved like a lightning flash through the night, clanging against the commander's, hurling him back until he fell.

Enickor towered over him. "And now the Kriell sends troops. Why? Haven't enough of us died? Are the Houses of Jeffires and Hadilka killing Chiy-une and her people too slowly to suit you?"

The anger inside him bellowed through the scrawny trees and seemed to touch the clouds. The rain halted.

The commander released his sword.

Enickor straddled the man's chest. The point of the Harcel Holy rested lightly over the commander's heart. He stared down at him for several long, quiet minutes while the anger ebbed, to leave the scum of disgust.

Abruptly he turned, lifted his sword at the men, sheathed it and began walking away.

He was almost to the sanctuary of the boulders when he heard the commander's warning shout and felt himself pitch forward onto the granite.

*   *   *

Illeuro reached the place where they had come to settle on this land and found only disappointment. There were no katelings here. No leah. The drones were gone, as were the papkoes. And Gaediv did not respond when he sent out a call.

How could this be? Where was the sentry? Had all life deserted him?

The nekka occasionally found him. Their thoughts were jumbled, erratic. Much had happened to alarm them.

He did not pause to rest. Rather he pushed himself to retrace his trail. Overland was fastest. The big suction cups on his pads held his mass to vertical cliffs guarding the inner Lyndirlyan. He sensed the ore deposits and noted the largest gem formations hidded by tons of rock.

Gorbich dogged him in the hills, their hoots confusion-filled. Any other Chiy-uneite would have collapsed by now, but Illeuro kept going.

The nekka called from deep within the mountains.

He would go to them, calling all the way.

Prior to the downpour Enickor did not think dryness could feel so good. He heard voices before he was able to open his eyes. The words were merely words. Little registered through the fuzz which had grown over his brain.

Besides being dry, the place they had taken him to was also comfortable. He was lying on an air bed and covered with a heat sheet. Sterilized air filled his nostrils. The smell of food brought a rumble from his stomach.

"Look at this sword."

Was that the commander's voice?

Yes, answered the waking part of his mind.

Absently he touched his left hip. He was naked. Defenseless. The anger started to surface again. He pushed it back, needing time to assess his predicament.

"This is special, not some decoration used for ceremonies or a symbol of religion." The Harcel Holy hummed into its scabbard. "Yes, Commander, that is more than just a sword. I've seen half a dozen Chiy-une made swords, but nothing like this." The second voice was strange, higher-pitched than the commander's.

"Ever see anything similar to it off-world? Maybe the Silenna system?"

"Sorry, no. Definitely from Chiy-une. Look at the quality of the metal. Even with their primitive smelters they produce a steel superior to what we've been reworking decade after decade. This stuff has a tensile strength we can't touch even with electron injection."

The commander chuckled. The sound was lost to the singing of the sword being drawn and sheathed again. "You cannot beat the original."

"Have there been survivors? Other than maybe the one in there?"

The commander unleashed a stream of curses in a low, jumbled tone. "No. That bastard Hadilka wiped the area. I'll bet he put his helix ship to work without even checking the ground for inhabitants."

"And you would like to be able to prove it, too?"

"I have other things on my mind." The commander dismissed the man formally, leaving no doubt that the military traditions were deeply entrenched in his personality.

Enickor turned his face to the wall and opened his eyes. Unshed tears fought their way to the surface, only to be held back.

The Harcel was dead.

Slaughtered.

The legends had been true. He had walked out of the sea and the loag died.

The Star Followers knew of the Harcel's death.

They all knew. And no one cared. No one would do anything.

Mining would continue until the last rich deposit was pulled from the muscle of Chiy-une. Until the Star Followers had it all and there was nothing left. Nothing. And he did not know how to stop them or how to save anything for the future.

"Are you all right? Feeling better?"

The commander was over him looking down. Concern filled both his words and his expression.

Enickor turned his head and glared back. He hated all the man stood for, and the man himself.

Like the predators he stalked in the Lyndirlyan Mountains, he took stock of his foe. The commander was an average-sized man, whose age showed only in the map lines of his face and the gray sprigs at his temples. The majority of his hair was black, like the neatly trimmed moustache framing his mouth and descending down to his jawline where it met with his sideburns. Hazel eyes under long clusters of black eyebrows

70

possessed a compassionate quality. He thought he detected a sadness about them.

"I am Commander Ahandro Magaikan of the Kriell's Personal Guard."

When he received no response, he turned slightly and gestured to a place on the floor. "Doesn't mean a damn thing to you, does it?

"There are your clothes." He turned and took several steps, muttering, "'And the Overeechy shall extend a hand to those in need . . .'"

"'. . . and protect the less advanced peoples of the galaxy from exploitation,'" Enickor concluded. Even trying hard, he could not sustain a hatred of Commander Magaikan.

Watching the older man, Enickor sat up, plagued by a body-wide painful stiffness. He dressed, rose, and crossed the small room. The whiteness of his surroundings flaunted the alienness of the place to Chiy-une, as did the glowing balls of light randomly fastened to the furniture and walls.

Unspeaking, he followed Magaikan's retreat into the next room.

A combination of living quarters, mess hall, and office, the room was neatly kept. The panel of lights slowly winking in the corner caught Enickor's attention. It was similiar to the one from the wreckage on the island mountain.

In the center of a table partially cleared of order-types and computer balls was the Harcel Holy.

Without breaking stride, Enickor reached out and picked it up. He met Magaikan's gaze, withdrew the sword a dozen centimeters, then slammed it back into the sheath.

"Special to you, huh?" Magaikan looked away, half smiling.

"It is a Holy of a people you murdered without thought for anything but what lay inside the ground they lived on."

"Sit down. I'll send for some food. You look like you need a meal."

Enickor's hand remained on the sword hilt. "I need to be free."

"To do what?" Magaikan punched several commands into the complex.

Enickor did not answer. Instead, he scanned the order-types lying on the table.

"My compliments on your swordsmanship. You're quite a master."

71

"I did not fight like a master. I fought with anger. That is not good." He glanced at an order-type labeled "HADILKA."

"It was good enough." Magaikan rested his hand on the sword hilt slung low on his left side. "I'm not easily beaten."

"Am I a prisoner?" He read quickly, excited.

"You're not exactly a prisoner. In fact, I was letting you go after our duel. It seemed fair enough. You could have killed me. And didn't."

There was a tapping at the door. Magaikan excused himself and answered. At the door, he lingered to engage in a muted conversation.

Enickor used the time to ponder on the order-types arrayed before him. He looked up once, then changed them around and scanned as rapidly as he could for content.

Both Houses had imported Quniero gem finders. The significance became a personal injury to him. The reptilian creatures would sap the marrow from the bones before the helix ships sucked the bone out of the crust. Bits of information uttered by the Hadilkan soldier began to make sense.

Would Chiy-une have nothing left?

He feared not. The mining of gems did not bother him as much as the symbolism. She was being systematically stripped of everything of value, including life.

Through his resignation to Chiy-une's plight came an ire spawned of indignation.

"Here you go." Magaikan placed a steaming tray of food in front of him.

He tried to eat with some self-restraint, and managed to do so only after he had consumed more than half of the meal.

Enickor felt the narrow hazel eyes study him and avoided the order-types.

"Who are you?" Magaikan's voice was flat. He meant business.

"Does it matter?"

"Yes, it matters. I'm looking for a man."

"I am not the man. I'm a Chiy-uneite, which is something less than a man in the eyes of the Star Followers. Isn't it? Just another one for you to kill." He met the commander's gaze and detected a flinch. Disappointment found him again when he realized he had baited Magaikan to deny his allegation.

"You continue to accuse me of killing people. I assure you, I have killed no Chiy-uneite." Magaikan pulled a chair around and sat across the table from Enickor.

"Any man who stands by and does nothing while people are being murdered, animals are being slaughtered, and a world is being made barren, her forests made sterile, is just as guilty as the man running the mining operation. He is merely a killer of a different conscience."

Magaikan yielded little in the way of mannerisms, but enough to let Enickor know he had hit a sensitive nerve in the commander. Sadly, he smiled to himself. Few Star Followers would have any qualms about the mining efforts on Chiy-une, or the cost paid by the natives.

During a brief silence, Magaikan folded his hands and looked at them, unable to meet Enickor face to face. "Sometimes, sometimes things happen in a way that some men are powerless to intervene. This is one of those times." He looked up, his expression open. "Were circumstances different, I might be tempted to take up your cause and fight with you. Perhaps not in the same way, or even on the same battlefield. But I would do it, because you are right.

"Instead, I must spend my time looking for one man whom many think is already dead and has been dead for a long time."

Enickor's eyes narrowed. "What has this man done?"

"Nothing, except to be born alive."

"Star Follower justice? His crime is living? What will you do? Kill him?" He could not halt the sarcasm which surfaced so easily since experiencing the ruins.

Magaikan adopted an impartial attitude. "No. I'll send him to the Kriell."

"And he will kill him. You will have done your duty. You won't be the killer."

Magaikan nodded slightly. He looked old, out of lies and too tired to play the Overeechy game. "It looks that way."

Three sharp knocks and the door slipped open. Magaikan rose immediately and turned.

Two soldiers entered, followed by two more herding half a dozen wet, dirty stragglers from the Harcel into the room. A young woman cradled a baby in her arms. The child was rigid and blue. An older man, white-haired and thin, emitted a strength on which the other five seemed to draw as they remained clustered around him. Two men, a middle-aged woman, and an adolescent boy who looked like her completed the survivors.

As the stream of warm air from the blower dried the mud and filth to their bodies, their burns and wounds began to show.

73

Enickor rose, unstrapping the Harcel Holy from his waist. He carried it, palms up, to them, and extended it to the aged man.

The old man shook his head. "I know you. You are the Man Who Walked out of the Sea.

"I am old and tired. Take them. Lead them. Save them from the purge the Star Followers ruin our land with." He reached out and touched Enickor's forehead.

His touch was icy, his hands purple. Enickor froze. He stared into the dead blue eyes of the Harcel Metaliary, healer of the sick, beseecher of the weather, controller of fate, and guardian of the loag in the leader's stead.

"Adaia?"

Adaia continued staring, his hand outstretched. "I know you. And I give you what remains of the Harcel, my friend . . . lover of the land . . ."

A chill passed through Enickor. He did not know how he knew, but he did know that Adaia physically died long before the Kriell's guard brought them here.

Calmly, he strapped the Holy to his side and approached the young woman. For a moment she was a stranger. Time had changed them all and made even the young much older than their years. When he recognized her, he shuddered and was determined to help her.

The young woman stared at the Holy.

"Elisif? May I take your baby?" His arms were ready to receive the child as though it were alive.

She responded to her name the second time, and looked at him. "He is my brother." A tear ran down the drying mud on her cheek. "He is my brother." She did not seem to recognize him, though she did not reject him as she would have a stranger.

"Elisif, you have done all you can for him. Adaia will cherish his spirit now. Let me have him, and I will pray the words which free him to the Wind."

She looked at the babe. The bluish features were contorted by death. The child's eyes were clouded and dull. His mouth remained open in an oval shape, his nostrils flared.

"You will pray to the Wind with me? He is so tiny . . ." Elisif's voice trailed. She opened her arms and let Enickor take the child.

Magaikan cleared his throat and began giving orders for the care and feeding of the survivors. His discomfort was great when he dismissed the soldiers.

Enickor began to leave with Elisif.

"After they have eaten and been cleaned, ask each of them about Enickor val Densu. Somebody has to know about the man!" Magaikan turned away.

He looked down at Elisif.

Recognition brightened her eyes. She opened her mouth. The slight shake of his head kept her silent.

She bowed.

He was the Harcel.

Chapter 9

FOR THREE DAYS FRIEDO PAYNDACEN WAITED FOR a sign from the tauiri beyond the ridge crest. The roh had returned once. He had wanted relief from the burden he carried. After Friedo had obliged, the roh double-sneezed and ambled back to the two torna-pok guarding the ridge.

On the other side, Pam-ella fought for her life. The poisons and multiple infections caused by the gorbich's claws and urine were difficult for even the torna-pok to neutralize. Two, one on either side, kept the chill from her small body. She was attended and licked clean throughout the day and night.

A malodorous smell wafted from the tauiri when the wind stilled. It went out to the gries as an invitation to a free meal. All they had to do was wait for it to be served. One by one, then two at a time, they circled in the sky. They seldom ventured close to the tauiri. The younger torna-pok played on the cliffs and narrow ledges. Natural enemies of the gries, they delighted in making the birds veer away sharply by lunging from the cliffs. Occasionally one of the youngsters was quick enough to catch a gries.

By the fourth day the number of gries in residence dwindled. Only the most desperate remained.

Pam-ella regained consciousness. A flicker of panic touched, then fled when her eyes opened. A dozen jade fangs half a meter long greeted her. Saliva dripped from the ends and rained on her naked body. The dim light winding into the tauiri gleamed on the inside razor edges of their fangs. A bull torna-pok who was the leader opened his eyes wide, showing the whites.

Unsure, she lifted her hand and extended it to the bull.

He lowered his head.

It was true—the black bull leader Hadilka had killed had touched her mind in some way. He had left a mark recognized by how many others of his kind?

A dull throb remained in her right shoulder. The talon wounds in her arm ached only slightly. She petted the beast in the center of the soft triangle formed by his eyes.

"Thank you," she whispered, sitting up in spite of the fires trying to rekindle in her leg. The three-eyed torna-pok had her attention. "Thank you." She gazed at him distantly, aware of the tears of gratitude rolling down her cheeks.

Later she cried openly, hard, part of her wondering why she was still alive while another part wondered what reason she had for living. This land, which Star Followers—her family—sought to destroy for the riches hidden inside the lithosphere, had a beauty few would ever see.

On her knees, she embraced the torna-pok, putting her arms as far around him as she could manage. "So much giving here," she sobbed. "So much beauty. And they are so blind..."

The anguish of her fruitless quest poured out to Chiy-une's creatures. And they empathized, huddling closer and closer to her and one another in the tauiri. The light was blotted out until only the darkness and the moist aroma of their breath conjured an invisible vapor of kinship.

When she stopped crying the tauiri took on the rhythm of breathing like a chorus hummed a song. Occasionally the bull licked at the puncture marks still oozing a mixture of poison and blood.

"I am one of them, the Followers, and you still help me. You are too gentle, too good. Such beauty of soul is not prized in the civilized parts of the Overeechy." Head bowed, "Only misunderstood and killed.

"And I let you down, too." In her mind's eye Hadilka stood over the carnage at the gateway to the Upper Lyndirlyan.

The bull snorted. He seemed to be trying to convey something.

Surprised, she asked, "Can you really understand me?"

He exhaled through his mouth, fluttering his great lips where they split for the fangs.

"I wish you could talk to me, tell me things, give me guidance. I wish..." Eyes closed, she visualized Enickor. "I wish so many things." Exhausted, she lay down. Sleep claimed her immediately. The fever had returned.

The days passed. She slipped in and out of consciousness. The protective beasts foraged analli roots, distasteful to them, but necessary to Pam-ella for the protein and healing agents they contained. When awake, she ate the bitter pulp of the analli. Strength returned gradually, waned, then returned to stay.

Time held no significance for either Pam-ella or the torna-pok. The sun rose daily. The cold crept along the ground from the north. Quakes rattled the lofty mountains, deposed whole cliff faces and altered the courses of rivers.

By the time she managed to remain awake for an entire day her leg had healed over. The swelling was down, though her breeches were a tight fit over her enlarged thigh.

Long curls from the bull's side were gathered into her right hand for support. She hobbled through the tauiri and into the morning light.

Theller uttered a cacophony of delight, each head complimenting the other and trying to out-screech it.

Pam-ella reached for him and hugged his black neck. "You have been so good to me, Theller. So good." She stroked him, noticing that the remaining light spots of his coat were changing to a solid black. "The coat of mourning..." She kissed his neck, reached over and scratched his other head near the ears.

He sneezed.

"The man...what happened to the man...?" She turned and looked up to the dark ridge ten meters over head.

Flanked by two torna-pok, and leading the delicate beast with four spindly legs, stood the Follower. He looked bigger than she had visualized him.

For a moment all her eyes would focus upon was the lithe creature beside him. It did not seem right. She remembered him as being larger. The beast had carried both her and the man for how long?

She shook her head.

The round head and pan-shaped face with two slits hosting the eyes was alien indeed. She noticed the flare of the breast where the neck joined the body. A short-cropped coat of chestnut hair covered the beast. Muscle rippled from the upper leg into the foreshoulder.

She felt the beast's gaze on her, and looked directly at him, recalling the terror incited by a song. Shrugging away the eerie feelings associated with the memory, she addressed the man.

"I guess you told me who you are and I forgot."

He cleared his throat, glanced at the herd of torna-pok, and managed a half-smile. "Friedo Payndacen," he said nervously.

"Thank you, Friedo Payndacen, for bringing me here."

"I didn't bring you here. I merely put you on your, your . . ."

"Roh. Theller is a roh."

"Your roh, so you wouldn't die on the ground. It seemed to be what you wanted." Uneasy, he narrowed his eyes as though studying her. "You certainly did not want me to take you to Shirwall."

"No. Not Shirwall." *What happened to the letter?*

"Pam-ella Jeffires?"

She nodded, bowing her head to rest on Theller's warm coat. The letter really did not matter. Shirwall was out of the question. Her father would understand. They were very much alike in some ways, stubborness being one of their more common traits.

"I've waited quite some time for a sign from down there. I didn't know whether you were dead or alive." His short laugh startled his beast. "Actually, I wasn't sure I was free to leave. And now, now I have too many questions I would like for you to answer to leave now. So, if it is all right, I'll wait until you are well enough to talk."

Scrutinizing him, she sensed the same kind of uncertainty Enickor had been prone to exhibit. Though he knew exactly what he wanted to do, he lacked the verbal finesse to do it. It seemed a temporary thing with the man before her. He looked uncomfortable at not having a total command over his situation. Yet he possessed an aura of patience that allied with the tenderness he had shown to her during the difficult time for them both. And he had yielded to her wishes.

Those were demands, she mused wryly.

But he was a Star Follower. On the land, that was not a good omen.

"What makes you think I have any answers to give you?"

79

"I know that you do." His smile was quick. "Whether or not you choose to give them is another matter."

"What do you want here?"

"The same thing you do. I want to find Enickor val Densu."

She stiffened. "Why?"

"When you feel well enough to discuss our mutual search, then I will tell you all you need to know."

"Star Follower," she muttered under her breath like a curse. "Imperious, righteous, smug bastards!"

"I beg your pardon?"

She glared at him, wishing she could unleash the venom she felt on him. "I have nothing more to say to you. You had better leave. Go back to Shirwall." She nudged the roh toward the tauiri opening.

"I'm not leaving without you."

She hobbled toward the tauiri, leaning heavily upon the roh. Suddenly, she was very tired.

The torna-pok began to close ranks. A line edged toward the Star Follower and his beast.

"Faelinor!" Payndacen's voice echoed against the mountain.

His beast opened his mouth and began to sing. His bone structure changed shape and size as the melody poured from his throat. The song created excitement in the air.

The torna-pok paused, openly fascinated. Theller faltered, then stopped to look.

The music split into a harmonious series of chords which immobilized the listeners, save Pam-ella and Friedo.

She glared back, angry at her physical weakness and his strength.

An impish smile that could not be repressed grew over Payndacen's face. He moved from the ridge and made his way carefully through the maze of basaltic pillars to get to the flat ledge at the mouth of the tauiri. The torna-pok glanced ruefully at him, but did not move. They listened to Faelinor sing a spell over the land.

Payndacen was still smiling when he reached Pam-ella and brushed the dirt from his pants where he had slid the final meter. "You really are as unapproachable and stubborn, as they said you would be."

She turned toward the tauiri, tired, her leg aching from the strain of her weight.

"Allow me." Payndacen picked her up before she could

80

protest, carried her to the farthest stone ledge beside the tauiri mouth and set her down. "Better?"

She began to rise, glancing inside.

"Faelinor left you out of his spell intentionally."

She exhaled sharply, then sat back to relax against the stone. "You made your point." Looking up at him, "Tell me, do you always need him to captivate your audience in order to get someone to listen to you?"

The smile disappeared. "No. Usually I make a request and it is obeyed."

"Well, I'm not in your service. I am not in your realm, and I am not one of your beasts to command. And if you do not have the power to stop the mining and the battles taking place across this planet, I don't have time for you.

"As far as I'm concerned, this conversation is over. I don't need some stumbling, curiosity-seeking Star Follower crashing through the brush with me. Go home." She turned her head away to take in the birth of spring in the valley below.

Faelinor's song floated down the mountainside. The land seemed warmer, the sun brighter, the sky blue again, not tinged with dusty brown. Listening to it, Pam-ella could not sustain the ire which ate at her inner feelings.

"You were not a student of the Overeechy? Nor of its lineage?" He rested his right foot on the rock beside her and leaned on his knee with his forearms crossed.

When she did not answer, he continued. "There might come a time when I can stop the mining here."

She looked at him, disdain and disbelief written in her expression.

"I am the Uv-Kriell of the Overeechy."

"Sure you are. I'm Lord Hadilka. Pleased to meet you."

Again she had amazed him with her indifference. "You really don't believe me?"

"No. I believe you. I also believe that the Overeechy has heard of the Porintel Loag and are practicing the manhood ritual—a bit late in your case, but maybe you needed the time. They want to make sure you can handle the promotion when the Kriell is assassinated." She tried to stand. "I know its always a case of gross misunderstanding, but aren't Kriells usually killed by their kind, devoted, loving subjects?"

"You are really a very nasty person, Lady Jeffires." Even as he said it, he could not help smile. "I've never met anyone like you."

"That lived," she added, standing and holding onto the rock.

"Ouch!" He stepped aside for her to hobble to the maw. "Tell me, why are you so, so nasty? Good Lord! You thanked me for saving your life. If you really believe that, don't you feel any gratitude or anything?"

"You mean, don't I feel I owe you something?"

"Yes."

In the split second that she glanced his way she lost her footing. He reached out and caught her before she fell.

She steadied, then looked straight at him. "No."

Her blatant honesty stunned him. She was worse than they had depicted her at Shirwall. Abruptly he straightened and thrust his hands deep into the pockets of his warm, knee-length coat. "I'll be waiting for you, Lady Jeffires. We have far more in common than you might think. When you are stronger, we'll talk again. Perhaps there is something I have or can do that you might find some value in."

He walked back to the steep, pillared slope and began climbing back to Faelinor. This time the torna-pok did not even acknowledge him.

Pam-ella watched, unable to close him out, wishing he would go away, knowing that he would not. The strength laced with a mild show of arrogance bespoke a high place in the echelons of the Overeechy. For a moment she wondered if he was the Uv-Kriell.

So what? Even if he is, he's still a Star Follower and he cannot possibly follow me through the Lyndirlyan Mountains. An inner smile lightened her dismal mood. *Especially if he's the Uv-Kriell! He would be too soft.*

Payndacen reached Faelinor and glanced back at Pam-ella. She was thin, even thinner than when he first saw her. Childlike in appearance, she was old in her knowledge of the ways to survive so harsh a land. He wanted to know what had driven her from Shirwall, and why she chose the cold, unyielding land over the splendor of the Overeechy. The will of iron was incongruous with her tiny physical stature.

He stroked Faelinor, whispered at the laid-back flap arched over his ear, then turned away. The walk back to camp would give him time to think. The terrain was rugged. He could not imagine Lady Jeffires surviving this dismal land for more than three years alone. He could not imagine himself living off the land unaided for half a year. Damn, but it got cold here.

Faelinor's song changed subtly.

Neither the roh nor the torna-pok seemed to notice.

Pam-ella felt the music touch something deep inside her. Enickor filled her mind. She sagged against the maw of the tauiri. She tried to conjure the fantasy of seeing him again, touching him, feeling him close. In that special place where dreams are born and fantasies nurtured, she returned to the beach and felt his mouth on hers, the excitement of their hearts thudding in unison.

Eyes closed, she was herself, yet saw herself with Enickor, embracing, touching, exploring one another openly as lovers, not as brother and sister.

Without warning the fantasy ended.

Faelinor had stopped singing.

The sound of crying hung in the mountain air.

Pam-ella opened her eyes and looked at the tarnished sky.

It all seemed so futile.

The sound carried through the mountains. Illeuro paused to listen. Never had he heard such tones. The range of notes belied an individual source.

The mountains smelled different here. The nekka had come this way. He could taste their passing in the stone.

The madness he thought would close in on him did not come. Now his concerns took another direction. How could he think for himself? Without Gaediv to guide him? To absorb his experiences? It was not possible. It was happening.

He scooped a mouthful of soil, separated the nutrients and voided the rest, then mutated it into nourishment.

The song ended.

Illeuro pulverized pebbles, chewed on a fallen ipcar branch for several minutes, then moved on.

The changes coming over him left him ambiguous much of the time. This was a strange land. Not at all like Alidanko. There was a thing here he equated with what the caretakers had called "freedom." While they did not believe they had it, Illeuro embarked on the discovery of what it meant.

The heartbeat of the land slowed as he moved north to the interior mountains. When night came, he tasted the old Gaediv's death in the rock and knew entombment had been completed, the rock purified around her. He understood the reasons for his isolation.

Change was always hard for the Quniero.

Here, it would be greater and swifter. He hoped the native-born Gaediv had many katelings, and that he would live to see them with his nekka.

Chapter 10

THE COMMENDATION OF THE YOUNG AND OLD souls to the wind god Ieuchna took place in the evening. Sleet, driven by the very wind the remnants of the Harcel invoked, kept the Star Follower security to a mininum.

Those dressed in all-weather gear mumbled to themselves about the lunacy of such a ritual.

Enickor led the chant. As a loag, they called upon Ieuchna to gather up the two waiting souls. Toward the end of the ceremony, Enickor added verses for those slaughtered by the mining ship. Belief in their religion was only a part of his greater concept of a deity. It made him feel better to verbalize the atrocity the Harcel Loag suffered. If the wind god existed as a separate entity, and happened to extend his hand to the roaming, lost souls who had not received the benefit of a formal ritual, so much the better.

Elisif ended the incantation. She knelt and tossed rocks into the pit formed by a *kalase*. The loagers followed, returning the dead to the ground which had given and sustained their lives.

They stumbled into the sleet-ridden night to gather stones for the grave. No one spoke. Even the soldiers were lulled by the frozen rain piling in the nooks and rock breaks.

Enickor squinted into the black grave, trying to see if they had covered the bodies. Sleet and darkness obscured the bottom.

Elisif emptied her burden of stones and turned to gather more.

Enickor held out his arm to stop her. Though she tried to keep her anguish private, a sob escaped. Head down, she waited for him to remove the barrier. Instead, he put his arms around her, felt her shivering and the ice upon her skin. Enickor held her closely, remembering the last time he had seen her at Keladine Ornasive's side.

Keladine had been so pleased with her. After nine sons, all of whom he had been proud, he had been blessed with a girl. Elisif had been more difficult to rear than the boys.

He drew his cape around them and felt her arms reach over his ribs. She was crying without shame now. "I'll take care of you, Elisif. It will be all right."

He felt tears of his own pressure his lower lids. It would not be all right. Nothing would be all right again. Not for Elisif. Keladine Ornasive was dead. The greatest Leader the Harcel had known throughout their history was gone. His sons were gone. Only this fragile daughter remained. *No, it won't be all right.*

The loags were being annihilated, the Leaders killed one at a time, as Keladine must have seen. He had not thought about how the Holy might have survived a mining over, but the proximity of the grave affected him. The great Leader had been slain by soldiers.

He wished the Hadilkan alive so he could slay him in his own way—with the Harcel Holy.

Cold inside and out, he held Elisif closer.

"Please, come inside."

The voice disturbed his island of thought.

Enickor nodded at Magaikan, then freed Elisif's right arm and kept her wrapped in his cape while following the commander into the temporary shelter.

The brilliance of the light hurt their eyes. The instant warmth let them know how cold they had become during the burial ceremony. Pain from waking, thawing nerves in bright red-and-blue-tinged fingers and faces was evident in each of the loagers.

Magaikan looked like a brewing storm about to wreak havoc in the controlled environs of absolute comfort. "I don't un-

86

derstand you people. You practically get killed, then go out and damn near kill yourselves by burying the dead in a sleet storm."

The rage that had begun beside the burial pit grew as Enickor listened to the commander. He removed his cape and ruffled it to get the loose water beads off. "Of course you do not understand us. It's easier that way. There is less guilt involved. If you cannot comprehend our life-style, you cannot be held accountable for what you do to destroy us. And in that way it becomes our fault that your mining slaughtered us, the natives of this world, the animals which we depend upon for existence, and the very land we grow our food on."

Elisif retreated a step involuntarily. Her eyes widened with fear. Yet her bright red fingers, flexing to regain feeling, reached out for him.

The new Leader of the Harcel pushed her gently behind him and stepped toward the commander. "And if it is our fault, then we must be something less than human, something not equal to you. But if we are not human, than there can be no guilt of any kind if you murder us for personal gain, strip Chiyune down to the mantle rock and ruin everything in between. When you are done here, you will move on to the next planet."

His left hand came to rest on the hilt of the Holy sword. The deadly calm in his voice put the the guards on alert. "Perhaps *they* will be cunning enough to kill those you send in the survey ships, instead of welcoming them with open arms and sharing what they have with them."

Enickor's words humbled Magaikan and quelled his ire in the face of one greater.

"Settle them down. Feed them. Whatever they need. I want a medic to look at the kid and the young woman." Magaikan gestured to the pale, wet loagers without looking at them. "You." He pointed to Enickor. "You come with me."

A sob escaped Elisif. The loag woman, Udia, pulled her behind the two men and into the protection of their small mass. The youth moved in front of her. He was shivering uncontrollably.

Magaikan glanced at her, then at Enickor and back, turned and led the way down the hall to his office. He did not break stride as the door retracted.

In the silence of anticipation hanging over the Star Follower settlement, Enickor's footsteps were loud on the synthetic floor. He neither hurried nor dallied to the commander's quarters.

There was a determination about him which added to the heavy tension.

No sooner had he entered than the door closed. The distinct sound of the mechanical lock followed. Enickor approached the heat blower, glad the temporary status had not included the usual radiant, even units built into the walls. He felt Magaikan's eyes on him as he held his cape in front of the warmth and watched it dry.

"Who are you?"

"I am the Leader of the Harcel Loag. What is left of it." He did not turn.

"That's what you are now, not when I found you." Magaikan's tone was steeled with patience.

"You did not find me. I was not lost." He turned the cloak.

"No, you were not lost." Magaikan poured a broth into a cup and inhaled the steam. "Nor are you from the Harcel Loag."

Enickor did not answer.

"I've been around, my friend. Even a place as godforsaken as this one has characteristics in each of its pockets of civilization. You do not fit into the Harcel. Damn near every one of them is blond.

"You're not a natural. Not like they are. The sun or some homemade brew has streaked your hair." He rested on the edge of the table and half way crossed his arms, never taking his gaze from Enickor. "I also know they don't cross-breed . . ."

"We don't breed. We have children the same way you do. We don't marry to increase our holdings, or for wealth like Star Followers do. We marry because we have vowed to care." He looked over his shoulder and met the commander's interest. "Emotional and primitive by your standards, huh?"

"Oh, I don't know." He sipped at the broth. "There was once a woman from one of the loags who did not require marriage for having a child. The Porintel Loag, I believe."

Enickor's heart began a faster cadence. He could not control it.

"I've heard it told that only a few, perhaps four, people knew why she chose to serve the Star Follower men," Magaikan continued.

"I suppose you are one?" Enickor asked, his tone even, his knowledge of the answer complete.

"No." Magaikan chuckled. "She, of course, was one. The son she had also knew, or so I have been led to believe by the Porintel Metaliary. The boy's father was a third."

88

Enickor folded his cape and let the blower dry him. He turned slowly, meeting the unwavering gaze of the commander steadily.

"You are possibly a bit older than the man I'm looking for. But you also look very much like I think he would look. You have a number of Porintel characteristics. Yet I think there is some Star Follower in you."

"My compliments for being able to tell one loager from another. You may be the only Star Follower on Chiy-une who has taken the time to learn such a trivial distinction."

"Who are you?" Magaikan's curiosity persisted, nagging him to press the dangerous loager with the sword.

"Just a man who does not want to die." He stopped turning and folded his cape over his left arm.

"Where were you going when we came across you?"

"To see the land, to know its suffering, to try and find a way to survive." He straightened the last fold and walked away from the blower, denying his instinct to turn it off. "Why am I a prisoner?"

Magaikan exhaled sharply. A sad half-smile flickered and died. "We're all prisoners here."

"You did not answer my question."

Magaikan laughed heartily. "I like you. You've got more balls than any battle-hardened commander I've faced in one damn long time."

He set the cup down and stood. All traces of amusement were gone. The storm had returned. "What in seven hellstones do you mean, I haven't answered your question? I don't even know who you are, let alone where you're from and a dozen other things I need to know about you. And, dammit, yes! You're a prisoner! You killed one of my men."

Calmly, Enickor walked towards the door. "Your own man killed him. I did not. It was unnecessary. Even savages, primitives if you please, have the capability to survive without murdering. Let the murderers kill themselves."

At the door he turned around. "What do you want of me, Commander Magaikan? Do you want me to say that I am Enickor val Densu? Will that take the mining ships away? Will it restore Chiy-une? Will it bring back the dead? Will it appease the Overeechy? Yes, we know a great deal about you. Much more than you have bothered to learn about us. We know, first-hand, what you can do to a man's mind or a woman's body. You have no idea how glad we are that those killing us are civilized. We might be in trouble if you were not. You want inside my head? You know how to go there. Do not expect my cooperation."

For an uncountable period of time the two men glared at each other without speaking. A man who made critical decisions daily, Magaikan was distressed as he struggled to make one now concerning the loager at the door. When words did break the spell, they were softly spoken.

"Those people, the Harcel Loag, need rest. In two days I'll release you all with some survival gear. I suggest that you head for the southern plains."

Enickor turned to go.

"Val Densu!"

He did not turn back.

The door opened.

The survivors used loag sign language for communicating. Legends of Star Follower settlements with ears in the walls had grown over the seasons. Now they believed them.

Magaikan sent a medic to the rooms assigned to the loagers.

Initially they protested, then relented when Enickor insisted the boy be treated. His silent entreaty included Magaikan's word that they would be leaving the following day. The boy, Landah, had to be well enough to travel. No one could carry him.

Landah responded quickly to the treatment. Before night, his lungs had cleared sufficiently to permit him a restful sleep.

Enickor checked on Landah and his parents before bidding Zaich a good night and returning to his room.

Elisif watched him enter without making a noise. "I waited for you."

He had hoped she would not. Sleep did not come easily under the Star Followers' roof. The desecration taking place on Chiy-une worried him. It further complicated his position. Assuming leadership of the Harcel was yet another imposition upon the task to save his Mistress.

He undressed and slipped between the warm, smooth heat sheets. The dull lamp glow tempered the starkness of the small white room. A steady flow of purified air laced with disinfectant moved through the room.

Elisif turned onto her side to face him. She seemed to be waiting for the right time to speak. Minutes passed. Finally she took a deep breath and let it out. "Buelthar saw you walk out of the sea."

"Your fourth brother?" Inwardly, he found a bit of comfort in her statement. Another question answered.

"My fifth brother, married to Zaich's daughter, Miyerva. He told us what he had seen." Sniffing, she paused. "I feel I must tell you these things. You should know the fate of the Death Loag you lead."

"It is not a Death Loag. Do not call it that, Elisif." He had not meant to be harsh, but it sounded so.

Meekly, she continued, though she was trembling. "We were going to the sea for the naming ritual. My father was very proud of his tenth son. Had my mother lived . . .

"It was a hard trip. Some of the land we had to cross to reach the sea had been destroyed by the Star Followers. We watched for them. Buelthar was scouting the night he saw you. He ran all the way back to warn us.

"My father, my brothers, except the baby, and almost everyone else returned to the loag. They ran all night and . . . I guess they didn't make it. If they had. . . . You now wear the Holy."

The sword glowed beside the bed. "I took it off a soldier. He died."

She went on as though she had not heard. "We hid when the sky darkened. It was like the end of the world, Enickor. The end of our world. It was terrible. We found a cave near the sea.

"There was a beast in the ocean just off the cliffs. He watched us for a long time, like he was waiting for something. There were twenty of us then, mostly men to protect us from the soldiers, those who knew the hidden trails of Chiy-une. But . . . part of the cliff fell . . ." The memory burned anew. The muscles in her throat worked, tightening to keep her from crying. She swallowed repeatedly while staring at a place over Enickor's head.

When composed, she continued. "We wandered for a time. I'm not sure for how long. I thought I heard Ieuchna calling us, and I felt the death cold in the wind whispering our names. The land had changed, Enickor. Once we were away from the sea, it was impossible to tell where anything was or where we should go. All the landmarks were gone. The land was gone. . . . You know?"

"Yes," he murmured, "I know."

"The soldiers found us. We thought they would kill us, but

they brought us here. I don't understand all the different kinds of soldiers."

"Don't try. It's a waste of time. Most are your enemy."

"I am not your enemy, Enickor. I would be good for you." The fear was gone from her voice. A glimmer of hope hung on her words.

At last Enickor turned to look at her. The additional warmth her body radiated affected him. He wanted to know her intimately without knowing who she was inside. No talk. Just feelings. He did not love her, nor did he know if he could love her.

He closed his eyes. Pam-ella stood in his mind. He wished that he did not want her. He wished that he were free of Shirwall once and for all, but knew he would never be free as long as the deep yearning he had for Pam-ella plagued him. It needed a resolution. One more answer to find, he mused.

Timidly, "Master?"

His eyes opened. "What, Elisif?"

"We are bonded, are we not? You are Leader and I am the Ornasive family . . ." Her words trailed. Her courage flagged when needed most. Flustered, embarrassed, she was unable to continue meeting his gaze. There was a trembling in her hand when it slid over his upper arm, across his shoulder, and through the hair on his chest.

"Yes. We are bonded." He took her hand from his chest and held it while raising up on his left elbow. The stray clusters of lustrous blond hair on her cheek were soft to his touch. There was so much he wanted her to know, but could not say.

"Elisif, I will care for you whether we consummate this bond or not. This is not something that you must do. Nor is it something that I must do. Understand?"

He knew she did not, but she nodded anyway.

She looked afraid. "You do not want me?"

Want? I need! The soft curve of her breasts where the heat sheet fell across them filled his vision. He cleared his throat and forced himself to look at her face. "Elisif, I want you very much. But I do not love you. I do care for you, and will continue to care for you for as long as I live because it is my duty as the Harcel Leader. If you want children, I will give you children. When you want comfort, I will always try to give that to you also. I will give you all of me that I am free to give, but there are parts of me which do not belong even to me. I am not my own man, and I will do things which you will not understand. There are places I must go. And I go for one purpose only. My life is not my own, Elisif. It belongs to Chiy-une. She has called me."

Wide-eyed, Elisif gaped at him for several seconds before reaching out to touch his cheek. "You are truly a special man to be chosen by the Life-giver Mistress. Will she help us? Will the summers turn warm? Will . . ."

"She is dying."

Elisif rocked back as though she had been struck. Color drained from her face. She appeared more fragile in the dim light, her expressive eyes impossibly wide with disbelief. A fresh crop of tears caught in her lower lids.

"There is no hope for us?" she asked after a time, then slumped beside him.

"Only if we give up the hope we have, Elisif. We must help her now.

"Magaikan said to go south. I perceive he means us good. He seems to be a rarity—a decent man. Nonetheless, we must go north."

"He is a Star Follower." She spat out the words, letting her hatred show for the first time, startled by its intensity. "They killed the loag. They killed my family." Looking up at him, "How can so many of them be so brutal?"

At a loss to explain the complexities of the civilized worlds, he shook his head. Elisif had moved until she was pressed tightly against him. His body began to demand satisfaction or her total removal. There was no compromise in the offering. He no longer thought of Pam-ella, only of Elisif, her softness, her nearness, and how much he wanted her.

"Elisif."

As though reading his needs, her manner changed. The hatred and outrage became shadows. For a fleeting moment she recalled the first time she had seen him. She had been only fifty seasons, well into puberty, gawky. And he had not been much older, but his size did not give him the gangliness associated with adolescence. His eyes were wise. His wits had been sharp; honed by experience. He had spoken with her father every night for ten days, talked with her in the afternoons, then left and no one would tell her where he had gone.

"I will care for you . . ." she began.

She had cried that night.

". . . and understand when I do not understand. I will question only when I cannot accept what I do not understand . . ."

93

It had been impossible to explain why she cried for so long a time after his departure. Her father had understood, even then he understood.

"The sons that are a fruit of our bond will be raised to do you honor . . ."

Enickor had been different in ways far greater than the birthright, she knew.

". . . and deny you nothing which is in my power to give."

The vows completed, they looked at each other for several seconds. The air of uncertainty lingered in the gap between them. Anticipation moved them closer, breeching the rift.

Elisif smiled and put her arms around him and sought his mouth. She hesitated for a half a moment. "You do not need to love me. I love you enough for both of us, and have for a long time."

Chapter 11

ENICKOR WOKE AND SAT UP QUICKLY. THE TIME flashed on the wall. It was early.

Relaxing, he gazed at Elisif. A smile started which would not quit. With her at his side the long journey north would be easier, and surely the nights would be shorter. He touched a blond curl lying on her shoulder.

Keladine Ornasive's daughter had grown up.

His smile broadened.

Yes, she has grown up.

He rose and dressed, then left without waking her. A guard met him in the hall with a request to follow to Commander Magaikan's office. Reluctantly, Enickor complied.

The commander's appearance was that of a man who had forgotten what a good night's sleep was like. His uniform was spotless and unwrinkled.

"Come in. Sit down." A casual wave indicated an empty chair near the blower.

Enickor almost felt sorry for the man and could think of no reason, other than himself, for the commander's obvious duress.

"Have breakfast with me." Magaikan reached behind him

and brought a tray of steaming food over the piles of order-stets. He set it off to the side between them, pulled up a second chair, and sat near the blower.

Enickor delved into the food. He attributed his hunger to the physical workout he had with Elisif. Better keep up his strength. A small grin remained bright on his face.

When all but the hot protein was gone he sat back and waited for the commander to tell him why he had been summoned.

Sensing the cue, Magaikan relaxed a bit. "I intend to keep my word to you. I'm going to let you go. And if you are brought into one of my bases again, you will never leave again."

A tense moment followed. Each man searched the other; one for understanding, the other for certainty.

"Things have changed in the last day and a half," Magaikan continued, then sipped hard at his mug. "There is a conflict out there for the mining plots and rights. It is a conflict just short of a war. We cannot call it that, because if we did, we would be forced to do something. And if we did that, our presence here would be revealed to the entire Overeechy.

"Regardless, Chiy-une would not be spared. In fact, she might die a little faster.

"The peace of the Overeechy is a fragile thing, perhaps even more so than a newborn child. Like that child, it must be pampered, nurtured, fed, and catered to during times of temper.

"Right now, there is still another contributing factor in the balance. Both houses have brought in Quniero miners. For a while it looked like the House of Jeffires was going to resist.

"They have also had to bring in more troops to protect the Quniero miners from the natural predators, expand and protect the supply lines, and half a dozen other good reasons.

"The more troops, the more likelihood of escalation in the fighting.

"A severe rift right now could split the entire Overeechy in half. The Kriell is not ready for that. Not yet." Magaikan set his mug down hard. "It will come. Make no mistake about that. The Houses of Hadilka and Jeffires have spent too many decades fighting one another for it to be avoided now—even if the two of them made peace between themselves. The seed has been sown.

"The House of Hadilka is not all evil, my friend. Certainly no more so than the House of Jeffires is good. There are a dozen smaller houses who would voluntarily lay down the lives of their sons out of the love they bear each man.

"Lord Hadilka is not a stupid man. While he is more self-centered than those who have ruled the House before him, he is every bit as much the politician. Right now, he seeks to maximize his investment in Chiy-une. For him, it is good business." His hand waved Enickor's protest silent. "This is not a personal thing for him. It is business.

"The attempt to ease the situation with a marital bond failed. Neither House will return to the Overeechy and leave the riches of your planet, as well as those beyond, to the other.

"The Overeechy rises and falls on political whims. If there is ever to be any hope of stability and autonomous planetary government, we have to hold tight now. We, too, are striving for a massive form of survival. Neither house can afford to show weakness where it comes to joint mining rights, or they will weaken their position across all of the Overeechy. In the long run, Chiy-une is a brief business venture which is paying off handsomely for both Houses, even with the importing of the Quniero miners. We know little about them except that they are a passive culture, which is a relief. Conflict is expensive. For everyone. Think of what your lands would look like after one of our wars.

"So you see, we cannot admit there is a problem here, or that we are here." A sardonic smile twisted his face and deepened the wrinkles which ran from the sides of his nose and disappeared into the corners of his moustache.

Hands pressed together, Magaikan rested his elbows on his thighs and leaned forward. "Have you any idea what kind of far-reaching effect knowledge of our presence here would have?"

Enickor studied him for a moment, then shook his head. "No, I guess I can't. Why are you here? Really?"

"I have told you. We are looking for a man. A very special man.

"The woman I spoke of, from the Porintel Loag, remember?"

Solemn, Enickor nodded.

"She had a son. The father of that child was the Kriell. I am supposed to find this man and send him back for the safety of the Overeechy."

"That is why he is special?"

"He can lay claim to the Overeechy." It was said. Magaikan leaned back. He relaxed. The burden had been shared.

"Why would he want to do that?" Enickor asked slowly, trying to assimilate the answers.

"He may see it as a way to save Chiy-une from the rest of the mining schedule. He would be wrong. It is not that simple. Neither the Uv-Kriell, nor the Kriell could successfully dispute the Houses of Jeffires and Hadilka claims. They are legitimate in the eyes of the court."

"I guess I do not understand." And truly he did not. It made no sense. Him? A claim to the Overeechy? How?

"The governmental procedures of mining rights . . ."

"No. That is not what I mean." Carefully, "What I don't understand is how can this man possibly lay a claim against the Overeechy? It is my understanding he was a bastard. A Chiy-uneite."

Magaikan laughed heartily. It was a good sound that deteriorated into sadness. "Yes. The poor bastard was really a bastard. That was no secret. The secret was whose bastard he is.

"When the Old Lord Jeffires sought to clear his title for his son Hoyiv, he succeeded. But he stirred up a mess that no one thought possible. The complications only began when Pridain analyzed the chromosone cultures. The Old Lord threw val Densu out of his house, and that was the last anyone has seen of him.

"Trouble is, we need to return him to the Overeechy for what is called safe-keeping."

"Safe-keeping sounds like a prison." The darkly spoken words tumbled out thoughtlessly.

"Worse. The only way the Kriell's lineage is safe is to eliminate val Densu.

"According to Standard Chronometrics, val Densu is several days older than the Uv-Kriell, and therefore has the right of succession."

"What if he doesn't want it?"

"Won't matter. He can become a dangerous weapon in the hands of Hadilka, Jeffires, Corphlange—a dozen of the powerful Houses."

Enickor met the commander's bloodshot eyes. *So this is the struggle he faces? This is the decision he has trouble living with. He has given me his word and cannot go back on it. And he knows who I am.* "Suppose he refuses them?"

"He will not be given a choice. I thought you said you knew what could be done to a man's mind."

Absently, Enickor nodded. He knew. Magaikan was right. There would be no conscious choice. They would have the body. That was all they needed—make the physical determinations line up, and any one of the powerful Houses who caught him would own the Overeechy. "What about a block? Don't the lords and the Overeechy hierarchy have blocks put into their brains?"

"During childhood. Before they're six. Val Densu did not have one implanted. He was still with the Porintel then."

It did not fit. If Magaikan were as smart and dedicated as Enickor perceived him to be, he should be on his way to "safe-keeping."

"Why?"

Magaikan stared at the floor, head arcing slowly from side to side. "Some men have causes which are right. Causes which other men would take up if the circumstances were even slightly different." He stopped moving and looked openly at Enickor.

Enickor froze. The candid show of emotion touched him, yet made him apprehensive.

"Men who follow such causes, who stand against the odds, are rare. They would die rather than compromise themselves.

"I am banking on that.

"I am hoping that Enickor val Densu will kill himself rather than be taken by a House . . . for any reason they may give. Of course, that is, providing he is not already dead." An ironic smile reinstated the beginnings of the hard exterior Magaikan often wore."

"Yes," Enickor said slowly, "he probably is dead."

The commander stood. He was hard military. He seemed able to live with his decision and accept the circumstance that it would always haunt him. It was part of the consequences of one of life's choices.

From out of the desk came the weapons Enickor had taken from the Hadilkan. "You know how to use these?"

Enickor nodded, lackluster. His mind spun with information trying to coalesce into a sensible form. In the foreground was Pam-ella and a fresh wound. *It could have been . . .*

The katelings under the Lyndirlyan broke through their eggshells. The drones rejoiced. Gaediv and her head papkoe were fruitful. The future of the Quniero on Chiy-une was insured.

The rock changed from sedimentary strata to granite masses. Illeuro tasted the change in the vegetation. The skirmish that had separated him from his nekka hung in his memory. He wished for Gaediv's wisdom to impart the meaning of what had happened.

The caretakers had brought many Quniero to this new, alive place. Why should they suffer discord over so few as his nekka?

Questions filled his thoughts during his alone time. In the darkest moments of loneliness he doubted that Gaediv had the answers.

Ahead of him the great mountains split. The vertical cliffs paralleled one another, wound into the distance, and disappeared. They rose three kilometers straight up and fell another four straight down. Others before him, probably native caretakers, had carved a ledge into the northern wall. The wind whipped through the opening, moaning and whining for freedom, seemingly too confined by the granite walls.

Illeuro started out on the ledge, found it too awkward and unpredictable, and moved along the cliff face using his suction pads. His secondary lids closed over his eyes. The veiled protection dimmed the light. It was a minor inconvenience. Illeuro tasted his way through the passage.

The wind screamed louder and louder the deeper he penetrated. Though Illeuro worshiped no deity, he felt the presence of a great life force between the walls. He hurried.

Under the auspices of the bull torna-pok, Pam-ella recuperated quickly. She ached to commune with her benefactors, to share their thoughts, their feelings, and to say all that was so urgent inside her. For the most part they seemed to anticipate her feelings, though she had not verbalized them.

Evenings they gathered in the tauiri and circled her. She sang the songs of her childhood. They were strange, enchanting lyrics that rode on the moods of the wind.

Faelinor answered back of his own accord; harmonizing, crooning, empathizing with the loneliness in her voice and the yearning in her tone. On rare occasion, Friedo's baritone entered the tauiri on a whirlwind.

The brief interim was a friendly time steeped in peace and harmony. The death machines in the sky were someplace else, and the land was ripe with contentment.

Yet, in the light of day, when Friedo and Pam-ella con-

fronted one another the hostilities resumed. To her, he repré-
sented all that was ill and, in addition, he was a leech. Most
days, it was easy to hate him. At times he reminded her of
Enickor. Those were the best times to hate him. They left her
empty and aching inside, revealing once again how futile her
quest had been, how hopeless.

The last night in the tauiri was filled with songs, sad ones
of unrequited love and the sorrow of parting. The torna-pok
knew she would leave in the morning. It was a certainty like
the drab sun rising in the east and the ribbons of cold which
snaked along the ground. The bond between her and the dead
torna-pok leader had brought her to them for help. The aid
created a deeper dimension to the bond, one which she did not
wholly comprehend, but accepted. She would always be a
special friend of the beasts, just as each and every one of them
would be for her.

At dawn she bid the torna-pok farewell. Tears slipped down
her cheeks and into the muffler wrapped around her chin when
she hugged the bull as best she could. He was so large her arms
could not circle his neck. His snorting and the increase of saliva
drippings from his fangs indicated his sharing of emotions.

The roh was strong. The time of Pam-ella's recuperation
had been well spent. He carried the pack, lightened as much
as she dared, and the saddle. Of all the bundles on his back,
Pam-ella was the lightest.

A light snow blew down from the north. It filled the granite
crevices and coated the lee side of the trees and rock stands.

Pam-ella did not look back once underway. The lump of
sorrow choking her throat would burst forward if she relented
to the temptation. A gray morning sky mirrored her mood.

Theller moved steadily down the mountain. His gait and tilt
changed very little with the slope.

Spring had teased winter and lost. Delicate leaf buds, half
unfurled, froze on their slender limbs and began to fall. The
cold reached through the bark to the marrow of life and tightened its stranglehold. Withered grasses, iced flowers that would
never produce fruit poked bright-colored petals through the
snow. The wind shook the trees and whistled through the
branches.

They descended into the valley. The weather was kinder
than on the exposed slopes. A spring had turned into a river,
and already began to recede, with ice forming along the banks
of the calmer meanders.

Pam-ella's destination was vague—more vague than her route. She wanted to get away from the Star Follower camping over the tauiri. The storm had provided excellent cover.

At dusk she made camp in a cavern high above the stream and facing away from the force of the wind. She found spagus and analli tubers, ate because she knew she had to, then gathered more for future meals. The analli would keep indefinitely in this weather. If they were kept dry.

Theller stood near the cavern mouth, asleep on his feet, yet keeping watch. As she slipped into her heat bag, she smiled, thinking of the advantages he had with two heads. "Just goes to show that two heads are better than one."

"Ah, indeed they are!"

Startled upright, the *kalase* filled her right hand. She listened for a quick moment, then took aim at a figure entering the cavern.

The flash was blinding.

"Damn!"

She fired again.

The winsong began a melody that struck fear into her heart. She fought back, refusing to be captured, yet very relieved to know who invaded her territory.

"Get out! Go away!" she screamed, covering her ears. She maintained a deadly hold on the *kalase*.

"Okay, okay," Friedo hollered back.

Faelinor quieted, snorted, then approached the roh. A couple of sneezes and silence returned.

Friedo lighted the cavern and moved closer to Pam-ella.

Distrusting him, she kept the *kalase* in plain sight and pointed in his direction.

"May I stay the night?"

"No."

"Surely you can't be afraid of me."

"I'm not afraid of you. I hate you. I hate all you stand for, Uv-Kriell Payndacen, heir to the Overeechy." The words were as harsh as sputum, and spoken with the same violence as a cough.

"Somehow when you say that it doesn't quite come off as something desirable." He squatted in front of her and dropped his pack on the floor.

"I said before that we should talk. I meant it. There are things you should know, Pam-ella. Things I want to tell you." He placed the light between them and returned to Faelinor. The

102

saddle, small and light, slipped from the winsong's back. He placed it beside the roh's, noting the size and contrast of largest for the smallest. The craftsmanship on each showed the dichotomy present upon Chiy-une.

Irritated, he swore under his breath and returned to his pack.

"I don't want you traveling with me, nor do I want you following me. You would not be accepted at the loags. Your presence would endanger us both. Do you think these people are eager to have you decimate their world?" Her face was flush with anger.

"Simmer down. I can't stop that, and you know it." He pulled his heat bag from his pack, sat on it, and removed his boots and greatcoat. Shivering from the abrupt temperature change, he slipped into his bag, pulled it up to his neck, then turned on his side and continued talking to her.

"You aren't going to let me be tactful, are you?"

His question netted a glare.

"Your father is dead. Hoyiv controls the House of Jeffires." His flat tone bounced off the walls.

She wanted to be surprised, but was not. Lying in the Gorbich hills and waiting for death, she had a great deal of time to ponder over the House of Jeffires soldier's reference to her father. The worst thing she could think of was that he was dead. Always she conjured the worst and prepared to meet it, but it was still the worst when it came.

Slowly, she pushed the *kalase* into its spring-loaded home against her arm. It was time to talk. "When?"

Payndacen softened. "About seventy-five days ago, give or take a few."

"Almost midwinter. He hated winter here. Too cold for him. He hated Chiy-une." She looked at him. He was a blur. "She hated him, too."

Friedo was silent.

"How? How did he die? Do you know?"

"I know rumors, Pam-ella. Nothing first hand. Only secondhand information that does not go together." Pained, he wished that he had not told her. The questions would continue until all he knew was out in the open.

"Tell me." She sniffed hard, saying: I can take it, with her attitude.

"Well, like I said, it's uncertain. One of the most prevalent rumors says that he was poisoned while recuperating from a heart transplant. Others say he died of heart rejection. Still happens sometimes.

"All the stories have one thing in common. Your father more than likely had a heart attack, and, for one reason or another, his death soon followed."

"That narrows it right down, doesn't it." The cold exterior returned.

"Look, that's what I know. Granted, I'm not a wealth of information, but then the House of Jeffires has not been heavy on the details. Charges and counter-charges were flying between them and the Hadilka House long before I got here." He reached for the light. It turned off with a touch, signaling the end of the conversation.

She turned it on, glaring at him. "My brother Hoyiv?"

"Some think he did away with Lord Jeffires to gain control."

She gasped. "How can you say such a thing?"

"Damn! I can say it because you asked!" He turned his back to her and pulled his long coat under his head like a pillow.

"I did not ask you that! I asked you how he was!"

"Alive!"

"Thank you!" She turned off the light.

"You're welcome."

Both lay awake for a long time. Pam-ella cried softly. Friedo listened, hating Chiy-une and what it did to people.

Chapter 12

THE RAIN HAD STOPPED DURING THE NIGHT. FOR the first time since rejoining the land, Enickor felt the joys of Chiy-une's communion with the sun. The days of confinement had cast a solemnity among the soldiers and loagers that the warm rays melted. There was a secret gladness in the blue eyes of the Harcel people.

Fourteen figures attired in all-weather gear gathered in the rock-paved compound outside the temporary base. Landah carried a small pack containing the majority of the medicines and bandages Magaikan issued to them. A second such pack was neatly tucked away inside Enickor's gigantic burden.

The Kriell's Personal Guard had been generous when it came to outfitting the Harcel Loag for their journey across Chiy-une. More than a few soldiers had found it difficult to look the dispossessed natives in the eye.

The company medic administered one last injection to Landah. He gave it to him in the neck. Soon the lad's eyes were glazed, his cheeks pink.

"Watch him closely. Go easy. He can't travel very far on foot without losing some of the progress he has made," the medic said to Enickor, patted the boy's shoulder and returned to the ranks.

Magaikan dismissed his men and remained alone in the compound with the loagers. He cleared his throat as he approached Enickor. "I have found that being right doesn't mean you'll come out on top. Just the opposite, my friend."

"I know," Enickor agreed, motioning to his group to begin. "But it is far better than not believing in anything at all and still not coming out on top."

He smiled at the commander. "Thank you. You have been most generous, Commander Magaikan. The Harcel will not forget. If you find yourself in need—look for us and we will find you. For I have found that the price of being in the middle can be very great, also."

Enickor started on the north-by-north-east journey across Chiy-une. His destination was the Alizandar Loag, by way of the Lyndirlyan Mountains. He felt Magaikan's gaze upon him for a long time.

Great consideration was given to Landah and his health. They camped early the first and second days. Though the lad protested greatly and suffered personal embarrassment, he kept his silence in the face of Enickor's dictates. The tents provided by the Star Followers sheltered them better than anything they had in the Harcel. After some grumbling by Zaich, they accepted that too. Acceptance was becoming a way of life.

The land was flat, graduating to gently swelling hills in the east. The mire caused by the rains wiped out the old trails marked hundreds of seasons ago and maintained by the youth journeys from one loag to another during manhood excursions.

The eradication of their living history cast a gloom.

On the tenth day they reached the Monolith of Decision. It was still early in the afternoon, but they made camp. That evening Zaich, Enickor, and Omagar swapped stories of previous nights spent in the Monolith's shadow, the signs they waited for and the secrets whispered to them by Ieuchna on the wind.

The gries called back and forth, relaying messages with a single cry. Late into the night Enickor tended their meager fire, made with damp wood that still did not seem dry once it became charcoal. He watched the high clouds play games with the stars and listened to the gorbich hoot from the other side of the hill. The sound possessed a frantic quality. It was new. It was part of the changing. Part of the end.

106

Try as he might, he could arrive at no new solution to Chiy-une's problems.

He gazed at the three tents. Muffled sounds coming from Omagar and Udia's tent brought a smile to his lips.

It had been a good idea to insist upon Zaich and Landah sharing a tent.

He gazed at his own shelter. In his mind's eye he saw Elisif curled in her heat bag—waiting. It was so easy to lose himself in her. Her need for him was not the same as his need for her.

It made him feel guilty. He fought the desire to make love to her, pretending that she was Pam-ella. The ghost came into his mind before and after. Thus far it had remained at a distance during their lovemaking. Unknowing, Elisif always chased it away until he thought of nothing but the present.

The moon rose, full and brilliant. The motion of the orange color served as a reminder of its continuous voyage; of the ever-thickening atmosphere.

Enickor climbed the Monolith of Decision and waited for the moon to look straight down on him.

The last time he had sat upon the smoothed top under the gaze of the night eye to make a decision, the results changed his life.

No.

He should not have returned to the Star Followers.

The choice had been made.

Any loag would have taken him in, with honor, after his manhood excursion. He had done well. Very well. It was an earned right. They could not deny him. Not after the manhood ritual had been complete.

The Harcel would have accepted him with open arms.

The Porintel, too, would finally have accepted him.

But he chose wrong then. He had returned to Shirwall. With the exception of Pam-ella, he had received only ridicule for his endeavors.

It had seemed the right thing to do at the time. He wanted to be part of a family and felt compelled to return to the tattered shreds at Shirwell. A man did not desert his father and peers for the company of those who were not his family. That would be a wrong.

How important it had been for him to belong to the House of Jeffires. Not for wealth or power. Certainly not for the mining, which was ultimately responsible for the destruction of Chiy-une. But for his family. A place to belong, to be taken in and cherished, as he cherished those who dwelt within the magnificent stone walls, the santuary where one could go when cast out by the rest of the world.

Sadly, he realized that even then he did not want to leave Pam-ella. She had been the driving force, the prime motive. When did he start feeling so deeply for her?

He recalled the day he arrived at Shirwall. The dryness returned to his mouth. Fear churned his gut. Again he felt the sadness of the Metaliary Ardinay, whose task it had become to turn him over to the Star Followers.

He had wanted to tell the old man not to worry. He knew why his mother had violated the taboos. Maybe he even understood. A little. Maybe. He had wanted to with all his heart.

Today, he understood. He wanted a family as desperately as she had, but on another level. She had made her compromises, reaped their rewards and found the aftermath bittersweet. The Star Followers had used her, and she used them. Their ability to heal the wrongness in her body was what she wanted. Too many husbands had already borne witness to her infertility. Then came the Star Followers. For a price they healed her, allowing her to bear life—the one thing she wanted above all else.

At the time Ardinay took him to Shirwall, her death was still fresh in his memory. She had wanted to die. The gladness in their small home filled the room and smiled from the walls as death crept over her body.

Now it reminded him of the joys to be found in lovemaking.

By the Great Lords, how she had wanted to die!

During her final moments, she had asked for his understanding; not his forgiveness for being left alone, but his understanding.

Too young, he did not understand. He was being abandoned to a people who did not love him, did not even want him. Only the old Metaliary seemed to understand.

"You will know the truth in the light it has been spoken, young Enickor. Then you will comprehend the compromises and the burdens your mother has lived with."

A gorbich hooted at the moon. It was close.

Enickor peered into the night.

Shirwall had never been able to replace the love and feeling of well-being he enjoyed in the presence of his mother. It was the feeling of family. She had been his family. She had wanted him.

The child of forty seasons who went to Shirwall was tolerated and accepted like a punishment for a crime. But from the first there had been the girl, small and delicate, who watched with warm eyes and a quick friendly smile.

"Family," he whispered. He looked down at his tent.

Elisif was his family now. She needed in much the same way he had when he was first left at Shirwall.

He sat on the Monolith for most of the night. When he climbed down a decision had been made and sealed in quiet ritual and ancient words saved only for this place upon the land.

Pam-ella Jeffires was banished to the past. She had no place in either his present or his future. What might have been was not. It had died, like the Harcel territory, contaminated by Star Follower ideals.

He entered his tent and undressed. When he slipped into his heat bag he found it was connected to Elisif's.

"I love you, Enickor," she said in a timid voice.

He turned and gathered her into his arms. "And I will try to love you the way a man should love the woman with whom he has exchanged vows."

"I do not even ask that. Just let me love you."

Pam-ella's ghost has been vanquished.

There was great joy in the leah when the katelings emerged. Blind, dim-sensed, they scurried and stumbled across the corbancoob floor, over Gaediv's feet and into the halls. Drones gently returned them, feeling privileged at having discovered an errant one.

The kateling wail was song in the leah. The few drones considered it reward for the long labors imposed upon them. Idle papkoes groomed Gaediv and kept the katelings clean.

Never again would the Gaediv leave this new leah site. It was their home on the living planet. She wandered through the passageways, tasting, anticipating, seeking the future of their new world and the Quniero's place in her impending history.

The history of Alidanko was just that—the old world's history. The differences between the two planets were vast. The Quniero of Alidanko had outlived their desert world. The mountains had been pulverized to sand. The core of the planet had cooled. Motion in the mantle had ceased. Only the wind and the Quniero moved the sand.

Gaediv moved through the leah and ventured out into the

109

night. Although she was surrounded by drones, she remained close to the leah opening. She tasted the air and knew the danger riding Chiy-une's future, the Quniero future.

She called upon the memories of her predecessors, and could not find anything which might shed knowledge on the sensation. It was new. So much would be new. Perplexed, the Gaediv knew her time would be like no other.

She returned to the corbancoob and summoned the Quniero. The land on which they had spawned katelings was a wounded one. She did not understand the reason for the caretakers' assault. Then, she did not understand caretakers. They were so new in the Alidanko common mind, only three Gaedivs old. So strange.

Gaediv communicated to all. The katelings were silent, innately knowing she was the life-giving authority. *This land of our leah is called Chiy-une. She is a wounded entity, assaulted by those who delivered us to this living place. We owe the caretakers homage and price.*

It is Gaediv memory which tells us this.

The drones bowed. *Life of leah,* came a common thought response.

Our nekkas mine the gems they covet. They give of themselves for the leah.

Life of leah, came again.

We have begun to establish the leah. But it is not enough. We must go deeper. We must find the barren places of this land and rebuild the leah underneath. There is havoc in the rock, fear in the soil and danger in the air. I have tasted these.

Another Gaediv shall be birthed. She will not replace me, but complement me. This land is alive and suited for many leahs. It is Gaediv wisdom.

Life of leah. This time the katelings bowed also.

The nekka of Illeuro asa Khatioup had moved seven times in as many days. The absent leader sensed the caretakers' frustration and subsequent brutality toward his confused charges, but he did not understand. He had surmounted the highest, most dismal peaks of the Lyndirlyan. The exertion, lack of rest, and the constant pressure had taken a toll. He had begun to molt two furins early.

When at last he caught a strong direction to his nekka he summoned them to meet him.

The caretakers prevented their departure.

He hurried even more, entered the forest basin, and experienced sensory deprivation for the first time. The density of the forest oppressed him. Darkness had never presented a problem to a Quniero. Taste and smell became their unerring guides.

But this forest was different. It neither tasted nor smelled like anything in the nekka leader's memory. When he entered the basin forest the sun had been in the sky.

Illeuro became lost, an impossible thing for a Quniero. He had tried tunneling, but the rock defied him. At last, he felt defeated. He had crossed the open spaces of this planet, survived the hazards of its peaks, worn the inner part of his suction pads down to their sensitive layers and now could go no farther. He had even survived isolation and adapted. It should not have been possible, but this place seemed filled with such things.

What should have been a two-sun-rotation journey had turned out to be impossible. Here, everything was different. It was beyond a simple nekka leader's comprehension.

His head tendril coiled and lay down above and between his eyes. His tail curled to the right. Illeuro hunkered against a boulder stand. And waited. For death, he thought.

The days following the Monolith were difficult. The gorbich grew brave, though they had not even touched upon the fringes of the Gorbich Hills. At night they stood watch in pairs, no two being tent partners.

The rains returned, further hampering their progress through the extended predator territory.

Half a mark into the Hills the weather changed. It had rained steadily for three days. The ground was a quagmire in the lowlands.

On the seventh day the clouds receded. Brown haze filmed the sky. The sun was orange, its beautiful yellow light obscured by another layer of filtering agents in the atmosphere. The depression that settled upon Enickor put him in a foul mood.

By the ninth day they saw the Lyndirlyan Mountains. Tomorrow, twenty days after they began their journey, they would be ready to enter the ominous mountains. Few had ever returned from them. Even manhood rituals took the participants through carefully charted passages. Most of those circumnavigated the backbone of the Lyndirlyan.

The following day they made camp at the base of the mountains. During the evening meal the gries were very active. A sense of excitement rode the late afternoon air.

111

Zaich and Elisif had first watch. She kept busy cleaning up the remnants of their communal meal, made of fresh greens and gries.

Enickor listened to them for a while, then dozed.

He was wakened in the middle of the night by human screams and gorbich hooting. Elisif was beside him, still clad in her all-weather gear.

Without speaking, she handed him his weapons and clutched her own knife in both hands. *Kalase* in his left hand, the Holy of the Harcel unsheathed in his right, he rushed from the tent and into the battle raging in their compound.

Someone had lighted a Star Follower torch and thrown it into the camp center. Enickor barely had time to be grateful for that advantage when a gorbich lunged. His reflexes went to work. He slashed at the head, sidestepping the extended talons aimed at his chest.

There was no time to see if he had killed the beast.

Another came from his left. He fired the *kalase*. The beast tripped over his taloned forelegs and tumbled away.

He shouted at Elisif. She came out of the tent and stood back to back with him. Together they moved toward the three battling the army of gorbich.

Landah lay on the ground, bleeding, trying to get up. He reached through the flexible bars formed by his companions' legs and retrieved his sword. Armed, he staggered to his feet and filled in the fourth side of the phalanx.

Elisif melted into the line. Her knife was good only in confined quarters. Combat that close was almost certain death.

Enickor crowded in beside her.

The *kalase* lit the night. The arc of brilliance brought cries from both the gorbich and the loagers. A slice of quiet followed.

Two gorbich lay dead between the three tents. Their grotesque shapes were worsened by the stench rising from the smoke originating somewhere between them.

The horde withdrew. It was a slow retreat, one which lacked finality.

After the night was quiet and death hung in the breeze, the moon ventured out from behind a high fog bank. They remained in phalanx position. Their breathing grew heavy, their fear a burden.

The brightness of the moon aided the light coming from near Enickor's tent. The trails left by the gorbich were lustrous. The sheen of crimson blood on the rock cast a strange beauty.

112

They waited for the gorbich to regroup and launch another attack. The cold of the night seeped into the bones of the three who had not been standing guard, and therefore were not prepared also to battle the frigid north winds. Only Elisif had been too afraid to give up her gear before going to bed.

The silence held.

Enickor slipped away. The ranks closed. Cautiously, he entered the nearest tent, whipped out a set of all-weather gear and tossed it to the phalanx.

Zaich caught it and handed off to Landah.

The lad returned to the center, leaving the four to watch each direction of the compass. He stood beside his sword and pulled on his gear. Hair flopping, he tried to keep his own watch in every direction. He was dressed and in his father's place when the next suit was tossed through the air.

Enickor disappeared into his tent, and emerged seconds later with the last set. He paused long enough to set the light so that it shone into the thickest part of the forest, the place where the gorbich were most likely to emerge.

He stood, glanced back at the solid phalanx, then at the forest.

The wind blew stronger. The gusts whipped the tender leaves clinging to the scrawny twig branches. Trees bent toward the south. They looked as though they would migrate if their roots were shallow.

Migrate. The notion struck Enickor with the force of the ice on the wind. For an instant he heard the sweet voice of his Mistress winding out of the forest. She, too, was in the south and safe from the icy north wind.

Out of the west came a scream which put an end to the brief reverie Enickor indulged.

He turned.

A gorbich leaped from the dark and struck him in full flight.

He went down, Elisif's shriek in his ear.

The clearing was alive with the beasts. The screams and wails were a collection of mockery and laughter.

The sword was ineffective against the beast. Enickor's bulk had been sufficient to unbalance the beast before they ended up in a heap on the ground. He could hardly move under the great weight, but knew he had only heartbeats to react.

He released the sword and heaved against the beast. The gorbich responded sluggishly and tried to get on his feet. As soon as there was room, Enickor grabbed the Holy and jammed the *kalase* against the soft underbelly.

The light flash was obscured by the filthy fur hanging over him.

The agony in the beast's cry spread the fear of death out to every corner of the darkness.

Two more gorbich converged on Enickor.

Time afforded him a lone glance at the phalanx. It was breaking up. The gorbich were winning.

The oppressive weight pinning him became his shelter as two sets of talons began to rip away at the fur and the ground to get to him.

He fired, aiming upwards, hoping to hit the chest or belly.

Yelping, the one near his head retreated.

Another took his place.

Blood ran down the sides of the gorbich and covered him. Flaps of hide stripped by the beast's comrades began to form a tomb around him. Each time he tried to move them he was met by a flurry of talons. They played with him, eating time as though it was meat, not allowing him to escape, but not converging on him for the kill, either.

The stench grew formidable once the entrails were exposed. Finally, the enormous weight pinning him to the ground began to shift. The tugs and pulls see-sawed his cover.

They're coming in through the top! He struggled, turning onto his back.

The battle sounds were muffled by the envelope of blood-soaked hide and muscle gradually burying him.

He took a deep breath of the foul air and began firing. He was wild.

Another corpse fell across his legs.

He waited, lungs burning, eyes stinging. The horde attacked the fresher kills with vigor.

When they resumed sorting flesh to get at him, he moved the *kalase* in a circle.

The hide across his legs caught fire. Bowel acid ran through the holes. He kicked at the carcass and tried to burn a clear path into the night.

Unable to see what was happening outside his tomb, Enickor gambled and rolled to his right. During the time he decided to flee, the Holy had returned to his left hand. He scrambled out.

Still on the ground, his eyes not adjusted to the light shining directly at him, he continued firing. He managed to get to his knees before one came from the direction of the phalanx.

The Holy swung around and sliced the gorbich's throat. Blood spurted a two-meter arc before the beast hit the ground, twitching, trying to crawl forward.

He brought the Holy around in front of him.

An old gorbich glared at him.

The incessant hooting filled the night to the exclusion of all else.

Enickor did not fire, did not strike with the Holy. He met the glare with an even ferocity.

Without warning, the old gorbich turned and left. He did not run, nor did he walk. His head was high.

The dim gray light spilling across the sky and down the Lyndirlyan Mountains gave a stark reality to the carnage-strewn camp.

During the battle the phalanx had collapsed. He could not see any of the loagers.

"Elisif!" He ran toward the spot where they had stood their ground. The dead gorbich posed hurdles which he leaped. In the center where he expected to find five corpses he found only emptiness.

"Elisif!"

He wandered around the clearing and into the forest. The Holy remained in his left hand. The *kalase* hung in his right hand at his side.

He shouted until hoarse and roamed the nearby countryside the entire morning, and found nothing.

At noon he returned to the compound. The gorbich had been there sooner. Their dead were gone. Two of the tents and a large portion of the gear were also missing.

Enickor quickly threw his things together and gathered what remained of the Harcel's belongings. After cleaning his all-weather gear, he shouldered the enormous pack and set out to follow the trail left by the gorbich.

It led to the highest peaks of the Lyndirlyan Mountains.

Chapter 13

I WAS WONDERING...DO YOU, DO YOU KNOW IF my father mentioned anything concerning Enickor val Densu before he died?" Pam-ella continued looking into the fog rolling down the mountainside and filling the valley.

"Like what?" Payndacen asked. *Damn, but her moods are hard to predict.*

"Like whether or not he had changed his mind, you know, reconsidered and given him a place in the House of Jeffires."

"Not that I know of. And if he did, I don't believe your brother Hoyiv would find it advantageous to reveal that kind of information." He lifted his hand, hesitated for a moment, then reached over and touched her leg.

The roh halted. She stroked the vee of Theller's necks, ignoring Payndacen's offered consolation.

"I know this is difficult for you to accept, Pam-ella. But if your brother did make such a claim, I would be highly suspicious of his motives. If Enickor val Densu did return to the House of Jeffires under such an enticement, I would not give any odds on his chances of leaving Shirwall again, or on his chances of living to see the next season."

"You can't seriously believe Hoyiv would harm him?" Her tone was flat.

Payndacen stroked Faelinor's neck and gazed at the black roh head staring at him. "Yes, Pam-ella, I do. To be honest, I do not think much of the young Lord Jeffires. Coping with the pressures of his Overeechy holdings and Chiy-une has changed him. He has few loyalties. As for inflicting harm onto Enickor, the Enickor you knew—yes. Killing him outright would not be a sound move on Hoyiv's part. And he's too smart to consider it. But . . ." There seemed no point in detailing the consequences. A subtle flinch told him that she understood quite well.

She hated admitting that he might be right about Hoyiv. It was a reality of which she had not wanted to be a part. But it was there now, and could not be denied. The competition, the defeats Hoyiv had suffered at Enickor's hand—at last they could be atoned in a special way. All Hoyiv needed now was Enickor for one last go-round. Would victory really taste as sweet as Hoyiv thought it might? She doubted it. Hoyiv was intelligent, but he did have his blind spots.

"I think he is dead." The muffler wrapping her chin muted the words.

"I beg your pardon?"

"I said"—she pulled her chin up from the wrap—"I think he's dead."

The cold fog made Faelinor restless. He moved on the scant trail. The roh moved beside him, sneezing, until Faelinor stepped back to let Theller lead.

"Why do you think that?"

"Because of the way the Ocandar have treated me from the start. At first, I knew so little about the land and her people I did not know that they were acting strange. I interpreted their fear as resentment.

"It would have been justifiable on their part."

"But they helped me the first days after I left Shirwall. Without them I would probably have either died or returned."

"Why didn't you ever return? Sorry, go on about the Ocandar people."

"They knew Enickor, of course. He had visited each of the loags recently. But the proximity of the Ocandar to Shirwall was something he took advantage of. When he needed to get away, or he wanted to be alone to think, he went to the mainland. Usually he stopped at the Ocandar. So, you see, they knew him well.

"I had hoped . . . no, I was certain, when I left Shirwall, that Enickor was either camped on the beach—and I knew the exact spot—or he went to the Ocandar." Head hanging, "It wasn't until later, much later, in my journey, and my learnings about the loags, that I found out how truly dispossessed he was. The only hope he ever had was Keldine Ornasive and the Harcel Loag. They were the last ones I visited."

Payndacen tried to follow the loag names and put them into place on a mental map he formed out of memory. It took him a moment to find where the Harcel Loag fit. "Had any of them seen him?"

"No. The Leader of the Harcel, Keladine Ornasive, grieved. Loag doctrines would have given him a place in any loag he chose right after he passed his manhood ordeal. I think Keladine wanted Enickor to marry his only daughter after he passed into manhood. He believed in Enickor. The Harcel Leader was a big man in many ways. He was compassionate."

She looked back at him. "The manhood ritual is an ordeal. I seriously doubt you could pass it."

The lack of sarcasm in her voice made him almost believe it.

"He chose to return to Shirwall. Therefore, he had no place among the loags. Do you follow me?"

"Yes. He had severed his birth ties by going back?"

"That's one way to put it. To the loags, he had chosen to align himself with a people who had taken advantage of them, abused not only their hospitality, but the very land which sustains their lives.

"Enickor did not see it that way. I know he didn't. And he thought he had a place where he belonged, a family. But he never fit in with Father's and Hoyiv's ideals of what a younger Jeffires should be.

"Oh, physically—there wasn't anything he could not do. And he's a quicker thinker than Hoyiv. And . . ." Her voice faded.

"If you believe him dead, why do you continue looking for him?"

"I don't know. I feel drawn to the land. It is nearly impossible to explain, but I *need* to be here. Oh, I am not waiting for some great purpose to drop out of the sky, or anything like that. I just need to be here.

"Besides, where else is there for me to go? Shirwall? Then to honorable Lord Hadilka? No, thank you. I have not yet had my fill of life's enjoyment and pleasures. Here I am my own. No one else's."

"One more question, Pam-ella. Were you in love with Enickor?" The words were faint, as though coated with the unexpected.

She nodded.

It began to make sense. She was not a sister searching for a man who was her half-brother. She was a woman searching for her lost lover.

"I don't know." Her voice was strong, her head high. "Maybe I am, was, in love with him. Now I have said it out loud and nothing has changed."

"Hasn't it?"

She looked back at him and smiled. "No. You do not matter to me. I hardly care what you think."

A quick smile warmed his face. "I have noticed. Please continue your story."

A thoughtful silence was broken by her light laugh. "No. I have said as much as I want to—maybe more than I should have. It's your turn to do the talking."

"I don't have much to say. I had better save it."

"For what? Marriage?"

He laughed out loud, startling Theller. "No," he said, drawing a deep breath, "I don't plan on doing much talking that night."

Pam-ella nudged Theller into a faster pace. "On second thought, maybe you had better save it for then. It might be the only way you're able to keep her awake—with sound."

Payndacen stopped laughing. Her attacks came from the strangest directions. Head shaking, he prodded Faelinor. "You know what I like about you?"

"Nothing."

"No," he called over the clatter of hooves on the stone trail. "Your stable, predictable moods."

"I did not ask for your company."

He could not help smiling. She looked so tiny sitting atop Theller. What she lacked in size she more than made up for in mouth and wit. He considered telling her that, then dismissed it as a bad idea.

"You had better watch yourself, Lady Jeffires," he said

119

when he caught up to her. "You almost acted human back there."

She uttered an obscenity learned in the Porintel and tuned him out.

The forest darkness took on a new feel. Illeuro asa Khatioup opened his eyes. He tried to get his feet under him. They would not obey.

A beast of immeasurable proportion illuminated the dark. His size belied the close proximity of the trees. A row of pearl fangs reached out of the beast's upper pan-shaped maw, meshed with the bottom and looked to stab the composting debris on the forest floor.

Illeuro's struggles ceased.

All three eyes focused upon the Quniero. *Death is not yours today, strange one.*

Illeuro did not respond. Nothing in his memory, or of the memories he had shared with the Gaediv upon becoming a nekka leader, had prepared him for a response to so magnificent a creature as the one before him now. The soothing thoughts which communicated with him dissolved the strange emotion a caretaker might have called fear. Illeuro did not know its name.

He knew caution, openness, not fear.

The beast's eyes grew to be giant yellow orbs with black centers. *You take from the land. But you give also. You are an old species. Not as old as the rangtur, but older than the Star Followers, and wiser in your ways.*

He looked away. *Follow.*

Illeuro did so.

The land rangtur lacked substance when he moved. *This is my forest, my link in the evolution chain of the rangtur. I will permit no violence inside her embrace. Nor will I permit you to mine here. Guide the Star Followers back into the peaks. Keep them away, strange one.*

I will do this, responded Illeuro, proud to be of service to so great a creature. Gaediv memory lessened in recent knowledge of species who met violence with violence, but were otherwise peaceful. The Quniero knew not the response to violence. In that, they were at the mercy of those who shared land with them.

The rangtur guided him to the fringes of the forest and seemed to dissolve in the air. Illeuro wasted no time.

The nekka called frantically from a place half a kilometer straight up. His being filled with joy.

The finds and losses of Enickor's life rolled through his memory. He sensed no justice in the things which had befallen him, nor could he see their reasons.

Dazed, he wandered through the Lyndirlyan Mountains. They were rugged and deceived any who gazed upon them with smooth, lush outer faces. But once beyond the friendly facade, the interior turned harsher than a seasoned traveler would want to imagine.

Stark granite cliffs rose out of the deep valleys and snagged the clouds. Black stains streaked the mountain walls. At times fog lay trapped in the valleys for days before the sun could burn it off. But the power of the sun upon the imprisoned mists of the Lyndirlyan Mountains was dwindling on a daily basis. The rusted sky reflected the heat and cast it back at the sun, unused.

The sun no longer heard the land's needs.

"Am I the only man to hear the land?" Enickor shouted at the sky.

The mountains picked up his voice and hurled it down their walled corridors and let it whisper to the heights.

Enickor followed the trail made by the gorbich. There were no side trails, nor was there any debris to alarm him. He did not understand why the gorbich would follow the five from the Harcel, if they lived. He refused to think of Elisif as dead, torn apart by the fierce predators. He pictured them running from the beasts, knew their weariness and despair. They thought him dead. They must have, or they would have waited . . . Or they were dead.

He stood on a ridge. Before him lay an enormous bowl-shaped valley where once a glacier stood for thousands of seasons. Soon another glacier would be born in this open womb. Now it was lush. The invitation it extended carried a foreboding.

The gorbich would be waiting. The most likely spot was just inside the tree line on the down slope.

Debating what course he should follow, a dread-filled idea struck him. What if they had not been followed by the gorbich? Suppose they had hidden, returned, and hid again, to wait for him? Then returned to the camp and found him gone?

The questions came. They built a panic fueled by doubt.

Light ricocheted from the white wings of a gries leading half a dozen more across the valley toward him. Enickor noticed and failed to register their significance. He sat and watched the lowlands, part of his mind reveling in the untouched beauty of it. It was the beginning, the starting place of the Hedshir Forest, the place from where the rest of Chiy-une's great forests were birthed. The valley was marked on loag maps as the Head Forest.

Here, the land was accustomed to the ground-slithering ribbons of cold. The flowers were hearty, the trees broad-limbed, flat on the top and green through all the cycles. The small, spiny leaves had an aroma peculiar to the Lyndirlyan Mountains. And for a moment Enickor considered starting a fire and burning some ipcar leaves. The euphoric sensation their burning produced would have been welcomed.

Weariness scratched at his bones. He had walked steadily for two and a half days. So had the gorbich.

Gorbich could go as many as eight days without sleep.

Enickor could not.

The serenity below relaxed him. Twitches and jerks beset his thigh and calf muscles. The pack straps were suddenly heavy, and cut into his shoulders. He wanted to sleep. The sun was racing to the west. Vibrant colors streaked the horizon and shared their profusion with the high clouds in the eastern sky.

The sound of a landslide rumbled from the distance. The noise rolled over the valley and shook the trees. Dust plumes carried on the breeze rambled along the granite walls. Far eastward, a dark pillar rose into the orange/blue sky.

The noise no sooner died than another followed from approximately the same place.

Squinting, Enickor tried to see what was causing the slides.

The gries cried as they circled overhead.

"Oh, no. Not the Lyndirlyan. Not the mountains, too." He covered his face with his hands, not wanting to know of the destruction slated for the peaceful valley.

The pitch of the gries' cries changed. They sought a higher plane on which to circle.

Enickor lowered his hands and visually sought the source of their fright.

The gorbich were backing out from the tree line. They did not run, but neither did they stand and fight whatever was rousting them from their ambush spot.

Enickor slowly pushed to his feet. The aches and twinges

122

his muscles set upon him diminished quickly after the first few steps upward. He sought higher ground. His moves were slow, planned. The gorbich would not be distracted.

The wind shifted. He smiled.

Once out of sight, providing the errant wind did not shift again soon, the gorbich would not be able to sniff him out. Downwind of them, the gusting breeze carried their stench to sting his nostrils anew.

He climbed and circled around the irregular granite thrusts which overhung the valley. Below was a gravel talus peppered with boulders. It spread fingers into the base of the magnificent ipcar forest.

Enickor moved through a narrow passage and had to take off his burden to force both it and himself through two high granite thrusts. Inside, he could see the valley, the trail up the near slope, and the far eastern ground which the Star Followers were sampling.

The gorbich snarled. They alternated standing their ground, clawing the dirt and the air, and retreating.

The sun left the sky. The colors faded. No longer did the third-magnitude stars twinkle and tease the watcher. They were dim. The first-magnitude stars were scattered across the night sky, still rich with the splendor the universe granted Chiy-une. These, too, had faded, and would eventually be consumed by the death haze.

An absolute darkness settled over the valley. The gorbich were no longer visible. Not even the tree line could be seen.

Enickor closed up his all-weather suit. The night chill promised to be well below freezing. Hunger was a vague sensation. The shelter he had chosen was good. He felt safe.

The gorbich continued snarling and hooting.

Enickor wanted to sleep. It seemed the best course, since he had no chance of seeing whatever it was that managed to both taunt and unnerve the beasts. He hoped the horde would not retreat during the night. He wanted to watch and study the unseen perpetrator.

Loneliness settled over him. He slept, dreaming of Elisif, of Pam-ella and of Meiska. The piercing howls of the gorbich roused him several times, but not for long. Once he woke from a dream crying. The dream had been of Elisif.

A dense fog hung on the eastern rim of the valley. The area directly below Enickor was clear.

Eating slowly and washing it down with a few sips of water,

Enickor studied the tree line. The gorbich were still there. Two were on the ground, either wounded or dead. He could not tell.

The stubborn beasts were cowards at heart. Why did they stay? Could it be that there was not more than one of whatever it was holding them?

Stroking the thirty-day growth hanging from his jaw, he wondered if the creature was a land rangtur.

He secured his bundle, speculating on where Elisif had slept during the night.

Once beyond the safety of the thrusts, he set his curiosity aside, changed direction, and concentrated on the climb ahead.

By noon he could no longer hear the echoes of the hooting gorbich, and he had found another way into the valley. He moved down the rock ledges that traversed the cliff face and into the ipcar. The breeze played music in the trees. The notes spanned three octaves. The gries cried overhead. The density of the ipcar was such that he could not see any part of the sky.

Dark shadows filled the forest. As he walked the valley floor seemed to change. When he thought he was going down, he was actually on level ground. He brought out his compass and followed the needle. So strange a sensation to lose the sky.

Night came early in the Head Forest. The wind blew hard through the upper reaches. The forest floor remained calm.

Enickor took his bearings, then turned to his right. He walked for a kilometer, stopped, put away his compass, and stepped from the forest.

It was dusk. Straight up against the colorful trails in the sky he could see the perch where he had spent the previous night. To his left, along the treeline, were the gorbich. He had thought himself in error until he stepped into the open night.

He proceeded cautiously. The two felled gorbich were in sight, their pungent masses stiff. Enickor walked around them. He halted sharply. His heart thumped in his throat.

To the left were the remains of the gorbich killed in the camp clearing. They had been dragged along as food.

On the right were the shredded remains of the rest of the horde. These had been freshly killed. Blood still glistened high on the smooth tree trunks. There were pieces of hide in the branches. A trail of gorbich pieces and slippery mud led into the Head Forest.

Enickor bent and retrieved a bright object. He turned it over in his hand and wiped away the blood.

It was a medallion, like the one Zaich wore to show his rank in the loag.

His heart sank. He grabbed the light from the pouch on the side of his all-weather suit, pressed it on, and lit the trees' limbs.

There were stringy pieces of gorbich flesh everywhere he turned. A head was jammed between two branches ten meters above the ground. Two forelegs attached by a breastbone were stiff and protruding from a tree trunk twelve meters ahead and ten up. The extended talons impaling the wood kept it in place.

"What could do this?" His voice was a whisper, though it sounded loud in the forest. A shiver passed over him.

He shone the light on the crimson-flecked medallion. Without a doubt, he knew it to belong to Zaich.

The sun set, plunging the valley into darkness.

Enickor turned off the light and put it away with the medallion. He listened for several seconds, knowing he had no choice but to follow the trail of his family.

He called Elisif's name over and over.

No response came out of the dark.

Chapter 14

THE CARETAKERS HAD BEEN RELIEVED TO SEE IL-leuro. While it was true that they could not tell one Quniero from another, they saw his importance evidenced in the greeting he was given. The nekka was whole once again. Damaged. Some almost dispossessed of mind and sanity, but physically whole.

The caretakers did not force them into the tunnels this time. They went willingly, led by Illeuro asa Khatioup, the only nekka leader in Quniero history to survive so prolonged a time of isolation. They revered him.

The morning after Illeuro's return he signaled the need to move the caretaker camp farther into the mountains. The nekka had spent the night sealing the gem deposits.

Reluctantly, the House of Jeffires began to pack.

Illeuro stood at the edge of the cliff overlooking the forest basin. Approval scented the air.

Enickor moved in the night, surrounded by carnage and the hum of gathering insects. He was afraid.

What kind of creature could stop the gorbich from entering the Head Forest? And when they did not retreat, tear them limb from limb? How large he must be! How powerful, Enickor mused.

There were Star Followers in the valley, true enough, but this was not their handiwork. They would have used *kalases* and killed the gorbich on sight. Toying with them, giving them an opportunity to retreat, was not their style.

Zaich's medallion lay heavy in his pocket. Zaich was alive. Elisif? He wanted her to be alive so badly that it hurt to think she might not be. They had to have traveled this way. But where were they?

He squinted into the absolute darkness of the forest interior. A chill reached back and raced along the ground. His first reaction was to inhale. He stifled it. A cold ribbon could freeze his lungs.

Waiting for it to pass, he sent Commander Magaikan a mental thanks for the all-weather gear which kept him warm and dry.

Gradually, he formulated plans.

He turned away from the forest, climbed the slope, and continued upward until reaching the thrusts. It seemed wisest to make camp in the same sanctuary as he had the previous night. Certainly it was high enough and sheltered from predators.

Before first light Enickor climbed down to the timberline and waited for the sun. Anxious, he chewed on a handful of spagus sprouts.

The first hint of the sun's approach became a signal. Enickor straightened and entered the Head Forest. He skirted the insect-infested gore and kept it to his right. Circling, he returned to the far side. The stench was nauseating. He glanced back. The cold morning light trickling into the valley showed the full extent of the carnage.

The night had been kind.

Fear caught in his throat and choked him before he reconciled it.

He entered the land where the great forests were birthed and legendary monsters cared for the land. Often, he reassured himself with thoughts of Meiska. The rangtur had been a feared entity until time proved him a friend. It was a flimsy thought, but he clung to it when strange noises followed him.

Somewhere ahead was his family. The hope of seeing Landah, Omagar, Udia, Zaich, and sweet Elisif kept him going.

His *kalase* remained ready in the palm of his left hand as though it had grown there. His right hand rested on the Holy.

A morning breeze sang in the upper branches. The rhythm was slow, enticing. Enickor fought the lull.

It was not long before he had to replace the sword handle with a light. The farther he penetrated the Head, the denser became the forest growth. There were places where only a hint of light penetrated the upper branches. Here none of the sun's warming rays touched the ground. Season after season of debris lay in various stages of compost. Not an unpleasant smell. In fact, it smelled clean. It had been a long time since Enickor had breathed natural Chiy-une air. The moisture cleared his sinuses and refreshed his breathing.

His fear dimmed.

The faint sounds of the gries in the unseen sky lent comfort. Their nearness took away some of the loneliness eroding his soul. The hum of insects on the way to the feast at the forest's edge provided an additional familiarity.

He walked at a brisk pace, detouring and climbing over fallen branches and moss-covered boulders colorfully decorated by lichens.

Small game, anittes he figured, darted from tree to tree just out of reach of his light. They toyed with the beam like small children daring one another to get the closest.

He kept moving through the Head. The day passed, marred only by the distant sounds of the Star Followers sampling the mountains.

Finally, Enickor decided to check on them. It was possible they had guests from the Harcel. Possible, he knew, but not probable. Better for Elisif if she were lost in the forest maze.

Sleep came easily.

The following morning he ate while traveling toward the blasting sounds.

The Star Followers had moved also. When the demolition resumed, it was farther inland.

Enickor smiled. Something was finally going his way.

What he calculated as half the morning passed before he was close enough to guard against detection. He removed his pack and hid it in a group of boulders with a tree growing out of the center. A sheet of moss scraped from the rock made a perfect camouflage. It was so good that he decided to mark the surrounding trees to be sure of finding it later.

Movement through the Head became easier as he approached the periphery. A choice of more than one path opened up as the trees stood farther apart.

He felt watched.

He did not turn. The pace he had chosen remained fixed.

There was something else amiss.

Silence.

There was a total silence; no cries, no insects, no blasting.

It required great effort to blend the rustle of his progress with that of the quiet forest.

Daylight played intermittently through the stout tree trunks. Fine rays poked beam-fingers into the darkness. Patches of mist floated and danced in the light.

He stopped and listened.

Faintly, from a distance, he heard people. They were not laughing or talking, merely walking on the land. Enickor squatted and braced his left hand against a tree. He cleared away the composting debris and placed his right hand, palm down, on the bare ground.

The vibrations, faint even to a Chiy-uneite, running over the land and into the ipcar, were the kind made by people. They touched lightly upon the land, almost reverently. He wondered if they were loagers, or land-skilled Star Followers located a great distance away.

The watched sensation returned in force.

He stood, looked around, saw nothing, and started forward. The day brightened. Magaikan's warnings marched over his memory with an awesome clarity.

He angled right to parallel the tree line in order to maintain the camouflage the Head provided. Regular pauses to check the ground and the wind for sound slowed his progress. When the tread of feet on the land became steady, Enickor departed the land and climbed the first tree with a branch low enough for him to leap to for a hold.

The lower branches were easy. The middle became difficult. As he neared the top, the bending and swaying under his weight caused him to gauge his motions very carefully. It would not do for a spotter to alert the Star Followers.

He waited.

The blasting did not resume.

By noon he caught a glimpse of the first Star Followers. They were crouched in the rocks above the cliff face.

It surprised him. He had not thought to look for them there. Below, there were more Followers. These, too, were en-

129

sconced in rock and boulder cover. They seemed to be watching each other.

He caressed the smooth ipcar trunk with the tips of his fingers.

There were still people on the land, close, perhaps almost directly below him.

He began to descend. It was even slower than the climb. The need for care had become critical.

Heart beating rapidly, he moved through the middle branches. Had he dared, he would have called out to those below. But he was not certain enough that they were the missing Harcel Loagers.

He was in the lower branches, and able to catch glimpses of the floor, when a ruckus broke out.

Screams, light flashes, smoke and shouts fractured the silence of the Head.

Enickor changed direction and tried moving through the branches. It was difficult.

Near the edge he dropped from the tree. A thin line of trunks was the only protection left.

A soldier in Jeffires battle garb was wrestling Elisif to the ground.

Enickor lifted his *kalase*, took aim and fired.

The man collapsed. A gaping hole smoldered across his back from shoulder blade to shoulder blade. For a split second, time stopped.

In his mind, the man Enickor had killed collapsed again and again. He did not think it possible he could do such a thing, but it had happened so quickly, so decisively, and so easily.

Zaich came running around a boulder, heading for the forest. His pack bobbed up and down. A hail of shouts and a burst from a *kalase* followed him. He ducked into the shelter the dead man had been using.

Enickor called to him in the secret language of the Harcel.

Startled, Zaich stood up. He grinned. Without warning, a hole appeared in the upper left arm of his all weather suit. He buckled to his knees.

"Get Elisif! Get her!" Enickor ran up the forest line to the direction from which Zaich had come.

Stunned but cognizant, Zaich nodded and helped Elisif roll the corpse off of her. Her sobs were woven through the melee.

When at last he shed the cover of the forest, it was with a burst of speed. His goal was a trio of yellow all-weather gear

130

lying in a huddle inside the beginnings of a granite column fall. The broken rectangles were piled like twigs in the lee of a enormous ipcar after a storm.

Eyes focused upon his destination, Enickor ran, weaving left and right. There was no time to look up, no time to check for the enemy.

When he reached the pile of yellow all-weather gear he was panting. "Landah," he said, glad the boy was alive. He grabbed the boy's shoulder.

Terror-filled eyes gazed back at him. The boy's mouth opened, worked grotesquely, but no sounds were uttered. A flicker of recognition crossed his face, then fled.

"Landah? Come!" Enickor pulled him off his parents. Landah shook his head and reached for Omagar.

Enickor turned Udia onto her back. Her pale blue eyes were lifeless, her face contorted with surprise and the disappointment of death. An ugly pattern of holes seeped red down the front of her suit.

The boy gripped Enickor's arm.

He looked up.

Two soldiers were approaching through the rocks. Both had weapons drawn. They did not seem to be aware of Enickor and the boy. The path to the forest had been strategically severed.

Landah turned back to his father. Gently, he pulled the hood back. He folded it neatly into a triangle, smoothed it with both hands, then stroked his father's hair. It began to mat at the nape of the neck where a beam had fused the spinal column before it lost all of its energy against a rock. Omagar's blond hair steadily gathered the crimson stain. Landah's stroking hid the once-golden sheen under layers of drying blood.

They had come in much the same manner as before. But now Illeuro asa Khatioup knew what to do. Experience had taught him. It was something he knew, and marveled that he knew without Gaediv's assimilation and interpretation.

The nekka surrounded him, lest he be separated from them. They insisted that he tasted of wisdom. He was close to being Gaediv. For them, he functioned as one.

The caretakers had a violent way of settling their disputes. They took life and threw it away. The Quniero could not embrace this concept and therefore did not want to be touched by it.

The nekka retreated to the bottom of their tunnels and mined gems. They filled the pouches, moving the displaced rock into the caretaker's machines. It disappeared and reappeared on the surface. Their productivity had increased steadily since Illeuro's reunion. Now they worked faster, harder, having tasted isolation from their leader and not wanting it to happen again.

They sent up filled pouches, thinking simply that if they produced enough all the caretakers would be appeased, and peace would return to their tunnels. When death tinged the air they worked even harder, Illeuro hoping they had not failed in labors.

Enickor kept his *kalase* down and waited for one of the two to be exposed enough to get a bead on him.

The openness of their position gave him a naked feeling. Waiting ground his nerves. Subconsciously, he backed up, pressing harder and harder against the granite.

The wait continued. Surrounded by the deposed columns, he felt safe, yet knew he was not.

The conflict ceased. No one left their cover. There were calls and counter-calls, each a set of signals and battle language. For the most part Enickor understood the House of Jeffires. Parts had been changed.

Landah was still petting Omagar's hair. It was now completely crimson. Blood dripped off the ends. Landah's hand was stained up to his wrist and well across the back.

The sight further sickened Enickor.

He looked back into the forest. For a moment he thought he saw Zaich carrying Elisif into the depths. He blinked. The image was gone.

"Landah," he whispered.

The lad did not answer.

"Landah, you must be ready to run. We are going to run to the trees." He glanced at the boy, then at the long, naked stretch between the boulders and safety. It had not seemed that long when he ran this way. Now it looked like a kilometer.

"Landah?" He checked the rock the two Jeffires soldiers used as a shield. "Are you ready?"

The boy continued stroking his father's head.

"Where did those Hadilka troops come from? I think we're in real trouble this time. Those are mercenaries in with the regular guard and the Hadilka engineers," came a tenor voice from the shield rock.

Enickor pressed harder against the granite, wishing he were one with it and invisible to the rest of the world.

"I don't know. We should have picked them up kilometers from here," responded a deeper voice. "Who were those people who ran out of the forest? Natives?"

"I don't know. We can check on that if it stays quiet. A couple of them fell over there in the rocks."

"Our fire or theirs?" asked the tenor quietly.

"Does it matter, if they're dead?"

"I guess not." They shifted in the rocks.

"We should never have taken their miner-beasts back in the hills, Vaich. Those lizard things are bad luck. Look at the trouble we've had since then."

"There is no such thing as luck. Besides, look at the diamonds they've found and mined. That new one? The leader they were crooning for? Did you see the size of the emerald hunk he carried up in his jaws?" His laugh was low, like his voice. "I thought Commander Pentik was going to choke."

For a moment it was quiet.

Abruptly both men came from behind the rock.

Enickor expected to be annihilated instantly. Instead, they exchanged looks of bewilderment and continued pressing toward Landah.

"He's not Overeechy. He's a boy. What do we do with him?" asked the tenor.

"I don't know. Maybe the kindest thing to do is shoot him. It looks like those were his parents...He'll die wandering around the mountains, or get killed walking out, the way they did to start with."

"Yeah," responded the lower-voiced man. "They look human. Are they sure they don't have real intelligence?"

When the tenor was half a dozen meters from Landah he stopped and raised his long *kalase*.

Enickor also changed the direction of his slightly. He loosed two quick flashes.

Both were dead before they could scream.

Landah skipped a beat in the regular stroking of crimson hair, looked empty-eyed at the bodies, and returned to his father.

Enickor could not explain why they had not opened fire on him, or why they appeared not to have seen him. He listened for the consequences of the double killings.

There seemed to be none.

He gazed into the forest.

His heart pounded wildly in his throat. Three enormous green eyes looked back at him. Yellow slits in the center widened, then contracted.

He blinked, looked away, then back to confirm the vision. It was gone.

He pressed against the granite. The solidity of it seemed to envelop him with safety. He closed his eyes, trying to make a decision. If they stayed here they would be discovered. He could not kill all the soldiers from the House of Jeffires. Even if he could, there would still be the complement from the House of Hadilka overhead to consider.

The yellow-slitted green eyes stared into the tableau of his mind.

How could he take Landah back into the forest? There was little doubt the beast was the same one that tore the gorbich limb from limb. And a man could never fight as well as a gorbich.

He debated, waiting, knowing that remaining in the granite fall became more dangerous each moment. Afternoon passed. At dusk, he decided they had to move, before the evening rally call was sounded by the House of Jeffires.

Part of the time he wondered if he was losing his mind to consider entering the Head once again. Before he could figure it out, voices rang out in the night. Both sides wanted to negotiate.

Enickor put away his *kalase* and grabbed Landah. When the lad fought leaving his parents, Enickor physically picked him up and threw him over his shoulder. On the cliff top a bonfire ignited.

The cloak of night shielded them. Enickor carried the lad deep into the forest. The wafting scent of ipcar leaves burning in the signal fire dulled the urgency of their flight.

Enickor fought the sensation by counting his steps, gauging the distance to the boulder group, and feeling the trees for a sign. The darkness was still oppressive. The clear memory of the eyes Enickor had seen went a long way toward stifling the effects of the burning ipcar.

Moderate surges of adrenalin kept him alert, ready to run with Landah on his back. There had not been any signs of the beast, no broken trees, no spoor.

He searched the same area of the forest for half the night. Landah was quiet, possibly asleep. Enickor continued feeling trees until his hands were sore. His muscles ached from carrying the boy. His mind felt tired, too tired to think about anything but the marked trees.

As the night ebbed, the search became mechanical, its purpose almost forgotten. When he did find the markers, he almost passed them.

He rested on his feet at the boulder group, slipped Landah from his shoulders, and set him in the center, against the tree. Enickor maneuvered his pack to the side, lay down, and slept.

The stone fort with its ipcar ceiling felt safe from the outside world. His sleep was untroubled by the creature in the forest and the monsters representing the Star Follower royalty.

When he woke he felt rested.

He turned the light on to its dimmest setting. Landah was sitting up, his features barely recognizable. He was stroking a round, moss-covered rock about the size of his father's head.

Enickor cracked several ipcar pods which had not been on the ground too long. The husks were damp and moldy. The insides were dry, the nuts crisp and tasty. He stuck several into Landah's mouth, one at a time.

Abruptly he snapped off the light, shouldered his pack, and pulled Landah to his feet. He continued holding the lad's hand until Landah paused, then turned away to take care of his needs.

Enickor was slightly relieved. As a second thought, he untied a small coil of rope from his pack and secured it around Landah's waist.

The lad was reluctant to go.

"What is it, Landah? What do you want?" The gentleness in Enickor's voice surprised even him.

He had to turn on the light to its dim setting again to see the thin gloved finger point back at the boulders.

"No. We must move on now. We have to find Elisif and Zaich."

Landah untied the rope and returned to the boulders.

Before Enickor could decide what to do about the lad, he came out with the moss-streaming rock.

Enickor refastened the rope and led them through the forest, well away from the battleground of the Star Followers.

Twice, he looked back. Tears stung his eyes.

Landah followed. In the dim light Enickor held to show the way he had seen the boy's pathetic smile and the steadiness with which he held the head-sized rock and stroked the green/yellow moss.

135

Chapter 15

IF YOU FOLLOW THAT RIDGE AND STAY ON A westward heading you should reach the sea in four, maybe five days." Pam-ella gestured to the near ridge leading around the Gorbich Hills.

"Why would I want to do that?" Payndacen asked.

"Shirwall is there."

The tense silence lasted several minutes.

Theller's right head watched Faelinor. The left one grazed.

"I am not going to the sea or Shirwall, Pam-ella."

"You are not going with me." Her voice was even. "This is not an Overeechy holding, Friedo. It should not be a Jeffires or a Hadilka holding either. You have no say."

He shrugged and waited for her to start her journey.

Pam-ella considered stunning him, but could not inflict that kind of brutality on him.

He would complicate things for her. How could she take him into the Alizandar Loag? They barely extended hospitality to her. How could she justify bringing along an outsider, especially a Star Follower?

The last several days had been pleasant, even made bright and enjoyable by his wit. She had laughed for the first time in a long, long time, so long that she could not remember the sensations in her lungs and stomach.

"Friedo, don't you think you had better visit Shirwall? You have been gone for some time now. Perhaps the Overeechy is concerned for your safety." She smiled to herself. "I certainly would not want to be blamed for your disappearance, or branded as a kidnapper. I understand the rewards for such things are rather, uh, drastic."

"Death is always drastic." He did not smile back. Instead, he studied the west. "I'm certain that they are concerned for my welfare, Pam-ella. I do not care. What I'm doing here is for me. Not the Overeechy. They will get the majority of my life, anyway. Now, while I'm the Uv-Kriell, I still can enjoy a little freedom before the yoke of responsibility passes to my shoulders. And this is something I must do, or regret for the time when they own my soul and I am committed to my father's plan.

"If we are successful, he and I, the Overeechy will never be the same. We will have changed it."

He gazed longingly at her. It bothered him that he had grown to care so much about her. Conversely, it pleased him when the diligent training she had undergone for presentation at the Overeechy came out from behind the hard exterior Chiy-une had molded upon her with time. The sharp contrasts in her personality were endearing. Gradually he was beginning to understand the complexities governing her. Leaving for Shirwall would take her away. She would not wait. Nor would he ask.

"Good-bye, Friedo." Her small gloved hand touched his shoulder.

"Pam-ella . . ."

She did not look at him. A nudge set Theller on an inland course. The Lyndirlyan Mountains rose straight up and scraped dirty clouds from the sky.

The wish to continue alone had been made very clear. Friedo watched her go. *How had she survived better than three years out here?* he marveled. *She must have a will forged out of Chiy-une iron.*

The sounds of ships high above the oppressive clouds blotted out the drone of insects and the echoes of hooting gorbich. The noise indicated that they were eastward bound.

Pam-ella peered up at the cloud cover. There was nothing to be seen, only sound. The self-confidence so painfully acquired during her stay on the land had been badly deteriorated by the incident with the soldiers. Attacked by her own House. It was still hard to accept.

Now she was alone again, just as she had been season after season. It was different this time. Fright seemed to hover over her.

She had not realized how nice it had been to travel with a companion. Sharing the workloads left more of the day usable. She did not get as tired. Her leg had grown stronger, though it was not completely restored. The scar would be there long after the limp diminished.

She smiled.

Friedo was not as bad as she had made him out to be. *In fact*, she decided, *I like him. As much as I can like a Star Follower.*

The smile broadened. She looked up, surprised by the moisture on her cheek.

It was not raining.

She touched the corner of her eye. She was crying.

Illeuro led his nekka through the tunnels. They fawned over him, each wanting consolation, each remembering their collective experiences the last time the two caretaker houses gathered in one camp.

He consoled them as best he could. The sour taste in the air thwarted his efforts. They sensed a strangeness about him that put him apart from the leah. He thought without considering the Gaediv.

The nekka's collective need for leadership lessened the importance of his separateness-thinking.

They emerged dragging double pouches steadied by their head tendrils. The fire had burned out, but not before the ethereal aroma affected the caretakers. Their disagreement had been settled without further bloodshed.

The pouches had been emptied and sorted into four piles. The two leaders each took one of the smaller piles, wrapped it in soft fabric, and hid it in their colorful skins over skin.

Illeuro waited to be acknowledged. The nekka lined up behind him.

One of the caretakers motioned to him. He responded.

Each Quinero followed and deposited his pouch against a growing pile.

When they returned to the main tunnel they found it blocked by caretakers with what Illeuro knew were weapons. He halted.

They do not mean us well, he communicated to his nekka. *The Gaediv bid us to obey the caretakers. We must do this. But we must also preserve nekka.* He felt their agreement.

The House of Hadilka engineers began sorting Quniero.

Illeuro soothed them, promising they would not be a broken nekka again.

When the sorting was finished and the count even the engineers clapped a chain collar on the one they had designated as their lead Quniero.

The entire nekka panicked.

They began tunneling.

Illeuro waited, making sure they were safely hidden by the rock. The response of his caretakers was puzzling. As soon as the guards moved from the tunnel he entered. No one tried to stop him.

Deep inside the mountain he collected his nekka. They gathered around him while he mutated the caretaker collar into crystalline powder.

Before he led the nekka even deeper into the mountain he returned the chain, which had been an attachment of the collar, to the surface. It tasted of following.

Gaediv would not want the nekka broken. Nor would she want us to be dispossessed of mind for the caretakers. Therefore our service must continue. However, we shall have little contact with them. Their fears of this land and one another emit hostility. Our work will be done without them, our bond fulfilled. When it becomes possible to send a messenger safely, we shall seek the leah and instructions. The nekka caught his thought of katelings and concurred heartily.

The wind whipped the trees into a frenzy. The songs played by the branches lacked direction. It was a cacophony of broken notes. The intensity became painful to his ears.

Landah cherished his moss rock and trotted to the pull of the rope around his waist.

Enickor used the light at full force to pick their way through the close-standing trees. The uphill climb grew steeper. Debris made the passage slippery.

Landah fell often, but always protected the moss head.

At last they came to a rock thrust padded by moss and large

enough to give a level cast to an area of ground on which to set the tent.

Thunder and lightning raged above the trees. Some flashes were so bright that fragments of their light penetrated the dense weave of branches. The air thickened. Mist settled on the trees, sifted through, and began streaming onto the ground.

"Stay right there!" Enickor yelled at Landah and held him against a boulder with both hands.

The lad clutched the mossy rock and smiled, oblivious to the perils of the storm.

Enickor bent into the wind. While the boulder grouping promised safety, it also opened up the trees and exposed them to the wind. The velocity was far more severe than any natural storm he had endured. If it were not for the greatly diminished protection afforded by the ipcar, the wind would kill them in less than a hundred heartbeats.

The freezing mists swirled around the granite thrusts like a powerful river surging down the mountain in spring. For each step he took toward the center of the boulders the wind put up a hand and tried to send him back two.

A bolt of lightning struck an ipcar ten meters ahead. A cracking noise, and the tree exploded. Splinters became arrows shot by a thousand archers. Simultaneously, steam hissed above the storm. A great portion of the tree leaned upon its neighbors. They tossed it back and forth, none of them wanting to carry the dead burden.

More determined to locate a good shelter, Enickor redoubled his efforts. The smooth thrusts became closer and closer, winding a spiral inward. He pursued them until they were almost too close for him to wiggle between. In a flash of lightning, he saw an opening ahead. He knew that on the other side would be a flat space large enough for the tent.

He did not wait to explore further.

The wind propelled him back to Landah. Ipcar and low boulders were his stopping points. They kept him from being hurled down the slope and into a treeless ravine which would fill with water once the rains began.

Landah watched, offering no assistance, only interest at the way the wind tormented Enickor.

Their return was even slower. The rains started. The ground became slick. The compost was matted by the rain and polished by the wind.

Three-quarters of the way up the final slope Landah balked

and refused to move. Enickor returned to him. He cajoled, promised and finally threatened at the top of his lungs.

The young face remained blank and open-eyed to the rain.

Swearing, Enickor closed Landah's all-weather gear. For several minutes they stood braced against the wind. Then Enickor moved faster than the lad could register.

Grief filled his blue eyes. A soul wrenching scream came out from the closed suit.

Enickor held the moss covered rock tightly, turned uphill and resumed the climb.

Wailing, Landah followed, arms outstretched, fingers opening and closing. His obsession to retrieve the rock gave him a phenomenal strength against the wind.

Breathing hard, glad the end was in sight, Enickor pushed the last few meters, ducked into the shelter of the thrusts and rested. He set the rock between his feet and pulled on the rope.

Landah rounded the boulder, spied the rock in a flash of lightning and dove for it.

Enickor stood unmoving until he caught his breath. The pack seemed heavier, the air thicker and the temperature colder. The wind shrieked around them in all directions except down.

"Come on, Landah." He gathered the rope into a coil and put his hand on the lad's shoulders.

The roar of the storm swallowed his words, but Landah nodded agreement. He would have agreed to anything as long as he had the moss hair to stroke. He was content, his attention divided between following the stone passages and making sure his treasure had not been damaged.

Enickor selected the best way into the center.

Lightning struck just outside the thrust perimeter. There was a fire flash. The rain extinguished it immediately. A tree burst into several parts from the strike and crumbled onto the thrusts.

Enickor ducked as soon as he heard the distinctive pop and crash of the branches. He pulled the lad down with him. The tree bounced nearby, carrying with it the charred scent of ipcar leaves. Branches flopped wildly in the air above their heads. The wind dissipated the ozone.

They waited for the tree to find a steady roost. It rolled to the left and right, bounced over the tops of the rounded thrusts, and finally settled. The wind stripped the smaller branches and leaves exposed above the stone.

The light guided them deeper into the granite maze. Around the last turn the thrusts looked as though they stood farther apart. The dip of the wind into an open space slammed off the granite and wore the moss to a thin layer.

Relieved and ready to set up the tent and sleep away the storm, Enickor charged into the clearing.

He shone the light across the open space, wavered, then stopped when it snagged upon a soldier from the House of Hadilka holding a *kalase* steadily pointed at them.

Friedo Payndacen found a strange reluctance growing inside him. He traveled through the night, letting Faelinor select the best course to the sea.

The winsong found the terrain comparatively easy. The gentle, rolling slopes seaward of the Gorbich Hills would have been considered level ground on his native planet.

The kinship between Payndacen and the winsong was not unlike that of Pam-ella and her roh. It was a friendship dependent upon an emotional plane no outsider understood.

Payndacen knew that his close ties with Faelinor had made him the brunt of many whispered jokes. The fact that he had not selected a wife, nor allowed one to be selected for him, fueled the insinuations. These were made by the jealous who coveted his place in the Overeechy.

By afternoon of the fourth day they could smell the sea. The salty air moved sluggishly over the ground. Late afternoon of the same day the ocean was in sight. A thin line distinguished the gray sea from the clouds.

He did not go to Shirwall.

The base quarters he had established were located well beyond the House of Jeffires's scan lines, and safe from overhead visual detection.

He hummed an old song his mother used to sing. Faelinor chimed in, harmonizing.

Vaguely interested, he watched the sun set. Dust made such beautiful reds.

The song brought back memories of his childhood. There were so few times when his mother was well. Of late he wondered if it was because she had no heart to be the Kriell's wife. It was a difficult role.

Long ago he gave up counting the myriad physicians, psychics, healers, and even medicine men who visited her chambers to effect an often-promised cure. The ailments remained. Even her pregnancy with him had happened in a laboratory.

The lack of love involved bothered him, though he knew it should not. The Payndacen lineage needed perpetuation.

Consequently, he had no siblings. His had been a lonely childhood, filled with adults, lessons, preparation, more lessons, combat training, even more lessons, and machines whose technology he knew from the lessons. It was not his idea of a happy time.

Ruling the Overeechy made his father inaccessible much of the time. During adolescence the Kriell became a stranger Friedo no longer knew. What he wouldn't have given over those years for a brother or sister...

Even now, remembering the loneliness hurt.

He had been fifteen standard years old the first time he took matters into his own hands and found a secret way to leave the palace grounds. By the seventh time he ventured beyond the Overeechy walls he was ready to investigate the city proper. It was a quick, almost instant, education that all the days crammed with lessons had failed to touch. Quickly, he learned how to play the opposite side of the Overeechy roles and the advantages of being what others expected him to be, all the while getting exactly what he wanted from them.

He continued sneaking out for better than two standards before Commander Ahandro Magaikan caught him.

Remembering, he grinned.

Magaikan had not revealed his identity. It would have been an unwise thing, considering his companions. Instead, Magaikan accused him of a series of crimes, grabbed him by the shoulders, and kicked him at the complement of guards surrounding them. The act served only to heighten the esteem of the surly crowd whose membership he enjoyed. Later that same year, Magaikan took him to Akiols, where he found Faelinor. The oppressive monster of loneliness devouring his soul began to die when Faelinor entered his life.

From the street life he had learned to fight without ethics, bargain without faith and speak the dialects of the uneducated. Yet the finery of the Overeechy had taught him the identical things in a different light. The insipid manners of degeneracy were also useful. Sometimes it was easier to get what he wanted by playing the role in which the person he bartered with saw him.

Someday he would have to play the game with Hoyiv Jeffires. He looked forward to it. Jeffires had gutter principles packaged in royalty.

143

The grin faded as the lights of his camp brightened. Faelinor yodeled their approach.

Magaikan. He was here, too. Somewhere.

The last time they saw one another Magaikan was leaving for Chiy-une. He stood in the throne room beside the Kriell. A veteran, Magaikan showed the Kriell none of his misgivings over his assignment. But Friedo knew. He remembered the single tic in the Commander's right eyebrow, the quick tightening of his jaw behind the neatly trimmed beard.

The ensuing confrontation between the Kriell and the Uv-Kriell had been brief. It had also been a painful ordeal.

"Father? Am I to believe I have a brother? One my own age?" How happy the news had made him. The stern faces looking down from the throne could not dampen his ecstasy.

"Yes, my son. Unfortunately, Kal Pridain proved beyond any doubt that the boy is mine when he cleared Lord Jeffires's line for Hoyiv. His results were accessible to several of the Great Houses before I was able to put a clamp on them." The Kriell had turned away, mumbling about errors of the past, damning Lord Jeffires as being a paranoid old fool.

"How can it not be good?" He knew, but he did not want to admit it.

"He is older than you, Friedo. Granted, the time is small, but by birth, he is the Uv-Kriell, and you are second in line."

"He can step down," Friedo said quietly. "You do not know if he will want to leave his homeworld. You cannot be sure . . ."

"I am sure that he is a threat!" The Kriell's mouth drew into a tight line. His bellow echoed in the enormous room. "Did I raise an idiot as well as sire a bastard?" He turned on his heel. "Son, you will die of terminal stupidity unless you start thinking with your head and leave your damn emotions aside."

Softer, "I know you wanted a brother. I know you have not had an easy time." He looked Friedo directly in the eye. "I know you think you can and will do better with your children. I hope so. I hope so."

The Kriell shifted. "And I hope that what I have set in motion throughout the Overeechy will continue with you, Friedo. There are changes being made. Slow. Subtle. Widespread.

"I have fought many battles. Some I have lost. Most I won. It is not easy. Being Kriell makes me responsible for billions of lives, not just the Great Houses, or yours—or of my bastard on Chiy-une.

144

"Compassion and justice are great qualities in any leader. And a wise leader knows when he can afford them.

"The Corchi are pressing Hadilka's settlements in the Sellbic system. It is costing a great deal to hold them back, but it must be done. We need that quadrant!

"The Overeechy cannot afford to be pulled apart over a lineage dispute. Think of it, Friedo. The House of Corphlange, House of Aidfel, or even the House of Dorors scrambling for power, tearing down the careful political alliances I've spent my life building just to get the changes we need across the board.

"Should I live long enough to see my grandchildren, I would like to believe I have left a legacy of a better life, more fair and just." He looked away. "Yes. I am idealistic. It's one of my vices, but I am also realistic."

The Kriell turned to Magaikan. "You have your orders."

The commander bowed deeply, clicked his heels and mumbled the necessary proprieties. He did not glance at Friedo.

"May I know what the commander's orders are, Father?"

The Kriell aged before his son. "No, you may not."

Friedo had turned and left the throne room. He had not seen his father since. His plans were covert and well executed. Even his domestic duties were being attended.

"Friedo!" A loud voice filled with mirth called into the darkness a second time, breaking the reverie of distasteful memories.

Faelinor fluttered the dying notes to a song and stopped to unload his rider. The strain of the past four days showed on him.

"Banter? Is that you, my friend?"

"Aye, m'Lord. We have much news about the mining operations here." Light from the camp reflected from his slightly uneven teeth exposed by an over-generous grin. "It seems to have worsened." The grin faded a bit with the news.

Banter was a stocky man approaching middle age. He was fond of Faelinor and Payndacen in that order, and would have laid down his life for either one.

"The camp is still secure? No intruders?"

"No, m'Lord. It has been quiet here." He glanced at the young Uv-Kriell, then back to the trail they were wearing through the knee-high grass. "It has been busy at Shirwall. The Quniero miners m'Lords Hadilka and Jeffires brought in have

145

become a difficulty. They have been disputed, moved back and forth, and, I believe, stolen from one another."

"And Hadilka? Any reports on him yet?"

"The last word Akasu was able to sneak out said that Hadilka has launched his own search, one independent of the soldiers he has in temporary bases across the continent."

"When was that?"

"Ten days ago."

Friedo shook his head. The whole thing was nothing more than a game between two powerful Houses. He understood. It was hard to swallow when involved so keenly on this side of it. The plight of the Chiy-uneites had been made very clear by Pam-ella. While there was nothing he could do to alleviate their problem, he could understand and respect them for their courage. It would have been easy to despair.

"Everyone wants val Densu, and no one has seen him for better than three standard years."

"Oh, no, m'Lord. Hadilka is searching for Lady Jeffires. It seems the old lord had promised her to him in marriage in return for the Hadilka holdings on Chiy-une. Running supply and guard lines to protect his Quniero is costing him dearly. Though the profit is well worth it, only he knows what he reaps." Banter stroked the winsong. "Lord Hadilka is no longer young. He still requires an heir."

Friedo glanced at Faelinor. The winsong neighed. Banter was more correct than he knew. The House of Hadilka had the Corchi to deal with in the Sellbic system, and the Overeechy needed a victory there. Hadilka was an excellent strategist. The odds improved with him closer to his troops.

"What is he using for guards? Where is he searching?" he asked quietly.

"Mercenaries, m'Lord. He is searching in the Porintel Loag territory." Banter paused, head cocked, eyes narrowing. "Are you all right, m'Lord?"

"Yes." He knew Faelinor would be ready to travel hard in a day, two at the most. Time was what he needed most. So did Pam-ella, but she did not know it.

Chapter 16

UTTER DISBELIEF SETTLED WITH THE RAIN. THE light shone on the *kalase*. It was several dozen heartbeats before Enickor took a second look beyond the weapon at the man pointing it.

Minutes passed as they stared at one another. Some time during the first few seconds the soldier had turned his own light on the intruders.

He was a young man. The cold put a pinched look into his features. Blue traces ran through his cheeks. His mouth was purple, and it was evident he was suffering chills.

Violent shivers jerked the snout of the *kalase*, heightening Enickor's trepidation. Gradually he moved the light over the man's chest.

"No!" he called.

Enickor returned the light to the man's face. A flash of pain came and left.

"Who are you?" Enickor yelled over the storm. He felt Landah pressing against his back.

"Who are you, I might ask?" The voice was strong, determined.

"We are from the Harcel Loag, on our way to the Alizandar, on the other side of the Lyndirlyan."

"Loagers? In all-weather gear?"

Enickor took a step closer, pausing when the *kalase* jerked a separate command. "There are not many from the Harcel left. The Kriell's man gave us gear and food for our journey." He kept the hatred he felt out of his voice.

"Conscience payments..." The weapon wavered.

"Please. Put away the *kalase* and let me set up our tent. There is plenty of room. The three of us can be warm and dry in a very short time. Please."

He considered for a while, then finally nodded.

Enickor went to work immediately. Some of his weariness vanished. Quietly, he plotted what alternatives he had and which ones might be useful against the stranger. It did not matter that he was young, nor that he had not declared either his House or his allegiance.

There was a dangerous quality about the man. He was a survivor. Star Followers shied from the Hedshire Forest. The Head was worse. But this one had chosen to penetrate deeply, and had sense enough to seek the center of a boulder group for protection against the storm. Few Star Followers were that far-sighted. A myriad of devices that did everything, including predigesting food in some cases, were what they relied on for survival, not their brains.

Once the tent was set up and the pack secured inside, Enickor removed the rope from around Landah's waist and pointed to where two rocks came together. The lad understood.

A heat blower changed the internal temperature by at least forty degrees. A blast hit Enickor when he pulled the flap back to enter.

The all-weather suit peeled away. He folded his, then Landah's, and waited for the stranger. The flow of warm air dried everything quickly. It ruffled Landah's fine blond hair. Delight blossomed on the lad's face as the moss dried under his touch. He did not seem to notice that it was shredding onto the dome-tent floor.

The flap flew back. The cold night sucked hot air from the tent, replacing it with its own frigid blast. A concentration beset the man's thin face. Not until he was all the way inside, crouched over, and Enickor reached to secure the flap, did the long tear in his all-weather suit become visible. It had been burned away by a *kalase*. The rent began at the man's right hip in the front and ended in the middle of his ribs on the back.

"Are you injured?" Enickor asked, fastening the tent for the night.

"My suit damage is the worst. It's so cold here." He pulled around a small pack he had pushed into the tent ahead of him. The *kalase* remained close to his hand at all times.

Enickor indicated a place near the center for Landah. The lad spread his heat bag, crawled inside and adjusted his moss rock beside his head.

The stranger stopped undressing and looked from Landah to Enickor.

Enickor looked back, noting the House of Hadilka emblem on his Independent Worlds uniform. *Escalation? They're bringing in the mercenaries.* Bitterness welled up from his empty stomach. "What is the matter with him?"

"He could no long accept life with those he loved dying all around him."

The stranger met Enickor's cold gray eyes and looked away. "He's very young."

"Only his body is young. His mind suffers the plight of the very, very aged."

"There are treatments, procedures which might help."

"They are Star Follower things. Star Followers caused him to be this way." The hate came through when he spat out the words "Star Follower." Suddenly, he did not care. He hoped the stranger would go for his *kalase* so he could shoot him with his own concealed weapon or, even better, break his neck with his bare hands. A little revenge would taste sweet for dinner this cold, lonely night.

There was an awkward silence, during which Landah's breathing took on the rhythm of a deep sleep. The innocent look belonging to the young no longer returned to his face. Tiny lines that usually waited until ninety seasons to show their beginnings already ran to his temples from the corners of his eyes and formed commas on the sides of his mouth.

The soldier picked up the *kalase* by the tip and offered it to Enickor. It hung in the air between them.

"My name is Strom Aknel. I am a hired soldier who has no business here anymore."

Enickor made no move to take the weapon, nor did he speak.

"I'm tired, too. Take me with you as far as the forest edge.

I can make it from there." He smiled quickly. "Where? I don't know. All I want is to be away from here and the Houses of Hadilka and Jeffires."

Enickor turned away. "I would rather hate you."

Aknel threw his head back and laughed. It was a harsh sound that lacked authenticity. His reddish hair flopped and caught the blower current as it dried. "Because I am a soldier for hire?" He did not give Enickor a chance to answer. "Many people hate men like me. Usually it is because they fear us. But I do not think you are afraid of me. You just hate soldiers?" He stopped laughing and became serious. A hint of terror hung in his expression and words. "What they did . . ." He looked at Enickor for understanding. "I . . ."

The electricity in the air heightened as the lightning flashes intensified. The thrum of rain on the outside of the tent added to the charge. Enickor turned back to face Aknel. He, too, had the look of a man aged before his time. A glaze covered his eyes as though he were seeing something against the domed wall.

"Who are they? The House of Hadilka?" Enickor was curious, his tone soft, as he sought to take advantage of the man's inner demon trying to get out.

"Yes. They attacked a group of travelers carrying mining pouches. They were helpless . . ."

A new hollowness beset him. "The Porintel? Were they loagers? Tell me, man!"

Aknel grieved silently and fondled the *kalase* as though he planned on using it. "There were only a dozen of them, swinging east. They must have found the pouches where the Quniero left them. They were carrying their possessions in them. Not gemstones. And they were unarmed, except for those swords, like the one you have there. Harmless.

"They stopped them, took away the pouches and made them repack." He paused. The words came hard. "Like those people, I thought they were going to go on down the valley.

"But the Hadilka men were on edge. Their Quniero had taken to hiding inside their tunnels. They took out their frustrations on the travelers. They waited until the people were in the valley between them and the House of Jeffires soldiers, then opened up. They ran a target practice.

"Some of those men went crazy. Crazy.

"I went crazy.

"I retreated. I fired at my own . . ." He set the *kalase* down

150

with a finality. "Then I ran." Looking at Enickor, "I didn't want to die. I didn't want them to kill me."

Enickor reached over and took the *kalase*. Hate grew a bit stronger. Yet he felt compassion for the man sitting across from him. Had he realized that Aknel was a mercenary when he first faced him in the little clearing he would have been more afraid, and with good reason.

"Maybe I wasn't cut out for this kind of work." Aknel pulled the heat bag around him and continued staring at the tent wall.

"Was this your first time out?"

"No. I have fought in wars the likes of which you can hardly imagine. The killing did not bother me. It was different from this. They were trying to kill me. It's . . . it's different. This is my last time, though. Never again like this."

Enickor turned off the blower and the light, lay down and listened to the storm. The one inside seemed louder than the one outside. "Maybe you weren't cut out to be a mercenary," he whispered. *Neither was I cut out to do what I'm doing.*

More katelings hatched. The largest egg, speckled and green, was the last of the hatchlings to emerge. She was treated with even more gentleness than the others. Gaediv favored her.

The drones prepared to leave the first leah. Three papkoes of the Gaediv's choosing accompanied the drones and their infant leah leader.

There was little time to waste. The young Gaediv grew even as they finished preparations. She could not win a battle against the present leah leader and her instincts prohibited cohabitation.

The Gaediv punctured her own tongue and dripped blood into the youngling's mouth. The memories of ages were shared, along with her own intent.

Katelings clacked and chittered around the corbancoob, oblivious to the change in the ancient Quniero way of life taking place.

Drones watched, certain that, as always, the Gaediv was right. She was leader. She gave birth. She was history, and therefore always wise.

In darkness the drones, young Gaediv and papkoes struck out across the land and headed south. They would pay no allegiance or obedience to caretakers, nor would they mine. The Gaediv had designated them future-carers. That they would be.

* * *

The storm lasted another two days. The first morning was awkward. Aknel was openly embarrassed by the deep emotion he had shown the previous night. But when Enickor pressed him, he detailed the incident, admitting that he had killed three of his own troop and wounded several more before they returned fire and he ran into the forest.

The second day they spoke of Orinthia, Aknel's homeworld. He glossed over the particulars of his deceased family. There seemed to be a relief as he spoke, an unburdening long overdue. He talked for the entire day, purging the demon within him.

"I wanted to see other places, visit new worlds. I wanted some excitement. I thought I was cut out for that kind of work. Besides, if I survived to retire, I planned to settle down and work an agri-spot." Aknel continued mending his suit, glanced up, then at Landah. "Somehow, I never considered that I would be asked to kill anyone who wasn't . . ."

His gaze shifted to Enickor. "I am very good with a *kalase*, death with a long-snouted one. I have an eye for it. There are several dozen weapons I'm equally good with. That means I can break them down, maintain, side circuit, and use them to kill in half a dozen different ways.

"Death was a reality. It was a risk that went with the territory." He inhaled deeply. "I did not know it would bother me to kill people who were not . . . who were already victims."

Aknel's manner betrayed the awe he felt when returned to the careful task of mending his suit. "It seems I picked an inconvenient time to find that out, didn't I? I have no idea how to get off this planet."

"Learning about yourself is seldom convenient." He believed him. He was unsure why, but he approved of the unlikely redhead. Enickor studied him, trying to find what made him trustworthy.

Aknel approximated his own age. Perhaps older. A fine splatter of freckles washed his nose and cheeks, negating the soft beard trying to grow. For an off-worlder he was small. A quiet power ran through his body. Strength showed in his arms and chest when he spoke adamantly on any subject. The blue of his eyes were startling. Those eyes seldom rested. They sought out the specter of death in every shadow.

The third morning broke with no rain and a soft, warming breeze. The decision to take Strom Aknel with them evolved subconsciously. It was just there, like the morning and with just as much certainty.

152

Once suited, they broke camp. Aknel offered to share the burden Enickor shouldered. He received the decline with a shrug. There was no mention of the spare *kalase*.

"What direction?"

"East."

"Good." Aknel gathered Landah's rope and gave the lad's gear a final check, pausing only to adjust an uneven strap holding his small pack onto his shoulders. "Good," he repeated, then started off after Enickor.

The nekka continued to mine. Once they exhausted the mining pouches their leader had gathered from the outskirts of the camps, they left the treasure in piles. The Gaediv had told them to mine gems for the caretakers. They would not shirk their duty.

Illeuro knew the hostility of the caretakers who followed the surface trail they left. Only once did he encounter a caretaker.

The man had spoken to Illeuro in the hisses and throaty rasps of the drone. "You do well to avoid the main camps, nekka leader. There is conflict there."

"Why do they not leave and join their leah at the place where the ships land?" he had asked.

"They do not have unity in leah. They have many, many leahs. Each is his own leah."

Illeuro did not comprehend such strangeness. Gaediv would give guidance if she knew.

"You do well to mine and leave the stones." The caretaker removed the pack he carried, opened it, and spread out the contents. "For you, nekka leader, and for your miners, I have brought a small payment. Taste."

Hesitantly, Illeuro complied. The taste was good. It was nutrition, and pure. "I will take." No more transmutation for nutrition while the supply lasted.

The caretaker wrapped it up and stuffed it into the gem pouch harness Illeuro had put on. He folded additional pouches and harnesses into the sides.

Illeuro sensed that this caretaker had touched upon Alidanko. He could still smell the air which had kissed the man's face and filled his insides. This one was different from those in the camps who neither spoke his language nor acknowledged the nekka unity.

"I would say one more word of caution, nekka leader. Count

153

the suns in the sky. Keep good watch. Let five more pass. Then, you are released of the Gaediv promise of help. You are free to return to the other nekkas. And you must tunnel deeply. The chaos which will touch the mountain will also touch its roots." Saying this, he had scurried into the shadows.

Illeuro tasted others in the wind, turned and disappeared into the tunnel maze the nekka had created to confuse the caretakers.

The next morning a lone miner watched the sun rise, and counted, one.

Theller picked his way through the narrow mountain passages. His light burden would have allowed him to move faster if the need arose. The ledge carved into the desolate cliffs narrowed hazardously in places.

On the left, the gray wall rose two hundred meters. It dropped more than five hundred to a river snaking the valley floor. Its banks bore scant evidence of vegetation. Sunlight glittered off the water. An occasional glare shot back at her.

Fear was her companion. She had ridden this ledge before and sworn that she would never do it again. That time she had had a guide, one who knew where it was treacherous before it became so, and the location of the strong places used for resting spots.

Theller sensed her misgivings and tried to compensate with a steady, quick pace over the wide places.

The sun was high. The end was visible from the out curve they were rounding. Thus far it had been a much better ride than she had feared. The gries cried and played air games overhead.

Soon caves began to appear on her left. She could see many of them across the valley on the right. Dismayed, she realized that she had forgotten about this part of the trip. How could she? She hated the caves. Just standing inside one of them gave her claustrophobia.

"Good Theller. Let's get out of here before midafternoon. I hate this place."

Theller snorted. Then sneezed. He stopped.

Afraid, her head moved like a swivel as she tried to see all directions at once.

Theller sneezed a double.

She urged him on for the next forty meters, to a cavern maw large enough to accommodate them. Her alternatives were gone. She entered a cavern. Theller's warning system was the best they had going for them.

Theller experienced breathing difficulties. He tried to stifle his allergic reactions, and keep moving over the narrow ledge.

Pam-ella jumped off the roh as soon as they were hidden in the shadows. She stroked his necks and let him bury his noses in her clothing.

At the sound of falling rocks and voices they retreated deeper into the cavern. It wound and changed elevations. Parts were so steep they had to sidestep. Theller moved slower and slower, gradually putting himself into a trance.

"No, no, not yet, Theller. A little more. A little deeper."

The voices seemed to follow them. The grating sounds of combat boots crushing the fine gravel coating the floor sounded loud.

She prayed to the Chiy-une gods for the Star Followers' continued merriment. Their sounds covered Theller's hoof clatter. Perspiration broke out in a rash over her body. The sudden heat made her head swim. Desperate, she pulled Theller into a narrow offshoot.

At first he balked, then turned and backed in. The jet black of his coat made him invisible in the shadow.

"Okay, Theller," she whispered, then felt his snouts against her long jacket. A deep inhalation, then the long, slow exhalation that told her he was well within his trance.

Involuntarily she pressed further into the shadows.

"The way I see it, we abandon the search for val Densu," came a voice with a slight whine in it.

"I agree. Finding the Uv-Kriell would be worth our time. We must also make sure we have a way off this planet. Without the Quniero we won't be a welcome sight for either House." A sinister laugh preceded the slap of a thigh. "I don't think they will like us buying passage on one of their ships with their gems."

A third, smooth voice took over. "The Overeechy will pay well for the Uv-Kriell's safe return. But there are no guarantees here, my friends. Perhaps our best leverage is to keep him once we find him.

"When last I went to Shirwall I thought I detected a small camp north of there. If it is still there, we might start there. Also, I heard on the squawker there was a skirmish involving a few natives at the Head Forest. That was five days ago. The

155

description of one of the men fits both val Densu and Payn-dacen. He wore all-weather gear."

Their voices began to fade. Pam-ella ventured closer to the opening.

"A couple of them were killed. They were dressed like natives and carried Kriell gear. I doubt it was the Uv-Kriell. They would have known his face and print type."

"That's right."

Pam-ella waited, apprehensive, wondering what else was in the cavern besides three mercenary soldiers plotting against the powers that ruled. Her heart beat wildly. It seemed a good idea to find out where the soldiers were going, yet it also seemed foolish to leave the safety of the niche.

Indecisive, she retreated into the shadows.

Chapter 17

THE SUN SET EARLY IN THE HIGH CLIFFS OF THE Lyndirlyan. The last bits of light retreated from the cavern walls long before they abandoned the sky to the errant moon and brighter stars. Pam-ella waited in darkness.

Finally she roused Theller and led him out of the safe niche. Moments later the refreshing aroma of river mist rose to greet them. Clouds played with the stars. The moon cast a fickle light.

The claustrophobia she had been battling since she entered the cavern relented. Sadness found the inadequacy she felt and further depressed her. A constant reminder that she owed no one anything did not quite alleviate the growing guilt for the opportunity she had turned down. *Who knows how many lives are involved? No one. Besides, Friedo can take care of himself. All he has to do is get in his ship and leave.*

A new form of loneliness added to her depression.

I don't owe Friedo anything. He chose to help me only because he thought he could use me. I have no answers! He's a Star Follower...He means nothing to me.

Theller hugged the cliff face and moved slowly along the ledge. The wind was quiet in the mountains for late spring.

Cold permeated the air and settled into the rock. It sank, sending more river fog crawling up the steep valley walls.

The moon had disappeared from the sky before Theller reached the end of the ledge trail. Their progress slowed. Fortunately, the weather held. The night cleared of even the highest clouds.

I am responsible for myself, and only myself. I owe nothing to the Overeechy. Nothing to a system which would have forced me to marry Hadilka if I had not rebelled. Why should I be the sacrifice? Once I give him an heir my usefulness to him is ended. One marriage cannot change centuries of discord. Not this marriage. Mentally, she shivered. Although she had searched, she could not find a life form or a word low enough to express her opinion of his character.

What do you mean, owe something to humanity? The Overeechy isn't humanity.

You don't believe that, Pam-ella, came the smooth voice which always warred with the harsher side of her nature. *The man is in danger. He helped you. Saved you from the gorbich.*

For his reasons. Most of which he kept secret. He's looking for Enickor, too. Not once did he say why.

Must all motives to help another human being be pure? Must they lack any and all notion of reciprocation? Must they be dependent upon the sole desire to aid another simply out of love for their fellow man?

The harsher side did not answer.

She laughed out loud, startling Theller.

Man would be extinct by now if that were the case.

So man would be extinct. So what? He isn't. He's conniving, treacherous, callous, greedy. Shall I go on? Those are the men who are civilized, cultured in the ways of the Overeechy. Sensitive individuals systematically killing every living thing on planet after planet.

It was the gentler side's turn for silence.

Anger prodded her awareness. She had not known how strongly she felt, nor how threatened. For the first time she realized the significance of her alignment with the people of Chiy-une. By rejecting the Star Followers she had become sentenced to the same fate as the loags. She had escaped her obligations in the Overeechy. For a moment she wondered what had really induced her to leave Shirwall—Enickor or her obligation to marry Hadilka.

Tears blurred her vision. She tried to hold them back.

And the loags.

They did not want her. They wanted to be left alone. They wanted the life-style the Star Followers had robbed from them; the land, the sun, and warmth. They wanted their culture back undisturbed, unaffected.

Would it ever be warm here again?

Their gods were deaf to prayers, blind to suffering, and unsatisfied with their sacrifices.

The hoot of a nearby gorbich refocused her view of the world.

The sun was beginning to throw warning colors over the eastern peaks. Theller had left the ledge well behind and put another ridge between them and the caverns of the mercenaries.

Pam-ella looked over her shoulder as they reached the ridge top.

Was there activity down there? A light reflection? No. The sun wasn't high enough for that.

She squinted, bemoaned her inadequate eyesight, then swung around on Theller's back to rummage in one of the bundles.

The roh paused, quite used to his rider's abrupt changes.

She found her binoculars and keyed them to infra-red.

Soldiers moved over the cold, dark tones of the rock, which had yielded its heat to the night. The men were brightest around their heads. Their all-weather gear and the enormous packs they carried retained the last dregs of the cavern heat.

They were moving out. The sizes of their packs, the burdens suspended on poles between double sets of shoulders, attested to it. Forty-five in all.

She sagged for a moment, weak-kneed. To think she had been in there with that many . . . so close . . . It made her afraid all over again.

She changed the magnification and dimmed the infra-red.

They were well armed and marched in a fast, orderly manner along the ledge trail. The crisp morning carried the sounds of their feet on the rock. They moved like a supply line. After some thought, she concluded that was what they were, though she did not understand why they were on foot. Ships could have picked them up just about anywhere.

She winced, wondering why they were marching in cadence. It should be broken. The vibration could shatter the rock.

Closer, another sound caught the morning zephyr.

It was difficult to pinpoint. She looked without the binoculars, then with them. Not until a company of men on foot started onto the ledge trail could she see them.

The stress lines on her face tightened.

Theller had picked his way through two groups of Star Followers and stayed far enough away from them to suppress his normal reactions. All the while she had been oblivious to the danger.

She patted him. It was indeed a fine arrangement they shared.

She lifted the glasses again and watched for a time. Neither group seemed aware of the other. The conversation she had eavesdropped on was her only key to who or what House might dominate this area.

Jeffires.

She led Theller to a better vantage point, where the rocks stood on end, to offer greater protection from any eyes gazing back at her.

By noon the lead group approached the other end of the trail. Even with high resolution they were difficult to track among the rocks. The second group had nearly caught up. They stayed half a kilometer behind. It was just enough for the turns and quirks of the trail to hide them.

There would be a battle. No doubt. *The Hadilka mercenaries will win*, she thought sadly. *The others are outnumbered.* She stood and packed her glasses on top of the bundle, where they would be easy to reach from the saddle.

Ah, yes. A political situation. Neither House wants the other to know how many supply lines they're running. No wonder they don't use ships. Each would know the other's location. Head shaking, a dark scowl contorted her face. "Why, if there was conflict there could be no mining. No mining—no profit. Certainly, we do not have any problems at all here! Just ask the Overeechy!"

The Overeechy. Again, Friedo invaded her mind.

She swore in the secret language of the Porintel and mounted Theller.

"The Uv-Kriell left too many questions unanswered."

They headed north instead of east. There was another trail, one more dangerous than this one. It could take her through the Lyndirlyan escarpments and down into the Gorbich Hills in a matter of days.

She would warn the Uv-Kriell. All debts, regardless of how ridiculous they were, would be marked "paid." She would owe

160

him nothing. He would owe her answers, for the information she carried affected more than one life.

So much for pure motives and human kindness.

The sun rose five times.

The Quniero ceased mining.

The reduced caretaker troops grew angry. Illeuro watched them from a hole in the shadows. They did not understand why their numbers had been so drastically reduced. He tasted fear in the air and thought them insecure in the absence of a large leah.

The nekka had tunneled to the base of the basin forest. Illeuro was the last through the maze. He had checked each of the miners, and made sure the nutrients given by the special caretaker had been consumed.

He led them into the Head Forest, the land of the rangtur, a place without violence. They did not have far to travel before the land rangtur greeted them.

Illeuro did not know how they crossed the magnificent black land in less than a day when it had taken him and the beast two days last time. The special aliveness of this rock affected the nekka collectively and individually. While he did not communicate with the rangtur, he felt changed when they reached the opposite side.

He led the nekka over the last ridge and into the first valley.

They traveled through the night, sensing the undefined threat at their backs.

Toward the end of the second day they contacted another nekka.

That night they joined and continued westward.

The Head Forest was confined to a high basin. An opening of half a kilometer in the granite walls allowed the ipcar to spill down a mountain slope and spread over the Lyndirlyan Mountains. The area where growth was the most lush, the trees the tallest and strongest, and semiconfined by more ancient glacier-formed walls, was known as the Hedshire Forest.

The Hedshire poured out from the Head, through the remaining expanse of the Lyndirlyan, then into the Great Iyigna Valley. A mighty river that never lost its anger ran through the valley and out to the Plains of Akatna os Egra.

This was the eastern borderland of the Alizandar Loag, Enickor's destination.

A sense of relief washed over him when they crossed the narrow spill gap of the Head without incident. The basin valley had become alive with soldiers, geologists, machinery, and the shaking ground wrought by the blasting probers. Most were on the move. To where, even Strom Aknel could not guess.

He did not understand why they had reverted to the old-fashioned, outmoded form of blasting to tunnel for samples. At least it was slower than a high-powered laser. He thought they were searching for the Quniero and caches of rare gem-stones. Why else would they send men and machinery in at all?

Strom Aknel became their scout once he caught on to the tactics Enickor used to get through the forest, and learned how to recognize the paths. He was good, just as he had said he was. Better.

The agility of his runs through the dark forest and between the ipcar branches to spy on the Star Followers impressed Enickor. There were not many so gifted.

Landah's condition improved when the moss died and his stroking denuded the rock. He wept openly. Enickor chanted the ceremonial words imploring Ieuchna, god of the wind, to cherish the spirits of Omagar and Udia.

Strom had stayed in the background for the first part, then moved to stand beside Landah, and hummed the rhythm of the chant.

Later that evening they ventured to make their first campfire since leaving the Gorbich Hills. The damp fog made ignition difficult, but also provided an excellent visual camouflage for the smoke. For even if Star Followers did smell it, they would never find them in the heart of Hedshires realm.

Landah stared at the fire. He rocked back and forth, his arms wrapped around his legs.

Enickor finished eating and checked the tent. "We don't need the blower tonight."

Strom agreed, nodding, "It would be best to save the solars." He pushed the burning log farther into the fire, then watched Enickor sit down across from him. "It is time we talked."

"About what?"

"We have put a large section of mountains between here and the night of the rainstorm." He looked away and nodded. "Yes, that we have done." Glancing at Enickor, "I still don't know who you are." His hand rose in a gesture to keep silence.

162

"What I mean is, I don't care who you are, it would be nice to have a name to call you."

Enickor thought for a while. A silent meeting earlier in the day came back to him.

Enickor.

Mistress? Is that you? It had been a great relief to hear her. She was faint, weak. To think that he had begun doubting her existence and his own sanity now seemed absurd.

Her presence was more physical in the Hedshire than it had been on the island. It was almost as if she reached out of the ground and tried to embrace him. Startled by the sensation, he soon found it enjoyable. He no longer felt alone.

I do not seem to be accomplishing anything, Mistress.

You are alive. That is much, my valiant soldier. That is much.

Is there not anything you can do upon the land to thwart the Star Followers? Can you not make them ill, or inflict a plague on them? Is there nothing you can do to make them want to leave, Mistress?

I will try, Enickor.

He felt her smile, and reveled in the joy it gave him. Impressions, feelings, sensations flowed between them. The conversation had ended. The warmth of the northern latitudes once again hosted her presence. The southern summer had been cold. The places she could abide and manifest her life's drive were limited. Her struggle to maintain control of the massive body called a planet took all her energies. She was losing. She extended hope for Strom Aknel.

The mining in the southern hemisphere, where water and ice shielded her crust, had intensified. The rangtur no longer freely roamed the oceans. They, too, were growing weak, and had ceased bearing offspring. Their evolutionary chain had come to a standstill.

The urgency was there. But Chiy-une did not press her warrior. She soothed him and left him determined and reassured.

"You already know my name. It is spoken in every military installation on Chiy-une." He smiled quickly. "And some off Chiy-une."

"There is only one name spoken that widely." His eyes narrowed as a grin spread over his face. The fire light cast deep shadows in his beard. "Enickor val Densu? Are you him?"

163

"Yes. I am also Leader of the Harcel Loag and Chiy-une's Warrior."

They exchanged looks for several minutes.

Enickor rested his left hand on Landah's shoulder. "It is possible that he is all that remains of the loag."

Strom caught the wistful tone that belied his exterior stoicism. "Is it not also possible there are others?"

The fire danced between them. Enickor warmed his hands. "Yes. There may be a young woman and a man traveling toward the Alizandar. Or they may have died in the storm, or been taken by the soldiers."

"I would hope they died in the storm if there was a choice," Strom said quietly.

"I know." He put his head down, hating the image of Elisif's fate if the soldiers took her. Out loud, "He really is civilized."

"Who?"

"Magaikan."

"Commander Ahandro Magaikan of the Kriell's Guard?"

"Yes."

"Why do you say that?"

Enickor looked through the flames at Strom Aknel. "Because he can feel. And because he can look at a woman like Elisif, young, pretty, afraid, and feel compassion, not lust. He can look at a man and see justice where the universe has sentenced him with injustice.

"It is strange, these truths we realize about people after we can no longer see them."

"What do you see in me? Civilization or barbarism?" Strom was smiling, leaning forward with his elbows on his knees and his hands folded in front.

"A bit of both. Would it surprise you to know I trust you?" Strom did not answer.

"The reason I trust you is because I have been told you are worthy of such trust. I have been told you are sincere in your wish to help me."

"Who is this excellent judge of character who advises you?" Enickor grinned and leaned closer to the fire. "Chiy-une." The joviality lining Strom's features wavered. "The planet?" Enickor nodded.

"The planet speaks to you?"

"She does." It felt right to talk about Chiy-une with Aknel. He had become an ally. A much-needed ally. "I am her army."

"An army of one man?" It would have been a ludicrous

notion not long ago. It still was. His respect for the man across the fire practically forced him to believe. The small glimpses of Enickor's sense of humor did not fall in line with this. He rubbed his palms together and blew into them, all the while watching Enickor nod. He thought of the hundreds of religions strewn across the Overeechy. It was not that unfeasible. "I believe you."

"Why?"

"First, because you say it. I don't trust many men, but I do believe what you tell me. And it is not the strangest thing that I have ever heard. Why shouldn't the planet talk to you? I grew up believing in a religion where God talks to everybody and He is invisible. This planet has substance, and yet, who am I to say this is not the same God."

Enickor chuckled. "I know of that religion. I could not believe in it when I first went to live at Shirwall."

"And now?"

He shook his head. "I still do not believe it." Soon he realized he was laughing alone.

Strom knew abject terror for the first time in his adult life. The thing looming at the fringes of their campsite looked invulnerable. No off-worlder weapon could touch it. It did not seem to possess any substance. Fog rolled through the trees and hid the creature for a moment.

Strom forced himself to look away; self-doubt and disbelief filled his mind. His eyes were wide and returned to the spot well above Enickor's head.

Enickor turned.

The fog parted. Three eyes illuminated the heights. The same eyes that Enickor had seen at the battle. He had been found.

Chapter 18

THE BEAST HUNG IN THE FOG AS THOUGH SUS-
pended. It was impossible to tell his dimensions, or how he
might be entwined among the trees. The three eyes formed a
triangle, wide-set at the base and rising sharply to the apex.
Night allied the mist in hiding the rangtur's true color.

Unconsciously Enickor rose to his feet. He did not turn from
the specter.

"Careful." Aknel's whisper was cold, thoughtful.

Two of the eyes focused on Enickor. The third watched
Aknel.

Enickor lifted his right hand, signaling his friend to remain
still.

Strom complied, dividing his time between watching the
creature and Enickor and the nervous flickers of consciousness
stirring Landah. The lad was transfixed; enticed and deeply
affected by the presence.

The two eyes shone more brightly upon Enickor. The mass
holding them tilted slightly, favoring the big man.

The edges of his fear crumbled. Curiosity strengthened his
resolve until he showed nothing of the turmoil inside. There

was something benign, almost familiar, about the way the creature regarded him.

It drew Enickor. He did not consciously want to go, nor was he able to prevent one foot from moving in front of the other. It merely happened, and could not be stopped.

Just as steadily as Enickor approached, the creature retreated, luring Enickor into the cold night until the fog swallowed him.

Remotely, he registered an awareness of Landah's urgent cries and the worried call of his friend. He heard himself answer with reassurance, but did not know what words were spoken.

There was light. More light than at the camp. It came from all around them. The intensity was not such that it permitted a better view of the creature, but merely to see where they were going and what lay in the path.

A granite knife had been thrust through the ground eons ago. It split the forest bed. The flora never forgave it and had since worked to erode and cover it in soft greenery. This was the place the creature chose to halt.

Enickor took his gaze from the eyes looking back at him for the first time. He did not know this place, but felt that he should.

The air was warm, humid.

He looked around. The circle of light centered upon him. Its presence added to his discomfort.

The creature kept his third eye, the one on Enickor's extreme right, focused into the fog, as though still watching Strom and Landah.

Such a thing did not seem any more improbable than the presence of the rangtur himself.

Soon no sound penetrated the circle. Not even Enickor's heavy boots crushing the forest lichens and twigs reached his ears. There was no ringing in the absolute silence like that which existed everywhere else. Only by its absence was it conspicuous.

The world began to recede. It melted away from the island of soft illumination. There was nothing but the man and the eyes, to the exclusion of all else. Large, green orbs, slits of yellow in the center; no eyelid passed over them to moisturize or protect. No reflex action showed.

The yellow slits widened.

Enickor felt his body rise. A stab of fear returned his solidarity.

167

The slits grew even wider; the bows in the center of the two eyes focused on Enickor each framed small black ovals.

He wanted to run. The desire grew stronger. For an instant sound returned.

There was an agonizing scream. It echoed, even though the mist engulfing the forest tried to swallow the resonancy.

He knew the voice and the agony it carried.

It belonged to him.

The black ovals grew larger, spreading the yellow well into the green.

Something choked the outcry.

Again, there was only silence.

He looked away from the green, yellow, and black, but found his gaze pulled back to the creature. The nothingness around him was more frightening than the thing looming before him and growing.

The ground fell away at his feet. He remained. Suspended.

The space between him and the upper eye began to shrink. The lower left orb disappeared.

Resignation swept him. He hated it. It tasted like defeat.

The proportions of the creature underwent a slow change. The area around the eye lost solidity and expanded, taking the size and shape of the green with it.

Enickor tried to detach himself from what was happening. He wondered if insanity was like this. He began concentrating on little things and noticed the steady film of moisture running down the yellow. The green was not a constant shade. It changed to become much darker at the edge he could still see. And finally he looked at the black.

The oval matched his height. Its width corresponded to the breadth of his shoulders. From deep within the black oval another set of eyes gazed upon him. They belonged to a naked man, scarred and bloody.

A ubiquitous depression radiated from the very center of his soul.

He watched as the man approached, suddenly very much afraid.

The man climbed a mountain and checked the black sky overhead. A puddle formed wherever his foot touched. It took an atrocious amount of effort and time to finish the climb. When it was over a sword filled his hand. It was the Harcel Holy. He began to fight.

He was hurled back, then lunged, parrying, sparring, thrusting, occasionally holding the sword in both hands. The enemy was unseen, yet seemed to be everywhere. The blows he suffered were manifested by new wounds and fresh blood flows.

The foe struck three times for each blow hurled at it.

The flesh on the man's thighs and back fell in strips around his calves and buttocks. Yet the pain emanating from him was far more than physical. The crux of the agony was in his psyche.

The one-sided battle captivated Enickor. By gauging the moves, the parries and the balance, he could determine how the blows were being struck, and the angle. He could find no flaw in the warrior's tactics, other than the tragic fact that he was so thoroughly outmatched.

The fighting continued even when the man had been brought to his knees. Time and time again he found the strength to rise and resume his defense. The pinnacle on which he made his stand provided no room for retreat. Death belonged to the defeated.

While he could not see it, he knew the man was slipping in his own blood. His chest was crimson. Gaping wounds over his entire body bled freely. The left eye was gone, carved out by an invisible hand. The right one wept blood.

Outraged, Enickor tried to send encouragement. He felt each of the moves and winced in expected pain every time the man received another blow.

Ultimately, it was over. The warrior was beaten to the floor of the stone pinnacle.

He was missing an arm. His left foot was attached to his leg by a flap of skin above the inside of the ankle. Blood streamed from his toothless mouth. What had been his nose was sliced away, the remains splattered across his face. The gray eye weeping blood gazed at him.

It grew, filling the black oval, then spread to encompass the yellow and finally swallowed the green.

It happened so rapidly that Enickor could only watch. Terror struck his soul. He wanted to yell, to protest.

Suddenly he was on the ground. The gray receded into the moss-covered invading rock. With it went the creature. The dim glow surrounding him dissipated.

Shaking, Enickor sat upright, covered his face with his hands, and wept for the valiant warrior, and wept in fear. The naked man fighting the unseen enemy was a replica of him and a personification of Chiy-une. The creature who had shown what might be his fate left a certainty in his stead. The rangtur, ocean and land, could do little to aid his battle to preserve Chiy-une.

The activity at Shirwall increased. Payndacen and Banter spent the morning after his arrival in walking among the scrawny vegetation and dunes across the water from Shirwall. The venture was far from a leisurely stroll.

In spite of the increasing activity on behalf of the House of Jeffires, the lines were amazingly simple to cross, and their territory easy to penetrate.

They did not stay long. The false security the House of Jeffires soldiers had been lulled into was too advantageous to jeopardize.

That afternoon Friedo checked on Faelinor and returned to the small camp Banter had organized.

While the memories of his trip and subsequent involvement with Pam-ella were still fresh, he recounted them to Banter. The older man listened with more enthusiasm than the recorder, which also took in every word.

"She went on? Alone?" Banter asked, incredulous. "The Lyndirlyan Mountains are filled with soldiers, deserters—God knows what else."

Friedo smiled at him and poured another half a glass of wine. He held it up to the light, glad he had not gone totally spartan. "You forget—she has been traveling across this land since val Densu left Shirwall. Take my word for it, she has learned many things during that time."

Banter noted the fondness in the Uv-Kriell's voice when he spoke of Pam-ella. He had watched Friedo from the time of childhood, through the tortures of his adolescence and into manhood. This was the first time he had seen what might be akin to love for a woman. There had been many women. That was commonplace for royalty, inescapable for royalty the stature of the Uv-Kriell.

A frown darkened Banter's generous features. There was still an unspoken message. He begged permission to leave.

When he returned, the Uv-Kriell was sorting his packs and replenishing his supplies.

"M'Lord, you are leaving so soon again?" Worry intensified the volume of his question.

Payndacen stopped in the middle of stuffing a pack and

turned to face his man. "You knew that I was. What bothers you, Banter?"

Wordless, Banter shoved a paper at him.

He opened it slowly and read the scrawl. It was short and simple.

They had been missed and ordered back.

"How did they find us?"

"They did not. It was a general broadcast. Everyone with a ship-set on the whole planet received it." He reached out and grabbed Friedo's arm. "It is as good as a hunting license, Friedo. You are the game. You, val Densu, and Mistress Jeffires. I'm sure your father did not realize what he was doing when he authorized the broadcast."

"I will pretend I did not hear that. But you are probably right." Was the Kriell that out of touch with what was happening on Chiy-une? Did he know so little about the nature of the men who shared this mining claim?

He had hoped his position and title would help him if he were dragged into a confrontation with some of the battling troops. Certainly, he never counted on it being a shackle which might lead him to be sold or traded.

The short-sightedness of the Kriell kept returning to his mind. Did the Overeechy's ruler know the number of mercenaries fighting in the mountains and hills of Chiy-une? Did he even know they were there?

No, he could not know that the multitude of Quniero had deserted their caretakers, or that the supply lines had been run manually. News of stolen miners, the trading back and forth, and the need to use mercenary protection around the camps themselves had been kept from the Overeechy. Surely the Overeechy had not even known about the Quniero import.

By Banter's estimation of the gemstone wealth pulled out of the Lyndirlyan, the expense of mercenary guards and the secretive supply lines were incidental expenditures. Small wonder both Houses indulged in such tactics. A planet rich in minerals or high grade ores was a prize. One rich in gems and ores was a dream come true.

Each wanted his interests to come first. Even the Kriell had invested a stake in Chiy-une, in the form of Commander Magaikan's search for Enickor val Densu.

He started to laugh. It all seemed absurd.

*　*　*

Six nekkas had joined Illeuro's. Each nekka leader had tasted of him, then bowed to his leadership. The rangtur mark lay upon him. This he knew without knowing why he had been singled out. He was not Gaediv.

When they reached the sea Illeuro sent three messengers to the leah. Each tasted of the nekka leaders and of Illeuro. They, too, knew of the time in the forest, the special caretaker who spoke the drone language, and the freedom from caretaker service.

The messengers would precede them. Other caretakers sought them. Illeuro did not understand why this was so, only that he should guide his nekka away from them.

He thought of the corbancoob and the katelings. His spirits lifted. While he did not know how he knew there had been katelings, he did know it. Once this knowledge had been shared with the nekka, they revered him in almost the same light as Gaediv.

Gorbich hooted in the hills above the sea. Illeuro listened and heard their hunger. He would hold the nekka within the safety of the living rock when they rested. The rock knew him.

A herd of torna-pok traveled with Pam-ella and Theller all the next day. The following morning she walked, stretching out the cramps in her muscles from riding.

Theller showed no signs of fatigue by afternoon. The torna-pok disappeared as stealthfully as they had come.

This was Porintel Loag territory.

She gazed at the narrow mountain pass before her. It ran a straight east-west line. The Porintel called it the Birthplace of the Wind. In the valley lay the relics of countless Harcel pilgrimages. It was sacred ground.

She ate while they walked. The ledge trail was far more hazardous than the one which she had used to get to this side of the mountain wall. She would walk the entire way. First, all the packs Theller carried needed to be strapped into her saddle and piled upright. Nothing could hang over the side, not even the stirrups. There was not enough room on the ledge for excess.

Something glittered between the vertical walls.

It caught the sun again.

She brought out the binoculars. A harsh inhalation lifted both of Theller's heads.

"I don't believe it." The glasses lowered, only to be raised again.

Several dozen loagers were leading roh and carrying packs through the Birthplace of the Wind territory they avoided because of its sanctity to the Harcel.

Her mind began to run with the implications their presence brought. Surely they were desperate. That was fact.

Theller picked his way down to the plateau adjoining the side of the mountain wall at the end of the trail. They waited.

As the loagers neared, the strain of their journey began to show. The wind caught the smallest fragment of clothing and beat the wearer with it. The looks of determination had been hardened by pain. Their movements were mechanical, neither hurried nor slow.

Pam-ella waited at the farthest point from the ledge. The faces were familiar. But where were the children?

Where were the little ones? Where were the babies? They were missing. Why?

Heart thumping, her stomach hardened. Terror was an old acquaintance. She swung her leg over Theller's two necks and dropped to the ground. As she ran down their ranks and sought the Metaliary she suffered the empty stares and a gauntness no amount of harsh weather could impose upon the strong-willed Porintel.

Not a head wasted the energy to see where she was going.

"Ardinay? Ardinay!" she called when near the old man.

The Metaliary departed the line and walked slowly to where she stood. There were few seasons left behind the dull gray eyes awash with tears from the wind. The steel gray of his hair was solid now; no trace of his youthful brown remained. The scrolled staff denoting his position filled his arthritic left hand.

"The fraen-spu of the land has come to see the handiwork of those who spawn her?" The bitterness in his tone was unusual.

"I—I don't understand. What has happened? Where are the children?"

"The Porintel have no children left. They are dead—like the land, like the crops.

"We have paid a great price for knowing you, Pam-ella Jeffires."

Head shaking slowly, her gaze was held by the old Metaliary.

He nodded. "Yes, the children. We are all that is left."

Oh, God no! He isn't saying that . . . She grabbed his arm.

"Tell me! Ardinay? The Porintel were more than a thousand strong..."

"We were. There is what you see now." He pulled away and joined the end of the caravan. "Not responsible... In my heart I know you are not responsible for the deaths of the children, but I cannot help but blame you. You have brought us nothing but evil.

"You live on the land, but you are a Star Follower. Everywhere you have gone there has been sorrow, death, and grief. You look for a man who should never have taken his first breath.

"Now, fraen-spu, they look for you. They want you, the men in crimson. They leave no peace in their wake, only sorrow and emptiness."

Stunned, she watched them increase their distance from her.

Ardinay turned around. "I would run if I were you." He returned to the procession winding up the side of the mountain to the east.

Chapter 19

Aknel and Landah found Enickor late the following afternoon. Dazed, he spent the rest of the day mumbling about the end of the world.

For Landah, the sight of the land rangtur, coupled with the sudden need of his help, diminished the effects of the scare and increased his cognizance. He became aware of the happenings around him and compensated by thinking out what he should do without having to be guided or told to do the basic camp tasks.

Aknel took charge. They continued traveling toward Alizandar Loag territory.

Enickor led. He did not speak much, nor did he do any more than walk and commune with his Mistress in a separate, silent world. It was enough. Aknel continued to scout, set up, and break camp daily. He foraged, using Landah's criteria of acceptance as to what was edible and what was not.

Roh came to visit. They remained a respectful distance from the threesome and ventured in close only during the Star Follower's absence.

The passing days were much the same, but the dispositions of the travelers changed. Aided by the strength Aknel shared,

Landah grew more alert. The hero-worship the lad developed for Aknel was initially shunned by the Star Follower, then cultivated as a means to further enhance Landah's return to normalcy.

Enickor, too, changed.

Once they were beyond the Hedshire and into the Great Iyigna Valley, Enickor found the first of the many answers he needed. Summer was upon them, but the days stayed crisp and the nights were cold.

Serpents, whose skins were bright with a fine array of colors rivaling the most spectacular sunsets, hung in the trees and slithered over the ground. They were the Keepers of the Valley.

Enickor warned his companions to stay close to him. The scouting ventures were curtailed for the duration of their descent into the Upper Iyigna Valley.

They did not pause to camp, nor did they linger when eating. The perpetual hissing and the rustle of tree limbs served as a prod to keep them moving.

"Chiy-une grants us this passage. It is a blessing she offers to her chosen," Enickor had said to Strom when they were almost through the high valley. "I would not have led us here without some assurance from her."

The serpents showed themselves openly. Tongues flicked nervously, eyes fixed. The smallest reptile the travelers saw was three meters long and fifteen centimeters in diameter.

Star Followers would not venture far into the Upper Iyigna. If they did, their stay would be brief. Even loagers stayed away. The forest changed into a gnarled, malodorous, disease-ridden place. The sparse branches allowed plenty of light to reach the lower planes. A continuous mist swirled around their ankles. It seeped upwards from the rot on the murky ground.

It took three days before they crossed into the Lower Iyigna, and another full day's traveling to be rid of the malediction of the serpents' territory. Once in the Great Iyigna Valley they paused for two days. They slept.

Here the ipcar stood tall. Leaves turned black to match the rich virgin soil at their bases. The perpetual flux of moisture rising from the river below and rolling over the heights above kept a fine mold growing on the trunks and in the rock crevices.

The second day of their respite Enickor departed from the camp and communed with his Mistress. Strom and Landah had come to accept his unpredictable goings, and listened without a doubt in the farthest corners of their minds to the strange directions Enickor often gave them upon his returns.

That evening they sat huddled around a small fire they had dared to build. Their camp was close enough to the Keepers' land to impart a relative assurance that Star Followers would not be around.

"Three days through the Great Iyigna, down to the river, and then another two to make a raft. That should take us out of the Lyndirlyan," Enickor said, drawing a crude map in the ashes pulled around a stone firebrace.

"How long will we stay on the river?" Strom asked, concerned. The land's unpredictabilities were one thing. He could run or fight. But water?

"If fortune rides with us, we will be able to ride through the rapids and out through the Plains of Akatna os Egra." He glanced at Landah's slow smile. "You will see them after all, eh?"

Landah nodded. "Perhaps I will be the last to go that part of the Manhood Trail."

"Perhaps." Both loagers knew the sad truth in the words. "You have had a difficult Manhood Trail to follow, Landah. And you are yet too young to have been expected to undertake it."

Enickor gazed at the lad, glad to see the sparkle in his blue eyes and the life in his smile. Decisive, he stood and withdrew the Holy of the Harcel. It sang as it left the embrace of the scabbard, then gleamed in the firelight as he held it in both hands, straight out and away from his body.

"As Leader of the Harcel, Friend of the Land, Warrior of the Mistress Chiy-une, I declare that from this day forth Landah, son of Omagar, beloved child of Udia who was cousin to Keladine Ornasive, greatest leader of all times, be known as a man. Landah Omagar shall be your full name, and by that will you be known to all men."

The Holy descended with ritualistic slowness.

Landah had moved to his knees. Quickly he stripped away his tunic. Arms extended, his hands, opened palms up, he waited, smiling, happy.

The sword edge came to rest on his forearms. Two red lines appeared. Gradually the weight of the sword slit Landah's forearms.

Strom watched. A sense of pride he had not known for many years filled him. While Landah was not a child, he clearly was not a man in physical terms. His survival of the crisis series which had banished him to the place where nonliving eventually became death earned him the right to manhood. His estimation of Enickor heightened. Strom did not think it often happened that another's evaluation of a man matched his own.

The moment when Landah received the sword and eagerly accepted the pain of manhood, casting aside the joys childhood should have enticed him with, would forever be graven upon Strom's memory. The communion of spirit between the lad and Enickor, the common bond he wished he could share, the tie sealed forever when the Harcel Leader reopened the vertical scars on his own forearms and pressed them crosswise against Landah Omagar's: these things could not be truly shared by any watcher.

The brief, impromptu ceremony salved the last healing ointment onto Landah's scarred emotions.

"I will uphold the standards of the Harcel. I will not refuse the Land her proper due, and I will lay down my life defending her in the war the Star Followers have waged upon her."

The smile had vanished. He was truly a man now, one with a cause that smacked of vengeance.

Moments later they were regrouped around the fire. The night's cold touched their backs.

"I wish it were that simple, Landah."

"What?"

Strom tossed another broken log onto the fire and watched the flakes of ember rise with the heat. "The siege by Star Followers." He glanced at Landah, then Enickor before staring into the fire once again. "You see, if it were not the Houses of Jeffires and Hadilka mining this planet, it would be one of the others, or two, or three. If the House of Jeffires quit its claim here, Hadilka would take over."

"Yes. There is still time to save the planet if they can be halted," Enickor said absently. "The backlash has already begun."

"I do not understand," Landah said.

Enickor became thoughtful for a short while. "It is like this. You have a roh, all right?"

Landah nodded.

"You feed him nothing but grasses. He will use only his cud-chewing head. His offspring will be smaller, and require less food. If that is continued for long enough, generation after generation, his teeth will become adapted, and both heads will grow short, grinding teeth. He will have no use for the sharp carnivore ones. He will have learned to eat only grasses."

Landah nodded again. "After many, many generations."

"The point is, he will adapt to maximize his assets to his environment." Landah took over. "So will all of nature. The alternative is extinction. A roh cannot eat enough grass to maintain his average size and weight using only one head, so he will adjust. Once he has, he will again grow larger with each generation, since his capacity to feed himself will improve.

"They use the helix ships for mining. They are fast. And they're efficient when you consider the cost of not using them and reverting to the old ground machinery and lasers. They pull the ore out of the ground, accelerate it by using the very energy in the atmosphere, and put it in orbit. From there, it's pulled onto barges.

"Getting back, they are fast," he repeated wistfully.

"When a planet is stripped of its heavy elements there is a reaction in the crust. It adjusts, taking bits of energy from here, giving some there, changing, rearranging, trying to establish a balance. There is pressure outward, pressure inward and all of that is disturbed when there is an energy reaction like those created by the helix ships."

Strom tossed a pebble at the fire. "That, my friend, is a rather oversimplified explanation of isotope formation, molecular transfer, and element mutation."

"I almost understand, but I do not understand why they chose Chiy-une and why . . ."

Enickor sighed heavily. "They do not value the land, only what it will buy for them. They have recycled their steel, their iron, and have beat the soul from it. There are still some things they cannot synthesize. Even if they could, they would still mine Chiy-une.

"It is their nature, Landah, just as it is ours to take nothing from the land without returning something. It is a difference that cannot be reconciled."

"Strom, on your world, did no one give back to the land? Was it dying, also?"

"Yes, Landah, we gave back, but not as you do. I came from an agricultural world. We grew foodstuffs. We gave nutrients to the land so it would produce more and better crops for us."

179

"That is not the same." Landah folded his hands between his knees.

"I know." The smile on Strom's face did not look happy. "Not then, but now I know." He looked at Landah. The young man contemplated the firelight. "You are the only people I have ever heard of with a culture based on taking, needing, providing—buying and selling."

"Are we truly so rare?" Enickor asked, amazed.

"Yes. And that is why the loags do not understand what the Star Followers are about. And why you are a dangerous man, Enickor. You have lived in both worlds."

"True, but I fail to understand . . . So many things I do not seem to grasp the way the Mistress wants me to." He slapped his upper arms and glanced at the tent. "It will be cold tonight."

"Cold as the scaffold on the eve of a hangin'
Hard like the steel when the smitty's done bangin'.
The heart of the maiden whose lover's been killed
Cries into the night, 'My love is not stilled!
It is something I've given that can't be returned.
I hope that in hell your black souls will burn.
You've shattered my life, though I'm kept alive.
Through the days that you live, remember—I died.'"

Finished, Strom cleared his throat. "I don't know what came over me."

"That is sad." Landah's whisper was nearly lost to the sputter of the fire. He looked at the outworlder in awe. "There is such sadness where you come from?"

"Yes, but there is unhappiness everywhere. And there is happiness, too. I believe that it usually balances out." He snorted, then stood. "Landah, it may seem bleak, but it could be worse for you and Chiy-une. They might have colonized you."

"An optimist," Enickor said, getting to his feet. "A poet and an optimist. A rare commodity on any world."

"And a mercenary, and a munitions expert . . ." Strom turned sharply. A cloud of dust flittered onto the fire and crackled. His green eyes were bright.

"Time . . . time . . . time the window . . . close the window and the time is over . . ." He appeared to exist in a world away from the Iyigna Valley, one far from Chiy-une.

As abruptly as he changed, he did so again. The manner

180

in which he seemed to look through Enickor raised the fine hairs on the nape of the Chiy-uneite's neck.

"Your planet must be alive. . . . Why else would I be here?"

Enickor and Landah traded glances and waited for the next mood to crest.

Excited, Strom clapped Enickor's shoulder and pulled him back down to sit beside the fire. "Time. That is what we need, is it not? Time to gather the loags together?"

"Yes. I want to get them south." The words were distant, as though spoken by someone else.

"And time is what the helix miners need. They need to complete their schedules. Those cannot be revised. They have pulled too much ore out of here. Volcanoes are popping up, rifts, quakes . . . The change window is set. It cannot be altered."

"So?"

"I would require a guide, Enickor. I would need to get across the land to the mining camps. They have the munitions, the . . ."

"What are you talking about?" Landah asked.

Strom turned on his log. A big grin stretched the freckles on his cheeks. "I did not think of it before, but there may be a way to buy a small amount of the time you must have." To Enickor, "I told you I was good with weapons. I can also put that ability to work on a helix ship. And if I can get to even one long enough to sabotage it, it will be worth the attempt.

"Expensive as they are, I would bet my life they will immediately call a halt to the mining until they figure out what happened, and how. Then they will reevaluate security, change it, and resume. Any interruption we can cause is to Chiy-une's benefit."

"Bet your life? That is what you would be doing, Strom." It was dangerous, but the potential was appealing. Why had he not thought of it himself? At last, a positive step. Any delay, regardless of how small, bought a piece of time. Time was hope. *Mistress? Do you hear? Do you know? There is hope. The man is right.*

Strom went on to explain how he would go about sabotaging the helix ships.

"Of course, it will have to be fast work. I will get only one opportunity—if I'm lucky."

"Security is very heavy, Strom. Very heavy."

"I know. And I can fit right in. Both Houses have contract

services for maintenance on their ships. The hardest part will be obtaining the right uniforms." The impish grin returned, broader. "As for security, most of it is hired. Mercenaries handle the security." He looked earnestly at Enickor. "If anyone can do it, I can. Do you think you can trust me that far?"

Nodding, "Why would you do it?"

Several moments passed before Strom answered. "I would be dead if you had refused my company on this journey. Without knowledge of the land or a destination, I may have wandered through the Head Forest until I reached a mining unit. Then what?

"But you did take me along. For a reason I do not understand, we have grown very close. Like brothers. Like a family. This thing with the helix ships is something I can do in return. To you. To your land. Maybe it will help me feel cleaner inside again."

The decision was settled when Landah handed them a slate and marker. Slowly at first, then faster, they mapped out the land, its barriers, paths, major trails, and the known Star Follower mining camps. Enickor's information was old, from pre-island days. Landah had little to contribute.

Forming plans to strike back at the Star Followers bolstered their pride. When the time came, they would be ready. Not all of Chiy-une's children would fall to the helix ships.

Strom would go, but not until they migrated to the Southern Rohn and were secured for the winter. It was agreed that they would seek a guide from the Alizandar. But Enickor worried that the loag had isolated itself, as the Alizandar had done many times in the past.

The night was half gone, the cold heavy upon the ground and the fire nearly spent by the time they put aside their plans and sketches.

Morning put them underway once again. There was a new vigor in the gaits of the trio crossing the Great Iyigna to ride the back of the wild river. Hope sweetened the Chiy-une air. The day felt warm.

Gaediv received the nekka leader's messengers with mixed emotions. She could not doubt the validity of what Illeuro asa Khatioup had experienced in the primeval forest of the high mountain. The blood taste bespoke the truth.

Also, she knew their release from servitude had been a false one. Memory recalled the bond made on Alidanko. Such a bond could not be severed by only one caretaker. His face did not match the one to whom the Alidanko Gaediv had bonded them. Illeuro asa Khatioup could not have known that without benefit of Gaediv consultation.

She pondered long, searching her memories and applying logic. She, too, tasted of the rock and sought the special presence which gave life. It existed. Yet it gave her no answers, nor did it shed light on her course of action.

Many katelings had been hatched. The leah was small for her rapidly-expanding numbers and the abundance of katelings in stair-step growth patterns. The drones labored ceaselessly. And still their efforts fell short of the leah needs.

It was only a matter of time before the first katelings reached maturity and assisted in leah expansion. But the horde of miners would arrive before then.

The hazards of discovery would be great. Caretakers might overrun the leah. The katelings faced death in that event. Gaediv would be slain immediately. There would be no leahs on this place. No propagation. There was to be only mining, then a return to Alidanko.

The air had tasted of deceit at the time of bargaining. The Gaediv memory had preserved the sensation for one of her successors to analyze. The caretakers failed to understand that the Quniero could not survive without a leah. Leah was home, hope, direction, and the common mind. The absence of a leah was dispossession and darkness.

Sorrowfully, the Gaediv sent out the messengers who had tasted of her blood to seal their knowledge. They moved cautiously into the night. The leah must be preserved.

Chapter 20

THERE WAS ACTIVITY IN THE LYNDIRLYAN. THE
evidence of haste, ship noise and fires in both the Head and
the Hedshire, caught the easterly wind and further blackened
the sky.

A newfound enthusiasm, bolstered by Landah's zeal to justify his manhood by taking on more work, cut the time needed
to build the raft down to a day and a half. Time was a foe as
well as an ally. They did not wait until morning to embark.

The rapids proved awesome. If Strom had known how bad
they actually were, he would not have agreed to run them.
None of the three were experienced in either rafting or river
travel. Their only communications were shouts; *lean this way,
check the lashed packs, push, pole that way*.

Once the white water lay behind, life seemed a little dearer,
a bit more precious, and far more fragile.

The Plains of Akatna os Egra flattened the terrain beyond
the gentling hillsides marking the end of the Iyigna Valley.
The river moved rapidly, carving meanders, changing the land,
and leaving fertile soil in each of its previous beds.

A cloudless sky mellowed the temper of the river and spread
a contagious lethargy over the three men. They basked in the

warmth of the sun. Time slowed on the plains. Weeping trees and long-leafed grasses lined the banks. The vegetation competed for space. The losers were forced into the water.

Inland, there were fat-leafed dark green trees poking out of the oris grass. Clusters of scrawny ipcar tried to survive in bare spots. Old river bed meanders cut into the plains and left dead trails marked by bleached tree copses.

Strom and Enickor lay on their backs, heads propped by the packs and bodies spread to receive maximum heat. Landah steered the rudder tied to the rear, and watched the river ahead.

"When I was a boy, Chalton would have opened my back with his belt if he had caught me doing this."

"Who's Chalton?" Enickor asked, eyes closed.

"The man my mother married after my father died. He would have made a great mercenary." Strom chuckled. "A truly great one. The man had no conscience. None." He moved away from the river, from Chiy-une, and returned to the four-room white fabricated dome of his youth.

He had not thought of Chalton for a long, long time. Nor had he wanted to.

The light, floating world he enjoyed on the raft disappeared. The scars on his back, buttocks, and thighs came alive with a will of their own. *He would have killed me*, he thought again. *Instead, he killed her. But he had already robbed her of life bit by bit, until even though she was dead inside, she continued to do as he told her to do.*

He remembered being on the floor of the tool garage. There was mud everywhere; funny-looking stuff. The pain of Chalton's belt hit his body again, again. Distantly, he heard his mother scream. It was a strange sound for a woman who had not spoken above a whisper since Chalton came into their lives.

His mother's scream was drowned by a barrage of yells: bass, relentless.

The belt no longer struck his naked body, though its ghost continued to do so.

Dazed with the rhythm of pain, Strom heard his mother scream again. Vaguely he remembered seeing the curved blade of the garden knife. It seemed to be growing from her hand. She moved like a fuzzy dream, screaming his name, telling him to run.

But he could not run. He could not even walk. He crawled to the tractor, pulled up on the side of the hover guard and fell into the control pit.

Off to his right, Chalton loomed over his mother. He was a madman. Those big, hairy fists, which had hammered every part of Strom's body, now rose and disappeared into the light dress his mother wore. The lumpy mass beneath the flimsy material did not resemble anything human. It did not fight back, did not make a sound. The garden knife lay on the floor. It was clean and shiny.

The battery light came on and burned brightly on the tractor panel. Strom pulled himself into the seat. The lesions across his back, buttocks, and legs screamed a pain of their own. Then, inexplicably, the pain stopped. He reached over the guidance system and turned on the furrow maker. It pivoted slowly to the right. A small readout indicated readiness and power availability.

Strom waited. Tears rolled down his freckled cheeks. His mother's lifeless eyes appeared from behind Chalton, then disappeared.

"Chalton," he said. His voice no longer belonged to childhood. It was calm, deadly, sure.

The big man did not turn. His oaths and curses about women who interfered with a man's right to discipline faded. His fist stopped, poised in the air.

"Chalton."

His left hand released the woman's arm. Her body fell to the floor with a thud. Her head bounced off the hover fender of the tractor.

"Chalton."

He turned.

Strom grinned at the terror in Chalton's eyes. The moment seemed to freeze in time. How he loved seeing fear in the big man's face, and knowing it was as great as the fear he had lived with daily. His finger moved ever so slightly on the activator, now fully charged for furrowing and pulverizing stone.

Twelve Orinthian years old, and he enjoyed killing Chalton. He felt bad when it was over, only because it was, indeed, over, and he could not kill Chalton again. He had been even younger than Landah was now. *Some mercenary I turned out to be.*

"Yes," he said slowly, "old Chalton would have killed me." He opened his eyes and shook his head to loosen the past from the present.

"Strom?"

Enickor sat up at the sound of Landah's voice. All three watched the thin column of smoke begin to rise into the flawless sky.

Strom grabbed his pack and quickly stuffed it with an all-weather suit, a few provisions, and a heat sheet. He glanced at Enickor, then took the better of the two *kalases*.

"Must be Star Followers," Enickor muttered. "We are still too far from the loag."

"We will soon know." Strom pointed to an outswing in the meander. "Pull her in there, Landah, then out, and keep on going downriver. I'll catch up with you later."

"Two days, Strom. I will expect you at the Alizandar in no more than two days."

Strom grinned at his friend's concern. "I'll do my best not to disappoint you, Enickor."

Landah steered the raft close to the river bank. There was tense silence after Strom departed.

Strom did not look back. Once the river vegetation swallowed him, it gave up not another sound nor flicker of grass. It was as though Strom Aknel did not exist upon the land.

Enickor took the tiller. The raft hugged the shore opposite the smoke pillar rising into the sky. Shadows and the reaching arms of the trees helped to hide them from any who might be watching.

The spell of the great river had been broken. The needs of the Mistress, the strife upon the land, and worry returned Enickor to the harsh reality of the world about him.

The concern both shared for Strom imposed a silence.

He was right, Enickor reflected. *We have become like brothers, like a strange sort of family. Watch over him, Mistress. Keep him safe.*

Suddenly, he felt better.

At dusk familiar landmarks began to appear. They were far into Alizandar territory, and near the loag.

Pam-ella led Theller over the narrow trail etched into the vertical walls of the Birthplace of the Wind. It was a long, difficult passage. Invisible nimble fingers untied the straps fastening several of her smaller burdens to Theller. They crashed into the valley below. The loose straps and flapping stirrup beat the roh's left side.

The gods who dwelt between the cold walls were malevolent creatures. Time and distance distorted. For each step forward, her destination looked two steps more distant. The wind which had blown against the Porintel travelers now fought against her, even though she was traveling the opposite direction.

The faces of the Porintel haunted her. The dangers Ardinay had predicted were intangible. His warnings went unheeded.

Never had life felt so heavy, nor simultaneously so empty. Because of her, the Porintel faced extinction. In time it would be. The heart was gone. The soul of the loag had died with the children.

Hadilka. He's the key. I should have killed him. I should have done so many things. But I didn't.

She sobbed aloud. Only the wind and Theller heard.

The Uv-Kriell would be warned. That she would see done. Then...then it was time for compromise on her part. She wondered how long she would be able to tolerate Hadilka.

Perhaps she could not save the land, but she could stop the slaughter of the loags who had taken her in and offered warmth and food. She could end the search and leave the mining rights to Hoyiv. He would like that.

The messengers arrived at midafternoon. Illeuro tasted of their blood and knew disappointment. He could not question the Gaediv's wisdom. She knew best for the Quniero. The leah must be protected at all costs.

It further saddened him that the break in servitude had not been a true one. Gaediv had not ordered him to resume mining for the caretakers. She had decreed nothing.

Chiy-une had changed the Quniero. The difference imposed a burden. Nekka leaders should not have to be responsible for so many, nor should he have to make decisions. Gaediv must advise and tell him what to do.

But Gaediv had said nothing. Her existence and that of the leah was already a breach with the caretakers.

Illeuro communed with the nekka and felt their disappointment and estrangement upon this foreign land. *We will not seek out caretakers. But we shall continue to mine.*

Gaediv expands leahs to the south.

We will go through the mountains and venture to the south. As we go, tunnels, leah berths, and corbancoobs will form in our wake. The Quniero of tomorrow shall reap our labors. We will serve the leah and Gaediv. And we will mine. But the gemstones we leave for the caretakers will not be left near the future leahs. We will carry them far and prepare the way for peace around the leahs.

He chose the strongest of the former nekka leaders and permitted blood taste. The nekka split. Illeuro went into the mountains. Astakp asa Phoutk led his nekka south along the ocean.

The sense of duty that each Quniero shared with his brother enhanced the purpose in their undertaking. They were tunnelers, turned miners by the agreement with the caretakers, and now tunnels and miners, serving both masters on this strange living world.

Illeuro did not feel sold out or relegated to fend for himself and his nekka the best he could. Rather, he felt pride that they had been allotted so great a role in the preservation of the Quniero on Chiy-une. And on Alidanko. The home leah with the Queen Gaediv would be unmolested. The caretakers had promised it if only some of them would come to this new land. They were here. They mined.

Strom Aknel felt like a soldier. He was proud of his self-discipline, the hard-wrought expertise that let him move noiselessly over an abandoned riverbed. The stones remained frozen in the delicate silt moving like a tide from side to side when the winds blew. The gray/black powder was packed into every crevice, and labored to smooth the uneven terrain at the slopes.

It was warm in the old bed. Today, the wind did not blow hard enough to lap the silt. The dark stripes blended by time pulled the heat from the sky and shared it with the surrounding bleached stones.

The steep sides kept him practically invisible, unless someone came to the edge and peered over the side.

In his element, doing what he had been trained to do, Strom could not remember being quite as happy as he was now.

The heat that lulled them on the river now baked him against the black silt.

He moved downwind from the smoke pillar, then left the old riverbed. The oris parted for him as he entered. Wary at first, then resigned, he moved along the path. It closed behind him.

He mentally logged the readout on the compass strapped to his left wrist every time the path deviated from a straight line. Constantly, he listened to Enickor's advice replay through his head. The Chiy-uneite knew his world well. The oris did play funny tricks on both the wanderer and the compass.

Intrigued by his invisible guide and delighted by success, Strom paused long enough to mark a number of the largest stalks as a precaution.

On the other side of the oris lay open plains. The growth was less than a meter high, dry and brittle. Thirsty ipcar, stunted and gnarled, cast scanty shade on the dry land.

The smoke column rose a kilometer away.

The open ground presented an obstacle. Strom returned to the oris and moved inside the periphery until a trio of ipcar stood between him and the column.

He removed his pack and climbed.

The land was flat to the east. The last signs of the gentle rise and fall of the foothills had been ironed away. A heat haze made an indiscernable ribbon at the base of the Lyndirlyan. The Great Iyigna had been swallowed by distance. Trees were more scarce to the south and stood farther from the river.

The source of the smoke was a camp. It was still too far away to ascertain the strength, though it did not seem likely there were too many of them. The clearing hewn out of the scrub was small. An ipcar branch served as fuel for the fire. Four domed tents sat on each point of the compass.

To his rear, north, was the oris and the river. This would be his retreat avenue. Those in the camp could not possibly know the tricks that would take them through the murderous wall.

On the ground, pack reinstated, he adjusted the *kalase* and checked the position of the garrote forming the decoration on his uniform cuff. He made the Overeechy issue dagger on his utility belt conspicuous. The folded, spring-loaded one in the belt itself could not be seen.

He walked toward the camp, watching the scrub, waiting for an armed complement of guards to assault him. The prickly sensation in the back of his skull he usually got when the energy field of a *kalase* was turned on him did not come.

Strom was almost on top of the camp before the six soldiers, wearing House of Jeffires battle garb, saw him.

A bedraggled group, they showed only mild interest in his approach. Two, clad in soiled, torn uniforms, showed *kalases*. Even these were brandished with carelessness.

Among them was a man dressed much as Enickor and Landah had been. The simple shirt and breeches were native, the boots sturdy, hand-crafted. His face enlivened with interest. No weapons were visible on his person. The blond/white mop of hair hung down to his shoulders, and contrasted sharply to the deep tan on his lined face. The cobalt blue of his eyes remained bright and intent.

"How did you get here?" asked the soldier with the *kalase*.

"I walked." Strom kept his approach steady. There was a scuffle in the tent on his left. He ignored it and penetrated the heart of their clearing. "It was a long, hard way, too."

"You're one of the mercenaries Hadilka hired, aren't you?"

"I was. I quit." A flicker of relief came when the *kalase* pointed at the ground and the man nodded.

"Why?"

"I prefer to do my target practicing on targets I get paid for hitting. Unarmed locals who do not return fire are not sporting." He met the speaker's gaze with steely eyes.

"You were there, too?"

"At the gorge?" He nodded. "I was there." He grinned. "Right up until the time I left—which was early in the shoot."

"Pull up a seat and sit. We're not going anywhere for a while." He massaged his stomach with his fingertips. It was a gentle movement, familiar in its duplication by two of the other soldiers.

"Thank you. Sitting for a while would feel good." He adjusted a log well away from the radiant heat of the fire. Quickly he assessed the armament strength. Besides the one dressed like a native, two others had no firearms. Four of them appeared to be stricken by an illness. The tent backed up to the west had a pair of boot soles sticking out of the flap.

A foul pall hung over the camp. It was the stench of illness and decay.

"My name's Katchuk. Bern Katchuk." He put away the *kalase* and nodded for his comrade to do the same. "The way I see it, we need all the help and traveling companions we can get in this country. The real enemy is this goddamn land. It either freezes your gonads off or bakes the potency out of them."

The fever-ridden man on Strom's left cackled. His gums were raw and festering. Bits of teeth poked out of the swelling. "She fought you off, did she? Maybe you aren't man enough for her, Kat."

Katchuk's hand closed on his *kalase*. He glared the man into silence.

Strom divided his attention, a more than equal share given to assessing the reactions of the rest. A sneer passed over the native's face.

"I'm Strom Aknel," he said, hoping to break the sudden strain between the two men. It was not time for conflict. Not yet.

They both turned back to him. The tension broke.

Strom noted that the native was disappointed the two men had not taken one another to task. He gestured at him. "Are you their guide across these plains?"

Peals of knee-slapping laughter rolled out on the sour breath of the reprieved man on Strom's left. The question elicted a chuckle and a few smiles from the rest.

"I would be happy to serve as their guide—straight to the depths of Chiy-une." He rose slightly off his log. Red-faced in anger, he pointed to Strom. "If you touch her, Chiy-une will eat your insides and curse you with the slow death these men suffer. It is . . ."

Kat backhanded him. The man went sprawling over the top of his seat.

"Pay no attention to him. He doesn't know what he's talking about. He spent too much time wandering through the mountains, if you know what I mean. He rambles on about some savior we can't kill." Kat smiled, but was not able to bring off the laugh he wanted. "Here, there!"

An older man heavily bedecked with rank on his chest and shoulders exited the tent in which there had been a scuffle. He smoothed his clothes, took a deep breath, and stared into the fire with a smile pasted to his scarred face.

They watched him with ambivalent expressions of anticipation and fear.

"Not bad." He took two steps forward, eyeing Strom as he moved. Unexpectedly, he kept walking over the log benches, stopped, and pitched sideways into the fire. His eyes never blinked. His expression became stone carved. The graying hair sizzled and curled. Clumps of it rose, snapping in the smoke. More stench from his melting synthetic uniform settled into the clearing. It hugged the ground, not leaving with the rising smoke.

Katchuk shouted orders. Two men pulled the other man from the fire. They laid him on his back and turned away. Already he was unrecognizable.

Swearing, muttering, Kat picked up a rock and threw it at the tent.

A scream, followed by hysterical sobs came from the inside. "Shut up! Damn it! Shut up!"

The native went to the tent, looking a question at Kat before entering. The words spoken by him and the female inside were foreign, but Strom thought he had heard the language before.

As he analyzed what he had seen, Strom wished that Enickor was with him to tell him what was going on. The feeling in the air was an eerie one, but not a strange one to him. Regardless of what had happened here, he knew the loagers had not been deserted by Chiy-une. The presence reminded him of the night the beast appeared over their camp and took Enickor.

Kat ordered two men to drag the corpse away, then sat down and began chewing on a brown tuber. Strom had recognized the tubers as an abundant food source which Landah had declared poisonous until they turned green.

That is why they are ill. They are poisoning themselves, he mused, and risked a more analytical look of their condition. *That is part of it, but not all. Landah's warnings were different.*

The tent flap slapped to the side. The loager led a young woman from the inner darkness and brought her to sit beside him on a log seat.

Beaten as she had been, face swollen from crying, Strom thought her beautiful.

Chapter 21

SHE DID NOT SPEAK, NOR DID HER HEAD RISE TO see the new Star Follower. The rest of the men avoided looking directly at her. Only the native met each man's gaze with a quality of resoluteness that made them turn away one at a time.

Disquiet suppressed the group. The Plains of Akatna os Egra were silent, listening for the whispers radiating from the camp. The furtive glances each of the House of Jeffires soldiers took at the woman were worry-filled. The death of their comrade had shaken them, and left a new fear behind.

"Where are you people from?" Strom asked after a long silence.

"It is not important. You have killed the place of our birth."

"Answer the man, Zaich!" Kat turned a malevolent eye on the two.

"You would not know of it. It was called the Harcel Loag." Zaich watched the fire without seeing it, his memories alive and insulating him from those around him.

The news rocked Strom. All of the sudden it was not a simple matter of getting out of this camp alive; there were two he needed to take with him. Enickor would be happy to know they were alive. The Harcel numbered four.

"I have heard of it," Strom answered slowly. He felt the attention of the Star Followers on him and did not look away from the charred rock at the fire's edge. "And I have met the man who carries a sword he thinks is holy."

Two blond heads lifted and turned to him.

"What are you talking about? Do you mean there are more crazies running around down here?" Kat poked the man with the broken teeth with his foot. "You take first watch tonight. Go to sleep and I'll kill you."

Strom shook his head. A film of perspiration coated his body, though he was no longer warm. Casually, he picked up a dried ipcar branch and pulled out the loag knife which had been Enickor's before the confrontation with the land rangtur. That it would be recognized if these two knew the Harcel Leader, he was certain.

With short, even strokes he whittled away the bark. "Not around here, Kat." He looked up and smiled. "Do you mind if I call you Kat or would you prefer something else?"

"Kat's fine," he mumbled, then rubbed his stomach gingerly.

"Okay. No. I met him a long way back, up in the mountains. I sat in his camp one night and traveled with him for a day. He led me through the big basin forest at the beginning of the timberline."

"Damn, that's about where we found these two." Squinting, Kat scratched his sparse beard. "Got separated, huh?"

When neither loager answered, Strom spoke up. "There couldn't have been a lot of them to get separated from. The two men I ran into didn't mention that they were looking for anyone. They did not seem to be looking, either."

"Maybe the whole damn bunch of them is close-lipped." His dark eyes squinted as they focused on the loagers and Strom.

"It could be, Kat. I guess it could be." He turned the branch over and changed hands. He was equally good with his right and his left. He could not explain why he felt each of the men in this camp deserved killing. The certainty flowed over him in waves. He fought the loathing that agitated him and kept him talking. "By the way, where are you men headed? Is there a mining camp nearby? I could use some traveling supplies— on consignment, of course."

Kat caught his meaning and chuckled. "No. We're going east, then south. We hope to run into a Jeffires company. But

I don't think they're out in this part of the wilderness. It is so flat, and no cover, I thought we would have spotted an installation by now. At least a supply line. Anyway, we're safe for a while. There's no use in killing ourselves by hurrying through this heat.

"Hey, toss me one a' those brown things by your left leg, will you?"

Strom gathered the knife and stick in his left hand, picked up a poisonous tuber, and tossed it to Kat.

"Help yourself. They're tasty and they fill you up, too. It takes the ache out of your belly."

"I'll pass. Thanks." He went back to whittling.

Kat laughed, choked and coughed, then spat a wad of red mucus into the fire. "Not refined or processed enough for you? No matter. You'll get hungry." He jabbed one of the men to life with an order to remove the water boiling over the fire.

Strom took note of the men's movements, the subtle interactions, the mutual distrust, and knew that he would not last the night if he stayed in their camp. Kat was good. The relaxed manner and openness could easily have been taken as an open sign of friendship. But Strom knew men as good as Kat, and better.

The tide of conversation turned toward homeworlds and exaggerated accounts of battle tales. Strom alternated active and passive roles, careful not to say anything which might exalt his military prowess above any one else's. Through the rest of the afternoon the loagers stayed huddled together on one log. They were distant, untouched by the braggadocio.

The feverish man on Strom's left took to fixing a soupy dinner from a portion of the water boiled over the fire.

Cold crept out of the oris as the sun disappeared behind the far mountains. Strom accepted his soup graciously. He sipped it loudly, as did the other soldiers, but spat it back into the cup. Each time he returned to his whittling he sloshed more of the liquid over the edge. Soon it was gone.

"Since you came along and are our guest tonight, we're going to let you have the girl to keep the cold off you. Tomorrow you can start earning your keep."

Strom looked up from his whittling at Kat, then at Elisif and back. "Why don't you take her? I appreciate the offer, but I really prefer the guy, if no one objects."

There was a moment of silence before Kat howled and slapped his thigh. "You are one strange bastard, Aknel. Sure you can have him. Have the girl, too. Or don't you like women at all? Or are you afraid of that old man's prattle about the planet striking you dead?" Kat roared. The rest followed suit, pointing as they tried to laugh.

Strom waited for the empty-sounding guffaws to cease. "It has been so long I thought I would start out slow. You know, practice until I got it right. That way I wouldn't disappoint either one of us." He grinned back at Kat and ran his blade over the smooth end of his carving.

"Seven devils of Pithcath! You are the first switch hitter I ever met with his hands and his sex." Kat rose, stretched and rubbed his belly. "Take them both, but don't get any ideas about going anyplace with them." The seriousness heightened by the firelight on his face changed slightly. "Of course, you had better not sleep too heavily with one of them beside you, either. That girl already killed two of my men."

"Perhaps they lacked finese in their approach." He glanced at Elisif, met her gaze and winked. She looked away, disgusted.

Kat pointed to the tent Elisif had vacated. "You can have that one. And if you don't mind, I'll take your *kalase*." He grinned. "I'm sure you understand. I wouldn't want one of them to borrow it from you and figure out how to use it."

"I understand, Kat and I appreciate your concern. You are absolutely right. You wouldn't believe some of the things these natives come up with." Head shaking, "They are truly a deceptive lot." He removed his *kalase* and handed it to Kat.

"Jinne! You take first watch. And stay awake, or I'll flay the skin from your back in the morning." Kat staggered toward a tent, mumbling how tired he was and rubbing his belly.

The others followed suit, as though it had been an order to retire.

Strom put his knife away and palmed his carving. He looked at Elisif, then at Zaich, and jerked his head in the direction of the tent. He knew they were being watched. It was something he could feel just as keenly as if a pair of hands were resting on his shoulders.

"Are you going to go peacefully? Or do I have to beat half the life out of you and leave your lady friend without any protection? She looks like she might fold if she loses you." He stood. "You heard the battle stories we swapped. Mine were conservative. It does not pay to outdo one's hosts." He hoped he sounded convincing.

To his relief, Zaich rose. Elisif held his hand and walked

behind him to the tent. Strom followed, taking note of where Jinne had set up his post.

Inside, Zaich and Elisif faced him. "You saw what happened today. You will die just like that if you force her against her will," Zaich said quietly.

Strom groped in the dark. The prickly sensation of being monitored stayed with him. "And what if I rape you, old man? Will your planet gods strike me down for that?" He couldn't find the sender, but he was sure it was there.

He reached out and found Elisif. Startled, she screamed. He grabbed her head and brought her near to his lips. "Enickor val Densu sent me. He's gone with Landah to the Alizandar Loag."

Stunned, Elisif stopped fighting, then grabbed him around the neck.

"That will do you no good," Strom said, forcing the carved knife into her hand and holding her fingers around it until she brought her free hand to feel what it was. "We'll leave it dark, my sweet. Your turn will come."

He moved quickly to unsheath his knife and find Zaich. There was enough confusion to simulate the reluctance of the older man's submission. Strom continued talking while removing the garrote from his sleeve and retrieving his smaller knife from the decoration on his uniform. He put his pack beside Elisif and loaded it with the all-weather gear he found stuffed into the front of the tent.

Next, he directed her and Zaich into prone positions. It took several precious minutes to convey his expectations. Once they understood they began making passionless sounds. If things did not go well, they had a better chance of surviving *kalase* fire if they were lying down.

Strom went to work on the back tent wall with his knife. He figured it would take less than five minutes to eliminate the soldiers, starting with Jinne. The invisible audience cheered him on. Never had he looked forward to covert combat with the excitement he now felt.

Illeuro did not know that his plan was deceitful. He considered it evasive. The nekka moved into the Lyndirlyan in one solid flow. They moved quickly, pushing away from the leah, destroying traces of their presence. The dangers of the living land were as complex as the rituals of the caretakers who had brought them to it.

Once they were beyond the first line of peaks, scouts hunted for used, abandoned caretaker sites. They were easily-recognized blights upon the land.

The main body smelled out a diamond find. Illeuro left a nekka which had been a unit nekka to mine. The rest moved deeper along the range and sought a place for a new leah.

Illeuro climbed the cliff face alone. At the top he tasted the rock.

Caretakers were coming from three sides. He did not know how long it would take them to reach their site, or how far away they were now. Caretakers were difficult to judge, they had so many ways of moving over the land.

He perched on the edge of the cliff, his long head a spear in the air. His mouth opened. A cry that Chiy-une had never heard before shocked her mountain walls.

The danger message had gone out. In typical Quniero fashion, they would hide.

The final portion of the raft ride through the Alizandar territory was long. The well of conversation had run dry. Neither Landah nor Enickor relaxed after Strom departed.

The Alizandar Loag turned out *en masse* to greet them. Their openness and the untouched serenity of the prairie, was a world unto itself. Their enthusiasm dwindled once the word ran through the crowd.

Enickor val Densu had returned.

The Metaliary took his place at the lone wooden pier jutting into the river. No one spoke until Landah and Enickor secured the raft.

Wide-eyed, Landah stayed close to Enickor. He had only heard tales of the Alizandar and never seen one in person. Their rituals differed from the western loags. No Alizandar youth crossed the Lyndirlyan on his journey to manhood.

The whispers and murmurs of their cowardice rose to haunt Landah. These were a powerfully built people. Their short stature and tree-trunk legs made them look impossible to put off balance. The sun had bronzed their skin and bleached most of the brown heads to a dirty streaked blond.

Their clothing was brief and colorful. The elder loagers wore bright capes. Soft animal-skin capes were worn by the warrior-hunters.

Enickor went through the formalities with a somber air. He

presented the Harcel Holy, unsheathed, for the Metaliary's inspection.

Inorag cur Maha, Leader of the Alizandar Loag, bowed deeply, his displeasure lightly masked. "I bid you welcome, Leader of the Harcel. May our humble village accommodate your needs."

"We must talk, Inorag. You, Pindar, Landah, and I."

"Of course. And we will." Inorag waved his people away and led his visitors down the pier and into the village.

Enickor was worried. The Alizandar gave no indication that they were even dimly aware of the threats dooming Chiy-une. Life continued here as it had since time began, with few exceptions. They read. They kept records, made paper, smelted iron, plowed and irrigated fields. The Alizandar had kept itself untouched by denying the existence of danger.

Inorag insisted upon the entire ceremony befitting a visiting loag Leader. It made no difference, in fact, he chose to ignore the statement that the entire Harcel was present and consisted of Enickor and Landah. The long awaited excuse for a gala celebration was at hand, even if Enickor val Densu was not a welcomed sight in Alizandar firelight.

Pindar listened gravely to Enickor's pleas for a conference and said nothing.

The night had slipped away. A new day would soon break the far line on the plains. The formalities had been attended and finished.

"Inorag, there is little time. Please, we must talk." Enickor took the older man's arm and steered him toward the guest cottage he and Landah were to share.

"Ah, tomorrow. Tomorrow there is plenty of time. You sea coast people are all too anxious. You give no time to rest and entertainment." He paused and turned to Enickor. "You will like what awaits you in the cottage. She has been saved for just such an occasion."

"I do not want a woman . . ."

"Oh? The Star Followers have changed you. Perhaps a man? Surely we can accommodate."

"Inorag! I want nothing but for you to listen to me." The stubbornness of the Alizandar Leader frustrated him. He turned away. "Pindar. Will you listen to what I have to say? Will you have the wisdom to heed the warnings the Harcel is bringing? Will you grant Adaia's anointed leader an audience?"

Pindar gauged both men, then nodded. "I will listen. To me

you are still Enickor val Densu. Not the Harcel Leader. I do not understand why . . ."

Swearing under his breath, and at the limit of his patience, Enickor herded Pindar and Inorag into the cottage and dismissed the two girls. Both looked relieved. Landah was openly disappointed.

Once he sat them at the table and launched his tale of the Harcel, the Alizandar men listened. He spoke of Strom and what had become of him. The time passed quickly as the journey through the Head and finally down the river was recounted. Nothing was omitted.

"You have had a difficult ordeal, Enickor. Very difficult," said Inorag, rubbing the ends of his beard against his palm. "We will offer you sanctuary."

"I don't want sanctuary. I came to warn you, to implore you to go south with us."

Inorag laughed. "Uproot the entire loag? Travel thousands of kilometers to the south? Why?" He stopped laughing and leaned heavily on his elbows, his face so close to Enickor's that the heated breath warmed the other man. "Do you know how many people we will lose? Do you realize how many will die? The children? Pregnant women? The elderly?"

"Do you realize how many will die if you remain here?"

"You did not answer, Enickor val Densu."

"Yes. You are right. Some of the Alizandar will not make it." He met cur Maha's stare and felt the iron will of the man. "If you stay, there may be fewer survivors of the Alizandar than there were of the Harcel."

A beat of silence passed before the Alizandar Leader asked, "How do you know this? How can you be sure? Have you seen the great Star Follower plan to slay the Alizandar?" Inorag slumped back. "I find it difficult to believe you have been totally honest in your account, Enickor. I do not intentionally offend you, but you strain your credibility with the Alizandar."

"Perhaps we should discuss this between us, Inorag," Pindar said, breaking the rising spell of animosity.

There was another pause.

"You are right, Pindar my friend. It is Alizandar business, and not for outsiders." With that he rose and left the cottage.

Pindar also rose, but moved more slowly toward the door.

"There was no exaggeration in the story, Pindar." Enickor's voice was soft, cajoling. "I swear upon the Harcel Holy, there was not."

201

"I believe you, Enickor. And you are safe here—for the time being." He turned around. "He will not bend. He will not tell them to go. Just the opposite. Inorag is a good man, a fine leader..."

"You do not have to justify him, Pindar. And I have not given up with him, either." Compassion swept Enickor when he saw the hope in the Metaliary's face.

"Nor have I." He left, closing the door softly behind him.

Landah and Enickor sat at the table for several minutes without speaking. Finally Landah asked, "What if they don't go?"

"Magaikan said to go south. He must have some knowledge of the mining layout. I think he was trying to tell me the Alizandar would be wiped out. That the Harcel was not going to be unique." Resting his elbows on the table, he put his head in his open hands. "They are gemstone mining in the high Lyndirlyan. How long before the helix ships come in for the heavy ore? Then what? The Plains of Akatna os Egra? They don't have much time to wait."

Landah weighed his words carefully before he spoke again. "Enickor. You must speak against Inorag if he refuses to tell his people. You must bring them with us. They cannot go the way of the Harcel. They cannot..." The rest of his words choked.

Enickor put his arm around Landah. "I know, my friend. Cry it out."

Landah put his head on the table and cried for his parents and the Harcel Loag.

Chapter 22

PAM-ELLA WATCHED THE WINSONG RETRACE THE trail she had taken when Friedo turned seaward. It seemed the days of rain would have washed the land free of it. Apparently the winsong had even greater talents than singing and mood weaving.

A sigh of relief floated on the wind. What if she had taken another route? Would he have continued straight into one of the ambushes waiting ahead? It was too close. She became suspicious, questioning the coincidence in which she did not believe.

A series of sonic booms rattled the western line of the Lyndirlyan. Oppressive clouds, ready to dump their muddy loads, obscured the ships.

Theller brayed.

Faelinor paused, listening, then answered.

Pam-ella watched the terrain below for Star Followers. She expected them to rush Friedo either from the lowland or straight down the mountain trail. The anticipation filled her with resignation. She had come all this way to warn the Uv-Kriell, and now it might be too late.

Instead of being able to return to Shirwall and Hoyiv possessing a modicum of bargaining power with Hadilka, she would be caught and sold. It chagrined her to think that her three-and-a-half-year quest had wrought nothing. The fate she sought to escape presently seemed the only viable alternative to saving what she had grown to cherish on the land.

Something moved on the middle rock trail.

When she saw the soldiers she was surprised by their diminished numbers. A scant dozen, they were bedraggled, worn. They moved slowly on the mountain. The broken line of their advance disappeared into scrub and popped out again.

"Ohhhh, Theller. We could take them." The glee in her voice was almost urgent. The *kalase* warmed her hand.

The roh took her on an upward angle on the mountain face. Together they chose a path which accommodated their follower and provided maximum cover. The soldiers remained in view. The noise they made reached Theller first.

Constantly, Pam-ella checked on Friedo's position. He was moving into the heart of the ambush place.

When it seemed imminent that the soldiers would at last spot him, Pam-ella dismounted. She climbed onto a rock shelf, put the lead soldiers in the sights of her *kalase* and waited.

"Call Faelinor, Theller. Call him . . . now."

Theller used both heads to summon the winsong. His corrosive braying was so loud it echoed off the mountain face for several minutes after he had finished.

Alerted by the immediacy and intensity of the summons, Faelinor turned sharply and assumed a battle stance.

Puzzled, the Uv-Kriell failed to react.

Pam-ella picked off the lead soldier within heartbeats of their first round of fire.

She took a second, then a third, and wounded a fourth before they had her position and returned fire.

Theller brayed again. This time it was his mistress who concerned him.

Heeding his warning, Pam-ella slid off the ledge, quickly mounted him, and held on. Theller galloped over the shale falls, his big feet sure of their ground. They rode down-slope to come up still above and behind the soldiers.

Payndacen's return fire had a deadly accuracy.

While they had superior numbers, they were not aggressive. This perplexed her. Somewhere in the Lyndirlyan the bravado they had possessed in the caverns had been stripped away. As, perhaps, were the leaders.

204

Faelinor began to sing.

Pam-ella took aim from Theller's back, fired twice, and held on. They moved down until they were level with the soldiers.

She fired again, noting that they no longer had the full packs they carried from the cavern stronghold.

Faelinor's song filled the day.

Pam-ella was immune to the passive sentiments he invoked.

The firing from the soldiers tapered.

There were three of them alive with no visible injuries. Two others writhed among the rocks.

She took careful aim and fired three more times. Each flash scored a fatal hit on the armed men.

Ardinay watched, his expression vacant. His eyes were sorrowful. The heart of the Porintel was gone. Killed. The children were dead . . .

"For the babies," she whispered, took aim, and fired on the closest wounded man.

"For their mothers," she said, louder, and killed the second.

Nothing in the rock formation which had provided shelter to the soldiers moved.

How long she sat on Theller, she did not know. Dismay over the lack of any more soldiers to kill rested keenly on her. The hate and fear, living just under the self-willed control that kept her on the course she knew she must follow, put a chink in her armor. The totality of her hatred for the House of Hadilka, the mercenaries, and even her own house frightened her. Living as Hadilka's wife now repulsed her more than it terrified her.

Insects buzzed in the air.

Vaguely, she heard Payndacen approach.

"Now I can do it, Theller. I could kill Hadilka. I really could." Tears ran down her smiling cheeks. "How rich and powerful I would be. If I am good," she whispered, leaning over to stroke Theller's left neck and massage the vee at his breastbone, "if I am really good, no one will suspect. . . . Then I will be truly free. The loags will be safe from his men . . . the land will help me."

"Pam-ella."

Startled, she turned.

The *kalase* wavered in her trembling hand. Panic struck her. Did he hear? Would he tell? Could he stop her?

Faelinor crooned softly. His song drank the tension from the day and touched her panic.

She took a deep breath and let it out slowly. The *kalase* lowered and ultimately disappeared into her sleeve.

"Friedo." She bowed and came up smiling. "I would say this makes us quite even." Normalcy had returned. The twist in her features was gone.

The carnage in the rocks kept drawing his attention. "More than even."

Faelinor continued his low melody.

Theller responded to his rider's order to move. He kept his heads just slightly in front of the winsong's and Payndacen.

Pam-ella did not speak for the rest of the afternoon. Nor did the Uv-Kriell press her. The profound disturbance he felt about the senseless murders in the rocks grew deeper. Her silence was morose.

They camped on the outskirts of the Gorbich Hills. Pam-ella's carelessness caused him additional concern. She walked through the woods, touching trees, grass, bending to scoop up handfuls of soil. Her sojourn in the dark forest lasted until the moon was well into the sky.

Their warm fire fought the chill of night. Pam-ella returned to camp and sat on a rock near the fire. Hands out for warming, she stared into the flames. The profusion of tears on her cheeks, and the dampness of her collar, went unattended.

Finally, Payndacen asked, "What were you doing out there? It's dangerous."

She did not change positions. "Life is dangerous. And I was saying good-bye."

A chill rippled his flesh with bumps. "Good-bye? Good-bye to what?"

"To the land. To something I loved. To a dream that will never be." She turned her hands to warm the backs. "To myself."

"Where are you going?"

"To Shirwall. To Hoyiv." She swallowed. "Eventually, to Hadilka."

Friedo moaned. Head shaking, "Don't do that, Pam-ella. Please. There is another way."

She looked at him. Nothing but emptiness lay inside her. "What is it?"

"Huh? I don't know. There must be another way, though. What has happened? Why this sudden change? God! Not Hadilka."

"I know, Friedo. I know. I appreciate your concern.

"He has won. And why not? Enickor is dead. He must be, or I would have found him. All this time, and not even a word from the loags. I suspect there was a time when someone from the Ocandar knew, but they would not tell me. And I did not know enough to suspect at the time." She shifted on the rock to warm her right side. "Besides, I don't think we would have much to say to one another now. I have changed.

"Let me tell you what has happened since I last saw you." She turned back to look at him, and was pained by the misery she saw. "Friedo, will you be my friend? I think I need one."

He opened his mouth to quickly assure her of his alliance.

"Before you say anything, you should know I used you today. I let them fire on you. I could have warned you well in advance. But I did not." Dejected, she rubbed her palms together. "You could hardly consider that an act of friendship.

"I sometimes think I'm losing my grip on reality. I don't know what comes over me... but I know I need someone, Friedo. I need someone. And I do not belive it is Enickor."

Zaich led them eastward. The moonlight was bright on the prairie. The dried golden grasses reflected the beams, to further light the world. They did not speak for a long time after leaving the camp.

The death work had been performed in less than five minutes. Stains made by blood-spurting arteries ran down Strom's left side. The garrote was cleaner, but the knife was faster. And a man with a slit throat tended to struggle less than one under the garrote.

It was Elisif who spoke first when they rested beside the river.

"Did you kill all of them?"

Strom nodded without looking up from the water where he washed his hands.

She exhaled loudly. "I'm glad."

Now he glanced at her. "They, ah, used you pretty badly?"

Even though her head bowed he could see the shining tears caught in her lashes. "I am unfit for the place of honor I once held. I am soiled, tainted. And if I am with child, it would be a child of shame with many fathers. There is no honor there. I cannot sit beside the Leader, nor can I warm his bed again."

Startled, Aknel turned to Zaich. "The Leader? Enickor? She's Enickor's..." His voice trailed as the older man nodded.

"I don't think he would expect you to die before, well, you know."

Elisif cried quietly.

Zaich took Strom's arm and led him downriver a little way. "You are very good with killing, Star Follower."

"Strom, or Aknel, or both."

Nodding, "Strom Aknel. You know nothing about our way of life. Elisif made her choice. I believe it was a wise one. She chose to live when the soldiers surrounded us in the Lyndirlyan. There were twenty more then. We could not evade them. Perhaps she did not believe strongly enough that Enickor val Densu would escape them and survive. Perhaps."

"She has loved him for many seasons."

"You say that as though he does not share those sentiments." The mire became deeper with each exchange.

"He has vowed to care for her. He tries. But we know. We are the Harcel. And we are loyal." Zaich smiled faintly. "He is Leader, designated by Adaia as the strong one. His survival attests to the Metaliary's wisdom."

Strom sagged down to sit on a bleached log. Perplexed, he gazed upstream at Elisif. "I really cannot understand, Zaich. If every man on a colony under seige refused to have anything to do with a woman who had been ... abused, hell! Half the Overeechy would be out of Star Followers."

Zaich brightened, grinning. "Then it is truly a shame they do not share our practices and beliefs."

Strom smiled. The situation needed a sense of humor. In this instance, he agreed with the loager. "But things have changed, have they not, Zaich? There are only four of you. She is the only woman. I mean ..." Confused, he stood and looked straight at Elisif.

"Zaich, the Harcel is dead unless she has children from another from the Harcel, is it not?"

Sadly, "Yes, Strom Aknel. Elisif knows this, too, as I am sure Enickor does. He will probably give her to either Landah or myself. We are true Harcel. Enickor is not."

"Yet he is the Leader."

"Yes," Zaich answered simply, then turned upriver.

The conversation was over. Strom did not understand or accept their philosophy any better afterward than he had before. He did regard Elisif in a different light. She had chosen to live and preserve the Harcel, using her body as the crucible for that

208

future life, even though it meant losing what brought her happiness.

The remainder of the night passed in silence. They crossed the river at a line of natural shallows which spread the water over a small falls until it was a kilometer wide. Here the river was only waist deep on Zaich.

Strom carried the armory he had confiscated from the House of Jeffires camp well above the water. He urged Zaich and Elisif to help one another, totally unwilling to compromise the munitions booty.

The loagers asked few questions, and took more on faith with the utterance of Enickor's name than Strom thought anyone in their right mind should. Cultures founded on trust and peace were always short-lived. Yet the loags of Chiy-une had been going strong for a long, long time, according to the briefing he had received before coming to the planet.

The gentleness of beliefs, the passivity of their natures, tended to make the Houses see them as weak. Aggression equated to strength in the hub of a House, or its Lord, was an avenue of invasion. Only might and power spoke loudly.

But these people were strong.

He could feel their strength in the will to survive, to persevere in the face of the awesome powers roaming their land.

Lost in thought, Strom failed to notice the formation streaking across the dawn until the sound burst on them.

He looked up, color draining from his face. "Oh, God! We're in trouble now."

He ran to Zaich. "How far?" he screamed, his face red, his heart beating in genuine fear. "How far to the Alizandar?"

Zaich glanced at the streaks breaking the sky. "I am unsure. What is it?"

He hurried back to Elisif and dragged her by the arm until she was even with Zaich. "Helix ships. They're coming with helix ships to mine the Upper Lyndirlyan. That's the spotting crew. We have to run until we get to the Alizandar. Come on. We have to find shelter, or the aftermath will kill us." Again he grabbed Elisif's hand and began running, pushing the older man as he went.

Strom glanced behind once. In the clear dawn he could see the reflection of the sun on the triangle of ships high on the Great Iyigna Valley. It was brighter than the morning star on Orinthia.

*   *   *

Illeuro had watched the small caretaker slaughter the larger ones. Her scent was of the land, not of the stars, and yet it was also of the stars. It confused him.

Gaediv would know of those of two worlds. A nekka leader could only guess. The air savored revenge; sweet and deadly. The sensation elicted surprise in the Quniero. Again, another anomaly to present to Gaediv when he saw her.

From the shadows high over the valley where the roh and winsong rode side by side, the nekka leader watched. He sorted the messages carried over the land by the wind. The brine of the woman's tears contrasted sharply to the acrid perplexity of her companion.

Insects caught the scent of food and rushed from hidden nests in the rocks.

Gries circled, calling back and forth.

Illeuro felt safety return to the Lyndirlyan territory of his nekka. He descended the cliff face. He had tasted the man and the woman. He would know them again.

Before the nekka further penetrated the mountain they would cleanse the land of the caretaker carcasses. No trace would be left to ride the wind. Should a future Gaediv find this leah acceptable and grace the corbancoob with katelings, there would be nothing to draw danger to them.

By the time the leah was formed, those of the land would have feasted and stripped the bones clean. The remnants would be returned to a different cradle of life.

Chapter 23

THE HELIX SHIP BEGAN PRELIMINARY WORK IN THE eastern Lyndirlyan during late afternoon.

The Alizandar grew against the horizon at a painfully slow rate. Loagers came out to match steps with the three weary travelers. The urgency of the situation birthed new energy in Strom. Panting, carrying both his load and Elisif's, he found a last wind and pulled ahead of them.

"You must dig in! Lash whatever you can together. Gather food, water . . ." Fire crushed his lungs. His throat grated sandy when he yelled.

The Alizandar laughed gaily, making light of his demands. The children joyfully imitated his alien gestures. Shouting Enickor's name, he broke from the pack and ran the last two kilometers into the village at top speed. Zaich and Elisif tried to keep up. The throng of loagers rushing from the village swallowed them.

Once Strom reached the edge of the village, Landah and Enickor heard his shouts. Urgency knifed the afternoon. They hurried from the cottage.

Inorag cur Maha and Pindar followed, curious.

"Ah, your friend has arrived. He certainly could never be mistaken for one of us, could he?" The leader laughed. "Look at that hair! It is strange to these old eyes."

Enickor sniffed the air and looked westward.

Strom was too tired to speak coherently. He pointed at the Lyndirlyan. "Helix," was all he managed to say. Hands on his knees, he hung his head and tried to catch his breath.

"They're here. We are out of time to talk. Inorag, get your people together. It has begun." Enickor slapped Landah's shoulder. The lad went into the cottage and returned with two sets of all-weather gear.

Strom sat, elbows straight on his knees, his head low between them. He coughed a few times and spat out mucus.

"What can they do to us from the Lyndirlyan Mountains? We are days away from them. You worry too much, Enickor. You take this leadership of the Harcel too seriously. Relax . . ."

Enickor silenced the old man with a look. "Have you ignored everything I have said? All my warnings? Do you feel the Alizandar exempt from the tragedy befalling the rest of Chiyune? Can you really be that blind, Inorag?"

Disgusted, Enickor turned away. "Perhaps it is you who does not take your leadership seriously enough, Inorag. This is no political game for you to play with me. Death is coming. It is going to reach out of the sky and rip the bowels from the mountains." He turned back and glared harshly at Inorag. "It will touch the Alizandar. We cannot defeat it. We can only hope to outride it now."

"What is the matter with you people?" Panting, Strom used a porch support to get on his feet, then swung the heavy pack from his back. "I am a Star Follower. And I am telling you, if you don't do something quickly, you are all going to die!"

Red-faced, Inorag turned on Enickor. "I will not tolerate your insults, Enickor val Densu, and those of your friend are reprehensible. You are no longer welcome here."

"Before you try to throw us out of your little paradise you had better listen to what's headed your way." Strom's voice was low, his eyes unblinking. The menace of his presence began to assert itself.

"I do not want to hear about faraway ships. It is the word of the loags that Star Followers do not speak the truth. They say what is to their advantage to say. Nothing more."

"Listen, my old friend," Pindar said, and gently laid a hand upon the Leader's shoulder. "It cannot hurt to hear the words

212

of this man." He glanced at Strom for assurance. "Star Follower or not, he will suffer our fate if he is right."

Strom seized the opening. "Soldiers. Tired, hungry, sick, and desperate. They are on the Plains of Akatna os Egra now. There are not many. They eat the wrong things and are poisoned, but they have drugs, and live a long time after they should have died. If they survive the helix ship mining, they will come here, hungry, angry, and near death."

Strom pulled out his all-weather suit and began putting it on.

"With the helix over the eastern Lyndirlyan, the best thing that can happen now is that you will survive long enough for more soldiers to come. Once they arrive, they will take your women and misuse them. They will plunder your stores. As soon as they are rested they will become bored. A few will play deadly games, using your children as pawns." His voice lowered to a whisper for effect. "As I said, that is the best that can happen to the Alizandar."

He stood, keyed the last fastener of his all-weather suit and hoisted his pack. "I know this to be true because I have seen it done. Another time, another place, I sat and watched and did nothing. It was not pleasant, and the children were not mine. They belonged to the enemy. In the end, all of them were killed."

Landah followed Enickor down the two steps to the ground. Awed, he hung on each of Strom's words, wondering if he spoke the truth, or lied to scare the Alizandar into listening. He could not recall Strom ever lying.

Strom glanced westward and swore a long oath. Two heartbeats later he was beside Inorag cur Maha, his *kalase* shoved deep into the old man's ribs, and holding a wrinkled left wrist high up the man's back.

"As I said, I am a Star Follower, old man. A very particular kind of Star Follower. I earned my living by killing people. It did not matter who they were. Most of the time I didn't care, either. After awhile, one corpse looks like another. It is a very special talent, and I am greatly gifted with it.

"I'm going to take care of you, then your friend here." He looked at the Metaliary. "What's your name?"

No answer.

"What's your name?" he shouted and pulled hard on cur Maha's arm.

"Pindar."

"Pindar. Good. You want to see your friend tomorrow?" The steel in Strom's voice carried through the compound. Loagers gathered silently in the center. Their fear shone in the afternoon.

Pindar stood tall. "Yes. All of us wish to see him on the morrow. He is our Leader. Please, we will do as you ask. We are not a violent people. What you are doing . . . ?"

"I know what I'm doing." Seeing Pindar's sincerity, he eased the pressure on the leader's arm.

"Get those people into the strongest buildings you have. I want all the food, water, clothing, bedding this loag has sorted quickly and divided into the buildings. Get it there now!"

Enickor moved people, telling them what to get, and designating work groups. He deemed Strom's tactics effective, if politically unsound. He had contemplated drastic measures himself, even prior to the Star Follower's wild arrival.

Landah went to the storehouses and started covering the holes used as breather vents.

"Hurry up!" Strom's tone charged the meek Alizandar into action.

"You will pay for this," Inorag hissed.

Strom glanced north, then pulled his wrist higher to shut him up. "You watch what is about to happen, old man. Watch very closely so you never forget who saved your loag. If you live through it, you can thank me. And if we do not survive what is coming, I hope you rot in the Seven Hells for your stupidity."

A brown stain spread over the prairie. Clouds condensed and turned black in the east and south. They rushed at a phenomenal pace to close the gap to the Lyndirlyan.

The air thickened and turned cold. The bright afternoon disappeared. The wind blew, gathering speed, pushing the loagers.

Fear gripped the Alizandar.

A young woman threw herself at Inorag's feet. Arms wrapped about his ankles, she wept on his sandals and implored him to make the clouds retreat. She clawed at the ground, babbling and crying for him to take charge of the sky, finally demanding that he save her from the chaos riding in the wind.

Shaken by the sudden change in the weather, Inorag had few words to say.

Strom ordered her up and told her to get some bedding for

214

the building to which she had been assigned. Screaming hysterically, she ran toward to the river and threw herself in.

Mildly concerned, Strom asked, "Can she swim?"

"What is swim?" Inorag's voice was barely audible.

"Handle herself in the water?"

Proud of the Alizandar customs, the Leader straightened as much as Strom would allow. "Women are permitted on the shore for the washing of clothing and their bodies. They have no water skills."

Flat-toned, "You mean she just killed herself?"

"She has chosen the company of the river god to that of the Alizandar. She has no man to fend for her." His voice cracked. "She has despaired in her Leader." Softly, to himself, "The river god accepts all into his embrace."

Across the compound, Enickor sorted people and selected buildings. He made inspections to determine the sturdiest, and split loagers into more groups. When the chaos dwindled and the majority of them were quartered, he made the rounds of the cottages and huts.

He found an old couple clinging to one another. He could not bring himself to physically eject them.

They pleaded with him, wanting to meet the river god in the place they had shared their lives.

Enickor assessed them closely. If one died, the other would follow shortly. Should they survive the impending holocaust, they would never survive the raft trip or the badlands crossing.

Touched by their devotion to one another, he knelt beside them and prayed. "May the river god enjoin the god of wind on your behalf. May there be peace where the river and the wind meet the meadow."

The old woman gave him a toothless grin before he closed the door to move on.

The younger ones were forced to the main buildings, and reminded what price Strom would extract from Inorag if their cooperation faltered.

The Star Follower shouted more directions from the cottage porch, singling out workers, redirecting them, and deploying those who had unburdened themselves back to the storehouses.

The running columns diminished. The booty looted from their homes, the strongest storehouses were sealed for the onslaught ahead.

The sky had turned as dark as a starless night by the time

215

Strom pushed Inorag into the smaller common hut. He called to Enickor.

"Straight ahead, Strom."

He followed the sound. Enickor reached out and grabbed him. The two settled. Landah flanked Strom. His popularity had suffered an irreparable blow in the Alizandar, even if his actions did save lives.

Soon it became hard to breathe. There were cries, gasps, and the sound of choking for several minutes before it became too difficult for the sounds of fear.

Enickor reached behind Strom to give Landah a reassuring pat on the back.

The fury raged across the prairie with a force greater than Enickor anticipated. The open, flat land posed nothing to deter the blast.

He wondered how they could mine the Lyndirlyan, knowing they had people there, knowing the dire consequences. Try as he might, he could not remember anything in old Lord Jeffires's attitude which made him think he regarded life so cheaply.

Or was trust so lacking that miners and soldiers were kept independent and separate, ignorant of one another's plans? Was the political need to outperform the rival House so great for both lords? He could not imagine Hadilka wasting good guards and paid mercenaries if he knew of their presence. Loagers, yes. Soldiers, no. Soldiers were of value in the eyes of the Overeechy.

The rock told of a wrongness so great that it burned the Quniero. They clambered from the tunnels they were constructing for a leah. The stench of death made their nostril beards stick straight out.

The fear and sorrow which rolled through the rock and the wind struck at their hearts. They banded together, seeking solace, understanding, and possession of mind.

The gaping wound in the heart of the mountains rattled the spires. Cliffs fell. Valleys filled with deposed rock. Rivers changed their courses. The Head would not die without her progeny knowing who was the slayer. The agony of her death tremored the Lyndirlyan, rumbled the Gorbich Hills and stretched down the coast as far as the Southern Rohn. Tidal waves unbalanced the ocean. The rock bridge connecting Shirwall with the mainland crumbled.

Illeuro and his nekka huddled at the mouth of the crumbling leah. He cried for the living land as she fought her enemy.

By the second day hail beat through the roof of the larger of the three common houses. A few who were not trapped by the debris or killed outright made their way to the adjacent house. They were near death by the time the doors were unbarricaded to admit them.

Water began seeping upward, through the floorboards, on the third day.

The fourth day: the hail stopped, the rain began. The water was several centimeters high in the two remaining common houses.

A fetid aroma clung to the soggy ipcar walls of the common. Once the wind eased, tables and boxes which had been piled against the window flaps were removed. Even the outside air was oppressive.

Enickor left the common and waded out to what was left of the Alizandar village.

The other common house stood intact. A man and woman were arguing loudly. No one would interrupt.

The land was devoid of green. The murky river raced in its bed and continued to flood the upper land. On the other side it stretched as far as the dismal rain allowed him to see.

"Mistress?" he whispered. "Mistress, can you hear me?"

No voice rose from the dingy water to fill his head.

Mistress, please answer. Let me know you are still with me.

I am with you always, Enickor. She was weak, distant. Pain filled the aura she projected. *Save the rest of my children. So many are gone.*

He wanted to ask how she knew, who and where the survivors were. She left him immediately, the strain of a prolonged visit too great.

It took several minutes to collect his thoughts. The argument in the near common ended. He waded through the mud and knee-high water to the stairs.

"Open up. We must organize."

The only response was silence.

He banged on the door with his fist and demanded that they open it.

Timid sounds leaked through the cracks around the door. A harsh flurry of whispers and a loud protest followed. Steadily the barriers were pulled away until the door opened a crack.

Enickor forced it over the warped, waterlogged floor. The odor rushing out to meet him took his breath away. He stepped back and waited for them to come out.

Zaich moved toward the threshold, holding Elisif's hand. Both squinted against the light. Their all-weather suits were soiled. They had remained dry inside.

Stunned, Enickor could not speak. When he had given up any hope of seeing the two before him, he did not know. The sight of Elisif made his heart ache. She looked weary, troubled. Gone was the twinkle in her blue eyes, the pink which always rouged her cheeks, and the feeling of life that had surrounded her.

In his rush he stumbled on the stair, then reached out and grabbed her. She felt so good against him. Her arms went around his neck. Even now her kiss was sweet.

Elisif treasured the moment and lost herself in the constant whirl of emotion which always engulfed her when in his arms. The black events since their parting, and the awesome journey through the Head when they feared him dead, were kept at bay. Now was not the time for soul-baring honesty. It was time to feel the love, which seemed as though it was going to burst inside of her.

He had lived with losing her by not thinking about her, not thinking about anything that did not strictly relate to his goal of gathering the loags and moving south. What happened on the way happened. There was no changing it, no going back, no undoing it. The anguish when he realized just how he had regarded her loss lessened in her arms. Murmuring her name, wanting time to stand still so he could remain holding her, he knew he never wanted to be away from her again.

Zaich clapped him on the shoulder. Enickor reached out and gathered the older man into the circle of their embrace.

His family was together.

The truth of her situation crashed upon her. Would she ever be able to look at Zaich and forget the ugly time they shared? "We must talk, Enickor." Elisif's words trembled in his ear.

"Not now. But tell me how you got here." He leaned back and brushed the hood from her hair.

Zaich was surprised, and took a backward step. "Your friend, Strom Aknel, brought us. He is a strange, strange man, Enickor. I would not want him for an enemy," Zaich said, then grinned. Rain bounced off his nose and cheeks. "Did he not tell you of . . ." His voice faded, as did his joy. He glanced at Elisif.

She pulled back and turned away.

"Tell me what?"

"Yo! What is taking you people so long to get your things together?" Strom yelled across the breech. "We must build some rafts. In a hurry. By tomorrow, this rain will raise the water up to our shoulders. We have to be on the river by then."

Behind Strom came Pindar and Inorag cur Maha. The seclusion had not repaired the damage suffered by the Leader at the hands of the Star Follower, but it had given Inorag sufficient time for reflection. The fragility of Chiy-une and the delicate nature of the Alizandar had become painfully obvious. His self-confidence was shaken. Dazed, he prepared to listen and follow for the time being.

"Get all the men out here!" Strom ordered. "Pindar! Start the women and children to work wrapping supplies in waterproof sheets. You do have some, don't you?"

"Yes, Strom Aknel. We have some." Pindar returned to the common. Moments later the men began filing out.

Inorag lifted his already wet and filthy robes and crossed the breach to Enickor.

"Maybe you can help get people moving and working together?" Enickor asked him.

"Yes. Strom Aknel will once again have his way." His voice lacked its usual malice. He commenced giving commands. Men finished clearing the door immediately.

The walls of the commons were torn down and lashed together to make multitiered, reinforced rafts. Supplies were divided, wrapped in portions for easier usage and distributed among the four rafts. Two of the craft had lean-to roofs built on to them for the babies and smallest children to be sheltered.

A steady rain pounded on the loagers, turning their unprotected skin a dull red. They worked without a break. The day dulled further and became night.

The Alizandar slept huddled together on the remains of floors, under the roof shards supported by corner skeletons.

Morning came, bringing more water.

The Alizandar had shrunk to a hundred and forty-nine. Four from the Harcel, plus Strom, who did not belong anywhere and felt he was in excellent company with Enickor van Densu on that score, made the four rafts barely sufficient.

As a precaution, Enickor and Strom tied the rafts together.

The lead one, the smallest, was ridden by the heartiest men and women. The Harcel remained together, with Strom on the spearhead. Two ropes, one on each side of the rear, angled back to two additional rafts, each clear of the other in varying distances and attached to the last raft, which carried the elderly and youngsters.

Each craft had a strong complement of men for steering, poling and guiding, such as they could.

Once the rafts were loaded, their cargoes lashed tightly, and the passengers loosely fastened on lifelines attached to beams of the rafts, Pindar made a final invocation.

The Harcel and Strom remained stoic and unmoved by the Metaliary's chant. Sobs and crying jags were the only sounds before Strom called out that the first raft was free. The loag silenced.

The river caught it immediately and snapped the lines fast as it sucked it out to the center. The second followed, then the third, and finally the fourth.

Swirls and eddies bespoke the deep turmoil of the brown water. The rafts glided over the surface, bobbing gently, as though a sleeping beast allowed them passage to the sea.

The rain continued. By evening the shores were invisible, the flood basin of the river vast and growing as the highlands drained.

Night was fear-ridden. The rafts traveled the river's backbone, carrying blind cargoes. And in the midst of the darkness Enickor listened to Elisif and Zaich relate their escape from the Lyndirlyan and subsequent capture on the eastern slope on the outskirts of the Great Iyigna Valley.

The Harcel Leader knew his obligation concerning both the loag and Elisif. He had sworn to take care of her.

"Elisif, are you with child?" His voice was soothing, non-judgmental.

"I think so."

He felt her turn away and embraced her to pull her back. "Can you say with certainty that the child is not mine?" Her head moved slightly against his chest. "Then there is no point in discussing it. I know I am not true Harcel blood, and we can cross that later, after the child is born, after we are settled in the south.

"Unless you have changed your mind, and no longer wish

to be at my side, I would not dream of giving you away. I care a great deal for you, Elisif. I want you to stay with me."

She cried softly and held him, happy once again.

The next morning Strom ate Zaich's breakfast ration.

Chapter 24

THE MOUNTAINS RUMBLED FOR THE REST OF THE day and into the night. Quakes shook the hills. They chose a wide clearing for night camp. Neither had spoken since the afternoon.

"Why did you decide to come back to find me?"

Pam-ella took a long time before answering. "It mattered to me what happened to you. The danger, and all. There has been too much pain, Friedo. People I care about...

"I could not let you be one more, Friedo. Not while there was a possibility I might be able to prevent it."

She saw his perplexity and smiled. "I know. I did my share of black morality back on the mountain. It just happened. Maybe I have lost my mind, or part of it."

The tent was warm and dry. The saddles and burdens lay near the flap. The thrum of steady rain beat on the dome. Outside, Faelinor crooned at the night.

"To want to go to Hadilka? I am forced to agree with you on that score, Pam-ella. His questionable character aside, the man has the subtlety and finesse of a cannibal when it comes to his wives. On principle, many of the women in court refuse to stay in the same room with him." He grabbed her shoulders and shook her once. "He could hurt you, Pam-ella. Really hurt you, in more than a physical sense. Once you marry him, you are bound to him and the House of Hadilka. By law you will be forced to honor any agreement he makes in your name."

"I will have to live with that. Friedo, it is impossible for you to know how I feel inside. It's like . . . like I'm stagnating, rotting in the ruins of the Porintel. I saw their faces.

"They were ghosts marching across the land.

"I cannot carry around this guilt. Don't you see that he is already acting in my name, and what he is doing is worse than anything he could do to me? I cannot go through life knowing it was me they were looking for when they sacked the Porintel. I might be able to put an end to their hunt through the loags. It is within my power. I can *do* something! Can you understand that? Me. Pam-ella Jeffires, who has never really done anything for anybody my whole life. Now the time has come for me to act. Already I have enjoyed more freedom on the land than my life-plan allowed.

"I can stop this, this killing of loagers, this fighting on the land between the Houses. It is an atrocity. I must do what is within my power to preserve the rest of the loags from the fate of the Porintel, at the least."

Friedo exploded and shook her. "Damn! You, Enickor, me. What's the difference? To the Porintel—none.

"Hadilka's animals? Do you think it would have made a difference to them? They get paid to kill."

She touched his cheek. Her feelings for this particular Star Follower had become quite genuine, and very deep, somewhere along the way. He had been good to her. And he cared for her. Another time, another life, a different outcome, she was sure.

"It made a difference to me, Friedo. And that is where it counts the most. Those people trusted me not to bring ill their way. The loags looked upon me as something special. Yes, they feared me. And, sometimes, I was afraid of them. But I went. And they took me in again and again.

"Oh, Friedo. Have you any idea how many times I would have died if it had not been for the loags or their hunting parties? The first year alone ineptitude should have killed me dozens of times." She smiled. "But I lived, because of them, because I'm stubborn, and because I had a goal."

The rain hammered the silence. Payndacen released her but did not move away.

"Had? You really believe Enickor is dead?" He felt weak and mentally pleaded for her to say no.

"I must."

"No. He has to be alive."

"He may be. To me, he is dead. It must be that way. Even if he isn't, he was an adolescent fantasy, someone I loved, but not in the way I thought I did three years ago. My father and Hoyiv never approved of him. We clung to each other. Perhaps their disapproval drove me even closer to him." A vague smile passed over her lips. "He was a good brother. The best. The Enickor I set out to look for does not exist beyond the fantasy world of a lonely fifteen-year-old.

"Now I have an opportunity to do something for this land and its people who have kept me alive long enough to start knowing myself, Friedo. It is not so great a price.

"Besides," she continued, unable to hold her gaze on him, "think of the political advantages this marriage represents to the Overeechy. There will even be a temporary peace there. I hope your father makes the most of it."

"Hadilka? Marrying him is the equivalent of committing suicide."

Hurt, she nodded. "The alternative is more painful to me."

"Enickor val Densu is my brother, Pam-ella. Half brother." He had tried to prepare himself for her reaction. An inward flinching evident in her face touched him. Her head bowed a little bit lower. Softly, "I wanted to find him so badly I left the Overeechy. I will have to face the consequences for doing that later. It was worth it then. It is worth it now.

"I started by searching for you. When I found you . . . When I found you I wasn't quite prepared. I mean . . ."

He paused for a few heartbeats. "You affected me deeply. I was not prepared for anything emotional. I ended up caring for you. I listened to your rambling when you were sick. I worried about you when you were with the tornas. And . . ."

"Torna-poks," she murmured, not looking up.

"Damn it! Will you listen to what I'm saying—not the words?" His shout disrupted Faelinor's croon. The winsong began again, the tone more soothing.

She looked up, but did not lift her head. "What are you saying?"

"I am trying to tell you I love you, Pam-ella." He let the words sink into both of them. "I love you. And you were in love with my brother."

He breathed deeply and exhaled slowly. "For a time, I wondered if I would be able to kill him for you."

Her head lifted, horrified. Tears caught on her lower lids.

"I could have it done." The snap of his fingers was loud in the tent.

"You would not..." The arc her head made grew larger with each shake.

"No. I couldn't. But I thought about it. And I also knew you would eventually find out." He laughed sadistically. "I'd probably end up telling you—like now. I have a weakness for truth sessions with those I care about. It matters.

"Don't go back to Shirwall. Don't use Hadilka as a way out of the guilt you feel. He is a terrible weapon. Don't..." Voice cracking, the words stopped coming.

"I am stronger than I look, Friedo. Suppose I am not the one who loses at one of his games? What if it is the other way around? Suppose that were to happen after were were married, Friedo?"

He looked across the small gap between them. Her eyes shone with menace. A special kind of hatred radiated from her. She looked like granite, not porcelain. The true portent of her decision struck him like a blow. Fear for her became a mounting dread.

"I would be rich, Friedo, powerful—one of the most influential, possibly even *the* most influential, woman in the Overeechy." Her eyes narrowed as she leaned forward, sharing her conspiracy in a whisper. "Do you have any idea how happy most of Hadilka's enemies will be to be rid of him? How delighted some of the other Houses will be? The colonies will be too busy to mourn.

"You are right, Friedo. He is a beast; cunning and infected with the diseases of greed and sadism. He holds most life cheaply. Except his own. He lacks principles and morals. He cannot be counted on to lie or tell the truth in any dealings."

She leaned back, hands folded in the cradle of her legs. "I know all of this. I know it well. I have lived with the threat of having to submit to him for most of my life. The price of peace. That is what I was to be to both Houses. The bridge over which friendship would be extended. I know more about him than he's taken the time to learn about himself.

"His weaknesses are simple. The fastest way to his easy side is through his ego, through vanity." Sighing, "I also know he's the staunchest, best defender of the Overeechy in the

Sellbic system, and the only House holding back the Corchi advance. He is brilliant when it comes to military strategy. That has been evidenced too many times to question."

She sat up straight. The malaise of evil had disappeared. "Peace there will be. I have a definite feeling that my Lord Hadilka will not enjoy a long life after we are married."

The statement was so matter of fact, it shook Payndacen.

"Surely you are not serious, Pam-ella. He has a loyal complement around him all the time. He . . ."

"Would you like their names, ages, marital status, rank, years of service, pay, duties? Name it." A deadly calm settled over her.

"There have been many attempts to assassinate him. I sat in on one of the trials." He swallowed hard. "I also had to sit in on the execution. Hadilka picked the form. It took all afternoon."

As he spoke he watched her, and knew he was weakening. Her decision was firm. He could not change it. There was enough madness in her fanaticism to give her the necessary edge.

"How? How could it be done?" Fascination began to replace his anxiety.

Head shaking, she smiled. "I'm not sure, yet. It is something that I know without knowing how I know it. At the same time, I am certain that it will not be . . ." She paused, confused, then resumed slowly. "Maybe it will be natural . . . Don't worry."

The sound of rain again dominated the tent. Payndacen was deep in thought.

"You have thought this through?"

"For a long time. I simply did not know if I could live with myself if I were a party to something like this. And now I do, just as surely as the sun will come up in the morning and the rain is falling right now. It is something I have to do. A debt I owe. One the land will pay."

He took her hand and spread her fingers on his palms. So small and calloused, he noted. "Why?"

"Why? Because I saw the survivors of the Porintel. I can look at Hadilka and see the dead babies, the children. I know what was done. I have been a witness to his leavings." She met his gaze, remembering the torna-pok surging through the Arch to the Upper Creel. "My greatest concern is that it will be too easy and I will get anxious. The first time he touches

226

me . . ." She shuddered, steeled herself and regarded him in full composure.

"It will be easy, Friedo. Believe me."

He closed his hand around hers. "And when it is over? What then? Will you continue looking for Enickor?"

"No. Even if he were alive, I could not stand his judgment. He was even more strong-willed than I. He is also a Chiy-uneite. He believes in preserving life.

"I could never explain why it is a question of my survival or Hadilka's." A half-smile lightened her mood. She squeezed his hand in return. "There is a great deal you have to learn about the man you're looking for, Friedo. He is one of a kind. Chiy-une is black and white where judgments are concerned. And I am composed of a million shades of gray."

"It seems all of us Star Followers are made of the leftover shades of gray the Chiy-une people sloughed off. We are civilized, educated." Sarcasm did not become him. The truth he heard in his own words stung.

He lapsed into thought again. His father, his mother's ailments, the politics, were all in gray areas. Only the street life he shared with the down-and-outers had true black and white ideals. But there was also a vast middle ground filled with *almosts* and *maybes*. If the grays of that world grew too dark and touched the blacker hues—death was not uncommon in the civilized world. It was often the sole resolution to a problem, even if the magnitude of the problem was not great.

Pam-ella reached over and turned off the light. They disrobed and climbed into their heat bags. She lay still for a long time, and watched the dark dome of the tent.

The little traumas mounting inside her numbed many of her emotions. It was a sad thing, she knew, almost like willing a special form of insanity to keep from going crazy.

The stomach-churning fear that went hand in hand with an outpouring of sweat was a part of the past. She looked into the future and conjured the worst fate she could imagine at Hadilka's hand. Worst case: death. The alternative?

Ardinay's eyes looked through the darkness and into her soul.

Not a bad bargain, she decided. *It will preserve the loags.*

Enickor? At long last she had peace where he was concerned. When the answers came and soothed away the doubts, she did not know. She felt certain her brother—she smiled inwardly, for he was her brother, not the fantasy lover she had

imagined to find on the beach across from Shirwall—her
brother would have encouraged her to do just as she was doing.
The longer she delayed going to Shirwall and honoring the
nuptial bonds old Lord Jeffires had signed, the greater the
smudge on the House of Jeffires's honor.

There would be a brighter day, she hoped. If she survived,
she would always have a friend in the Overeechy. Friedo Payndacen would one day be Kriell. What had come over her on
the mountainside? She had used him as bait in a snare.

Friedo.

Her left arm came out of her bag. She reached across the
narrow strip of tent flooring and touched him.

"Friedo?"

"Hum?"

"Are you asleep?"

"No."

"Are you tired?"

"No."

"Are you angry?"

"No."

"Will you make love to me?"

He turned to look at her in the dark but could not see her.

"I've never . . . well. I want to give it freely for the first
time. Will you?"

Such a simple question. Two answers.

He found her groping hand and held it. How many times
had he wanted her? He couldn't count them.

Only in dreams did she ask him such a question. Always
the outcome was the same.

Now she was asking and it was real.

He felt like the one who would be left behind the next
morning when the great battle none would survive commenced.
One time. That was it. Over. Tomorrow everthing would be
changed.

Yet he was choked up, genuinely touched by the honor she
was trying to bestow on him.

As an answer he unfastened his bag and pulled her toward
him. She was only partially clothed, warm and unsure of what
to do.

"I love you, Pam-ella."

She wished she could reply in kind, but did not have to.
Friedo found her mouth and was in no hurry to end the reality
of having her and return to fantasy.

228

*   *   *

The nekka remained huddled around Illeuro for most of the night while the land cried in agony. Her wounds were grievous.

Clouds gathered over the Lyndirlyan and wept Chiy-une's tears. The loss of the land rangtur effected Illeuro far greater than isolation. The chasm of black aloneness ate at his being.

The nekka sensed his crisis and pressed closer, nearly crushing him on the outside while the bane's presence threatened the same inwardly.

Not until the gray dawn did Chiy-une ease her hold upon the Quniero. Illeuro was then able to separate himself from the ravaged land. Weakened, he reorganized the nekka. There would be no leah in this part of the Lyndirlyan.

The land called to them. Illeuro felt they must answer. She had absolved their commitment to the caretakers and usurped their allegiance.

The nekka began the long return to the remnants of the Upper Lyndirlyan. The land needed rebuilding, the mutated rock and elements required the expertise of the Quniero to mutate them back to their former compositions.

The nekka moved as one toward the dull eastern crags. They sang a dirge for the land and the living rock around them that had lost brothers beyond the peaks. The sound was rare even on Alidanko.

Chiy-une had found an ally among those who had come from the stars.

The rain fell more gently.

The rain had ebbed to a drizzle by midmorning. Friedo and Pam-ella spoke little after making love a second time. Desperation to achieve the solace of another person had crept into the act. When it was done, a heavier gloom descended over them.

Without saying so, each knew the other wanted to stay the day and forestall the inevitable.

Breakfast went slowly, after which Payndacen gave her an extra all-weather suit he had packed for her.

It took longer to break camp and load their mounts than ever before. Pam-ella refused eye contact.

They rode north for half the morning before the silence was broken.

"Thank you," she said, finally looking directly at him.

"Thank you, she says after I tell her I love her, beg her not to leave me, and give her my body." Friedo looked skyward.

She smiled in spite of his semiseriousness. "You know how we pseudo-Star Followers are: unprincipled, selfish, love and run."

"I'm afraid so," he muttered, wishing it were not true in this case.

Theller paused, sneezed, then sneezed again.

"Trouble." Pam-ella judged the terrain, berating herself for not being more defensive. Her plan worked best if Friedo was free and she willingly returned to Shirwall. A delay now was doom for more of the loagers.

Payndacen, too, had fallen into a self-deceiving lull, unaware of the pitfalls of the route they had taken to reach the sea. Quickly he gauged his position in reference to Banter.

Ten, maybe fifteen minutes. Long enough to get killed.

"Faelinor," he whispered, "weave fear."

The winsong began slowly. The melody spun a mood and grew louder. His face changed shape a hundred times in a few minutes, each note and mood painstakingly designed and shaped before touching the misty air of Chiy-une.

Friedo jumped, nearly unseating himself when a hand closed around his booted ankle.

"Call him off."

With a sigh of relief, Friedo did as requested. An eerie silence lingered.

Dismounted, he hurried to embrace the man. "Magaikan— am I glad to see you! I've hoped to run into you for some time. You sure look good!"

"And you, Sire, look terrible."

Sneezing, Theller retreated steadily. Pam-ella's eyes were wide. The rush of humanity through the scrub made her wary. The *kalase* warmed her hand.

"Pam-ella! Come on over. It is safe. We have an escort now."

The roh halted. She wondered what would happen if she turned and ran. To where? Freedom was too expensive.

When she did not prod the sneezing roh forward, Payndacen and Magaikan went to her. After a quick introduction she relaxed, but only because Friedo was so at ease.

At the Uv-Kriell's suggestion Pam-ella dismounted. She walked between the two men, through the appearing ranks of soldiers in front of them. At first Theller followed, finally passing the trio to walk alone, upwind from the Star Followers. Faelinor joined him.

"Where were you headed?" Magaikan asked.

"Shirwall," Pam-ella answered.

"Oh, you are returning home." He glanced at her. A hardness set her chin.

"No, Commander. I am going to visit Shirwall temporarily."

The commander digested her mood in silence.

"Have you any news of Enickor val Densu?" asked Payndacen as he looked at Pam-ella.

The pause made both of them look to the commander. "Not exactly. Rumors, mostly. If he is still alive he may be traveling with the remains of the Harcel Loag."

"'The remains?'" Pam-ella echoed, alarmed. "What do you mean, 'the remains'?"

Magaikan pointed to a fork in the trail. "They were mined over."

"What do you mean 'mined over'?" Payndacen asked.

"Exactly what you think it means, Sire. No warning. No envoy. Lord Hadilka's helix ship mined the land under the loag. The only ones who survived were near the ocean. My men found them and brought them into camp.

"We had a guest at the time, a rather interesting individual. The survivors knew him." He gazed down at the ground and held a branch out of the way. "What a sorry lot. Some girl carrying her dead brother, an old spiritual man who I swear had been dead for hours and was still talking."

"The Metaliary? Adaia?" Pam-ella asked, anxious.

"I believe so. Yes. They called him that in the ceremony they had. Damndest people! Went out in a sleet storm to pray to the wind."

"The Harcel religious beliefs revolve around the wind. The wind god, Ieuchna, roams the surface of Chiy-une, gathering souls, telling secrets, offering solace to the lonely with his songs. The name Ieuchna is sacred. His birthplace is revered by the Porintel and in their territory. His name is rarely spoken among the Harcel Loag."

"How is it that you know so much about their religion?" Magaikan was as interested in her vast knowledge as he appeared.

"I am fraen-spu to the loags, Commander. A witch who touches all the gods, believes in none, and speaks their names

231

without fear. It was ignorance on my part which won such a title for me."

She took a deep breath. "Tell me," and exhaled, "was there any mention of Keladine Ornasive? Have you have any news of the Alizandar, the Porintel, or Ocandar?"

"The Ocandar are headed south along the ocean. They are still intact; well, almost. The House of Jeffires chased them off."

"Oh."

"The Alizandar are also headed south and seaward down the river. They were spotted by one of our survey ships. The river flooded the long territory after the eastern Lyndirlyan were mined."

Pam-ella stumbled. "The Porintel went into the Lyndirlyan. . . ." They walked in silence for half a kilometer.

Magaikan slowed. "If they were as far east as the Head Forest line . . ."

"They would have been." She felt Ardinay's eyes looking at her again. Pausing, she gazed at the Lyndirlyan and heard the cries of the Porintel. "Friedo, they are gone now. Dead. The entire Porintel Loag."

His hand grasped hers. For a moment he thought he could hear agonizing screams coming from the Lyndirlyan. "What can I do to help you, Pam-ella?"

Astonished, she looked up at him. "Do you realize what you are committing yourself to? My God, Friedo, you are the Uv-Kriell! You cannot afford to know me, let alone help me with what I must do."

He nodded, not fully understanding why he felt so strongly about ridding Chiy-une of Hadilka, just feeling the unceasing drive which fueled his decision.

The screams reached his ears and did not leave the echo of his memory for a long time.

Chapter 25

Rᴀɪɴ ꜰᴇʟʟ ꜰᴏʀ ᴛʜʀᴇᴇ ᴅᴀʏꜱ ᴀɴᴅ ɴɪɢʜᴛꜱ ʙᴇꜰᴏʀᴇ
the rafts were carried beyond the zone.

The river had become an inland sea ranging to all horizons.
Occasionally an island appeared. Trees still clinging to such
rarities had been stripped bare by the hordes of prairie creatures
seeking sanctuary and feeding off what was left of their domain.

Gries circled, disappeared, and cried despairingly.

The rafts were pulled down the river by the eddies and
currents controlled by the deep water. The shallows on both
sides were also cajoled seaward by the might of the main flux.

By the sixth morning the prairie took on changes. The stark
guardian cliffs protecting the Qeakine Knolls were visible
against the gray sky.

The most dangerous leg of their journey lay in the hazardous
twists and turns formed by the cliffs guarding the rich land
known as the Qeakine Knolls. Enickor no longer worried about
the rocks which jutted above the surface when last he walked
the heights leading to the knolls. The river was high enough
to cover not only the rocks, but some of the lower knolls, too.

He and Strom discussed strategy, debating whether it was
better to thread the Qeakine collectively and remain tied to-

gether, or pull tight, redistribute the people, and run for the Knolls separately at intervals.

"Look at those people on number two. Regardless of how we divided them, we could not keep the children secure on that one and man it to make the crossing." Strom gazed at the raft behind them on the left. "Look at the water. It's too rough to risk it. They will have to make do the way they are." Worried, Strom tested the towrope.

"It won't be smoother once we pass the guard rocks." Enickor pulled hard on the tiller. "Landah!"

"Yes?" He stepped over Elisif and met Enickor.

"How are they faring? Is there anything else we can do?"

Landah visually rechecked each of his inspection stations as he spoke. "All the cargo is lashed. Everyone has a safety line. I have checked each tie-on. We are out of rope, though. If we need more, we will have to take it from the raft ties."

"No!" Enickor shouted louder than necessary. "No one touches those ties. These rafts may not make it as they are. If one bond is weakened, and we're tied together . . ." Enickor's voice trailed as he envisioned the disaster.

"Number four would never survive alone, not even with the six men we put at the tiller," Strom said softly, then filled his gaze with Elisif. It was hard to stay away from her at times. More than he wished she were not Enickor's, he wished that she did not love him. The double negative left him in the cold with only his growing emotions to keep him company at night.

"What will you do? See how the river narrows. We will be killed." Inorag cur Maha wrung his hands. The raft trip had daily aged him the equivalent of a season. And for each kilometer they traveled away from the Alizandar Loag, a new wrinkle etched his face. He had abdicated his leadership to the Harcel and Strom by the fifth morning. The days passed looking upriver to a place only his mind saw. Nights were filled with chants accompanied by the Metaliary's cracking baritone and tears.

"We do the best we can," Enickor answered. Gently he led the old man to his special place on the raft. "You must keep seated. Please, do not untie the rope again, Inorag. You are Leader of the Alizandar. They will need your wisdom and strength when this journey is ended."

The Leader sat, a beaten man, his eyes turned upward. A trembling attempt at a smile showed that he almost believed Enickor.

Pindar kept his fears more private than did the Leader. A position of strength, the Metaliary worked on forging plans for the future. As much as possible, he ignored the discomforts, the smells, cries, and heartache surrounding him.

The Metaliary put his arms around his old friend and Leader's bowed shoulders, and shared his strength.

"Oh, Pindar, we have outlived our women, the ones we loved, our loag and now, perhaps our usefulness." The Leader met Enickor's gaze and failed to hold it.

"Perhaps you are old and ready for the river, Inorag. But I am not. I am Metaliary. I must be ready to rebuild the Alizandar for my grandchildren. And I must finish training my successor."

The Leader turned to his friend and wept.

Enickor felt helpless, awkward. Brusquely, he moved aside and began shouting orders to the rafts.

Strom had already finished securing the main raft.

Ahead loomed the gates to the Qeakine Knolls. Two basaltic monoliths rose straight out of the angry water. The black stone had been smoothed by time and weather until it exuded a dull luster which made itself known even without the benefit of direct sunlight. The pillars appeared as the last warning signs. Any who passed beyond them entered a hell. White water formed a rampart between the entrance guardians; bubbling and churning.

Apprehension settled heavily upon Enickor. He questioned the wisdom in taking the rafts through to the Qeakine Knolls. But fighting the current to beach them had already proved an impossible task. There were no alternatives.

Mistress, help us. Let the rocks not be too hard or the river too cruel for us. His prayer ended abruptly. The pillars grew steadily as the rafts were sucked closer. They commanded the river and the countryside for kilometers. Staring at the gateway—to death or freedom, Enickor did not know—he recalled the many times he had sought the boulders and rock forests since returning to the land. Always there had been peril, but always there had been a special kind of peace. That same peace seemed to reach out to him from the ominous black walls. Still, it did not soothe him as it had done previously.

The Alizandar began to moan as a whole. The Metaliary's voice rose above their mounting fear with a chant. Soon the loag answered his intonations.

The white water line became visible at the top of a wall. It dropped a meter on the other side.

The pillars blotted out the sky with their mass. The first raft hit the fall. Simultaneously they were plunged into the deep shadows of the gate's arch.

Pindar's voice grew louder and stronger. "And the land shall grace us for the love and labor we have given."

"And pour forth the fruits of her kindness."

Elisif screamed. The raft tipped, then splatted down on the lower water elevation. The timbers groaned. Two cracked.

Strom immediately went to work. He whipped off the waterproof covering from one of the grain carriers and began reinforcing the weakening logs, mumbling about the underside he could not see. Water splashed over him, pulling at his clothing. He held on with his feet and one hand and worked the rigging.

". . . and the sun shall set us free from hunger," Pindar continued, dropping his voice at the end as usual.

Faintly, the loag responded.

Enickor patted Elisif's hip, smiled until she smiled back, then made his way to the tiller and Landah.

Tied off, Enickor, Landah, and two Alizandar men tried to steer the lead raft to the middle of the river and keep it there.

The second and third rafts made it down the water wall intact, thanks to their more rugged construction. The fourth split three timbers.

The roar of the water against the straight basaltic walls drowned out the Metaliary's chant. Fear returned to the loag. Their hopelessness, manifested in tears, was belittled by the spray off the narrow walls and the rush of the water.

The rising and falling action soon produced a new wave of illness.

Enickor watched the tumultuous horizon, straining to see the next turn, the proximity of the walls jutting into the river, and any changes in the water itself. Occasionally his gaze fell to Elisif. Wet, exhausted, Strom joined her and tore strips from his shirt for her to bind his hands with. Confident that his friend would take care of her, he ceased worrying about her.

The passage felt as though it would stretch all the way to the sea. Time ceased to have meaning.

Those at the tillers strained to keep their crafts away from the walls and in line with the lead. The water, once broken by the head raft, did not seem to mend as quickly as it should have. Each successive raft had a comparatively easier task if the tillermen kept it in the groove.

Enickor recognized a second landmark high on the walls. They were a third of the way through the gate. Beyond it a natural arch closed the sides and provided a sturdy footbridge. It was closer to the water than he remembered. True, the river was very high. Maybe it looked different gazing down at the fast-rushing water than watching the landmark approach from below.

Something moved over the top of the arch.

Enickor felt the cold fear of certainty touch his heart once again. It had been a long time since his old nemesis had put an icy finger on him.

"Strom!"

Strom looked around, uncertain.

"*Strom!*" he yelled again, taxing his vocal chords to their limits.

Strom looked back.

Enickor pointed to the arch.

Squinting, Strom examined the heights, talking to Elisif the whole time. Finally he saw movement. He unfastened Elisif's lifeline and tied her to an exterior timber before giving her Enickor's knife.

"If the raft starts to break up, cut that log free and hold onto it for dear life." He touched her cheek and smiled. "It will be the only chance you have. Take it. We'll meet you downriver." Still smiling at her bewilderment, he moved aft.

"Trouble?" Enickor asked.

"It could be," Strom shouted back.

"Pindar! Chant!"

The Metaliary was glad to follow Enickor's order, and began the Pledge of River Life Xota. The loagers on the first raft followed.

Strom moved to the left rear corner and secured his lifeline. "I never wanted a burial at sea or river," he muttered.

As they entered the bridge shadow the current's swirl reached from the edges of the arch roots and seized them. It beat the water into froth at the edges, then released it downriver in a vee which threatened the raft with another drop from the dangerous wake.

Aknel opened one of the waterproofed chests marked in his scawl and pulled out a long *kalase*. He kept it low, hidden from those watching on the arch; then waited. The more time that passed, the greater became his concentration. He did not expect them to fire on the lead raft. If they were Hadilka-led mercenaries, they would use the third and fourth rafts for their practice, then try to catch the first two downriver if they were still interested.

He felt movement beside him, glanced and was glad to see Enickor with the second long *kalase* pressed to his clothing.

"Can you use it?"

"Mechanically, yes."

"Can you kill with it?"

"Yes." His voice was soft, almost lost in the roar.

The first burst shattered the center of the third raft.

Aknel had the *kalase* raised and discharging before the timber splinters fell back to the river.

Broken logs, waterproofed chests, children, and corpses caught in the current matched pace with the second, then the first rafts before speeding on through the flux.

Strom saw only the arch and the movements at its near edge. He fired repeatedly. More bodies fell into the river. These were uniformed in Hadilka crimson and bright all-weather suits. A few of the men on the footbridge retreated.

Smaller assault weapons unleashed a barrage on the remnants of the third raft. One by one the remaining logs were severed. The loagers with lifelines attached were either pulled underwater as dead weight or struggled to grasp racing log fragments to keep from drowning. Their screams were lost in the rush of the river.

"Hit the arch edges at the cliff," Strom yelled to Enickor. "If we bring it down quickly we might be able to save number four. They're still target-practicing. . . ."

Enickor aimed at the far side of the arch and began to fire. He wished he could make the rock grow instead of killing it. He wished it would cover the river and protect them from the marauders overhead.

He wanted to hide under the Mistress's tender skin and float down a more gentle artery to the sea. How could he save her children with only Strom's help? There was no place to hide and no one to help them.

The *kalase* grew hot.

Swearing, Strom ejected his power supply and slammed in a second. He alternated firing at movement in the center and at the opposite point Enickor was weakening.

A few bursts of return fire boiled the water on both sides

238

of the raft. Ill luck ran on their side. Someone managed to hit the other rope link. It was secured to the second raft.

Suddenly they were moving faster, free of numbers two and four and rapidly increasing the gap between them.

Zaich, Landah, and the two Alizandar struggled valiantly to keep the raft dead center. The ropes they pulled bobbed in the water, the right one attached to three logs, all that remained of the third raft.

"Damn!" Strom lowered his *kalase*. Even with the power alignment scope mounted along the top he could not keep a steady bead. The twists of the river posed the final defeat when they cut off the arch from view and left numbers two and four vulnerable, unprotected.

Sharing his frustration, Enickor glared at the rock, as though he could will each side to rise up, bend to the middle and shelter the Alizandar.

The black walls spread downriver. The ire of the water eased as the width grew.

Most of the heads were turned to the rear, each hoping to get a glimpse of the second raft. No debris caught up with them, but Enickor was not optimistic. They were traveling much faster than previously. It would take the debris longer to reach them.

Elisif joined the Harcel Leader. Her hand wound into his. They kept vigil together.

It was late afternoon when the sedate Qeakine Knolls came into view. Green, grassy, tree-lined, and rolling to the sea, Enickor realized he had forgotten such beauty existed on Chiyune. The ugliness of destruction seemed to have permeated each isle of serenity he touched.

He and Strom took over the tiller. It was easy for two men, now that the water was calm. They guided the raft toward shore and looked for a place to land. The Alizandar needed to spend a night on solid ground. And they could wait to see what might have happened to the other two rafts.

Enickor chose a sharp bay with two exaggerated points jutting far into the lake basin as a place to camp. They were on the out-river side, ready for the swift water. The recessed spot afforded them the luxury of a blazing fire. The risks seemed minimal. Its heat dried out the soggy travelers. A warm meal rekindled their flagging spirits. Watchers dotted the river bank.

The sun was almost gone from the sky when the second and fourth rafts entered the enormous lake basin.

The last piles of wood were heaped onto the fire. The flames grew, sending plumes of smoke into the twilight.

Yells and screams carried over the water and bounced off the hills. Gries called from above, circling the lake in search of a twilight meal.

By nightfall the Alizandar were united.

After they told of their magical escape Pindar questioned them unmercifully. It was impossible for rock to grow. Yet the loagers maintained that it had done so. It had sheltered them from the Star Followers by growing out of the cliff sides and closing over them until they were safely around the bend.

Shaken, Enickor left the fire.

The night was quiet in the Knolls. Sweet air rose from the grass. He walked away from the camp, climbed the side of one hill and down into the valley. Slowly he ascended the next one. The moon illuminated a small patch of clouds and reflected off the water.

Mistress? Are you here?

Yes, my Warrior. You did well today.

No. You did. You spoke to the rock and the rock answered by saving the Alizandar.

Ah, Enickor val Densu. You think me mighty, and I am not. You think yourself small, powerless, and you are not. It was you who commanded the rock. For it is you whom the rangtur gave the power to rock-speak.

I do not understand, Mistress. What have the rangtur to do with rocks?

The rock is living, just as the grass, the trees, and my children. The rangtur know the rock, for they are as old as my bedrock. They were my first children. You, the loags, are my second children, the love of middle age, Enickor, and very special. The time of my respite between the rangtur and you was too great. I am weak, growing weaker.

I do not understand this rock-speaking thing. When did I have this? How? Mentally, he silenced. She was gone.

He climbed to the top of the knoll and looked across the water. A large fire burned brightly on the opposite shore.

The essence of the land rangtur led the Quniero through the decomposing passages of the Lyndirlyan. Deposed cliffs, crumbling aretes, and splintered ipcar decried the assault upon the land.

Volcanoes opened in the sides of mountains, blew off the peaks, and belched a fine black ash ten kilometers into the sky. The lopsided mushroom leaned east as the winds prodded it toward the Upper Lyndirlyan territory.

Tirelessly, Illeuro asa Khatioup led the nekka through the mountains. This was their home. Never again would they bask in the hot sands of Alidanko, nor would they serve caretakers. The land held the key to their bondage, one which they served lovingly.

The ruins were beyond Illeuro's ability to comprehend. He did not think even Gaediv could understand and explain the devastation of living rock.

The Quniero abandoned the surface and sought the quieter depths of the Lyndirlyan. One messenger went out into the mountains to retrace their trail. The land needed a leah here. It would be long, many seasons of katelings, perhaps many Gaedivs, before the land was mended.

Chapter 26

BEFORE THE FIRST FINGERS OF LIGHT REACHED over the eastern knolls, two of the rafts were downriver. The order had been reversed, and now the aged and the young went on without the strength to lead them.

Traveling alone, it would be easy for the lighter single crafts to catch the two-raft tandem on the smoothest part of the trip.

Strom had departed in the middle of the night for a scouting run. The firebuilders across the lake made him very uncomfortable. He did not return until the second raft was pulling away.

"This country is a hotbed of mining survey and sampling activity. They weren't afraid of us. Apparently they watched us pass into the lake area here, and figured we were no threat. And they were tired themselves." He cleared his throat and spat. The pinch in his face betrayed the agony of the long run he had made, as well as the exertion it demanded.

"We should leave quickly, though." Anxious, breathing hard, he glanced around at those listening to him and finally settled on Enickor. "I also think we had better catch up with the other two rafts. There is a lot of tension between the engineering groups since the Quniero went underground. Each

House believes the other one had something to do with the disappearances." He took a deep breath, trying to stretch his lungs beyond capacity. "I overheard that from their scouting party. They had fortified the supply lines, and staked out places where Quniero gemstone caches have been found.

"So we must hurry. There is no way of telling what waits downriver. You saw how restless the guards get."

"Was it that bad?" Enickor scratched his chin through his beard.

"In the knolls—I saw signs." He slumped to the ground and took a deep breath. "You were right. Star Followers are animals. They did not bury their leavings properly for a combat situation. Rank amateurs."

The last raft was loaded. The cargo had been shifted to provide a scant protection for the riders, should they be attacked from the shore lines.

Strom slouched against a chest, his right hand on his knee, his left leg straight. Small muscle quivers spasmed his thighs. Head back, he rested.

"Tired?" Enickor asked, switching sides on the tiller.

"Very."

"Why don't you sleep?"

"I can't." Strom shook his head.

"Why not?"

"My mind needs to run down as far as my body. Some parts of me don't work very well together."

Enickor glanced around. They were isolated and ignored by the rest of the riders. "How bad was it in the knolls?"

"Bad. Halfway to the inlet I came across what was left of a battle. It was not very old, few days maybe. The stench... Terrible. It was ugly, really ugly, Enickor. The worst I have seen.

"Frenzy was all I could think of, like animals who are starving and attack. Except... some soldiers had been dismembered. One choked to death on his own fingers. They had been cut off and shoved down his throat."

He paused, swallowed hard, and continued without opening his eyes. "This place does things to people not from here, Enickor."

"I do not understand what you mean."

Strom took a deep breath and let it out slowly. "I think you do. It has changed me. I feel it working, sometimes. Strange. The force, or whatever it is, the intelligence, has softened parts

243

of me and hardened other parts. It is as though she, Chiy-une, is molding me into what she wants me to be for her." His laugh was hollow. "Like being married for a while, I guess."

Enickor wished the answers would come so easily to him. He wanted to know the names of the thousand little feelings he had developed since leaving the island. The black stone and white beaches were empty now, like the promises of clarity in life. More and more he saw the middle ground where there was no solution, only more problems.

"She says that you are special, Strom, that you are a friend and to be trusted."

"Did she? She may be right—to a point. We will talk about that later. What I saw back there, Enickor—she did it."

"Chiy-une cannot kill . . ."

"No, perhaps not selectively or directly on her own. Not like that. They killed themselves in a battle, and what came after with those who surrendered was something else. She affects Star Followers in a way that they seem obsessed with destroying themselves after they've been here for a while. Violence is the key. That is her weapon." He yawned and let the air out of his lungs in a rush. "Yes, Enickor. That's it. It grows exponentially, like a disease rotting a man's guts.

"There was talk around the camps, but it was always hushed or shunned. Nobody believed in ghosts or living planets, or any native deities seeking revenge. After all, this was a good, clean, guard-duty assignment. All we had to do to earn our pay was escort supply lines and fend off wildlife which might attack the line or the mining groups. The inhabitants were subhuman."

He opened his eyes for the first time and found the steel gray of Enickor's centered upon him. "I didn't tell you that before, did I? That's what they told us—to a man. The natives are subhuman, and resemble humans only in their form. Case after case was cited about the way each loag lived, worshiped, and their persistent rejection of advanced technology was offered as evidence of their lack of intelligence."

Enickor stared through the man in front of him. How many times had those sentiments been bared, but never spoken aloud? The disdain with which Hoyiv regarded him still hurt. For all his physical superiority, the intelligence which allowed him to grasp things far above his educational base, Hoyiv considered him subhuman.

After so long a time he did not think it could hurt anymore. Yet it did.

Hoyiv. It had been a long time since he had even permitted himself to think about Hoyiv. He would mine Chiy-une until nothing remained, then be off for the Overeechy to enjoy all the luxuries he had beem missing at Shirwall. After that? After that, Enickor thought darkly, there would be another planet to mine, more ore to sell, higher profits, and greater prestige for the House of Jeffires.

Silently he thanked Pam-ella Jeffires for not marrying Lord Hadilka and padding the already iron lining of Hoyiv's coffers at the expense of her blood. She had been smart. She had run to the land. The land accepted her. Camp talk also bespoke an acceptance on the part of the loags, if somewhat reluctant and fearful.

Pam-ella . . .

Strom was still talking, but he did not hear.

Absently, he guided the raft to the center of the river and held it. The slow current did not fight him.

Where was she now? What had happened to her? Was she still alive? Had she returned to Shirwall when they began to kill the land faster and obliterate the loags? Was there any chance she might follow to the Southern Rohn?

His heart was beating fast, his mind racing in speculation.

"Do you love her?" Strom asked, not looking at Enickor.

"Yes." Enickor pulled back to the present. Pam-ella faded away. "What did you say?"

"I asked you if you loved her, and you said yes."

"Loved who?"

"Elisif. Who did you think I meant?" Confused, Strom glanced up and realized that they might not be speaking about the same woman.

"It does not matter." Irritated, he wanted to close the subject.

"I think it does." Strom sat up straight.

Enickor switched to the left side of the tiller and began the long, slow pull as they entered a lazy meander. The excitement of the knolls had faded with the knowledge of the carnage they hid.

"I had better ride on a different raft from now on," Strom continued.

"Why? I need you here. How can we talk if you are upriver from me? No one else knows . . ." He broke off, knowing he had missed something. "Why?"

"In a word—Elisif."

245

Bewildered, Enickor looked back at him and repeated his question.

"I think I'm in love with her. Either that, or I am suffering one of the strangest cases of lust I have ever had."

"Oh." He was not surprised.

Disbelieving his ears, he sat up straight. "That's it? Oh?"

"What do you want me to say? Elisif is a very nice young woman, pretty, personable. It is easy to see why you would be attracted to her."

"There is something I fail to understand here. I have just told you that I'm in love with your woman and you tell me—in so many words—that it is all right with you?"

Enickor looked down at him and shrugged. "Yes. That is fine. If she feels the same way and wishes to be free, I would free her. The day of separate loags is over. There will be intermarriages. Remember—the baby is mine." He grinned, glanced over the lines of people between him and Elisif. She smiled back.

"I don't understand you people." The weariness of his scouting trip caught up with him in full. He turned away, grabbed a ball of blankets and curled up. "I just do not understand."

"You are not alone," Enickor whispered, pulling the tiller harder. He watched his friend settle down and drift off into a fitful sleep, then smiled. "I understand you, Strom. I understand you very well."

A skimmer paralleled the narrow ledge linking Shirwall to the mainland. The sea was calm and gray, like the sky.

Hoyiv had been quick to send transportation for the Uv-Kriell and Commander Magaikan. He considered Pam-ella a bonus.

The time she spent searching the ranks for a recognizable soldier had been put to good use by planning strategy. She listened to the camp talk. The regard with which Hoyiv seemed to hold the Uv-Kriell, Hadilka, and even herself, was low. It was painful to realize how shallow her brother's feelings were, how easily bruised and fragile his ego had always been. Sadly, she knew he would lash out at the first threat posed to the House of Jeffires. Had not he already done so to the land in his duel against Hadilka?

None of the soldiers camped in the Ocandar village were familiar. She wondered what had become of her father's trusted officers. All spoke of the Quniero miners and their desertion.

Their idleness made them edgy. Without any miners to escort, supply lines to run or guard, they had returned to Shirwall territory.

It had saddened her to see the loag homes besmirched, then used for shelter because they were too lazy to pitch their own domes. Where was respect for another's labor? What had happened to the discipline the House of Jeffires had traditionally insisted upon?

As they neared the imposing fortress, she grew more reticent. She held Friedo's hand with a ferocity that numbed his fingers.

"Pam-ella," he said, turning to shut out the rest of the world from her view, "it is not necessary for you to go through with this. There are options."

"My alternatives have disappeared, Friedo. Would you promise me something?"

"Anything, Pam-ella, anything."

"If Hadilka . . . if this should take a bad turn for me . . . don't make it easy for him to forget what he has done. I want . . ." Her voice broke. She was afraid again. It seemed impossible that there remained any fear inside of her. So much, so often, yet there was always some left. It was a lot like love, she decided.

"I promise." No mention had been made of good-byes, but already the hurt was there and growing like an ulcer on his heart.

He framed her face in his hands, pushed back the hood of her cape, and memorized her face, dirt smudges included. "You know I love you. Nothing can change that. I said I would help, and I will. We will play this all the way to the finish. I would like to be wrong about Hoyiv."

"I know." She wanted to be wrong, also.

"I will also keep looking for Enickor." He glanced to the front of the skimmer. They were almost there.

He took his time kissing her good-bye, knowing the responses they invoked in one another compounded the difficulty.

The skimmer halted. Magaikan cleared his throat and braced himself for the scenario about to be played out for the benefit of Lord Hoyiv Jeffires.

Magaikan watched the sea, thinking this to be the saddest, most depressing planet he had ever visited. He could not define the lure it had for him. Strange place, he decided, damn near human in temperament.

Friedo held her tightly. "Reach inside my upper pocket. There's a sender. If you have need of me, use it. I'll come, no matter what, Pam-ella."

She did as he asked and palmed an object no larger than a button. "Friedo—" she pushed away "—if things had been different it still would not have worked."

He smiled. "It is that they were not. I am counting on the future."

A House Guard complement marched down the great stone stairs to the water. Magaikan exited, returned a salute, then stood aside for the Uv-Kriell and Pam-ella.

They strode between the gold and yellow of the House of Jeffires's finest.

Before they reached the top, the massive carved doors opened for a second time. Hoyiv came out to stand on the stairs and greet his guests.

Looking at him, Pam-ella thought it wrong for someone to be unchanged for so long. His hair was the same length, the same shiny texture. Not a wrinkle creased his face unless he smiled, and those disappeared when he resumed his natural frown.

Hoyiv bowed curtly to the Uv-Kriell, clicking his heels as he hit the lowest point. "It is an honor to extend my hospitality to you, Sire. Please accept what we have. Shirwall is yours."

"Thank you." It took only moments to analyze the young Lord's expectations of the Overeechy and its Uv-Kriell. He assumed a role which would allow Hoyiv to feel superior. The practiced demeanor of arrogance returned with a flourish. It was easy with Hoyiv.

"Commander Magaikan, I hope you will feel free to review the House Guard at your convenience. I'll have quarters prepared for you."

"He stays with me," Payndacen said evenly, and readjusted the gloves in his belt.

Hoyiv was uncomfortable for a moment, then resumed his easy composure. "Pam-ella. We've missed you." He held out his hand to her.

She hesitated, then took it. "Who is we?"

"Father and I—until he died." He motioned to the door and bowed. "I don't think he ever forgave you for deserting him."

Magaikan led the way, followed by Payndacen.

"How did he die?" There was no warmth radiating from the arm around her shoulders. It felt stiff, forced. When she looked up at him she saw a stranger, and wondered where her brother had gone. Even his pretended affection for her was a gleaming product of formality. Had ambition strangled all of his loyalties?

He chuckled. "You are still right to the point, aren't you? Your time among the natives has left you unchanged."

"No, Hoyiv. I see things more clearly now than I did when Shirwall was the whole sphere of my existence, and you and father were my mentors."

She stopped short, reached around and removed his arm from her shoulders. "My return has nothing to do with the love I might have for you, nor with any concern for the standings of the House of Jeffires with the Overeechy. I am ashamed to share the name with you. The atrocities performed in your name will condemn you from one end of the Overeechy to the other.

"My brother the murderer. I cannot begin to tell you how proud I am of your achievements in child-killing . . ." Once the flow began there seemed no end.

Hoyiv's face became flush. "Enough! This is my house! I will not tolerate your accusations."

"You will," Friedo said quietly and turned to Hoyiv, "and I will, because they are true. The House of Jeffires is drowning in the blood of the Chiy-une loags. This matter will be brought up at trial in the Overeechy."

The sudden color that had rushed to his face began to fade. "You would not dare such a thing! You would have to admit to being here and having troops here. How would the echelons of the Overeechy consider that? Your right to the Kriellship would come into question immediately. Are you ready to face that, Sire?"

Payndacen extended his arm to Pam-ella. "There is one vein in which we are quite similar, Lord Jeffires. Neither of us is like our father, nor do we share the same ideals they cherished. I, for one, am quite willing to open up Chiy-une, and the events which have transpired here, to the entire Overeechy—including the Enickor val Densu matter."

Hoyiv thought for a moment, and followed Payndacen down the long hall to the main room where a gourmet spread covered the center table.

"And what of Hadilka?" Hoyiv asked, selecting a fine wine and inhaling the bouquet. "Will you also accuse him?"

"What shall I accuse Lord Hadilka of doing, Hoyiv?" Friedo

shook out a napkin and laughed. "As you know, he is well looked upon in the Overeechy for his untiring battle to hold the Corchi in their own system. Would the House of Jeffires undertake his responsibilities on the frontier?"

Hoyiv refused to look at the Uv-Kriell. His hatred for the man broke its disguise.

"We have nothing but praise for Lord Hadilka's conduct here on Chiy-une," Friedo said and popped a small sandwich into his mouth. "My respects to your chef. These are excellent."

Pam-ella watched in amazement, then caught Magaikan glancing at her and knew her wonderment showed. The commander yielded a subtle, knowing smile. He is good, she thought, better than I thought possible.

Friedo rested his hand on Hoyiv's shoulder. The fine napkin dangled loosely over the Jeffires insignia emblazoned into the gold uniform. "As a matter of fact, I am giving serious consideration to recommending the good Lord Hadilka as the standard-setter and offering him Overeechy contracts for the exploration and development of the new mining starts for the Akopal Quadrant.

"A fine man, Lord Hadilka. Truly worthy of praise and honor." He left Hoyiv for another sandwich. "Don't you agree, Lady Pam-ella?"

She was on stage—and hated it. "Well, I do have to admit that there was a time I viewed him in a slightly different light . . ."

"You hated him!" Hoyiv said too loudly. "He's the one who mined over the loags. Not the House of Jeffires. We have always run surveys and given warning when we mine with a helix, Payndacen! Not me. I find this quite insulting."

Magaikan took a step forward and rested his hand on his *kalase*. "You will show the Uv-Kriell proper respect, or you will not live to regret it, Lord Jeffires. There is a limit."

Sullen, aware he had elicited the unwanted attention of the Kriell's protector, he managed a bow and retreated. "Yes," Hoyiv said, nodding and contrite, "you are correct. I beg you to accept my apology, Sire. This is very trying for me, the unexpected return of my sister and your presence . . . Please, I would take it as a personal favor if you would forgive me."

"Certainly. It would be difficult to hold anything as trivial as a deportment lapse against the man who acted as brother to my brother." Payndacen enjoyed the role, particularly when it allowed him to antagonize Lord Jeffires.

250

Hoyiv glanced sharply at Pam-ella, then at the Uv-Kriell. "Have you any news on him?"

"No," answered Payndacen. "Pam-ella believes he is dead. That is part of her reason for returning to Shirwall." He crossed the room and dropped into a large chair tilted toward the one Pam-ella occupied. He examined the room's decor and watched Hoyiv.

"You are certainly right, my dear. You could do worse than align yourself with Lord Hadilka—and there will be no stigma attached to your reputation once this nasty business of the loags comes to court in the Overeechy."

Pam-ella smiled, stifling a laugh. Was this the same man who slipped down the walls of the tauiri by the seat of his pants? Whose arrogance had been stilled by the mountain winds? He was so out of character to the sensitive, gentle man she knew, yet played his role with a finesse the greatest of actors would admire.

"Am I to understand that you have really come back to marry Lord Hadilka?" Hoyiv slowly sank to the edge of the chair.

As Pam-ella noted the gamut of emotions changing Hoyiv's face, she began to feel ill. How could he be so callous, yet concerned, simultaneously? Had he wanted the mining concessions on Chiy-une for the House of Jeffires badly enough to tamper with their father's recovery? Did he kill him?

Before today, she did not think it possible. Now, she did not know.

She knew he was in shock. But his gladness for her presence, and a solution to many of his problems, was evident. She wished there were more time so it wouldn't be quite as easy for him. "Yes, I hope to marry him as soon as possible," she answered, squeezing Friedo's hand. "I hope you approve. Friedo's going to stand up for me."

Dismally, she thought that before night fell he would have revised his mining schedule, called in an entire second crew and put a priority order in for an additional helix ship.

Of course he approves, she thought dryly.

Hoyiv Jeffires's attempt to appear confused and angry met with failure. "This is quite a surprise. Of course, it is what father wanted for you, Pam-ella. And for Lord Hadilka." He managed some genuine concern when he continued. "You are the only sister I have, Pam-ella . . ."

"Of course you will want to do what's best for me." She

251

had trouble bringing a smile to her lips. "You will take care of arranging for my future with this wedding, won't you, Hoyiv?"

"Yes, yes I do, and I will." Caught up with his own plans, he was unaware of the looks exchanged around him. "I will try to reach him this afternoon and persuade him to come to Shirwall and honor father's agreement."

"Oh, I'm sure Lord Hadilka is a man of honor," Pam-ella said. Her fate was sealed once the great lord knew she was at Shirwall. The momentary jocularity faded. A low level of fear returned, one that she did not think would leave until they reached endgame.

Chapter 27

ENICKOR COULD NOT FOLLOW THE LOGIC WHICH deemed Chiy-uneites inferior to the Star Followers. After a lengthy review of what he knew about the Overeechy life-styles, Enickor marveled that they had been able to make any evaluations concerning life. It was so cheap in the core of civilization, easily replaced, one life similar to another. There was mechanical life: androids, and some robots who looked more human, and probably acted thus, than their owners and designers.

The fabric of judgment has been warped, he concluded, *strained by greed and the consequences of supply and demand.*

The journey through the Qeakine Knolls gave him plenty of time to ponder. Gradually, he came to look upon the Star Followers as lost even to themselves. Loags knew and respected one another, never infringing upon another's rights or territory without a mutual agreement. Yet the Star Followers seldom agreed on anything without lengthy talks, documents, voice prints, and witnesses.

This quieter part of the journey became a time of reflection for Enickor.

The siege Strom had anticipated from the Knolls had come

the afternoon of the first day beyond the lake. The lopsided skirmish had claimed eleven lives, injured eight more, then ended. The rafts had escaped intact.

Rain fell. The river spread into the Knolls and turned them into islands. The water continued to rise even when the rains stopped.

Illness was no longer a stranger to the Alizandar. Several of the elderly had succumbed to their worn-out parts and slipped away during the sleep period, a few to the river in the dark of night. Their lifelines had been neatly coiled beside their belongings. Both were left for the use of the living. Not even their clothing had been taken back to the life-giver, Chiy-une.

The chants of the Alizandar Death Ritual were frequent during their trek to the sea.

Again and again the loagers beseeched Enickor to tell them how they were going to land. Their thinking horizons had been expanded by each new situation. An ever-present fear, one of the angry ocean and the legendary monsters who dwelt there, began as a whisper on each of the rafts.

Enickor remained mute on the subject. An answer would justify their fears.

Strom asked once.

Enickor grinned.

Strom did not ask again, but looked forward to whatever his friend had in store.

"He is the Man Who Walked out of the Sea," Elisif told her companions. "The sea knows him."

Her well-meaning attempt to console served as the catalyst for more fear. The Alizandar began to keep a distance from the Harcel Leader.

The estrangement disturbed him.

His family was secured. Knowing that eased some of his worry. He could stand in one place and see them; Zaich and Landah, Strom, Elisif—they were his world.

He continued to be attentive to Elisif, but knew his preoccupation with the loagers sapped much of his enthusiasm. The bounds of her understanding remained out of sight. Often, he wondered how he had been able to shut her out during their separation. He thought of her crossing the Lyndirlyan through the giant forests, down into the Iyigna, and the black time with the soldiers. It pained him to imagine the odious manner in which they used her. He did not ask her about it. Her nightmares told him more than he wanted to know. She cried in her sleep.

254

More than once Strom had relieved him early. All it took was his presence to allay the nightmare. Conversely, he needed her. He needed them all. They were a family. Together, they were strong.

Daily he communed with the Mistress. As they neared the ocean he sensed Meiska. The bond grew until they were finally able to communicate.

The nine days to the sea ended. The smell of salt and seaweed overwhelmed the dampened earth aroma that boiled from the knolls.

When the ocean was in sight, Enickor shouted westward, untied his lifeline, and dove off the front of the raft. He swam hard, using long, powerful strokes to pull ahead of the raft being sucked to the sea.

Meiska rose from the gray ocean, mossy and green, a sight that elicited true joy from Enickor and abject terror from the rafters.

The rangtur moved into the river, his long body curving, moving effortlessly against the strong current. As soon as he was close, he extended a tentacle and wrapped Enickor in the five tendrils on the end. Enickor wished he were as large as the rangtur so he could embrace the beast with all the affection their reunion deserved. He ran his hands over every part of Meiska he could touch, patting, stroking, sharing his pleasure and receiving the same in return.

They drifted toward the sea. Enickor swam around Meiska, walked up his back, dove off, and swam some more before catching a glimpse of the rafts moving swiftly toward them.

The outflow of the river extended far beyond the riptide.

Enickor climbed atop Meiska and began pointing to the south.

Strom commanded the tiller of the leading raft. Grinning in open fascination, he guided them southward. Zaich came to help fight the current.

Meiska positioned his bulk to form a sea wall, protecting them from the high waves and the rich brown river wake coloring the ocean on the other side of a frothy median. The murky sea hid his true length. The effects he wrought were vast.

The river calmed and rose. When he moved, the flux carried the rafts smoothly to the south and into the ocean.

With some effort, the second and third rafts closed the gaps between them and tucked into a neat line behind Strom. Meiska paralleled their course and labored to keep them centered in relationship with his body. By doing so, he was able to control the current flow. Waves broke over him. He rose higher out of the water.

It was a grueling day for the rafters and the rangtur. They utilized the smooth seacoast until the once-distant cliffs were beside them and the landing places appeared. The rafts could not continue.

Enickor was pleased at the distance between them and the river. No one could have caught up with them. Not on foot. They were safe from the old dangers. Ahead lay the new ones.

The Alizandar was unusually quiet after making camp. Many engaged in long periods of watching the Harcel Leader. Even the children did not venture near.

Enickor was happy. He ate his fill of the sea's bounty furnished by the rangtur. Tonight he would make love to Elisif. It had been a long time since they had had any real privacy. The world felt good. In the morning he would take Strom out to Meiska before they began climbing to the upper cliffs.

Only once did he think about the land between them and the Southern Rohn. The impending hardships depressed him. He banished the thought. This was his night to be happy, and nights like this were too rare to waste on circumstances over which he had no control.

Astakp asa Phoutk smelled the presence of the native caretakers. Theirs was vastly different from those who had brought them across the black void from Alidanko. Sadness and benevolence for the land had been captured in their scent. He tasted their need to travel and knew they were not a danger.

His nekka huddled deep within the sea cliffs, each wanting a glimpse of the awesome creature who was kin to the mountain rangtur that had touched Illeuro asa Khatioup and forever changed him, yet afraid.

He waited until the darkness cloaked the cliffs before sending a messenger north to Gaediv. They had begun a new leah beside the ocean.

They made slow progress up the cliffs to the sea plateaus. The children did well. The nine old men and women bringing up the rear could not carry packs. Enickor sent a dozen of the stronger men from the Alixandar on additional trips to compensate.

256

Much of their food stores had been depleted. The remainder was soaked, and rotting in chests.

The day passed.

Night saw them camped less than a kilometer from the night before, most of the distance being vertical. Below, Meiska lolled in the beach side of the riptide.

After the evening meal Enickor gathered the Alizandar around the common fire. He selected a place beside Pindar and Inorag.

He began by slowly explaining what he expected to find ahead. The vast wastelands would impose hardships no loag had endured. Lack of food and water was his primary concern.

"As you have seen, there is no turning back. We have no place to go except the Southern Rohn, where the sun keeps Chiy-une warm."

He stepped away from the leaders and drew a deep breath. "Some of you will not make it. Some will die." He looked into faces; young, old, afraid, resigned, trusting, skeptical. "As a loag, we must do everything possible to prevent those deaths. More than ever you will be called upon to give aid to one another, make sacrifices for the common good, and go when you think you cannot take another step."

"We can stay here!" cried a voice from the shadows.

"And live how? For how long? The Star Followers have overrun the Qeakine Knolls for mining. Strom found evidence of tortured . . ."

"He is a Star Follower. Do you believe him?" came a gently spoken question from a young woman directly in front of him.

Enickor smiled. "I am also half Star Follower, yet all of *you* are here."

The woman bowed her head.

Enickor touched her. When she looked up, she smiled meekly. "I would trust him with my life and those of the rest of my family. He is a part of my family. Would you not believe one whom you call brother and love?"

The young woman glanced at Strom, then back to Enickor, and nodded.

There were many questions. The time passed quickly. Some of the old barriers cracked, a few tumbled, and others remained steadfast. After the general gathering ended several dozen stayed to speak with Enickor. He was pleased, especially since these were the backbone of the loag, the vigorous and strong.

"What can we do to make the trip easier on the children?" asked the same woman who had challenged Strom's credibility.

"Keep them smiling when they are hungry. Make them laugh when they're thirsty. Do the impossible." Strom came forward, his gaze taking in the feline grace of the young woman. "Then love them when they are starving and want to eat anything they find on the badlands, and take it away from them."

"We will stay as close to the sea as we can," Enickor continued, lifting his arm around Elisif.

She snuggled closer, smiling, unafraid of what lay ahead and confident. Her world was complete. The battles she engaged in were gradually diminishing. The tide of victory was surging toward her. The changes were slight, but distinct. If she loved him a little harder, perhaps the return would be even greater. Keladine Ornasive did not raise a weak-willed daughter, nor an unimaginative one.

"The rangtur's ability to hunt for us is the best advantage we have. We will need only to climb down the cliffs to get food. There are places where he will not be able to reach the cliff base and the ocean is too treacherous to hazard."

More questions were asked and answered. Gradually, loagers slipped into the shadows to sleep. Several moved to the perimeter to change places with those standing watch.

Strom began to explain basic survival tactics learned in training. Constantly he stressed the dangers of the badlands and the necessity to cross them swiftly.

"Are you afraid of them?" asked the young woman.

"What's your name?"

"Jelica. Are you afraid of them?"

"Yes," Strom answered quickly.

She looked back at him for a long time. "Why? Have you seen something? Are there more Star Followers there?"

"No. There won't be any Star Followers there. There are pockets of radiation. Those are what I fear. And that is why we will not touch anything that lives there. Radiation kills, Jelica. It is far worse than thirst, or starvation, worse than just about anything you can imagine and it is not a quick death." When Strom looked around, knowing his words were frightening, he was surprised to find himself alone with Jelica and two others.

"Where did everyone go?" he asked.

"It is late," the young man answered, taking the hand of the woman with him. "We will talk again tomorrow night?"

"Or the next?" the young woman said with a yawn.

"I would like that." He smiled in response.

Jelica watched them go.

Strom watched her.

When they had disappeared into the night Jelica cleared her throat and shifted on the rock bench. "I do not understand Star Followers. No. I do not understand you, Strom Aknel of the Harcel. Perhaps I do not need to." She rose, smiling.

"But I would like to understand the Alizandar," he said. "And you are correct. We are very different." He grinned. "You could say that we're worlds apart."

"I suppose so." She turned from the fire, hesitated, then stopped. "Would you sleep with me?"

Surprised, he realized he wanted to make love with her very much. She was no Elisif, but she was attractive in an earthy sort of way. Smaller-boned than most of the Alizandar women, she looked frail in the erratic firelight. High cheekbones flush with color, her eyes were wide and pale. Straight brown hair highlighted by sun-bleached gold streaks framed her face.

"I think I would like that very much, Jelica. No conditions."

She did not move. "Conditions on pleasure?"

"This is for tonight, and no tomorrow? I do not want any kind of attachment." It seemed too good to be true.

She smiled. "You are like the Harcel and the Porintel. You think pleasure is something to be taken seriously."

He stepped over the log he had been sitting on, reached back and tossed it into the fire. "Oh, indeed. I take my pleasure very seriously and welcome the opportunity to show you." He held his arm for her to take. When she did not, he placed her hand on his and bowed for her to show the way.

The ceremony was elaborate. The House of Jeffires had spared no expense in obtaining the finest trappings. Dignitaries from several of the Great Houses were in attendance, and bore solemn witness to the political alliance sealed by the marriage. The brief celebration was notably devoid of women.

The two most exuberant celebrators were the Lords Hadilka and Jeffires. The pair had spent long hours in conference prior to the final signing of the marital agreement.

Pam-ella suspected that codicils had been negotiated, added, and modified. Hoyiv had never looked quite as happy as on

259

her wedding day. No worry shadowed his moods. His open friendliness, even to the Uv-Kriell, made her more wary of him.

Her misery faded into a limbo where she had forced the rest of her emotions. Memories of Enickor no longer troubled her. He was a part of the past, the prod which had sent her onto the land and showed her another way to live.

Commander Magaikan remained at the Uv-Kriell's elbow the entire day. The commander said little, watched everyone and stayed prepared to defend the Uv-Kriell.

The Uv-Kriell, richly attired, put on his court manners, added a dash of decadent arrogance, and arrived at the proper mix. It was part of the life an heir endured until the time he was Kriell. Then he could be himself—half the time; more if he married the right woman.

Smiles were cheap. Compliments, the substance of which politics are made and fortunes born, flowed as freely as the fine wines and rare liquors brimming carved emerald glasses.

Made up with all the tricks and skill her previous years at Shirwall had given her time to perfect, Pam-ella achieved a stylish radiance. The dark lines of doubt were hidden. Her smile glistened, unflawed at all times. She greeted her marriage guests with enthusiasm, wanting each to remember her as happy to be among the civilized culture of the Overeechy's finest.

Names and faces were committed to memory along with minute details about each new person she met. The constant lavishing of attention on Hadilka was part of the role she played.

As the evening came and left, and traded night for the small hours of the morning, the guests took leave for their rooms. Pam-ella consumed prodigious amounts of wine.

The hours before dawn were long for the Uv-Kriell and Magaikan. They were even longer for Pam-ella Jeffires-Hadilka in the adjacent suite of rooms. Friedo sat in the dark, sipping glass after glass of wine and listening.

Lord Hadilka's vociferous laughter shook the stone walls of Shirwall.

The images running through Payndacen's mind were grisly. He did not sleep, nor did the wine furnish any insulation.

Brunch the following day was an extension of the previous night's festivities. Instead of the low-cut wedding dress, Pam-ella was clad in a loose gown, high-necked and long-sleeved. Her smile remained radiant. Her make-up perpetuated the illusion. Only when she looked directly into Friedo's eyes did the mirage she weaved falter.

"I will be checking on you, Lord Hadilka," the Uv-Kriell said, chuckling a little. "I have enjoyed the privilege of giving you the beautiful Lady Jeffires for your own. Her interests are now yours, and the little conditions you granted must be fulfilled."

Hadilka tucked his left hand into the crimson sash running across his midsection. "Surely you do not expect me to postpone my wedding trip in preference to recalling my miners and their guards? Why, that's inhumane, Sire." His belly laugh shook the room.

The Uv-Kriell's smile disintegrated. His eyes narrowed slightly.

The room quieted.

"Surely I do. In fact, Lord Hadilka, I insist upon it. From this time forward, Pam-ella Jeffires-Hadilka will not join you again as her husband until your troops have been removed from Chiy-une."

Flustered, Hadilka wrapped his large left arm around his small bride, and pulled her against him. He gazed at her with open lust.

Demure, she smiled back at him and stroked his jowls with the back of her hand. An ugly purple bruise peeked out from the edge of her sleeve.

"You would hold such love apart, Sire? I assure you, the miners, and the guards I hired to protect them, will be lifted as soon as I return. Already I have turned over all mining interests to Lord Jeffires, as agreed."

"I am appalled you are so reluctant to honor your bond, Lord Hadilka." It was easy to be incensed with the man. "In good faith I have stood with Lady Pam-ella and allowed her to become Lady Hadilka. Eager, and justifiably so, I might add, as you are to be with her, I'm sure you did not spend the night in separate rooms."

Hadilka laughed again. "Most certainly not, Sire!"

A nervous round of laughter flurried the room.

"You have taken the goods, my Lord, and now are reluctant to pay the pittance she asked and I am honor bound to see fulfilled? Is this the sanctity that a man who loves his lady gives to the small premarital request she made?

"I have never stood at a wedding, and I take my duties as overseer of the agreement very seriously. It will be as I have said, Lord Hadilka. Surely a man of so much honor as yourself agrees?" He smiled and felt the tension in the room ease.

Quickly, he winked at Pam-ella. "I can understand your disappointment, Pam-ella." Apologetically, he continued, "It is Lady Hadilka now, isn't it. Please realize that I am acting in your best interests. And it is evident that your Lord is just as eager as you are," chuckling, "zealous, in fact, to get on with your beautiful future."

Hadilka also laughed, but with less vigor than before. "How right you are, Sire. Sweet woman that she is, I hate to be away from her. I have waited overly long for this, but you are correct again. Honor does come first." He kissed her forehead. "It will not take more than a few days to oversee the evacuation."

"Perhaps you can make it a joint venture with Lord Jeffires, and defray the expenses of the cruisers? Surely he will be able to significantly reduce the number of, ah, guards he has employed?" Payndacen nodded at the young lord.

"Excellent idea! I wish that I had thought of it!" Hoyiv came forward, again thoughtful.

Briefly Pam-ella afforded a glance at Payndacen. There was a great deal to him she was just beginning to realize and appreciate. *Should've and if*, she thought. *But I'm glad we had that night together, Friedo.* Knowing the Star Followers would soon be leaving Chiy-une made Hadilka's arm resting on her battered shoulders a little lighter.

Chapter 28

THE ALIZANDAR TOOK THREE DAYS TO COMBINE the supplies hauled up from the beach. Enickor had wanted to get moving as quickly as possible, but decided to avoid another clash with Inorag.

Meiska took Strom fishing the second day. The two took to one another like lost members of the same loag. The abundance of fish they pulled up the cliff that evening was enough for a massive feast and the morning meal, with plenty left over for drying.

Jelica sat with Strom beside the fire. Enickor was restless and pacing, watching the sky. Both men knew the dangers of having so large a camp on an unprotected cliff top. There was no place to hide or defend if the need arose.

"One more day," Enickor said, sat between Landah and Elisif and picked up his dinner.

"I will scout the northland in the morning," Strom said quietly.

Jelica glanced at him, concerned, but she said nothing.

"We have been here long. It is best to know if we are followed or have stumbled into a supply line route."

It was a restless night. Neither Strom nor Enickor slept well. Both were up before first light.

Strom returned at noon. He was winded, red-faced, and showed all the signs Enickor had begun to recognize as typical of a man who constantly demanded more from himself than others ventured to ask.

Away from the hub of activity, Strom threw up, coughed, and sat on the ground. His arms were wrapped securely around his midsection.

Enickor waited patiently. Too many times Strom had returned in this condition for Enickor to try to rush him into telling what he knew.

Finally, "They're coming. We must move. I mean—*move.*" He breathed hard, trying to catch the big one that would satiate his aching lungs.

Inorag cur Maha made his way through the tight circle around Strom. "What is this?"

Strom looked up and blinked hard. The sun was bright in his eyes. Perspiration running down his eyelids stung. "They're coming."

"Who?" cur Maha demanded, flourishing what was left of his cape.

Strom glanced at his listeners, squinting against the sting in his eyes. "A loag. Another loag is coming."

There was the briefest pause, then instant jubilation from the Harcel and a few shouts from those of the Alizandar who heard.

Inorag was both worried and happy. Another loag leader would provide a quorum to override Enickor's assumed leadership.

Strom pushed to his feet and swayed. He steadied against Enickor's shoulder.

"There is more? Tell us," Enickor asked, somber, reading Aknel's face. He scooped a cup of water and poured it slowly across Strom's shoulders.

Moisture flew off the ends of his hair when Strom shook his head.

The rowdy cheers died. Strom took half a dozen good lungs full of air before speaking again.

"They are being followed by a large company of soldiers. At this point, I would estimate that they are ten kilometers apart, and their trails have recently joined. The loag is coming

264

straight down the coast. The soldiers are coming out of the Qeakine Knolls, heading south.

"Both are headed this way." He looked straight at Inorag. "We have to move out. Now. We must keep the main body ahead of them both until it's safe."

Inorag sagged visibly under the weight of this new decision to be made. He had neither the experience nor the will to carry the burdens thrust upon him since leaving the prairie land of the Alizandar.

"I do not know. Pindar?"

The Metaliary shook his head and murmured, "Perhaps it is better to leave such decisions and judgments to those Leaders who have had the misfortune of experience in these matters. They would carry the greater wisdom in their actions."

Nodding monotonously, Inorag deferred to Enickor once again and took leave of the closely knit circle. He was a little more broken, a bit older, and seemed to have lost the scant amount of self-esteem recouped during the interim since the rafts.

Enickor stepped forward, nodding his thanks to the Metaliary for easing the difficulty in handling the situation.

Pindar did not deign to recognize the gesture.

The old anger, so dominant the first days back on the land, tried to resurface. Enickor fought it, though his mind saw the Ocandar's fate. And he knew Strom was right. Chiy-une did do something to the alien minds. Its name was violence for the soldiers.

He found himself gazing at Strom. Chiy-une had not affected him in the same way. Could she indeed choose which way the land influenced those who trod upon her? He would have to remember to ask.

The Alizandar was again reorganized. The aged and the young were sent ahead with a strong complement of men and women to help them fend off any predators straying out of the badlands and to carry the greater burdens. Every child over twelve seasons carried a pack. There were no exceptions.

The two dozen who remained behind dug in the top of the cliff. It was the only decent vantage point for kilometers. The top extended inland for six kilometers before the incline off the beach reached its elevation. Either way, they could see an army, or a loag, approach.

It was with some relief that Enickor slept that night. The first part of the Alizandar had departed. They were to travel through the night. Zaich, Elisif, and Landah were with them. Inorag, under the strong influence Pindar exerted, assumed his position as Leader. There had been a glimmer of pride in the old man's eyes when they left, him at the lead wearing what remained of his ceremonial cloak and headdress.

The following morning they waited behind piles of rocks. No fires warmed the fish cooked for last night's dinner. Fog sat heavily on the cliff, its damp mouth swallowing everything.

The sun moved high in the sky. The fog lifted. The day remained depressed. Still there was no sign of either the loag or the army.

By midafternoon Strom set out on foot and Enickor by sea on Meiska to chart the fate of the Ocandar.

Meiska moved swiftly through the water. He stayed in the edges of the haze oppressing the sea. The silence of the water was broken occasionally when the rangtur changed directions.

Enickor watched the shore. It carried a dreary sameness along the coast until they came to the river.

Meiska turned back, heading closer to the shoreline.

They were looking for a body of people on the move. "Perhaps they stopped. Or moved inland," Enickor mused, stroking the rangtur absently.

On the third and fourth sweeps they moved closer to the shore. The rewards for diligence were mixed. Smoke appeared against the distant horizon. It was black and billowing into the already-rusted sky. The temptation to deviate from the original plan and leave the ocean for the inland trails was great. After considering his own constant push for following plans and agreements laid out beforehand, he prodded the rangtur to take him back.

It was late by the time Enickor bid Meiska good night and climbed the cliff to the Alizandar camp.

Strom had not returned.

Enickor and Jelica sat side by side and waited.

A cold fog rolled over the sea, embraced the cliff, and squeezed the last dregs of warmth from the stone.

"I understand, at last," Jelica said quietly at about midnight.

"What?" Enickor did not move, and only partially listened to her. He remained tuned to the night and the sounds and rhythms of Chiy-une's nocturnal life.

"He fits nowhere. He is not a Star Follower—not like the ones who kill with no thought, or harm the Alizandar or the other loags. He makes pleasure with the same intensity and

266

giving with which he does everything else." She shivered. "But there is another side to him." Glancing up at Enickor, who was now giving her his entire attention, "Just as there is to you. A dark side, one as menacing and terrible as the side you wear outside."

She paused. He did not respond.

"His enemies should fear him greatly, as must yours, Enickor." She looked back into the misty dark and could see nothing.

A quarter of the night passed before Jelica spoke again. "He had better come back." Anger and worry filled those words.

"Yes, he had better. We need him," Enickor agreed in a whisper at the dawn.

The fog lifted at midmorning. The land was abnormally silent. Enickor had managed to doze once the camp was alert. Jelica maintained her vigil.

The first warning noises came from the northeast. Nothing could be seen through the lingering haze. The sky was particularly foulcolored. They could not be far from the reach of a mining zone.

Prairie dwellers seldom saw either a roh or a torna-pok. When the beasts came out of the haze a general pandemonium erupted.

Enickor was wary, but glad to see them. They were the backbone of the Porintel way of life. He was chagrined also. As a child he had yearned for a roh to choose him. It would have been proof to the Porintel that he belonged and deserved a family place. But he had never been approached by any of the numerous creatures.

As a mingling horde they erupted from the haze, hundreds of them, all sizes and colors. Gone were the territorial quarrels. The once-disputed land no longer existed.

They crossed the open terrain from the back side of the cliff. They jostled and parried, sorting themselves by rank and station. Tauiri leaders and herd heads took their places in the order of their contributed numbers. Dust mingled with the haze and thickened it.

Once aligned, a delegation of four roh and three torna-pok continued through the Alizandar watchers as though they were not there. They approached Enickor and lay down.

Enickor wondered what kind of a bleak state the rest of Chiy-une might be in for her finest to give themselves and their members to him for service. He did not want so much responsibility, nor the aching burden it put on him. All he had wanted was the acceptance of one single roh.

He considered rejecting them, but could not for fear of what they might do to themselves.

And what of the badlands? There was nothing for them to eat. Water had to be carried. They would have to make the long journey around.

He felt the thousand eyes of all those on the plateau staring at him and the wonderment of the Alizandar. Turning, he gazed down at the sea and Meiska. The rangtur did not let him down. A stream of confidence came from him.

Enickor stepped forward and touched each leader. The melody of the Porintel Archivar poured from his mouth and into the beginnings of a sea breeze. The strength of his voice grew with his confidence and the sureness of the old ritual imparted. Save for the melodious Archivar, the land and those upon it were silent.

Deep in the leah, Gaediv accepted Illeuro's message with dread and certainty that the land and with it, the Quniero, faced change. One so vast, so overpowering that they would be challenged more than at any time in memory to meet it.

Failure was the ultimate death of the leahs. Death to the land. Unilateral death. The kind of death a Quniero understood, not the singular decease of an individual. They were missed, but never in the memory of the Quniero had one individual made a significant difference to the leah.

Gaediv recognized that perhaps that time had come, too.

Illeuro asa Khatioup was like no other nekka leader. He thought separately from the leah. He sent messages to confirm his thoughts—but he thought beyond the task he had been given.

She wondered if it was a part of the changing and mourned their lost way of life.

Astakp asa Phoutk summoned his nekka into full retreat down into the bottoms of the caverns they were building in the cliff face. The thundering of the land just north of them shook small, weathered slabs of the cliff loose to fall into the crashing waves.

The melody of the caretaker's song wound through the black

tunnels and turns, following them, trying to lure them back to the sunlight.

The nekka leader remained in the bottom of the tunnel with his charges. Gaediv had said to avoid the caretakers, not to be fooled by promises. The song was a promise.

The days following the wedding at Shirwall were superficially relaxed. Members of the Great Houses were in no haste to leave, particularly with both the Lords Hadilka and Jeffires in absentia.

Payndacen spent much of the time with Magaikan on the mainland poring over the monitors on board his ship. Banter was delighted to see the Uv-Kriell in what he considered excellent company, bested only by his own.

The exact numbers of mercenary guards employed by each of the Houses would never be revealed. Payndacen doubted they knew for certain themselves. The manner in which they had been recruited, paid, and transported—extra-computer—promised to keep that information cloaked in total chaos. It was part of the price of a joint venture between traditionally warlike Houses, he decided. Those who survived to reach lift-off once again were paid handsomely, each on a different scale, in accordance with the terms of the contracts they carried. No contract—no pay. Men had been known to kill for the special medallion another carried, especially if the terms were seen as better than the one currently held.

According to the information Commander Magaikan had been able to obtain and piece together, the two Great Houses would require a minimum of four cruisers to evacuate their hired troops. Hadilka would need another for his own men and servants.

Now, three days after the wedding, Lord Hadilka had sent a communication asserting that the evacuation of his guards had been completed. His House soldiers and entourage would remain to insure his and Lady Hadilka's safety and personal comfort.

He and Lord Jeffires had employed the services of one cruiser. It departed filled to two-thirds of its capacity.

Payndacen sat in the lounge of his ship. The volumes of information Magaikan had gathered on both houses, the mining endeavors, and Chiy-une herself were piled in the room. Columns of memory molecules were neatly secured against the assist module of the computer.

"I cannot let her go with him—not like this," Payndacen mumbled, ran his hands over his face, through his hair and locked his fingers behind his neck. "Goddam. I can't let her throw away her future..." He wanted to shout at the ghost voices in the mountain, *She's not guilty! Let her go*.

Out loud, "When he has his heir, when he is through with her...what then?" He glared at the commander. "She will still be a Jeffries to him. She will not bend, and she will tire of the role playing. That will be the end. He'll kill her, Ahandro." The parallel wrinkles on his brow drew closer, deeper. "So help me, I'll bring him up on charges, and have him slowly put to death."

The eyes looking at the commander were bloodshot from strain and lack of sleep. "But she'll still be dead," the Uv-Kriell continued, to no one in particular. The term "misery" took on a new meaning when he thought about it. "She cannot survive long as a Hadilkan."

Banter brought a small meal and a decanter of wine.

"I must catch him at something. Anything. It's the only way I can put an end to this. Hoyiv has the mining rights—that is settled. It cannot be revoked.

"We have to find a way to void out the marriage agreement from Hadilka's side."

"You mean cheat him out of his wife?" Magaikan asked coldly.

Payndacen regarded him for a moment. Some of the rage had left him. "Yes, Ahandro, I mean catch him at a breach of contract which would cause him to lose his wife.

"I feel so damned helpless. There she is, throwing her life away to save the loags of Chiy-une and it's not going to work. It's all for nothing. The loags have been so dractically reduced—damn, what a bloodbath.

"Those hundreds of mercenaries who guarded and ran supply lines, and took care of the engineering surveys are not gone. Nor are they leaving. Neither Hadilka nor Jeffires have any intention of shipping them out."

"There will be no orders to bring them back. The disputes and skirmishes will continue, even though the House of Hadilka no longer presses a claim," Magaikan added, despising the wasted lives.

"No. And they will continue for how long? Until the planet dies, or they do?" He sat back and took a glass of wine. It was heavy-bodied, like his mood.

270

He gazed thoughtfully at Magaikan, sipped the dark red liquor, then said, "Once the last of the supply lines dry up, Jeffires mercenaries will begin making their way to Shirwall."

Banter cleared his throat. "If I may say so, Sire, I believe that will culminate in increased mining activities along the western Lyndirlyan. There have been uranium strikes there, marked and plotted. Residual radiation will keep the mercenaries from returning to Shirwall too quickly." Banter pushed aside the clutter in one of the larger chairs and sat down.

"He's right, Friedo."

"Yes. And an experienced contract soldier will know his fate—and his best alternatives. They will go after the remaining loags."

"They went south," Magaikan said into his glass.

"You have been so sure all along that they went south." Payndacen's eyes narrowed. "Why?"

"You will have to trust me." Magaikan became cast iron. "They went south. Use that information any way that suits you, Friedo."

There was a moment's silence.

"All right," the Uv-Kriell said softly, "they went south. So eventually the soldiers will go south, too. They will need food. They have no women . . . Eventually their clothing will wear out. Their weapons will run down."

"Not the weapons. Not for a long time," Magaikan said slowly. "Hadilka issued KS-2106s."

"So did Jeffires," Banter said.

"Okay. Okay." Pandacen rose and began to wade through the information and plan outlines scattered across the floor. It made the match even more unfair.

"Ahandro, you and Banter go south. Take this ship. Take yours, every one you can . . . No. Wait. Don't take this one. Banter can take it later."

When he turned around there was a glint in his eye, and evil in the smirk passing for a smile. "I believe I have it! By god, we will force Hadilka's hand and make him slip up yet." He picked up the cruiser's manifest, the one logged into the Overeechy files showing two trips, both to capacity, then the accurate one, and slapped them together face to face.

"Ahandro, you leave in the morning. Locate the mercenary strongholds, and prepare them for evacuation. We are going to shove them right down the House of Hadilka's crimson throat!" His eyes narrowed. "Find out if any of them knows

271

anything about Enickor val Densu. I still want to see him. In fact, it is more important now than ever before.

"Banter! Clean up this mess. Stash it where only you can find it. We are going to take a pleasure trip, and we will be having company. Lord and Lady Hadilka are about to begin their connubial life, and we are going to be a part of the send-off. For the time being."

Magaikan did not like the way the Uv-Kriell looked, nor did he approve of the tone of voice. He recognized it too well. Young Payndacen was as devious and single-minded as the old Kriell, once bent on a course. He hoped the woman he loved, and her ideals, were worthy of the Overeechy's most promising heir.

Chapter 29

PAM-ELLA WAS READY FOR LORD HADILKA WHEN
he returned. The three-day respite had permitted some of her
bruises to heal. Others were still dark and ugly.

The reprieve had been put to constructive use. Every scrap
and memory molecule in his collection had been pored over
as though her life depended on it. Not until the third day, hours
before his return, did she come across what she had been
looking for all along. Lord Hadilka's medical history.

She stood on the stairs of Shirwall and gazed out at the
mainland. The death cries emanating from the Lyndirlyan
Mountains fought the wind. They were relentless. *Friedo hears
them,* she mused in wonderment. *Why don't the others?*

It was a question with no answer.

She was sensitive to the bloodlust on the land. It chilled
her. The anger and sorrow Chiy-une exhaled cast a pall over
every living thing.

Across the water, Faelinor began to sing.

Tears rolled from her eyes. To return, even for a day and
a night . . . "I will come back, Theller. Wait for me."

Faelinor's lament blended with the constant shrieks pouring

from the Lyndirlyan. He could hear them dying forever, never stilled, never at peace.

"Ah, there you are, my sweet."

The voice instilled dread. She turned around and brought a smile to her lips. "You have returned quickly, m'Lord . . . Is your business taken care of?" She saw him through the results of his deeds on Chiy-une, perceived a monster, and shrank from his touch.

"Most certainly it is. I have conformed to the letter. My ground advisors and supply line escorts are well on their way home." His large hands dwarfed her shoulders. "What's this? Tears?"

She pushed the moisture from her cheeks. "I was listening to the land."

Amused, he asked, "What? Listening to the land?" He laughed and gently shook her. "And what does this land tell you?"

"I wish to go back."

All mirth faded from Hadilka. Stern, he shook her intentionally. "You are mine now, Pam-ella. No more land! No more running away. I thought you understood that."

"You misunderstood, my Lord. I wish to take you with me, and return for a day." She touched his face. "I will be at your side until the wind god, Ieuchna, lays claim to our spirits.

"I thought perhaps you might like to see some of the places I have lived, and partake of the wonders I found. It would be nice to take a day and share them with you. The time would be of special meaning between us.

"Of course, I would expect you to invite some guests for amusement during the journey.

"Besides, such a journey would permit me to bid farewell to a part of my life you are now replacing. Both are very special to me, you and the land, for different reasons."

She knew he did not want to have any more to do with Chiy-une. A heavy frown deepened the creases of his round face. On tiptoes, she kissed him. "Please?"

He relented, smiling. "All right. I have other matters to attend, which come first, Pam-ella." He embraced her, kissed her and let her go. "You are a delicate flower. I will have to be careful with you." He kissed her again, passionately. "Come. Let's find some privacy before the Uv-Kriell gets back. He seems quite unhappy to have you out of his sight. I certainly understand why. You are lovely, Lady Hadilka."

274

She glanced back at the mainland. Faelinor was on the beach and still lamenting. She wondered if the winsong's dirge was for her.

Not until a day after the arrival of the land beasts was there a sign of the Ocandar. They began filtering in, in small bands. The first few dozen were mothers and children pulling supply carts.

Using rope slings and harnesses, the loagers were brought up the cliff. The carts were a welcome addition.

Meiska patrolled the coast and found nothing.

Scouting parties ventured north to guide more from the Ocandar to the cliff.

Across the gentle rise of the land, away from the sea, a battle raged. It was not the usual skirmish, with no resistance on the part of the loag. Quite the contrary.

The Ocandar had been armed with Star Follower weapons. Self-taught, they had learned well both the value and the dangers of handling such awesome destruction power. They had no sense of battle tactics, yet they struck back at the core of the military force trying to press them against the sea.

The casualties were great on both sides.

On the second day of battle the Ocandar crushed the soldiers' right flank, and penetrated their supply line. They managed to come away with a fresh cache of weapons, a small ration of food, medical supplies, and a parcel of all-weather suits.

That evening a quiet celebration took place behind the Ocandar lines. They ate without benefit of a fire. The man who had become their battle leader spoke softly to the injured, and showed those tending them how to use the medical supplies.

Strom Aknel felt competent and fulfilled. Fighting and strategy had been the sane part of his life for the past eight standard years. He experienced a rush when leading his primitive troops into battle against the military giants across the strip. He loved the sensation. It was even more magnificent than when he killed the ailing soldiers holding Elisif and Zaich.

He decided that killing was a great deal like women. Only certain types were to his liking, and those he enjoyed with an open abandon.

Fog caressed the night. Strom woke and noted the time. Quietly, he roused his forces.

A score of minutes later they were on their way across the

strip. It was unseasonably cold. The night smelled of old death; rancid and abundant.

The Ocandar people rose to the occasion of defense better than any of the loagers with whom Strom had come in contact. He reasoned that they had lived among Lord Jeffires's troops long enough to learn the true meaning of hatred. They had learned well. Being pushed from their loag land made some of them real fighters. Those were the ones he selected as lieutenants.

They crawled on elbows and knees along the green strip separating the camps.

Strom could not remember who the leader was, or if he had ever been told. The Metaliary remained with the wounded. His skills extended far beyond the molding and fashioning of hardened ores. The handling of pliable flesh and compounding special mixtures of herbs were also a part of his realm.

The darkness was complete. Each member of the Ocandar force could reach in either direction and touch his flank-mate. They reached the gentle rise, and started down the inland slope.

Strom took out the binoculars confiscated from the soldiers' supply wagon. Fumbling, he found the infrared setting and looked through them.

Forty meters ahead the enemy camp lay quiet. The bright outlines of sleeping men ringed a cold fire pit. Sentries walked back and forth. He counted their steps, matched them to time, and halted his line.

Soundlessly, he removed the binoculars and secured his *kalase*. Enickor's knife came out of the sheath at his waist. He counted steps and seconds, angling to the outside sentry.

The surprise was muffled by Strom's left hand and the fog. It was a messy kill. He dragged the body back to the Ocandar lines, where it would be stripped of weapons.

The second sentry was more difficult. A big man, Strom came at him from out of the fog. He jumped. His heel slammed into the guard's solar plexus. A whoosh of air stifled a cry into the night. As a safeguard, Strom slipped the long blade between the man's ribs, and pierced his heart.

The third and fourth were easier.

There were more sentries at the far end of the camp. They were not overlapping with the positions of the dead men. Strom sent out the signal.

The Ocandar forces moved. As soon as they entered the

main depression of the camp they began to put space between them.

Strom waited, excited, feeling as though he were a sword of justice ready to drop upon the wicked. *A child of the Seven Gods*.

He stood and shouted.

The Ocandar opened fire.

Chaos churned through the fog and grew loud. The sentries on the opposing side of the camp returned fire immediately. Those on the ground took longer to respond. Some never did.

The Ocandar were careful to remain on the perimeter of the depression, lest they be caught in a cross fire of their own and the soldiers.

It did not last long, nor was it a complete rout. More than a score successfully retreated into the protection of the foggy night.

The casualties were heavy. When the Ocandar pulled back to their own lines, they found their new leader had been seriously wounded.

A wince passed as a grin when Strom addressed the Metaliary. "If you cannot do anything for me, let me go quickly. I am not one for lingering deaths." The pain in his left side came and went. He no longer had any sensation in his left calf or foot. "Please."

Surrounded by his lieutenants, Strom felt whole inside. Never before had he felt so much at peace as that moment. "Victory. You have tasted victory. You can beat them." He took a deep breath and let it out slowly. To the Metaliary, "Tell Enickor you found the equalizer." Painfully, he unfastened his *kalase* and extended it.

Strom drifted in and out of consciousness for the next several days. Sometimes the pain of being jostled in a cart became his passport to absolution.

Eventually he heard Enickor speaking to him. When he opened his eyes he saw Jelica and a torna-pok. He closed them quickly, doubting he could do what Enickor asked. He could feel his life slipping away a little at a time. Jelica undressed him tenderly. He kept wondering why, even after Enickor explained that he was going with the torna-pok to be healed. The sun burning inside his left ribs and leg went through what he considered the equivalent of a prolonged nova stage, confined only by his skin.

"It will be all right," Jelica said, then kissed his brow. "They are healers, Strom. Enickor says that they will take good care of you." Her eyes were red, but she did not cry. "They had better. There is no one else to teach me how to take pleasure seriously. You still will, won't you?"

He hoped so.

Enickor watched the torna-pok carry away Strom and a dozen other wounded from the Ocandar. Heavy-hearted, he listened to the accounts from the Ocandar. Strom Aknel had an army. If he lived, so did Chiy-une.

"Equalizing violence," Enickor whispered. *Mistress? Is that our only hope?*

The answer came in a burst of sorrow and anger.

The Lyndirlyan was dying.

The nekka in the sea cliffs felt the battle upon the land and tasted bitter victory in the rock. The wind bespoke sorrow and death. Ruin had touched the sea cliffs.

The nekka remained in the bottom of the leah they were building.

The novelty of role-playing for the two lords had worn thin for the Uv-Kriell. His disdain for Lord Hadilka and his host at Shirwall became more difficult to hide with each encounter. Seeing Pam-ella cling to the man's side, knowing her hard-muscled body was bruised under her unstylish and overly-modest dresses, did not lighten the task ahead.

Banter waited at the stairs. The ship was ready and hovering over the ocean on his right.

They marked the days of waiting. Magaikan's search for the remaining bodies of mercenaries was well underway.

Freido wanted something, anything, to use as an excuse to annul Lord Hadilka's marriage contract with Pam-ella. Proceeding without Pam-ella's knowledge of what he was doing troubled him slightly. There seemed no way to convince her of the futility in persisting with her line of thinking. Her objectives had been accomplished.

Yet Pam-ella had her own plans well underway. Each day with Hadilka was a special kind of hell. She hoped it would purge her soul of the festering guilt. Ardinay watched in her dreams.

As she stepped outside the carved doors of Shirwall she could hear the land calling, and the pitiful cries in the Lyndirlyan. She glanced at Friedo.

He met her gaze and she knew that he also heard it.

The ship was near capacity. The Lords Hadilka and Jeffires sat in the lounge with Pam-ella, Friedo, and two guests from neighboring Great Houses. House of Jeffires servants were jammed into the galley with carriers and exotic foods and beverages. Conversation was sparse, forced.

Pam-ella watched the land roll by on the viewer. The magnitude of the devastation in the heart of the Lyndirlyan astounded her. The eastern areas, the Head and the Hedshire Forests, were gone, the ground leveled to a gentle slope rising from the prairie lands.

The fate of the Alizandar worried her, but she said nothing.

Eventually the ship turned north. They traveled slowly over the mountain range until reaching a place which looked untouched by Star Followers.

Pam-ella knew the territory. Heart beating wildly in her throat, she asked the Uv-Kriell to land the ship.

The Lords exchanged muted comments. Payndacen was annoyed at the break such a stop would present in his schedule. Magaikan's cache of mercenaries was not far.

She asked again.

The Uv-Kriell conceded and ordered Banter to turn back and land.

A herd of torna-pok watched from the trees. Banter was reluctant to open the ship.

"Come, my Lord. This is a very special place, and I would like to share it with you," she said, extending her hand to Hadilka. Inwardly, she quivered. There was no stopping the events unfolding. She was committed. Their fate rested in the land now. She no longer felt in control of either her mind or her body. At best, she was a witness acting as a monitor pledged to signal the optimum time. She did not want to know the outcome of the events happening around her. The suspense gave it a frightening sense of excitement.

"You mean, go out there? There are beasts in the forest."

She smiled. "They will not harm you. Have you so little trust in me, m'Lord?"

"Lady Pam-ella . . ." the Uv-Kriell started, then stopped. He recognized the air of determination about her and ceased questioning.

It took more cajoling for Lord Hadilka to relinquish his comfortable divan for the meadow of Chiy-une. They sauntered through the ship down the ramp. The land was soft under their feet. The air was clean.

Pam-ella turned in the meadow. The sirens of death were still. Only the wind in the trees called. The puzzlement evident in Friedo's behavior bothered her. She wanted to ask his help, but did not. Instead, she asked him quietly to trust her as she returned to the ramp for Hadilka.

Payndacen's blood felt congealed in his veins. He did not know what she was planning, but he did not like it, either. The dread honing his wits remained just below the panic level. He felt the anticipation charging the air, a slight quaking on the ground. A thickness in his throat prevented speech.

He watched Pam-ella tease Hadilka and his guests into the center of the meadow. Unable to move, he heard her laughter and thought it tear-filled. Removed from the rest of the party, he wanted to call out, do something, anything but be frozen in time.

A tremendous oppression seized Payndacen in a powerful grip at the same time that he saw the torna-pok emerge from the forest. The loathing the beasts carried spread over the meadow like the ocean on the beach at high tide. It became a paralytic blast from a KS-2106.

Beside the ship, the laughter continued.

He did not understand how they could make jokes. Couldn't they feel the power in the air? It came from all around them, like thundering hooves ready to trample the life from their bones.

The men surrounding Pam-ella listened to her oration on the torna-pok migration and mating rituals, and noted where she pointed with open interest.

"I feel as though I have been here," Hadilka said, bemused. He took several steps toward the tarnished Arch to the Upper Creel.

"The torna-pok run comes out of the Lyndirlyan up there." She pointed at a glacier-carved pass. "Each year they come down to mate."

"You know, I am sure that I did some hunting here." Hadilka said, nodding.

Pam-ella glanced over at the torna-pok standing in front of the trees. Her nod was slight. She felt the essence of her being caught up and sucked out of her, like the gorbich poisons the torna-pok had pulled from her body.

"Yes. It was a magnificent hunt a couple of years ago.

Nothing to it." His voice trailed. He squinted at the Arch. The surface shed its blackened skin and began to shine as it had when thousands of torna-pok polished it with their long, flopping coats. Their ghosts hammered the ground, translucent and larger than life. His heart tripped over beats. The course of his blood through his arteries became complicated, the passageways plugged by minuscule red corpses with six legs.

Briefly, Pam-ella recalled that time in the tauiri, and wondered if she had known then the torna-pok were a large part of her answers. They knew her thoughts, but she was not privy to theirs. Was it their idea to come here, or hers? Did she want Hadilka dead? Or did they want vengeance? Or both? If they had gazed into her mind then, they knew what she had seen, what she had experienced.

She looked at Hadilka, at the torna-pok, back to Hadilka, and realized that it did not matter. The debt would be paid. It was beyond her or any other Star Follower's control.

The Lord looked into a triangle of three green eyes and saw his inner self. He grabbed at his chest, then his head. The little clotted images of torna-pok closed off the arteries. The black translucent leader ran over him, followed by the herd. He cried out in fear, then collapsed.

The royal party standing near him hurried to his aid. They worked feverishly to loosen his clothing and make him comfortable in the dew-dampened meadow. Once he was lying down, they tried to straighten his ponderous bulk.

Hoyiv shouted for a medical scan and diagnoser. Banter ran into the ship and came out carrying an armload of equipment.

Inexplicably, the pall lifted, and Friedo was able to move. He was shaken inwardly. He did not understand what had rooted him to the ground.

A dozen gries flew down from the Upper Lyndirlyan and passed overhead. Their song was light, cheerful. The hum and buzz of insects signaled the endless work to be done in the flower-dotted meadow.

Strangulated sounds rose from Lord Hadilka. Banter worked on him. The diagnoser read out symbols, lines of symptoms, and a final analysis.

Hadilka was given pop after pop of medication.

Banter and one of the guests worked on the lord long after the grotesque sounds had ceased. Soon, all five sat back on their heels and gazed up at Pam-ella.

"I'm sorry, Pam-ella," Hoyiv said, and meant it. "There was nothing we could do. I . . ."

She looked down at the corpse. Even in death she felt him leering at her. A tear slipped down her cheek. She turned away.

The torna-pok began retreating into the shadows. A black bull paused. His enormous green eyes focused on the lone woman.

For a brief moment, they shared understanding.

Pam-ella cried. Her tears were not for joy, nor were they for relief. She and the torna-pok had used one another to kill an enemy of the land. But both knew it was too late.

The Uv-Kriell approached her and spread his cape over her shoulders. He did not speak. The oppression had diminished, but he knew everything had been changed irrevocably.

Illeuro and his nekka unanimously paused. The radiation seeping into the rock from above tasted of death. Yet there was the taste of another death in the rock they transmuted.

It was a bittersweet taste.

It was revenge.

Only Illeuro knew its name. He felt the essence of the land rangtur smile upon him, and thought their work would go easier now.

Chapter 30

THE SUDDEN DEATH OF LORD HADILKA THREW HIS House into a state of chaos. Pam-ella, aided by the Uv-Kriell, brought his body to the heart of the Overeechy for the Ceremony of the Six Days and subsequent cremation. He remained controversial even in death. The throng witnessing the final days of the ceremony was a mixture of tearful sorrow and complacency.

Kal Pridain chose to wait until the ceremony had ended before approaching Lady Jeffires-Hadilka. He was a small man, with kind brown eyes and a thin-lipped smile. "My condolences, Lady Hadilka. Had he but listened to my constant words of caution, perhaps he would still be with us."

"I beg your pardon?"

"The autopsy scan—his heart transplant and the constant weakening of his arteries—is what I mean. He lived as he wished, with no heed to consequence."

Isn't that the truth, she thought. "I thank you for your concern." Inwardly she shook, not once having thought about the result of the mandatory autopsy for all nobles.

"Lord Hadilka had been under my care many times. Again, may I express my sorrow at both our losses. Any time you

have need of me, or my services, please call me personally."
The wiry man took leave with a bow.

The finery of the Overeechy hit her at last. She seldom saw
Friedo away from the Overeechy meeting rooms. He had his
own affairs to soothe and handle.

She delayed starting her year of mourning long enough to
become acquainted with her new household, the business as-
pects and financial projections for the coming years. There
were several meetings with the Kriell, the military advisors of
the Overeechy, and two House of Hadilka generals straight
from the Sellbic system. Pam-ella assured them all that Hadilkan military policy would remain unchanged.

The journey from Chiy-une, the strain of learning an entire
House language and routine, melded into the whirl of events
which never seemed to halt. For every two commitments she
fulfilled, four awaited. The time became a haze that she moved
through, almost comprehending each situation, but not quite,
able to bring it off, but without confidence.

Three marks passed, then three more. At last her house was
secure, its affairs straight, and she was ready to begin her year
of mourning.

She chose Chiy-une as the place, much to the disappointment of those whose concern and care she had elicited during
her residency.

Banter piloted the Overeechy ship on a course to Chiy-une.
The Uv-Kriell accompanied Lady Hadilka to her chosen place.
This time his departure from the Overeechy carried the blessing
of his father. For, since he had stood for Pam-ella at the marriage, he also carried an obligation in this matter.

They were strangers on the journey, seldom speaking, often
staring at one another. Banter avoided them, as did the few
servants and advisors accompanying them.

Two days prior to landing, Payndacen could tolerate the
strain no longer. He waited until she was ready to retire, then
followed to her cabin. He knocked softly.

She answered right away. Beyond her, on a wall chair her
pack was ready and waiting. Loag clothes lay on the floor next
to it. "Yes?"

"I want to talk to you."

Hesitant, she stepped away.

They were awkward for a few moments as they chose places
to sit, across the small cabin from one another.

"I want to know what happened out there."

284

"Where?" she asked, smoothing the coverlet over her pillow.

"When Hadilka died. I felt something happening, as though I was being sucked into a stream of events and made powerless to stop them." Rubbing his hands together, he tried to think of the right words to describe his feelings. There did not seem to be any.

"Symbiosis is the closest thing I can think of, Friedo. It just . . . happened. Me, the torna-pok, and something else."

"The planet?" It was a whisper. He wanted her to say no.

She hesitated, then nodded, not looking at him. "Please understand, that is why I have to go back. There is no choice for me. There never has been . . . not since the clearing and Hadilka.

"I need answers, too. I need . . . so much, Friedo, so very much. And I don't know where to start. I can make some of the parts fall into place for Chiy-une. You know, ship out the rest of the soldiers Commander Magaikan has found. I don't care whose they were."

She laughed bitterly. "My late husband's mining endeavors on Chiy-une ensured wealth for his House for generations."

She looked at him and no longer tried to hide her tears or the doubt gnawing at her. "Why did you come, Friedo? Are you still hoping to find Enickor? Are you, too, looking for the something missing in your life?"

"Yes, for Enickor, for myself. And I came along because you might need me. A great deal has changed, Pam-ella. The missing thing in my life is right in this cabin. But you're not ready yet, are you? I love you. I don't think that will ever change."

She cried hard.

He rose, started for the door, then stopped and turned back. Crouched before her, he removed her hands from her face.

"Don't go yet," she sobbed. "I still need you . . ." She reached for him, wanting to pour out her feelings, unable to continue speaking through her tears. How could she explain the intricate needs she felt for the land and the peace she hoped to find to him, when she did not understand it?

He held her, feeling her wounds to be as grievous as they had been after the gorbich.

They were three hundred strong before entering the badlands. Two hundred and thirty survived. Plagued by thirst and

285

hunger, they had moved steadily south and endured the parched badlands.

The eighty-seven days spent crossing the desolated land crushed most of the spirit from the loagers. Even the self-sufficient Ocandar failed to maintain the hard-won optimism which bolstered the Alizandar. The totality of the destruction bit into their hearts and found the places where each hid from his own fear.

After the crossing they were near the sea once again. Meiska waited in a lagoon filled with corralled fish.

The journey had consumed more than a hundred and fifty days. Summer slipped into autumn. The harbingers of winter had come and gone. The Southern Rohn was warmer than the Lyndirlyan or the ocean beside Shirwall. But the water still froze on the streams at night, cold snakes penetrated the primitive tents, and snow piled too high to hunt for anittes.

The place Enickor chose to settle was a large, gentle valley near the sea. No mountains pressed the fog against them. The open plateau lent itself to crop planting. The Alizandar were pleased by his choice, as were the Ocandar. Enickor considered their joint satisfaction a major victory.

Enickor hoped the two cultures would reinforce one another. They were dependent upon the sea until the first crops were planted and harvested.

The trek had cost lives and relationships. It had also put a couple back together, and cemented personal bonds.

Inorag survived the hardships of the badlands and actually appeared younger. When he had sought out the Ocandar Leader he met with personal disappointment, for the old one had been slain by the Star Follower soldiers. Now, the Ocandar followed their savior—Strom Aknel. And Strom followed Enickor val Densu, the Porintel Leader of the Harcel Loag. It ceased to make sense to Inorag. He left it alone and resumed the task of leading his people, resigned to being the only true leader of any people.

The torna-pok rejoined the loagers after they crossed the badlands. With them were Strom Aknel and eight of the ten Ocandar loagers injured on the northern side. They and the roh had skirted the waste. Strom was healthy, not sufficiently to embark on his plans for the Star Follower helix ships, but enough to plan on having a future.

He was reluctant to discuss his experiences. The glint in his eye and the constant smile he wore bespoke a time not solely concerned with healing. The herds trailed the caravan, disappeared totally several times, but always came back. More than once a torna-pok or roh was deliberately left behind to feed the travelers. It waited for death as though it were a blessing.

Elisif grew large with child. Enickor worried about her constantly. The hidden spring feeding the well of strength she drew upon seemed endless. When he had feared Chiy-une's children doomed, in the Lyndirlyan, she gave him hope and stroked his courage. Quiet, anticipating his needs, she remained constant at his side. Not until she was needed to attend a woman from the Ocandar whose time came to be delivered of her child did Enickor realize how emotionally dependent he had become on her.

He had waited a night, a day, and most of a second night for her to return. When she had returned to creep into the tent, she had been tired and drained. Old tear traces had marked her cheeks. Fresh ones clung to her lower eyelids.

Somber, she had said few words to him. Both the mother and the child had died.

The significance hit Enickor sharply. His worries about the child Elisif carried intensified. He thought he could survive the baby's death, but not Elisif's.

That night he lay awake and beseeched the Mistress to protect her. Elisif lay on his shoulder sleeping fitfully. The child moved against him. He wondered when the deep love he felt for her had begun and flourished to such great proportions.

Like the anger he felt when first upon the land, the love he held for Pam-ella had also faded away. *Perhaps it died from neglect,* he thought, *or perhaps it never really existed, and all it ever was, was wanting and not being able to have.*

Elisif had been right. She could love him enough for both of them.

The following evening they entered the valley where they settled. There were ceremonies of celebration and ceremonies for those who did not survive. Pindar bestowed upon them a simple eulogy for the Porintel and the lost Harcel.

The next morning they began felling trees to construct common houses and running barracks for living quarters. The season was well upon them, and the cold nights promised cold days in the not-too-distant future.

Gradually the differences between the two loags came to be something appreciated, instead of quarreled over. Zaich and

Landah courted women from both loags for a while. Then only Landah was seen moving back and forth.

Peace fit well into the journey-weary loags. The island of serenity they lived on was remote from the Star Followers. Ships did not disturb the sky here.

Meiska helped them through the first winter.

Elisif's child, a boy, did not survive the birth trauma. The tragedy drew her closer to Enickor. Together they cried and buried the babe, both praying to the wind and Chiy-une for a better second life for their son.

A hard winter; they lost twenty-three to the cold.

Spring brought warmth, planting time, and evidence of activity on the cold winter nights. More dwellings would rise on the green plains. A second crop, babies, would be reaped by autumn.

With the return of warmth came the Mistress. Her ailing call reminded Enickor where his loyalties had been placed.

He took Meiska and returned to the island. But there was no joy in the homecoming, only sadness and the knowledge of impending doom.

The north had been devastated, the Lyndirlyan Mountains leveled, the Birthplace of the Wind gone, as were the great forests that stretched and wound down through the Gorbich Hills. The Plains of Akatna os Egra had turned to stony rubble; barren, parched with radiation, the rich topsoil washed into the river and out to the sea. Even the far eastern mountains had been planed to the level of the flatlands which once stretched between the two great ranges.

The ice at the northern pole had been attacked by the helix ship. The continent covered by millennium after millennium of ice layering yielded a vein of pure nickel.

Enickor empathized with the Mistress, sharing her sorrow and the ire of each assault that stripped more of her tender inner tissue of its irreplaceable treasures.

Powerless to halt the Star Followers, a keen depression settled over him. Meiska delivered him from the island.

Elisif, Jelica, and several of the smaller children swam in the shallows.

As Meiska approached, Enickor thought once again how mixed life's blessings had become. He dove off the rangtur and swam to Elisif, anxious to be alone with her.

He held her with a fierceness that delightfully surprised her. "I love you, Elisif," he whispered vehemently, and held her

288

tighter, fearing her loss more than that of Chiy-une. She made him feel whole; needed, loved. For her, he would do anything Chiy-une asked. Without her, there was no future.

Gaediv had spread leahs over the continent. The katelings were fewer, their population controlled by something the great Gaediv did not understand. She remained supreme, each Gaediv remaining in contact with her, tapping her memories, using her as a central information bank. Always, they had to return to the source.

Gaediv was the source. All knew her to be so.

She was Most Revered.

Their work progressed slowly below the chaotic surface. Quakes, volcanoes, and the ancient business of mountain-building seemed to compress normal geologic time. The Lyndirlyan refused to stay buried. It was as if the rock gathered itself from across the plains and out of the sky, and struggled to rise above everything around.

Illeuro asa Khatioup wandered between nekkas and leahs. He had become what no other Quniero had been—a loner. Yet he was not dispossessed of mind. He neither became lost nor did he turn violent. He listened to the spirit which had touched him in the Head Forest.

Each Gaediv knew this, questioned, then accepted the anomaly for which there was no answer.

It was Illeuro who made first contact with the native caretakers living in the south. The spirit had directed him to the land's Warrior.

Illeuro did not think the caretaker appeared any different from the others. His taste gave confusion. He was of the stars, but also of the land. The spirits that touched upon this caretaker were greater than those who communed with him.

Illeuro offered gems.

The caretaker refused, having no need. In return, he offered grain.

Illeuro tasted of it, knew its value, and the sacrifice the caretaker made to offer such a thing, and left.

This place smelled of ore.

He wished to tell the caretaker of the caretaker treasure in the ground below them. Illeuro did not know how.

The ore smelled pure and tasted of death.

* * *

The seasons slipped by, and the year of mourning had passed.

No peace had settled in Pam-ella's soul. No answers had graced the ends to hundreds of questions.

Twice she had rendezvoused with the Uv-Kriell. The second time, their parting had been inexplicably painful for her.

It was winter of the second year. The land paths between the desolate areas of the north took her southward, as they soon would the miners.

Stray torna-pok traveled with her and Theller. Occasionally a gorbich wandered their way. The torna-pok always made short work of the strays.

Pam-ella slept securely at night. The creatures surrounding her were friends indeed, and would fend off the worst gorbich attack.

The gorbich had been forced into the badlands. The first generation to survive the radiation now tried to survive their first independent winter. They were a brazen lot. Night was their hunting and feeding time. They ventured beyond the fringes of dead trees and scrub marking the beginning of the badlands, and into the healthy land where small game thrived in deeply dug burrows.

The torna-pok represented a living barrier between Pam-ella and the grotesque gorbich creatures who haunted the night.

She moved south, looking for something she began to think was as dead as Enickor val Densu, but unable to leave Chiy-une behind and go home to the Overeechy. There always seemed one more trail which had to be followed, one more bend she needed to look around.

She knew Friedo Payndacen would wait. On the eve of their last night together, she had asked him not to, and feared his agreement. Even when he reluctantly agreed to leave her and return to the Overeechy, she was unable to shed the invisible shackles holding her to the dying planet.

Chapter 31

ANOTHER WINTER ROLLED OVER THE SOUTHERN Rohn. This one found them prepared. The fires in the hearths were large, as were the stew pots hanging over them. The granaries strained at the seams, and the ice houses were nearly empty.

A forge, primitive and crude, warmed part of the common with its sheltered heat.

Well-fed children toddled and crawled over the tables and benches of the common. Their parents remained lean from the last harsh winter and the rigors of easing this one.

During one of the recently-begun evening conferences came a sound which stilled Enickor's heart. It was a ship. Close. It sounded as though it was landing.

He and Strom slipped away from the group and the Harcel legend Elisif recited. She caught his look, then continued her culture-rich tale.

Enickor glanced at his people. They had grown since coming to the valley. There was no panic incited by the Star Follower ship. Panic would not make them go away. And there was no way to fight back. With what? Loagers could not fight a ship, not even with the *kalases* the Ocandar prized.

291

They had used their only available weapon, patience, hoping to outwait the Star Followers, and the ice bearing down on them from both poles, and the radiation pouring out of the ruined land.

Strom followed Enickor into the night. Rain beat the ground. It was a naturally heavy rain, void of Star Follower origin.

The ship became visible once they passed beyond the compound boundaries. The landing site was a place slated for domestic multicrop planting in the spring. Close to the low-walled semifortress, it would be the early summer garden.

Seven men departed from the ship. Six were heavily armed. The man in the center had no visible weapons.

The two sides approached each other steadily. Without warning, the six armed men staggered out in alternate steps and halted. The center man kept moving.

In the rain it was difficult to distinguish features beneath the all-weather suit, but Enickor thought the man familiar.

"How has the Harcel Loag and its Leader fared over this last cycle of seasons?" the man asked, extending his left hand.

"Fewer in number than when we last met, Commander Magaikan," Enickor replied. He hesitated, then took the commander's offer of peace between them. "Landah's parents were killed in the mountains by the House of Jeffires."

Magaikan swore under his breath. "I am sorry to hear that. I had hoped for . . . Never mind.

"What of the Alizandar? Were you able to get many of them across the badlands?"

"Yes. Many survived. It was difficult. Very hard on them. Most of our casualties were suffered on the Plains of Akatna os Egra before we took to the river." He and the commander walked idly in the rain. "We picked up the Ocandar north of the badlands. They have learned some of the Star Follower ways and emotions well." He gestured to Strom. "They follow Aknel. He led them into battle against a group who tried to rout the Ocandar and take its food, women, and clothing."

Magaikan stopped and glanced at Aknel with the certainty of a man who know men and their capacities. "May we go somewhere and talk? It is important."

Enickor glanced around. The land felt sacred to him. And while he trusted Commander Magaikan more than any other Star Follower, he did not want any Star Followers in the three rooms he and Elisif called home. Much had happened over the seasons since he last spoke with Magaikan, but he still could not open his loag to him. He appreciated the commander's rare quality of being a man of his word.

"Your ship? Providing I am free to go when we finish?"

"Certainly. I did not think it would be acceptable for you." He turned and led the way back to the light.

"Your men are quite safe here, Commander. There is no need for them to remain in the rain, armed or unarmed."

Magaikan dismissed half the guard.

Enickor matched stride with the commander and felt the silent presence of the Ocandar Leader on his left.

Strom was tense in the relaxed manner he had been trained to use when killing. He neither liked nor disliked entering the ship. It was a ship like a hundred others. The men were men. They bled. He would kill them or not, depending on the circumstances that unfolded between the two men on his right.

Inside the ship, they paused in a large airlock for several seconds to dry. Magaikan removed his headgear and led them down a corridor, passed four armed ship's crew, and into a conference room doubling as his office.

Magaikan tossed his gear at a holder on the wall and missed. He stripped down to his uniform before turning back to his guests.

"Make yourselves comfortable."

Both men removed the head portion of their all-weather gear.

The commander had aged. There was more gray in his hair. His clean-shaven face yielded more expression. His hazel eyes appeared to have withdrawn further into the sanctuary of his brow.

"It seems I find myself in a rather unusual predicament," Magaikan began. "In my search for Enickor val Densu I failed to count on the zeal that this man's brother—half brother—would have in his efforts to find him."

Enickor stepped out of his suit, straightened his torna-pok-skin breeches, and sat.

"It was unrealistic for me to think he would abandon the search. I should have known better," Magaikan said, disgruntled.

Strom remained dressed and standing. His *kalase* was ready and out of sight. He met Magaikan's gaze with steel.

It bothered the commander to have his every move analyzed by a stranger who was more of a loager than a soldier. The sharpness of his eyes and the feel of the man separated him from the others. "When did you acquire a bodyguard? A Star Follower? Mercenary, by any chance?" he asked Enickor.

"Strom is the Leader of the Ocandar Loag. He is a member of my family."

Magaikan addressed Aknel and relaxed. "I'm curious. Where did you acquire your battle strategy? I spoke to survivors of that skirmish and was amazed by your tactics. Impressive."

Aknel acknowledged the compliment with a nod and remained silent. Talking broke concentration. Every mercenary guard worth his medallion knew that. So did the Overeechy Commander.

"All right." Magaikan moved over to the head of the conference table and poured three cups full of steaming black liquid. He had answered his own questions concerning Aknel. To Enickor: "What happened to the young woman with the Harcel? Did she survive?"

"She is my wife." Enickor took a cup and nodded for Strom to do the same.

"Your wife?" Magaikan was surprised. "I would have thought . . ." His voice trailed. He looked troubled, doubtful.

"You would have thought what?" Enickor asked over the cup.

"Nothing. Nothing."

"When last we met you promised me permanent residency," Enickor said softly. "I am glad you have changed your mind. For both our sakes."

Strom shifted imperceptibly.

"Many things have changed." The faraway expression that came over Magaikan relayed the complexities of his world.

"Tell me of the changes. Do they affect Chiy-une?"

"Pam-ella Jeffires married Lord Hadilka, for one. The Chiy-une mining interests all belong to Lord Hoyiv Jeffires now."

"I see." The words came slowly. The news left him numb inside. He expected to feel something, anything, not as though the inevitable had finally occurred, and that it was unfortunate.

"No, you could not possibly see. I fail to understand any of this, val Densu."

Enickor glared at the older man. Quietly, he asked, "Why do you call me that?"

"Quit playing games. We both know I knew who you were when I let you go with the Harcel. As I said, much has happened. You are going to have to come forward now."

Enickor did not change his expression, nor did he answer.

"I attended the marriage at Shirwall. Lady Pam-ella married Lord Hadilka for only one reason. She wanted the soldiers off Chiy-une, and the loags safe from them. Hadilka had gone looking for her—starting with the Porintel." He paused and could not meet Enickor's unwavering gaze. "I am sorry about your loag. Had I suspected, steps would have been taken."

Surprised, he placed the empty cup on the table. The Porintel's fate had been resigned seasons earlier. The confirmation was unexpected.

"The politics became very delicate. Through it all the Uv-Kriell," looking at Enickor, "your half-brother, has been looking for you. He is as possessed as she is."

After an awkward silence Enickor cleared his throat. "What do you want from me, Commander Magaikan? Volunteer status for safe-keeping at the Overeechy?"

"No. That danger has lessened. This is now House of Jeffires territory. We have kept it sealed, and regulated the influx of manpower." Magaikan sighed heavily. "Lord Hadilka is deceased. It is only with his widow's backing and power that I have been able to operate this openly."

Enickor accepted the news with a quick blinking of his eyes. "Did marriage fail to agree with him? Or did one of his enemies finally breach his personal defense?"

"He died in the Lyndirlyan Mountains in the midst of his wedding guests and Lord Jeffires. Lady Pam-ella was there, too, as was the Uv-Kriell." Magaikan refilled his cup. "It changed them."

Enickor noted the difficulty the commander had achieving impartiality. The man's emotions ran deep, and his disturbance was great. It seemed that he groped with something far beyond the logic of his understanding. Chiy-une had touched his soul. Her mark did not rest easily.

"What I want—my reasons for being here—I want you to come north with me. Give me thirty days, val Densu. I want you to meet with the Uv-Kriell. See Lady Hadilka." He turned on Enickor, his composure as fixed as granite. His hazel eyes were fill with compassion. "Set them free from you, from this place, from this time.

"The mercenaries are gone." He glanced at Strom. "Perhaps a select few remain. The House of Hadilka has searched out even the smallest pockets of them, and transported them back to their homeworlds. Lady Hadilka has spared no expense."

The pause that followed was loud with the air circulation

system. "You know for sure this has been done?" Enickor asked.

"Yes. I have done it on behalf of the House of Hadilka. In this, I hold her power of attorney and sealing crest. She has endured much, and risked even more, to guarantee the safety of the loags from the dissension between the two houses."

Enickor rose and walked back and forth across the office. She had submitted to Hadilka after all. He stopped pacing. "Where did Hadilka die?"

"On a torna-pok run called the Arch of the Upper Creel." Magaikan spoke softly, following the other man's thoughts and lending his own confirmation without say it aloud.

"This brother of mine . . ."

"Is in love with Lady Hadilka," Magaikan finished.

"Then why does he wish to see me? He should go see her."

"It is not that easy, is it, Enickor?"

He did not answer.

"He would not harm you. Quite the contrary." Magaikan sat on the edge of the table and folded his arms. "Thirty days, val Densu. It's winter. There's no planting. No harvesting."

Enickor glanced at Strom.

"The Uv-Kriell will be here in three days. I'm rendezvousing with Lady Hadilka in two. Will you leave with me tomorrow?"

"What if I say no?"

Magaikan shrugged, palms up. "Then I will be forced to bring Lady Hadilka here to identify you. The Uv-Kriell will follow.

"We can do it here, or we can do it at the Overeechy base camp. It might be easier on your people, and your wife in particular, if this took place back at the base camp."

Instead of being angry, Enickor smiled. "You leave me little choice."

Magaikan kept silent.

It seemed inevitable that he would have to face the Star Followers again. "I believe you were the one who told me I shouldn't go with anyone, regardless of the reasons they gave. How do I know the House of Corphlange has not reamed out your mind and replaced it with a remotely controlled organism?"

Magaikan grinned. "I guess you have no guarantee of that, do you?"

"What about the mining?" Enickor asked slowly, figuring his position. "Can you open a way to put a stop to it?"

296

"Perhaps it is also time you paid a visit to your old House, val Densu. Lord Jeffires will see you, so long as you are in the company of his sister and the Uv-Kriell," he answered thoughtfully. "I'll work on arranging it."

"Now that might induce me to go," Enickor said thoughtfully. Chiy-une, free of the mining helix ships, still had a slender chance for a future.

Enickor shook out his dry suit and put it on. "I will give you my answer in the morning."

"Fair enough. By the way, do you need anything?"

He stopped halfway out of the conference room door. "Like what?"

Magaikan shrugged. "Antibiotics, medical supplies, a hard-ened steel forge?"

He turned to Strom. "Beware of Star Followers bearing both strong consciences and gifts, for they shall attempt to make you feel obligated."

"There is something else."

Enickor turned back. His smile had disappeared. "What?"

"Quinero were brought in to mine precious gemstones. I have searched, used heat scans, movement broaches, and everything I can think of to find them. They need to return to Alidanko in order to survive." Magakian slumped in his chair. "They, too, were victims."

"I have seen one, Commander. He visits upon occasion. Sometimes I think he tries to talk to me, but I have no idea what he might be saying. He does not stay long. And he is always alone."

Magaikan shook his head. "Loners do not live long. They are a hive culture, and must return to a group, travel together, and the like. If they become separated for too long a time, they suffer a kind of terminal insanity."

"How many were brought in?" Strom asked, speaking for the first time.

"I have no way of knowing. Neither House kept accurate records. Naturally."

"Naturally," Strom repeated.

Magaikan regarded him sharply. "Can you make a guess?"

"It does not matter. They do not want to be found," Enickor said with a finality that ended the conversation. "Let's get back, Strom."

* * *

It was a short night. Elisif did not sleep, nor did she cry until after he was gone.

The storm broke. Strands of white/gray clouds remained strung high in the sky. She and Jelica went down to the ocean and watched Meiska herd fish into the nets of the Ocandar fishermen. On the horizon were a horde of rangtur coming their way.

The ship lifted with a roar, and was out of sight before the beginning sounds reached the two women.

Theller halted, then pressed into the shelter of a rock outcrop. The pattern of mining ships overhead moved at an abnormally slow pace.

The torna-pok scattered in every direction. The sensor beam scanning for rich ore deposits pierced their eardrums and plunged them into a bath of pain.

The repercussions nauseated Pam-ella. She ate no dinner that evening, nor did Theller graze. The close proximity of the beam left them slightly disoriented and dazed.

She built a large fire as night approached. Without the torna-pok insulation against the mutated gorbich she felt a threat. Plenty of wood was piled near the fire. Ill, she would not sleep much. Her fear would keep her awake until morning.

Most of the night was quiet. In the small hours before morning the gorbich began their hoarse hooting. They had surrounded her in the dark, and now began to close the circle. She felt herself back in the Gorbich Hills, the paralysis caused by fear this time, not an attacker's weapon.

Huddled beside the fire, she sorted out her packs. The sender Friedo had insisted she take when she returned to Shirwall sat at the bottom. She picked it up.

A round of gorbich hoots shook the night.

She activated the sender. It was about time anyway, she decided.

The gorbich drew nearer.

She threw more wood onto the fire. The flames sloughed tremendous heat as they reached to the stars. Pam-ella held her *kalase* and faced the night.

Theller snorted. His hoof-falls were loud on the ground. His two heads carried on a conversation filled with fear and empty soothing.

The sun seemed frozen over the dark eastern horizon.

The gorbich grew more brazen in the torna-pok's absence. One leaped into the camp and caught his hide on fire when he braved the flames dancing in the air for ten meters.

Pam-ella fired the *kalase* and hit him in the side of his enormous, misshapen head.

He kept running, his side blazing. The screech and odor hung in the air like a portent of the foul miasma to come.

A second gorbich ventured into the firelight.

Pam-ella killed him instantly.

His comrades hooked him with their talons and dragged him into the shadows. She could hear them tearing the kill limb from limb.

They were quiet while they ate.

She began to relax a little. Knuckles locked around the *kalase* loosened. Blood rushed into her fingers.

With nothing to do but watch and wait, she counted the minutes until dawn.

Theller's nerve-curdling cry terrified her.

She jumped to her feet in time to see him being dragged away from the fire by half a dozen mutated gorbich. She began firing, turned back, and fired on the two more advancing on her.

She killed them both. The closest one fell into the fire and began to burn. Next she took aim and fired at two more in order to secure the area behind her. When she returned to Theller, he was hobbling back toward the fire circle, kicking, gnashing with his teeth at the beast latched onto his side. Pam-ella went for a head shot. The jaws released.

Theller returned to the fire and brayed victory.

"Theller!" she screamed, wanting to feel him for assurance and mutual protection.

She fired at the spot where the gorbich attacked from most frequently. The thrashing beyond the burning bushes ceased.

A lone gorbich hooted three times, then howled at the brightening line in the east.

From the west came a ship to answer her distress beacon.

She felt as far removed from reality as she had been after meeting Ardinay at the Birthplace of the Wind, and even more lonely. The land had held her captive, attacked her, loved her. Still she was empty inside. She opened her pack and started to clean Theller's wounds.

* * *

Elisif saw them coming.

Terror clutched her breast. She ran along the reef, unmindful of coral cutting her feet.

Three silver dots in the sky moved farther south, then returned. The nausea they emitted in the form of a wavelength was well known to those of the Harcel. It was the prelude to death.

Electricity soon filled the air. Clouds materialized out of a clear sky. The day became night. Wind lashed the sea and stripped the land. Trees were uprooted and tossed like broken sticks along the ground. They smashed into one another, small toys in a giant Star Follower's collection.

The air thickened, condensed by the gathering power. The molecules pressed against one another, generating more excitement and electricity. Pockets of fluorescent glow appeared and disappeared, the cascading electrons moved to rapid fall.

The roofs cracked and moved off the commons of the Southern Rohn. The foundations shattered. The walls went in four directions in pieces no larger than a small child. The sea jumped the reef, then hurdled the twenty-meter-high cliff network to wash out the settlement.

The ground opened in the far planting field. Just a crack at first, then wider.

The helix ship unleashed the gathering energy onto the ground.

Chiy-une roared and surrendered the Southern Rohn.

Illeuro asa Khatioup tasted the death of the Southern Rohn in the rock. His keen knowledge of what their fate had been came from the spirit of the land rangtur. With the destruction of the Rohn, Illeuro underwent another change. He felt the spirit engulf him. This time he knew it would remain. The spirit of the land rangtur had become a part of him.

The nekka revered and shunned him simultaneously.

Katelings retreated to Gaediv's protection when he traveled toward the heart of the leah.

He tasted the difference. Isolation. Dispossessed of his own mind, yet in possession of all his faculties.

Gaediv requested him to leave, for the good of the leah.

Unquestioning, Illeuro asa Khatioup reconciled himself and the spirit clinging to his consciousness to banishment.

In the cold daylight, he finished experiencing the death of the Southern Rohn. And wept.

Chapter 32

THE SHIP SETTLED A THOUSAND METERS FROM THE bonfire.

Pam-ella glanced at it, and continued tending Theller's wounds. She felt beaten. Her quest had ended, her year of mourning served. No longer did she know her goal. She could run no more. This last battle had stretched her limits until they had nearly broken.

The Overeechy vessel had come to scrape up her emotional remains and take her back to where the battles were more subtle, civilized, and the loss was only wealth or power, neither of which she cared for.

When the ship did open, shouts erupted into the morning stillness. The gorbich that had lingered in the middle brush scattered.

Enickor stumbled on the ramp. His eyes were glazed with disbelief, head moving from side to side in a futile denial.

The Mistress continued speaking to him.

The wind could not hear his questions, nor the Mistress's response. If it had, the sound would have been a faint whisper.

Dumbfounded, Strom stood beside Magaikan. Neither man comprehended either the significance or the provocation of

Enickor's outburst. A madman, he had begun to tear the ship apart. His words mingled with guttural cries until they were indistinguishable. It had been all they could do to subdue him long enough to get him out of the ship.

Enickor staggered at the bottom of the ramp and fell to the ground. Prone, arms spread, he shared the loss of the Southern Rohn with the Mistress. He grieved silently to the outer world and felt a greater part of himself be extinguished.

He did not respond to Strom's grip for several minutes.

Magaikan moved around the two men, left a guard, and took a complement across the open space to the raging fire.

Torna-pok began drifting through the hills and down the clear run leading southward.

"Enickor? What's happened to you? What is happening?" Strom had pulled him up by the shoulders and shaken him until his eyes focused. It was the first time fear had found a home in the mercenary's voice.

He was rewarded with silence and a vacant stare.

Strom backhanded Enickor and sent him flying.

One of the guards flipped the safety off his *kalase*.

Strom ignored him.

Enickor gathered himself up, pushed away from the ramp and stood. His face was bright red on the left cheek, like the lines shooting through the whites of his eyes.

Slowly, he turned to the Ocandar Leader. "Elisif... We talked once of finding a helix ship..." His voice trailed, his thoughts disjointed.

"I remember, Enickor. What about it? I can still do it," Strom answered thoughtfully, trying to analyze the events. They had planned on spring, but now he was much closer. It would be easier.

"Go with Magaikan." Enickor looked at him with a death-like expression. "Do it. It is the last time I will ask anything of you. After it is done, leave Chiy-une, Strom. There is nothing here for you anymore."

Enickor's fingers dug into Strom's upper arms. The wild rage inside him lay just below his control level. He felt the empty hole inside him grow, as though everything that made life worth living had been scraped out with a dull knife. "The Southern Rohn is gone. Dead.

"The helix ships are mining it right now—as we stand here. Elisif... Jelica... Pindar... They are gone, Strom."

He heard the words, but could not make the meaning sink

in. How could they be gone? "Jelica? Elisif?" They were there just yesterday morning. Gone? Dead? Couldn't be . . . Zaich?

"The Mistress has spoken to me. Her children are killed." Flat-toned, his words were hollow.

Strom pulled away, spun around, and peered into the south. "All? All of them?"

Enickor turned away from his friend and the Overeechy ship skirted by onlookers, and began walking north.

Strom pulled out of his trance and ran after him. "Where are you going?"

"I don't know. Where I can do something to help Chiy-une." The hesitant steps faltered. "Barring that, maybe to Shir-wall, to fight back at a man who called himself my brother once."

"I'm going with you." The promise of revenge sounded sweet. Anger sounded in his voice. Grief would come later, when he was alone and it was dark.

"No. Do what you know how to do best, Strom. Kill the helix ship. Take away one of their weapons. Show them . . . show them that we will not go down without a whimper. It will not stop them, but it will tell them they have not killed the heart of the loags. It is only a symbol, but it is all we have left." He extended his left hand to Strom, Star Follower fashion. "I have loved you, Strom. You have been my brother. Do this for the Mistress."

Strom took Enickor's hand, then embraced him. The loss they shared, for a brief minute, flowed between them. Each knew that no matter what faced them, their cause remained the same, their bond unbreakable. Chiy-une owned them.

Enickor's sense of failure dulled his will to live. The loags were dead. Chiy-une was dying. The rangtur chain of evolution had come to a halt, and was on the verge of being irreparably broken.

Strom returned to the ship. He glared into the southland. He did not blink. Not so much as a dark cloud betrayed the death of the Southern Rohn and the gentle people he had loved, and who had loved him. *Family.* There would never be another.

"Are you going or staying?"

The question brought him back to the present. He turned to see the dour commander on his right. He cleared his throat, but the lump remained. "I would like to go with you for a while. I have business in the mining camps."

Magaikan nodded. "I heard what val Densu said. I'm sorry.

Those were good people. So few people from the Overeechy understood anything about the loags."

The commander ordered his men back into the ship. After a pause, he spoke again. "Maybe I can help you, Aknel. Unofficially, of course. With the power of the Uv-Kriell and the Overeechy at my disposal, I still don't seem able to help anyone else." He looked to the north.

A small figure dwarfed by an enormous pack balanced on her shoulders followed Enickor val Densu. Two torna-pok flanked Theller and stayed on the edge of the path as they followed.

Strom followed Magaikan's line of sight. "Who is that?" he asked.

"A victim, just like val Densu. Only not like him." Magaikan pushed Strom toward the ship. "This planet is a bastard. I hate it."

Strom turned on the commander. "Do not speak ill of her, Commander Magaikan. She has touched your soul very gently and given you immunity. You have been spared a great deal, compared to other Star Followers."

"You, Aknel, are a Star Follower."

Strom grinned a frighteningly cold grin. "The difference is, Commander, she owns me. I am a mercenary. What is greater is that I have been given a holy cause."

"Mercenary, my foot," he said, coming around to face Aknel.

There was something about the man which raised the fine hairs on Magaikan's neck into a salute. The absoluteness that he was right reminded Magaikan of himself long ago, before the Overeechy got a hold of him, before the soft peacetime life the Kriell preferred. He knew he was going to help him, but did not know why. Perhaps there was something to the business of the planet being possessed by a spirit from the dead.

The leahs cherished the rock, gleaned the impurities from it, and mutated the poisons into allies. Chiy-une's wounds were deep into the bedrock; many breached her crust.

The skies clouded with fine ash and grit. The external wounds of the land cut into the mantle. Steam, gasses, and magma belched out of the great rifts and spread over the edges. Tremendous volcanoes grew higher each mark.

Quakes and tsunamis reshaped much of the seacoast in the south. Glaciers stretched down from the north, contrasting sharply with the kilotons and finely settling debris the Star Followers and the volcanoes had hurled into the atmosphere.

Chiy-une had become a foreboding land.

Patient, loving, the Quniero tried to salve her wounds in the safe places where they could persevere and begin anew, forever detached from their homeworld.

The winter howled out of the north. Strom Aknel destroyed a helix ship and left a clear message from Chiy-une's survivors before the spring thaw.

The House of Jeffires was in turmoil. Miners and engineers approached Hoyiv *en masse* and demanded transportation back to Overeechy territory. Inexplicable cries rode the winds and penetrated the soundproofed quarters at the sites, so they claimed.

Hoyiv had no one whom he trusted. He began personally overseeing the mining operations. He appealed to the Uv-Kriell through Commander Magaikan, and asked for clearance to bring in more contract guards for his camps.

He received no answer.

The Uv-Kriell came and left. The passage of events in the Overeechy prevented his regular return. His mother's death and father's illness whipsawed his loyalties. The time had come for him to assume more responsibilities in the Overeechy. His mounting obligations pulled him away from Chiy-une.

Events began to focus on Shirwall. In early summer, Magaikan's platoon returned to the Overeechy. Chiy-une no longer played host for a representative of the Kriell. He had given up on finding a single Quniero.

The solitary Quniero had roamed the land, and walked through the heart of what had been the Gorbich Hills. No beast, normal or mutated, approached him for battle. Instead, they ran, hooting, fear-filled, and sought sanctuary from him.

Chiy-une had taken the strongest of those who had come to strip her treasures for the caretakers, and given him over to the essence of her firstborn.

Not until spring did he find what he sought.

Recognition had been a painful ordeal for Enickor. The Quniero was from the past, from the Southern Rohn. He could not think of that time and place without the ache of Elisif and the loags rekindling.

The Quniero traveled with him. Enickor communed with

305

the spirit he carried across the land. That part of Illeuro which craved the unity of a leah was satisfied with the smaller human leah that traveled over the land.

It was fall. The morning held the bone-chilling cold and dampness that was unlikely to thaw before midsummer, if then.

Pam-ella coaxed the fire back to life. Around the small clearing the trees looked dead. Frozen branches turned at odd angles, black and naked against the rusted sky. The torna-pok dug deep pits into the ground, seeking the bottom chamber of the anitte burrows where they hid during the cold. They often accompanied the roh in their search for spagus.

Enickor left the tent and came to sit beside her. He picked up a long stick and thwacked Strom's tent.

"He has already gone."

"Where did he go?"

"He heard a ship and went to investigate." She stacked more kindling over the growing flame. "I'm leaving, Enickor."

It did not surprise him. "Where are you going?" He glanced around. Illeuro was gone. He shrugged, appreciating the Quniero's aversion to ships.

"To Shirwall, then back to the Overeechy. I have a House to run." She looked sideways at him. "We're into mining, you know."

He smiled at her empty irony. "Yes, I have heard of the House of Hadilka's success."

"It is hard to leave you, Enickor. It hurts me. I know we will not see each other after this parting. The finality . . ." Her voice trailed.

He exhaled slowly. "I will miss you too, Pam-ella. You have been more than a friend. You have been family. We were always family, weren't we?"

"The answers I need are not on Chiy-une. Perhaps they were at one time, but no more." She made spider tracks in the ash.

He did not reply.

"I loved you."

"I know. I loved you, too. And I wanted you so much that it almost cost me the knowing of someone else." He threw the stick into the fire.

"Elisif?" she asked in a whisper, knowing his ache for her would never fade.

He nodded. "I thought about you a great deal during our early days together. I had taken a oath to care for her, and did, in a physical sense. Not until much later did I come to know how much she meant to me." He turned to her and smiled. "You would have liked her." His smile broadened. "You wouldn't have been able to stop yourself."

She folded her hands and nodded.

"We should have started and ended it right there on the beach when we were kids, Pam-ella."

She too smiled. "You are right, but I am glad we did not. For then, I might never have left Shirwall. I would never have known Friedo Payndacen. Not like I do . . . the loags . . . Theller."

He rose and took several steps. "I have done a great amount of thinking since the Southern Rohn was destroyed. Sometimes answers are lying on the ground, just waiting for someone to come along and pick them up, like ore samples for a miner. It always seemed to me like I should know what to do and be able to do it. But I did not know—or I would have done it."

He looked back at her. "I know the answer now. I have been protected by it, sheltered, aided . . . It has been there all the time, Pam-ella, waiting . . . waiting for me to do something with it . . . waiting for me to act as the catalyst and draw all the scattered resources of Chiy-une—even Chiy-une herself—together. Even the Quniero know their lot in any future Chiy-une might have. They have worked, while I have stumbled over the salvation which has always been there."

He turned south. His thoughts drifted through memories. "I can wish with all my might that I had put the pieces together sooner and found the answer. So simple. But . . . I did not. And I cannot undo what time has done."

Strom called from the maze of trees.

Pam-ella shouted an answer, then asked, "Have you found your peace, Enickor?"

"No, but I know how to find as much peace as I will know. I have a form of an answer. I'll go to Shirwall with you, but you will be gone before I work it. It must be like this."

"I understand."

"Do you?" He hoped that she did.

"Yes, Enickor. I really do. You're going to kill Shirwall, aren't you?"

"That is part of it." He smiled. She knew him well.

She stood and brushed the seat of her pants. "I am glad you are not counting on that being all of it. You would be disappointed."

He chuckled, feeling good about verbalizing his intent. "I

am not going to kill Hoyiv. His intelligence and his greed are valuable tools, which I hope will work for me."

Strom and three others broke through the woods and entered the small clearing. He held out his gloved hands as he approached the flames.

Pam-ella took a step forward. Her mouth opened, then closed to a warm smile.

"It has been too long, hasn't it?" Friedo returned the smile and nodded slightly.

Strom cleared his throat. "Enickor? This finely dressed man is your brother, the Kriell of the Overeechy."

Friedo approached Enickor with long, even strides. He was openly curious. His bare left hand was extended.

The physical similarity of the two men had increased with hardships and age. They spoke softly, knowing the time which might have afforded them a relationship had long passed.

The day faded to night.

The following morning Enickor stood on the beach across from Shirwall. Strom had departed, as had Pam-ella and Friedo. His friend's allegiance to the Kriell would be a lifetime bond.

"Good-bye, little sister," he whispered. The gray morning swallowed the craft carrying away the last of his family.

Meiska swam in from the open sea. He rode high in the water.

Enickor took stock of the land. The mountains were flattened. The hills gone. The band of untouched land along the coast in front of Shirwall had shriveled from prolonged cold. Ice floated in the sea.

The stone fortress was lifeless. No one walked its wide corridors.

Illeuro crossed the rocks toward him. He did not question how the Quniero covered the distance from when he last saw him. Instead he took comfort in the nebulous presence of the land rangtur. Meiska kept a strange distance, his mood as foul as the weather. The power of the stone rested heavily inside Enickor.

He waited.

The day passed, as did the night.

Finally, he felt the wrenching of the mantle rock begin, and knew the helix ship was at work far on the other side of the planet.

The Harcel Holy, forged lovingly of Chiy-une's purest ore, filled his hands.

He spoke to the sword in a whisper, yet the living rock heard, and told the Quniero and the rangtur across the planet.

As one they battled the power being gathered in the atmosphere, defied the edict which decreed it must part, and held.

Cries of anguish poured from the rubble which had been the Lyndirlyan Mountains.

A thousand souls rose on the wind in unison and opposed the natural laws ordering Chiy-une to bare her ore. For those laws applied to the dead worlds, where there was no choice and obedience was inevitable.

All that was and had ever been Chiy-une, from the rangtur to the Quniero and the torna-pok, gave to the whole, and fortified the rock, locking the molecules into place, resisting the power and bouncing it back to the helix ship whence it was summoned.

When it was over the sun rose again in the east. The land felt a little stronger. The House of Jeffires was minus a helix ship, and Shirwall had been deposed to the sea.

A second, a third, and a fourth time helix ships came.

Each time the rock fought and resisted. And each time the ocean and the land rangtur joined forces with the Quniero, and were able to help a little more.

The Mistress grew hopeful.

Enickor remained beside the ocean for the remainder of the fall and through the winter, while the Mistress rested. He answered every new attempt at mining in the same way.

In early spring Hoyiv Jeffires recalled his ground crews.

Enickor val Densu remained at the shattered beach across from Shirwall's ghost, with Illeuro as company. They had won a victory known only to the Mistress and those Chiy-uneites still remaining.

Chapter 33

THE FRIGID SEA BECAME WARMER THE FARTHER
south Meiska carried his passenger. It made little difference
to the rangtur, though he personally preferred the more tem-
perate climes to those now in existence at the Shirwall ruins.
He had refrained from communication, not wanting to press
the Warrior into returning to the island before he was ready.

Enickor did not miss conversation. He had withdrawn to his
inner self at about the same time that he discovered the solution
to the Star Followers' mining techniques.

His service to the Mistress was complete. He wondered how
Illeuro would be rewarded, and could not imagine the Quniero
returning to the leah. He understood the special displacement
that serving the Mistress left. Perhaps he would remain with
the spirit of the land rangtur until his physical time ended. Then
the land rangtur would take him on yet another journey.

Chiy-une was free at last.

His rapport with the rock would keep them safe for as long
as he lived, perhaps beyond. Chiy-une would not be worth
fighting over again, nor was the House of Jeffires likely to
resume mining efforts here again. It would be too costly. Hoyiv

Jeffires was not a stupid man bent on taming any world. He was a businessman. Chiy-une was bad business now.

Enickor wondered what he would do with the remainder of his life. He could only swim in the lagoon and play with Meiska for so long. Besides, the ice would be in the lagoon in a few dozen seasons.

He embarked on a plan to bring down the wrecked ship from the mountain a piece at a time and reassemble it. *Why not?* he mused.

The island was a shining promise on the horizon. The day was clearer than any had been for more seasons than Enickor cared to remember.

He watched it grow, the black mountains flashing in the sun, the growing white beaches warm and welcoming. Peace flowed over him and took away the keen loneliness of being the last man on Chiy-une.

Meiska leaped the reef into the lagoon. The spray soaked Enickor. He slipped from his perch and swam to shore.

The sand was warm. He sat and gazed out to sea.

The most immediate necessity would be shelter. As long as Meiska stayed around he did not have to worry about food. The rangtur would help provide. Had he not always done so?

"Enickor?"

The voice was soft, like a treasured memory restored to life.

"Enickor."

It was not his imagination, nor was it the cerebral calling of the Mistress. It was a voice, a genuine sound. He leaned back, his elbow sinking into the sand, and looked around.

She was there, her hair glowing electric as the wind played it against the brilliant evening sun.

A small child clung to her leg and reached for her.

"We have been waiting," she said, scooping up the child and advancing toward him.

"Elisif?"

Her smile broadened.

"I thought you were . . . the Southern Rohn . . ." It was too much to comprehend.

"The rangtur came. They took many of us away from the Rohn when the ships came. Meiska pulled me off the reef and brought me here. The others are . . . I don't know. It was difficult, being alone, waiting."

Slowly he came to his feet. She had become a blur. He

311

feared she might fade away, but it was only the veil of tears which marred her image.

"Your son. I named him Keladine, after my father. I hope..."

She did not have time to finish.

Enickor was home, nestled safely in Chiy-une's future.